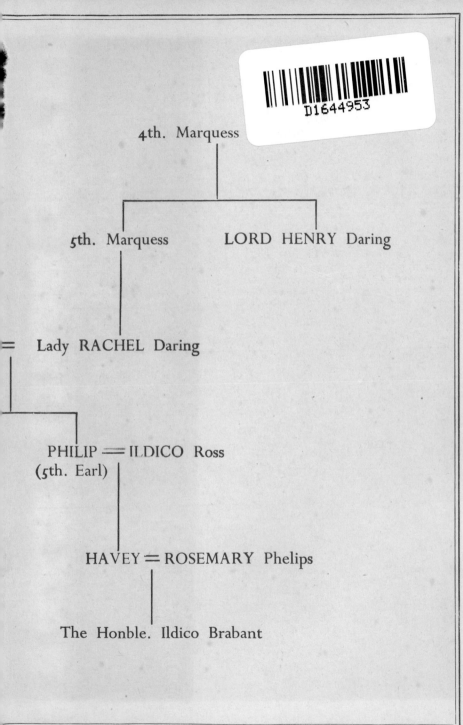

4th. Marquess

5th. Marquess   LORD HENRY Daring

= Lady RACHEL Daring

PHILIP ══ ILDICO Ross
(5th. Earl)

HAVEY ══ ROSEMARY Phelips

The Honble. Ildico Brabant

LOWER THAN VERMIN

LOWER THAN VERMIN

BY

DORNFORD YATES

WARD, LOCK & CO., LIMITED

LONDON AND MELBOURNE

First published . . . 1950

MADE IN GREAT BRITAIN

Printed in Great Britain by Butler & Tanner Ltd., Frome and London

To

The Gentlemen of the Old School

who, whether they were peers or ploughmen, masters or servants, shop-assistants or statesmen—whatever walk of life they adorned, justly commanded the respect of their fellow men.

CONTENTS

NOTE

It is sometimes suggested that the incidents of other days which I endeavour to record are figments of my imagination. Such suggestions are mistaken. It is true that none of my characters exist and that nine out of ten of them never did exist : but people exactly like them did live and move and have their being precisely as I have set down. To this, many persons, yet alive, could, if they pleased, testify. Indeed, I can remember no circumstance which I have ever set down (except in three of my books) which the spirit and manners of that particular period did not allow. If you were to tell a youth that, less than forty years ago, six hundred quail, among other things, were served at a private dance in Curzon Street, he would not believe you : but the man who roasted them was once in my service. Times have changed : that is all.

Dornford Yates.

Part One

'YOUTH'S A STUFF WILL NOT ENDURE'

"MARY SAYS," said Vivien, "that life's very dull."

"What's she mean?" said Philip. "I mean, it doesn't make sense."

"I think," said his sister, "she means that she doesn't have any fun."

"Well, we have," said Philip. "Heaps."

"I know. But she's older."

"I'm going to have more, when I'm older."

"So'm I," said Vivien, warmly. "But when I said that to Mary, she said, 'You wait.'"

"I'll bet we do," said Philip. "Look at Virgil. He's older than Mary and he has buckets of fun."

"That's just what I said, darling: and she said, 'But he's a man.' She says men are all right, but girls are always stopped."

Philip laid down his gun. Then he stepped to his sister and flung an arm round her neck.

"No one shall stop you, Vivvy."

The girl looked into his eyes.

"Promise, my lord?"

"I promise. I'll see you have all you want."

The above conversation was held in 1892, when Philip Greville Brabant, fifth Earl of Ringwood, was fourteen years of age, and his sister, Lady Vivien, was rising sixteen. The time was an August evening of singular charm; and the scene was The Great Hall at Poesy, the lesser of the two seats which the Earls of Ringwood maintained.

Philip and Vivien were orphans in the fullest sense of the word, for, though she was yet alive, Rachel, Lady Ringwood, fleeted the time abroad: this was, perhaps, as well, for, though undeniably charming, she could not have brought up a child in the way it should go. Passionately in love with her husband, within six weeks of his death she had entered a nunnery. She was received with rapture : she was dismissed with regret : but a novice who is found astride of the convent wall, discussing the points of a hunter with a young and attractive member of the Whaddon Chase, is clearly not of the stuff of which brides of Christ are made. A subsequent visit to an aunt whose palace in Venice was run as palaces should be run, revived an interest in life which had only been stunned. What is more to the point, it gave her a taste for the continental way : this was scarcely surprising, for in 1886 the continental way with a wealthy, English lady of high degree, was worth having. Faithful to death, she neither received nor married another man ; but, with this great exception, she sought and captured consolation for year after year. And so the mantle which she had so abruptly put off fell upon shoulders which, frankly, it better became. An aunt, a great-uncle and a cousin put on and distinguished the garment in different ways. A duenna did more. Though she never put on the mantle, it was she that adjusted its folds. Between them, they did very well, tempering duty with wisdom, if not with love, and riding their charges on the snaffle so far as they could. This was out of order in the era under review. But their charges were highly bred and they had the finest instincts. So the curb was left in its case, and very seldom came out. Whether such treatment was wise, Philip and Vivien Brabant shall show for themselves.

When at home, their lives were spent between Poesy, Brocade and Grosvenor Square. Brocade was half a castle and very fine ; Grosvenor Square had its points in the winter —it was, for instance, not far from Drury Lane ; but the precious manor of Poesy had their hearts. At the moment at which this tale opens, it had their flesh as well, and the great hall made a fair setting for such a striking pair.

It was thanks to Miss Carson, duenna, that 'the children' used the great hall. Many things were due to Miss Carson's excellent wit. Upon this particular point her letter shall speak for itself.

Poesy.   *1890.*
Lord Ringwood is now twelve and Lady Vivien fourteen. Although they are quite content to continue to use the nursery, it would, I think, be wise to promote them to the great hall. No other chamber is so convenient. They will, of course, honour such promotion by doing no damage and themselves clearing up any litter which their amusements may cause. They will, for instance, spread cloths upon the tables, if they are to use paste or something which might make a mess. I always think it wise to accord a privilege before it is sought : it is then more likely to be respected. Beside all this, it is time that they became familiar with their great surroundings. Most of their lives will be spent in handsome chambers, valuably appointed : I think it prudent that they should learn forthwith to take this as a matter of course, yet always to extend to their homes the consideration which they deserve.

Lady Ursula, their aunt, protested—

Is the great hall really convenient ? Supposing a caller arrives.

Miss Carson replied—

In that case the caller will have the privilege of passing through his lordship's and her ladyship's private room, and if either of them is caught unawares, so much the better. Nothing is more likely to teach them to be at their ease in any circumstances. I particularly commend the great hall, for, for one thing, it is spacious and, for another, it is, in a way, a thoroughfare. When

13

*they are given their own room, children are so much inclined to
shut themselves up and to regard visitors as trespassers. That,
I think, is undesirable.*

Lady Ursula gave way, and Miss Carson's judgment was
shown to be very good. Brother and sister were enraptured
and cared for their new apartment with a jealousy that warmed
the heart : occasional visitors chanced upon the two at their
best—and kept waiting either Lady Ursula or their horses,
while they inspected stamps and albums or actually joined in
games. As somebody said, ' *And those who came to call,
remained to play.*' For children's parties, of course, the hall
was ideal, while the oriel might have been made for the
Christmas Tree. Myself, I have always thought that it looked
its best by night, with the crimson curtains drawn and a
section of a trunk of a tree on the mighty hearth : oak floor
and panelling rendered the flicker of the flames, and three
oil-lamps, well-shaded, dispensed a pleasing radiance, kind to
the eye : four doorways, heavily curtained, gave one to the
terrace and one to the vestibule, one to the newel staircase
and one to a corridor : curtains and oak and beautifully
moulded plaster, the excellent address of portraits and the
glow of Persian rugs, the comfort of cushions and the peculiar
dignity of chiselled stone—these things were in the great
tradition, the same yesterday, to-day and for ever, enjoyed
by English commoners and fit for foreign kings.

But this was a summer evening, and all the casements were
open at half past six. The oriel itself was aflame with the
flare of a sinking sun, and all the chamber was quick with
the glow of the mellow light.

Vivien was the more striking of an unusual pair. Her
magnificent, golden hair was tumbling about her shoulders
from crown to waist ; her really beautiful features—aquiline
nose, gray eyes and an exquisite bow of a mouth—appeared
to their best advantage, for my lady was holding a slide in her
elegant hands, holding it up to the sunlight, and peering at

14

it intently, to see that it had no fault. Her frock was of gay, blue linen—full, long-sleeved and falling to, say, twelve inches above the ground : her feet, which were tucked beneath her, were clad in strong tennis-shoes.

Though at an age when boys are not at their best, her brother was good to look at and had the makings of a most handsome man. His hair was fair, but not golden ; his eyes, set wide apart, were unusually blue ; his nose was straight, his smile was very ready, his chin was firm. A cricket-shirt, gray flannel trousers and stout brown shoes became him well ; and a smear of oil on a forearm argued the business on which he was now engaged. His small-bore, single-barrelled shotgun was, naturally, the apple of his eye.

" She's a beauty," he said. " But I don't believe I'll ever be keen on shooting."

" Why not, Pip ? "—abstractedly.

" 'Cause I don't like killing things. I mean—that rabbit on Tuesday . . ."

Vivien shuddered.

" Don't."

" Well, there you are. And that's what guns are for. Hunting's all right, 'cause the fox has a pretty good chance. But shooting isn't fair. Even the rottenest shots kill stacks of birds."

" Yes, hunting's fair," said Vivien, restoring her slide to its box. " I don't like cub-hunting much—I can't bear the cubs being killed. They haven't a chance—really. But Arthur says the young hounds must be entered an' that's the only way."

" That's right," said Philip. " And it's frightfully good for us. 'Member last year, when the Master called to me to turn Havoc and Hero ? "

His sister nodded.

" He's a darling, of course. But I do hate Anderson." Anderson was the huntsman. " You were at school, when the Master was ill and Anderson hunted the hounds. More than once he was frightfully rude to me : and I was only well up—I'd done nothing at all."

Philip's eyes were blazing.

"That man was rude to you? I wish I'd been there."

"You couldn't have done anything, darling. When he's hunting hounds, he can say what he likes. But Pricket says he's a violent socialist and it's 'cause I've got a title that he's so rude."

"Yes, but that's filthy," said Philip. "To wait till he gets the chance and then, for private reasons, curse a woman for something she hasn't done."

His sister shrugged her shoulders.

"Pricket says they're like that." Pricket was Vivien's maid. "She says they've got one in her village in Worcestershire. And one day he went to church and went and sat down in the Betteshangers' family pew. Well, they couldn't have a scene in church, as, of course, he knew. So that was taking advantage, the same as Anderson. But the villagers waited for him and threw him into the pond."

"Well, I think it's filthy," said Philip. "We've always been perfectly civil to Anderson. Always. And he has a present at Christmas—that I know. Five pounds, I think. And each of the whips has two."

"That's what I said to Pricket, and she said that makes things worse. They hate us for being able to give them things."

"But they jolly well take them," said Philip. "If I hated a man, I wouldn't take his presents."

"Pricket says," said Vivien, "that hatred knows no law."

"That isn't right," said her brother. "We hated old Calder like blazes : but when he was drunk, we used to make a ring round him, if Sophie was coming by. I mean, you had to, Vivvy."

('Sophie' was the house-master of the Headmaster's House at Harrow. Calder had been the butler, until six months

16

before. Many times had he gone to the well; but at last he had been broken.)

"Of course. But you didn't really hate him: I mean, if you had, you wouldn't have covered him up. But socialists simply loathe us, because we're better than them."

"That's not our fault," said Philip. "And the village doesn't hate us. Look at old Tom and Blewitt and Mrs. Rone. They're far poorer than Anderson: yet they're terribly sweet."

"Yes, but they're not socialists. It's only the socialists that hate our class."

"But why should socialists hate us, if others don't."

"Because they want to be equal: they don't like us having things that they haven't got. All people should be equal, they say."

"I'll bet Anderson wouldn't like the whips being equal to him. He treats them like dirt."

Miss Carson's voice came floating in at the oriel.

"Come out on the terrace, darlings. I think it's the loveliest evening I ever saw."

The two went flying.

The broad, flagged terrace was commanding more than the park: a man who stood to its weathered parapet could look upon the face of the England that Gainsborough and Constable knew. This was a goodly countenance. Pasture and woodland—deep, luxuriant meadows, laced by a golden stream . . . the incomparable majesty of timber, full of years: the prelacy of hedgerow elms, the lusty seigniory of solitary oaks, the privy council of chestnuts and the delicate pageant of beeches, rising to the slope of a hill: thin spirals of chimney-smoke, betraying a hamlet embowered and out of sight: the thrust of a gray, old tower, commending gratitude to Him who made the paradise: and, over all, cast like a veil of gold, the mellow brilliance of the near-setting sun—long, clean-cut shadows and substance glorified; the effigy of post-and-rails, printed upon the sward; a copper beech resplendent

17

and the church's vane afire. . . . Painters have snared these things, to put my pen to shame; and yet there is one detail no brush could ever catch. . . . There, to the left, perhaps a mile away . . . a flourish or bravery of water—a ragged fountain playing above the willows, now high, now low, but always there and dancing . . . against a rose-red wall. Such was the fine abandon of the ancient water-wheel—a merry labourer, that slapped his master on the back and tossed him in the air, making a pretty parable, worthy of Aesop's pen.

"I can smell the brewery," said Philip. He snuffed luxuriously. "Gorgeous."

"Vandal," said Miss Carson. "All the same I must confess to a weakness for that particular scent. If beer smelt as nice as that, I should have a bottle on my dressing-table."

Philip was bubbling.

"I'd love you to come down to dinner, smelling of beer."

"Rude child," said Miss Carson. "Vivien, what do you see?"

Her gray eyes fast on the landscape—

"I don't know," said Vivien, slowly. "I mean, I can't describe it—I haven't the words. It's like an old English song or a Nursery Rhyme. I mean, I loved it last year, when we went to the Pyrenees. But this is the real thing."

"You're perfectly right, my dear. Lump all your show-places together, and they won't count beside the English scene. There's a permanence about it. Songs and rhymes were composed in country like this. There must have been a rhyme about a mill-wheel, but I suppose it's been lost."

"I know," said Philip. "Let's ride to the mill to-morrow and see Big Ben. We may, mayn't we, Miss Carson?"

"Of course, my dear. Take William."

"We'll take the ralli-car, if you'll come too."

"Yes, do," cried Vivien. "You know we'd love you to."

"No, sweethearts, I'd like you to ride. Perhaps I'll drive down with Arthur. I want to see Mrs. Trent."

Mrs. Trent was the rector's wife, who, in a mad moment,

18

had made herself a bed which would have made a *fakir* think. She had lain on it uncomplaining for fifteen years, bearing ten ill-favoured children, making ends meet somehow and always doing her best to keep appearances up. She had married her husband, because she had pitied him—a mistake that was sometimes made in the nineteenth century. He was more than uncouth and devoted his undoubted scholarship to the ' debunking ', with every circumstance of scurrility, of lesser lights. Jebb's *Sophocles* was good enough for most people, but not for the Rector of Peregrine. With a wealth of libellous incoherence which took him years to produce, which, of course, never appeared, he unmasked the slight errors which creep into every great work : but the savagery of his criticism was fatal. Homer may nod : but only one greater than Homer may, therefore, flay Homer alive. The faithful rejection of his efforts made a fanatic out of a caustic sage. The man became a crusader, whom nobody ever heard of, whose morning-star, save in the privacy of his study, was never fleshed. As for his living—well, services and sermons simply embarrassed the crusade, and his cure of souls was a burden he ceased to bear. Poesy did its best : but the Ringwood library had always been at Brocade : that being so, the lesser seat did not count. So Lady Ursula and Miss Carson turned to the rector's wife. That they were a very present help, there can be no doubt : but for their constant support, I do not believe that she would have been alive. And ' the children ' were very good. Whenever desired so to do, they entertained the Trent offspring with all their might, reserving until its departure the furious strictures which the latter's deportment provoked. (On one unforgettable occasion, Percy Trent had endeavoured to climb the Christmas Tree, and had brought the whole thing down —tub, lighted candles and all, in indescribable havoc, to the glory of hell.) Indeed, for the last two years, two footmen had stayed in the hall while the Trents were there, with orders to forestall violence.

"Why," said Vivien, slowly, "why did she marry the man?"

"Not 'the man', Vivien: 'the rector'."

"I beg your pardon. The rector. But why did she marry him?"

"I really don't know," said Miss Carson. "He may have been different then. Girls do make mistakes, you know."

"But all those children, Miss Carson. Pricket says that he doesn't know their names."

Making a mental note to have a word with Miss Pricket—

"Scholars," said Miss Carson, "are sometimes like that. They go the way of professors who get so wrapped up in their work that they forget time and custom and duty and everything else. I heard of one once who, on a dark winter's morning, got up and dressed—and then forgot what he had done and, finding himself in his bedroom with candles lit, supposed it was night and undressed himself again and went back to bed."

'The children' shrieked with laughter.

"But surely," bubbled Philip, "he saw that the bed wasn't made."

"That detail would make no impression upon a scholar's mind. They are above such things—as is Mr. Trent."

A great gong rumbled its summons to go and dress.

"Bags I the bath first," cried Philip.

"Well, don't lie in it," said Vivien.

"I trust," said Miss Carson, "that neither of you ever does such a silly thing. If I thought you did, I should have the hip-baths back."

"No, no, please," cried 'the children'.

"Then promise me that you won't. To lie in a bath's all right for the old and the sick—it certainly comforts them, and it may do them good. But it's really bad for young people."

'The children' passed their word—and made for the stairs.

20

Miss Carson strolled for five minutes before going in, reluctant to leave such beauty, thinking upon her charge.

So far all had gone well. Philip and his sister were quite unspoiled : natural, easy and upright in all they did. Their manners seemed to be perfect. As was right and proper, they were conscious of their estate : but they were also conscious of the penalty this imposed—an extra-special duty towards their fellow men.

Once, in Grosvenor Square, a cabman had given offence and Philip had turned on the man. Miss Carson, about to pay him, had closed her purse.

" Wait, if you please," she said quietly and led the way into the house.

When the door was shut, she called Philip into a room.

" That wasn't Lord Ringwood," she said. " That was a rich little cad. Lord Ringwood would never turn on a poor man who knew no better, because he'd forgotten himself. Think of his life and yours. You've come from a box at a theatre back to a lovely home : he's been sitting all day in the driving rain, and when he gets home to-night he's got to groom his horse and wash his cab. Then, again, he's much older than you. You hadn't thought of all that—boys of your age don't. But the Earl of Ringwood has *got* to think of those things. Others may do as they please about that sort of thing—thanking a servant, for instance : but Lord Ringwood has no choice. He must always thank servants for what they do." She opened her purse. " I was going to give him four shillings. Here are six. You will please go out and give them to him yourself . . . and I hope you'll say you're sorry for what occurred."

That Philip had done as she said is little enough : the point is that he did it handsomely. To the money she gave him, he added three shillings of his own—all, in fact, that he had : and when some minutes had passed and Miss Carson went to the door, he was standing bare-headed in the rain, deep in conversation with the cabman, who was telling him all he knew. Then the boy put up his hand, and the cabman uncovered and took it. " Good luck, sir," he said, " an' thenk you kindly. An' there's yer ma." He lifted his voice. " Thenk you kindly, m'm."

Miss Carson smiled and nodded, as Philip threw himself on her and put his arms round her waist.

" He thought you were Mummy, Miss Carson. I wish you were."

For once the duenna was gravelled. Had she been able to speak, she would have said the right things : but she dared not trust her voice. Instead, she stooped and kissed the upturned face. Then they shut the great door together, and Philip began to tell her all that the cabman had said.

I think that perhaps that will show how much it was thanks to Miss Carson that so far all had gone well. Be that as it may, the two had increased in wisdom and stature and in favour with man. For their Maker, I dare not speak : but I find it hard to believe that He did not look upon them and find them good. But now they were growing up. Vivien was a young lady, and Philip had been at Harrow for three full terms. That a critical time was coming, there could be no doubt. So far their lives had been sheltered—the barques had lain in the stream : but very soon now they must make for the open sea.

Vivien was taking notice—no doubt about that : and she was talking to Pricket, and Pricket was talking to her. Well, that was as it should be—girls did talk to their maids. Pricket was only nineteen, but that was, again, as it should be— youth to youth. And Pricket was a very good girl— dutiful, happy, utterly devoted to Vivien and honest as the day. But she must have a care. Gossip was all very well : (to forbid it was worse than useless :) but discussion of the rector's intensive, if careless propagation was out of place.

Miss Carson found herself smiling . . .

She stopped and turned, to sweep the exquisite landscape

with one last, lingering look : then she followed the 'children' into the house.

*　　*　　*　　*　　*

"Sally !" shouted Big Ben. "'Ere's 'er ladyship asking for you. An' 'is lordship's 'ere."

"Coming, father," cried Sally, from somewhere within the mill.

Sally was a true miller's daughter—apple-cheeked, buxom, gay. Together, she and Big Ben made the prettiest picture, the gray-haired, smiling giant and the maid with the dancing eyes. The miller's wife had died when Sally was born, and the two had lived by themselves for nineteen years : Big Ben had played mother, too, and Sally was the light of his world.

Now she came running, with flour all over her arms.

"Why, Sally."

"Good morning, my lady." She took Vivien's hand. "Oh, there now. See what I've done."

"Don't be silly, Sally. Nice, clean flour. I'll bet you're making a pie."

"No, my lady," said Sally. "I'm baking to-day. Good morning, my lord." Philip wrung her hand. "You've got a new horse."

"Isn't he a stunner, Sally ? I'm going to hunt him next year."

"Ay's a beauty. Ay looks so pleased with life."

Big Ben was chuckling.

"'Member the unicorns an' Rory—'e was a one. Faith, a can see you now—your lordship leading an' 'er ladyship an' Sally behin'. Don' seem so long ago."

"Oh, Big Ben, it's ages."

"Come my age, my lady, time sort o' seems to stan' still. It's quiet at the mill, you know, day in an' day out."

"How is Rory, Big Ben ?"

"Pensioned las' year, my lord. The rheumatiz brought 'im down—it gets mos' draymen in the end. But 'e was a mighty man. Knap a flint on his chest, you could, if you'd give him a quart of ale. A've seen it done."

"Sally," said Vivien, "next year I'm to put up my hair."

"Oh, it's a business," said Sally. "I used to cry. But Arabella will help you. She's very deft."

"I love Arabella," said Vivien. "She says . . ."

Pricket's aunt was maid to a lady-in-waiting. Wide-eyed, the two girls pondered the mysteries of the Court.

Big Ben and Philip were discussing the tickling of trout.

William, holding the horses, was standing a little apart.

Miss Carson arrived, with Arthur, behind a high-stepping cob.

And there was a scene for an artist that knew how to paint —men, women and horses, standing at ease on the greensward beside the rose-red mill, the sunlight brilliant about them, oaks in the background lifting their immemorial arms. . . . Of such was the English country of 1892.

Then Sally ran in for the 'washerwoman's cake'—moist and full of raisins, excellent fare. . . .

Vivien was folding a kerchief of emerald green. Then she put up her hands, set it on Sally's hair and knotted the ends together beneath her chin.

"Doesn't that suit her, Big Ben?"

But the father had no words and the daughter was overwhelmed.

"Oh, my lady." Sally fingered the stuff. "I've never had such a thing."

"I know. It's time you had. And it suits you better than me. I've only worn it twice."

"Oh, my lady. To make me a present like this!"

"But I want you to have it, Sally."

Sally made to kiss Vivien, after the way of a child. Then she remembered her state, and drew back with a blush.

"Sally, Sally," cried Vivien, and kissed her on either cheek.

Miss Carson saw and approved.

* * * * *

24

A jolly month had gone by, and Philip was due to return to Harrow School. It was, indeed, his last evening. To-morrow morning he would be driven to Blackbird, to catch the London train.

The boy was content, accepting his coming translation as part of the game. He hated leaving Poesy—anyone would : but he was happy at Harrow, liked and was liked. Had the choice been his, he would have stayed at Poesy all his days : and there was the rub—that nearly a year would go by before he saw it again. Christmas this year must be spent in Grosvenor Square : and Easter, as always, at Brocade. The weight of the coronet was beginning to make itself felt.

Coffee had been served after dinner in the great hall—this, to mark the occasion, for after-dinner coffee was not allowed. (*I think they might have it at Christmas : and if Philip has beer at Harrow, they might as well have it at home. A little, of course, at lunch. Much better to begin like that.*' *E. C.*)

Miss Carson had been invited : otherwise, she would not have come. And the three were about the slow fire which would never really go out for the next six months.

Philip lay, propped on his elbows, before the hearth, savouring the crystals of sugar to which the coffee belonged : her coffee forgotten, Vivien sat on a hassock, close to Miss Carson's knee, looking now upon Philip and now on the flicker of the flames : and Miss Carson was sitting back in an easy chair, sipping her coffee and watching her charges and finding the two to her taste.

The three were properly dressed—the rule was never broken, no matter where they might be. Philip was wearing Etons and dancing pumps : Vivien was wearing an old-rose, short-sleeved frock, full and low at the neck, black silk stockings and patent-leather slippers, lovely to see : the duenna was in full evening dress of unrelieved black, an almost sleeveless corsage, cut very low.

At the age of fourteen, Philip was dressed in Etons for most of his time : he always wore them at Harrow, except when playing games : he wore them every Sunday : he wore nothing else in London ; and, as I have shown, they made his evening dress.   That Miss Carson was dressed as became her, she owed to herself : the following correspondence shall make that—and other things—clear.

Poesy,
Hampshire.

My lord,
    I had not realized that the Earl of Ringwood and Lady Vivien Brabant would be left so much in my charge : it had not occurred to me, for instance, that I should take them regularly to the play and other entertainments, or even preside at table as often as I do.   Please believe that I am very happy to do these things and, indeed, count them a great privilege : but in these circumstances I feel that I should, so to speak, dress the part, and that I cannot afford to do on my present salary.   I think it would be, perhaps, convenient, if I were made a small dress allowance.   By buying wisely and well, I should be able always to appear, at home as abroad, dressed as becomes a lady attending two children of rank.   Of course I should regard any clothes so purchased as my livery and should not wear them on leave . . .

Carlton Club,
Pall Mall.

My dear Madam,
    I am shocked that you should have been embarrassed.   The Trustees have been unpardonably remiss in this matter.   In the absence of Lady Ursula, I am advised that the sum of two hundred and fifty pounds a year should put you at your ease. This will be paid to you by the solicitors as from the commencement of your engagement ; that is to say, the six months' arrears will be paid forthwith.
    You will permit me to say that the Trustees are more than satisfied with your interpretation and discharge of your duty : they are most favourably impressed . . .

(On her return from France, Lady Ursula was informed—and went off the deep end.

'You must be mad, Uncle Henry. I dress myself on a hundred and fifty a year.'

'More's the pity. And you can afford two thousand.'

'I don't think it's right to spend so much money on clothes.'

'Right or wrong, it's decent. You're still a good-looking gal : but what's the good of a picture without a proper frame ? '

Lord Henry Daring knew his world. From that time on, Lady Ursula Brabant was beautifully dressed. What is more to the point, Miss Carson took care to dress on two hundred pounds a year, always returning the balance to the solicitors.)

The duenna was very good-looking—her fine, classical features were greatly admired, and her figure was admirable : an excellent dignity sat in her level gaze : her mouth was firm, yet gentle : her dark hair was perfectly done in the Grecian style—she had, of course, her own maid : and everything about her was *soigné*—a word for which ' first-rate ' is the best I can do. Perhaps her greatest triumph was that all servants used her with great respect : this was largely because they liked her—her orders were always requests. But, then, she ' knew behaviour '. She could have married a dozen different men : but she was too happy in her duty to think of leaving ' the children ' she loved so well. And now she was getting on. She had looked twenty-seven for ages : but now she was twenty-eight. Still, few at that age have become an institution.

For a little, the three of them talked of unimportant things —Philip exhorting the others to keep him informed, Miss Carson desiring Philip to let her know when his boots showed signs of wear, Vivien proposing to write two letters only for every one she received. But Philip held the board.

" You will let me know about Trueboy (Trueboy was the new hunter) and Gola (Gola was a spaniel, now great with pup) and—and everything? And don't forget to tell Lister as soon as you know when they're going to draw Fantasy Brush. (Lister was the head gamekeeper, whose duty it was to see that the earths were stopped.) And ask Mr. Leith to write—he writes such jolly letters, all about everything. (Mr. Leith was Poesy's agent, a most understanding man.) Oh, an' . . ."

Vivien leaned back and looked upwards into Miss Carson's eyes.

" Pip has a month at Christmas. Can't we spend a fortnight in London and then come here ? "

" Oh, do let's," cried Philip. " Darling Miss Carson, do let's come here for two weeks. I got no hunting last year, except at Brocade."

" Ten days, perhaps," said Miss Carson. " I'll ask Lady Ursula."

" Can't you ask Great-Uncle ? " said Vivien. " I mean, I think he's more likely to understand."

" Lady Ursula's most understanding. Besides, if she says no, Lord Henry won't say yes. Any way, I'll recommend it. Ten days at Poesy."

Lady Ursula's writ ran at Poesy : Lord Henry's, at Brocade : Grosvenor Square served two masters. This, roughly, of course : uncle and niece always got on very well. Lady Ursula Brabant, spinster, possessed no home of her own, and so she lived at Poesy, where she had her own rooms. She could have had Poesy's dower-house, and would, I think, have preferred to make that her home : but a sense of duty kept her at Poesy proper most of the year. She had her own rooms also in Grosvenor Square. At this particular moment, the lady was visiting friends : she had, however, arranged to lie in London to-morrow, and Philip would lunch with her at Grosvenor Square : a sense of duty, again. Lord Henry Daring, bachelor, lived in Arlington Street—with a shooting-box in Norfolk, of which he was very fond. He had rooms at Brocade, to which he repaired as a duty three or

28

four times in the year. He always spent Easter there, to the great content of 'the children', whom it was his pleasure to spoil. He had no need of rooms in Grosvenor Square, but when his wards were in residence, he was a constant visitor.

The difference between Lady Ursula and Lord Henry was shortly this. Had Philip been about to lunch with his great-uncle, instead of with his aunt, he would have broached the question of spending ten days at Poesy during the Christmas recess. As it was, he felt it was better to leave the approach to Miss Carson, who knew her world.

Miss Carson glanced at the clock and rose to her feet.

"Half past nine, children." The two got up. "I've got some things to see to, and so I'm going up. We'll say ten o'clock to-night, but don't be later than that."

"You're understanding," said Vivien.

As the other stooped to kiss her, the girl threw her arms round her neck.

"You won't ever leave us, will you?"

"That's a rash request, darling. I like to think I'll always be somewhere about."

Philip had run before her, to open the door.

As he put up his face—

"Soon you'll be too big a boy to kiss."

"Not for you," said Philip. "I hope you'll always kiss me, Miss Carson. You see, you're different."

"Good night, old fellow. Sleep well."

So duennas have their reward.

As Philip returned to the hearth—

"It was decent of her," said Vivien, "to leave us alone."

"She's awfully decent," said Philip. "Always, I mean. Woodville thought she was our mother, when she was at Lord's."

This was hardly surprising. Lord Henry had provided a coach for the Eton and Harrow Match. 'I cannot climb on to a coach,' wrote Lady Ursula. 'Miss Carson must take my place.' Miss Carson had taken her place extremely well:

Lord Henry had been as charming as she deserved, and Ringwood's coach had been an immense success.

"I believe," said Vivien, "that we're to see Mummy at Easter."

"Good," said Philip. "In Paris?"

"I think so." She hesitated. "Miss Carson's said nothing yet, but I think I'll have to stay on."

Her brother stared.

"How long for?"

"I don't know: but I think I've got to learn French. Mary was there for a year."

"But, Vivvy, you can't! You've got to come up for Speech Day, and then there's Lord's. And—and what about here?"

"I don't know, Pip. Perhaps they'll let me come back for things like that. Any way, I'll tell you as soon as I know."

"You will write, Vivvy, won't you? I mean, about everything. I want to know all about the opening meet."

"Promise," said Vivien.

Philip frowned.

"And if Anderson's rude to you."

"I don't think he will be again. It's only if nobody's there, to hear what he says."

"I call it filthy," said Philip, violently. "If the Master knew, he'd sack him."

"Don't you worry, Pip. I won't give him a chance."

Still frowning, the boy left the hearth, to make the slow round of the hall, marking the points of the chamber he loved so well. Refectory table and portrait and high-backed chair, convex mirror and chest and tall-case clock—slowly he savoured them all. Then he returned to the hearth and flung himself into a chair.

"Ten minutes more," said Vivien. "Oh, Pip, I shall miss you so."

Her brother looked round, to see the tears on her cheeks.

In a flash he was on his knees and his arm was about her shoulders, his head against hers.

"Vivvy, darling, don't cry."

"I didn't mean to, Pip. But I do hate your going so."

"I hate it, too. I loathe it. Harrow's all right, but I want to be here with you."

"You'll write when you can, won't you? You know. Just say what you're doing. You'll have time when you're on Boy."

(To be 'on Boy' was to be at call, as a fag. The duty was taken in turn by the junior boys.)

"I'll find time, Vivvy. I'll write when I'm up to old Bogey. He gases for hours, and he thinks we're taking notes."

"As long as you write, Pip."

No more was said.

The boy sat down by his sister, and Vivien put an arm round his neck. And so they sat, till the clock declared the hour.

Then they got to their feet, and Vivien rang for a servant and led the way upstairs.

*　　　*　　　*　　　*　　　*

Lady Ursula rose and put out welcoming hands.

"Dearest child, did Freeman find you at once?"

(Freeman was the tall footman who shared the carriage duty with Wickers, the groom.)

Philip returned her kiss.

"Yes, thank you, Aunt Ursula. I think he saw me first. And he knew my portmanteau before I'd pointed it out. And Holly says the greys make a lovely pair. He's going to put Random in the brougham this afternoon."

(Holly was the Town coachman—a most important man : to drive a fine equipage as a fine equipage should be driven in the London of 1892 was demanding no ordinary skill.)

"What time will you have to leave?"

" About half past four.   There are always heaps of trains."

" How's Vivien, darling ? "

" Oh, she's all right.   When are you going to Poesy, Aunt Ursula ? "

" Early next month, dear boy.   I'm sorry you won't be there."

" So'm I."

" Your great-uncle's coming to lunch."

" Is he ?   Good.   Aunt Ursula ? "

" Yes, dear ? "

" I want you to see Trueboy.   He is a real stunner and looks as good as he is.   I rode him cubbing last week, an' the Master said . . ."

Lord Henry had not forgotten his Harrow days.   At half past two, despite Lady Ursula's protests, Philip and he left for Tattersall's.   Lord Henry being well known, Philip was introduced to more than one famous sportsman within those famous gates.   The boy had the time of his life.   Then tea in Grosvenor Square at four o'clock.   Finally, the farewell to greatness.

" Darling boy, you have warm things to wear ? "

" Yes, thank you, Aunt Ursula."

" Bet he don't wear 'em," from Lord Henry.   " I was at Harrow myself."

" Uncle, be quiet.   You will be sensible, Pip ? "

" Yes, I will, Aunt Ursula.   If it's really cold we *have* to wear overcoats.   I mean, they put it up on the board."

Lady Ursula shuddered.

" But you don't have to wait for permission ?   If you feel cold . . ."

" Oh, yes.   We can if we like.   You ought to see Frensham.   He puts on his coat if he thinks it's going to rain. But Dammy never wears one."

" Dammy," said Lady Ursula.   " Is that his name ? "

" No.   Duhamel, really.   He's French.   He's a master, Aunt Ursula.   He's frightfully funny.   He has fives-balls on

32

his desk, and if you aren't attending, he jolly well buzzes one at you. But he doesn't care if it snows. He comes in soaking wet and just says, ' I have my gown.' It does keep the rain off, of course.'

Lady Ursula covered her eyes.

" Good for Dammy," cried Lord Henry. . . .

The latter drove in the brougham to Baker Street. But there, at the portals of Hell, he bade his great-nephew goodbye.

" You don't need me," he said. " Men see themselves off." A sovereign passed. " That's just to oil the wheels. I'm glad to know about Dammy. He sounds a good man."

Philip took off his hat.

" Thank you very much, sir," he said. " And thank you awfully for taking me to Tattersall's. When I tell the other men . . ."

" That's all right, Pip. I enjoyed myself. How old are you now ? Fourteen ? Next time you're in Town you must dine with me at the Club."

" Oh, thank you, sir. I'd love to."

" The Carlton don't allow guests, but we'll try somewhere else."

" Can Vivvy come, too ? "

Lord Henry shook his head.

" We haven't come to that yet. But I can ask her to tea."

" I know she'd love it, sir."

" So be it," said Lord Henry. " That's an engagement, Pip."

Wearing his ankle-length coat, Freeman preceded his master into the depths.

They overtook Postlethwaite Minor, staggering under the bulk of a Gladstone bag.

" Hullo, Ringwood."

" Hullo, Possum. I say. This afternoon my great-uncle . . ."

"Allow me, sir," said Freeman, possessing himself of the bag.

Postlethwaite relinquished it gratefully.

33

Chattering excitedly, the children followed the footman, let him take the tickets and shepherd the porters along.

" There's your ticket, my lord, and yours, sir. Your bags are in the rack and the luggage is right in front."

Philip put out his hand, and Freeman tugged at his glove. Then he took off his hat, took Philip's hand and bowed.

" Thank you very much, Freeman, for all you've done."

" Thank you, my lord. It's been a very great pleasure."

" Don't stay now, 'cause we're keeping my great-uncle waiting."

Freeman put on his hat.

" Very good, my lord. Allow me to wish your lordship a very pleasant term." He turned to Postlethwaite. " And you, sir."

" Thank you very much," cried the children.

Freeman stood for a moment with his hand to his hat. Then he turned on his heel.

He was of the old school.

*　　*　　*　　*　　*

It was the fifth of December, and Vivien was going strong.

William, out as her escort, had fallen at Robin's Water and, though he had mounted again, was far behind. And all the field had been left, for Vivien was riding Blue Boy, and Blue Boy with Vivien up could not only jump like a stag, but go like the wind. The huntsman was there, and Vivien —but nobody else.

The Master was ill: he was up and about his house, but he dared not hunt. He would have to resign, of course. After all, he was sixty-eight, and had had a good run.

The fox was clearly making for Peppercorn Brake. He had been making for that for half an hour, but only one man had known it—old Mr. Rampus, commonly called ' Old Ram ', who had hunted since he was ten and was rising seventy-four. After sixty years, a man gets to know his country. . . .

And so Old Ram was up, though he had not followed hounds. By lane and bridle-path, he had hustled his mare along to Peppercorn Brake; and, but for a gate which gave him a minute's trouble, he would have been in at the death.

But he saw the huntsman striding to Vivien's side, with the bleeding brush in his hand.

" Never bin blooded, have you? "

" Oh, yes," cried Vivien, sharply. " The Master did it himself."

" Twice won't hurt you, you bitch."

He caught her right wrist. He daubed her brow and her cheeks and thrust the stump at her lips. Then he flung the brush down on the ground.

" That'll learn you to——"

" Stop, man, stop ! " roared Old Ram. " How dare you use a young lady in that outrageous way? "

Anderson swung about, glaring.

Leaning out of her saddle, Vivien was violently sick.

Old Ram came up with a rush.

" The Master shall hear of this, huntsman. Get to your hounds." He turned to the girl. " There, there, my dear. There's nobody here but me. The man must be out of his mind. Here, take my handkerchief."

" I'm sorry," said Vivien, faintly. " I think I'm going to fall off."

Old Ram contrived to hold her, till William came pelting up to lift his mistress down.

*　　　*　　　*　　　*　　　*

An hour and a half before Vivien had been so abused, her duenna was shaken and shocked by news which the house-keeper brought.

" But I can't believe it, Mrs. Hoby. You're sure it's true? "

" I think it must be, ma'am. Arthur had it from Lister, and they're reliable men."

" But Sally of the Mill . . . murdered. . . . It doesn't make sense."

The housekeeper shrugged her shoulders.

" They say that whoever it was tried to set fire to the body. Her clothes was burned."

Miss Carson put a hand to her head.

" How very, very dreadful. . . . And what of Big Ben ? "

" They say he's stricken, ma'am. He roused George Fitall, his man, and sent him for help. But when they got back, he was lying in the doorway senseless, and so he stays."

Miss Carson looked dazedly round. Then she took hold.

" Lady Ursula doesn't know ? "

" No, ma'am. I thought I should come to you first."

" Very well. I'll tell her at once and see what she says. I think she'll agree with me that, so far as ever you can, you and Mr. Watkin must discourage any discussion of this most shocking affair." (Watkin was the butler.) " Pricket had better be told, if she doesn't already know—and warned to say nothing at all to Lady Vivien."

" Very good, ma'am."

" At the moment, Mrs. Hoby, I can't think of anything else. Oh, yes. Who's out to-day ? "

Mrs. Hoby named the servants.

" Tell them that on pain of dismissal they're not to approach the mill."

" Certainly, ma'am."

Miss Carson rose.

" I'll see Lady Ursula now."

The interview was distressing.

Murder was one of the very many things that were not dreamed of in Lady Ursula's philosophy.

When she had digested the truth, she began to weep.

" In our village," she wailed " . . . in our lovely Pere-grine . . . at our very gates, Miss Carson . . . and poor, little, pretty Sally. . . . What monster has done this thing ? "

36

Suddenly she got to her feet and passed to and rang the bell.
To the servant who came—

" Tell the coachman I want the brougham in half an hour."

" Very good, my lady."

As the door closed—

" But Lady Ursula——"

The other held up a hand.

" I must go to Big Ben—I've known him all my life.
Poor, poor Big Ben. If he's unconscious, I can arrange
some comfort. If he's not, it may be a help to him to see
an old friend."

" Please let me come with you," said Miss Carson.

" On no account, my dear. Your place is here. Give
the best orders you can. I'm sure they'll be good."

Fifty minutes later Lady Ursula reached the mill.

God knows what it cost the poor lady : but she was
Ursula Brabant, and Brabants had their duty to do.

As the groom opened the door—

" Stay with the brougham, Akers."

Alone, she faced a policeman she did not know.

" Can you tell me where Big Ben is—the master of the
Mill ? "

" I think he's with neighbours, ma'am."

" You don't know their name ? "

The constable pushed back his helmet.

" Would it be at Bush Cottage, ma'am ? "

" Let's see. That'd be Mrs. Borrit."

" That's right, ma'am. Borrit's the name."

Lady Ursula drove to Bush Cottage.

Big Ben's brain was affected : he could not pronounce his
words.

" There, there," said Lady Ursula, laying her hand on his
arm. " You must come to us, Big Ben, and you and I will
talk about other days. You mustn't grieve for dear Sally—
she's happy now. All her troubles are over. I wish ours
were. Mr. Leith will care for the mill, and you will stay

37

at Poesy, till you're yourself again. After all, we're very old friends. You used to help me on to the kitchen-garden wall. . . ."

Mrs. Borrit's eyes were bolting.

" Oh, me lady, to think of such dreadful, awful things. Never in all me life. And to try to burn 'er poor body, to 'ide 'is crime."

" Who did it ? "

" Oh, I couldn' say. But I think she was in trouble, me lady. An' that's what she gets for it. Tryin' to save his-self, if you ask me. But the police'll get 'im all right."

" No doubt. We must leave it to them. Look after Big Ben to-night. To-morrow we shall be ready to take him in."

Lady Ursula drove to the agent's private house.

" You know of this matter, Mr. Leith ? "

" Only, Lady Ursula, that murder has been done."

" Justice must be done, Mr. Leith. The crime was barbarous."

" Be sure it will be, Lady Ursula."

" I don't like servants' gossip : so kindly report to me whatever you hear."

" That shall be done."

" And please look after the mill. Find someone and put him in charge. Big Ben is coming to us."

" To Poesy ? "

" Yes. I think he'd be best at the lodge. And I'm sure the Foys would be very good to him. I'll see them as I go back. Would a pound a week be too much ? "

" I think, perhaps, Lady Ursula, fifteen shillings would be better."

" Very well. And you will see to the mill ? "

" I'll do that at once."

He saw the lady to her brougham, wondering at a drive which he had never suspected, at the depths of the still waters which he had known so long as a languid stream.

38

The Foys, man and wife, were more than pleased at the prospect of lodging Big Ben. Their daughter's room was empty, for she was now a housemaid in Grosvenor Square. The chamber lay at the back, commanding the little garden, trim and retired.

"He'll be quiet here, my lady, poor Big Ben."

"Try and keep his mind on the old days, Mrs. Foy. I shall be down to-morrow, to see that he's settled in."

*　　*　　*　　*　　*

Miss Carson was at the stables, when Vivien returned. The duenna left nothing to chance.

One look was enough for her. Vivien did not seem to have fallen, but something was wrong.

"Are you all right, my darling? You don't look yourself."

Vivien smiled.

"Yes, I'm all right, Miss Carson. But I'll be glad of a bath."

Not a word about the hunt.

Miss Carson looked at William, whose face was a dusky red.

"Here's Pricket. Pricket, see to Lady Vivien. She's rather done up. I'll come in a minute or two."

As the two girls entered the house—

"What happened, William?"

"I was behind, ma'am. I fell at Robin's Water: her ladyship gone on to Peppercorn Brake. They killed jus' short o' the trees, an', excep' for the huntsman, she was the only one there. An' the—the blackguard blooded her."

"*Anderson blooded Lady Vivien?*"

"So Mr. Rampus said, ma'am. He got there jus' too late. Very rough he was with her, too. An' her ladyship fainted off, and when I come up, Mr. Rampus was holdin' her on. I got her down, an' a keeper's wife brought some water. . . . And a strange gentleman come up and was very

39

good. He had some brandy with him and saw that she took a sup. And that did her ladyship good. But, by the time I could leave her, hounds was gone.

"The gentleman wanted her ladyship to wait for a carriage to come. But she says, 'No. Put me up.' And so we comes home."

For the second time that day, the duenna felt something dazed.

*　　*　　*　　*　　*

Two letters shall speak for themselves.

Dear Lady Ursula,

I have seen Big Ben and the doctor. Mercifully, the former seems to remember nothing of the shock which laid him low. He has been told that Sally is with her cousins at Mockery Dale. The latter does not think that his memory will return, but thinks it possible that he will have another stroke in two or three days. This may be the end of him.

The police are reticent, but active. I saw the Chief Constable and gather that an arrest will be made any moment now. I think they know who it is, but he did not say.

Yours very faithfully,

John Leith.

My dear Lady Ursula,

As I may not leave the house, I write at once to express my horror and shame at what occurred this morning by Peppercorn Brake.

I have seen the huntsman in the presence of Mr. Rampus. As a result, the man has been paid his wages and will leave the country for ever before to-morrow mid-day.

But, as his employer, I cannot avoid my responsibility.

I can only beg you to accept and to convey to Lady Vivien my deepest apologies for what occurred. I hope you will believe that I had no idea whatever that the socialistic principles which I

40

had heard the man embraced, could have engendered such spite against an innocent girl, whose spirit is so excelling, whose manner to high and low is above reproach.

Yours very faithfully,
Willoughby Pouncet.

The second note was too much.

Poor Lady Ursula, who had been told nothing of Vivien's misadventure, felt that her world was crumbling before her eyes.

Letters in hand, she entered the great hall.

Vivien and Miss Carson got to their feet.

" Sit down," said Lady Ursula. " Why wasn't I told of this ? "

Vivien turned pale, and Miss Carson took a deep breath.

" I had meant," said the latter, " to tell you, Lady Ursula, later. I, er, knew how worried you were, and I felt it should wait."

Lady Ursula took her seat.

" I should have been told at once."

" Please believe, Lady Ursula, that, in the ordinary way, I should have come straight to you. But I felt that to-day . . ."

" Why to-day ? " said Vivien.

Lady Ursula swallowed.

" Perhaps you were right, Miss Carson. As it is, Sir Willoughby has written to me. What happened exactly, Vivien ? "

In a low voice—

" Anderson brought me the brush. . . . I thought he was going to present it. . . . He pushed it into my face . . . and said he was blooding me."

Lady Ursula's eyes were blazing.

" *Anderson did that to you ?* Who saw him do it, child ? "

" Only old Mr. Rampus. He ordered him back to his hounds and was terribly sweet. And when I was down, a stranger gave me some brandy out of his flask."

" Where was William ? "

" He'd fallen at Robin's Water. He got up as soon as he could."

" You'd better read that letter. It is addressed to me, but it's meant for you."

Vivien took the letter and read it slowly enough.

Then she lifted a startled face.

" But I don't understand," she said. " What's this to do with it ? Has someone attacked Big Ben ? "

Miss Carson's hand flew to her mouth.

Lady Ursula stared at her niece. Then she peered at Sir Willoughby's letter, still in her hand.

Subduing the impulse to scream—

" I made a mistake, my darling. I meant to give you this."

The notes were exchanged.

When she had read the second—

" I love the Master," said Vivien. " He's awfully sweet to me. Of course, it wasn't his fault, but it's like him to take the blame. May I show it to Miss Carson, Aunt Ursula ? "

" Of course."

The letter passed.

" But tell me about Big Ben." She glanced at the clock. " Can't I go down and see Sally ? She must be beside herself. And who would have touched Big Ben ? Was somebody drunk ? "

" Nobody knows," said Miss Carson. " Someone broke into the mill, and Big Ben was hurt. Sally is quite all right. You shall know all to-morrow—I promise you that. But don't ask Pricket, darling. I'd rather you waited for me."

Vivien sighed.

" What a day ! "

" Yes," said her aunt, faintly. " It's—it's been a bad day. Will you come to the Blue Room, Miss Carson, I'm going there now."

As the door of the Blue Room closed—

42

"I'm not fit for these things, Miss Carson. Five minutes ago I made the sort of mistake that must never be made. I'm going to wire to Coles Willing and ask him to come. I think we should have a man here, and Uncle Henry's too old."

Coles Willing was 'the children's' cousin—and third trustee. He was also a first-rate lawyer and a most able man.

"You're perfectly right," said Miss Carson. "Shall I write it out for you?"

"Yes, if you please, my dear. Just say 'Please come at once', and send it to Curzon Street. One of the men must take it to Hasted now."

*　　*　　*　　*　　*

At half past nine the next morning, Vivien was riding with Arthur to Oxney Hall.

She had said that she wished to see the Master himself. 'He's ill, and he wrote so kindly, and really I'm quite all right.'

Miss Carson consulted Lady Ursula.

"I think, if I may say so, that it's a good idea. With Big Ben arriving this morning, she will be out of the way. And she's quite old enough to see the Master herself. I have an idea that she hopes to beg Anderson off. Sir Willoughby won't have that: but it argues an outlook that I would rather not thwart."

"Quite right, my dear," said Lady Ursula.

"And Oxney's away from the mill."

"So it is. You'll have a word with Arthur?"

"I will, Lady Ursula."

"How soon d'you think we shall get a reply to my wire?"

"Any time now, Lady Ursula. I'm sure, if he can, Mr. Willing will come at once. I mean, he'll have . . . seen the papers."

Lady Ursula covered her eyes.

"Isn't it dreadful, Miss Carson?"

43

" It's quite the most dreadful thing that I've ever known."

" You've said nothing to Vivien so far ? "

Miss Carson shook her head.

" I thought, perhaps, after luncheon."

Lady Ursula pursed her lips.

" It's my duty, really : but you'll do it better than me."

" I don't think I shall, Lady Ursula."

" Yes, you will.   But . . . don't leave anything out.   She'll only learn it later."

" I quite agree."

" She's sixteen now, and she's going to Paris next year."

So Vivien was posting, with Arthur, to Oxney Hall.

It was a glorious morning—not too cold, windless, without a cloud in the sky. Foul weather must follow, of course, for weeks to come ; but here was the grateful assurance that Spring was not dead, but sleeping, and would arise again.

Miss Carson was perfectly right.   Vivien was going to try to beg Anderson off.

After all, the man was married : that meant that his wife and children would suffer for what he had done : and that was unfair.   Besides, if he had to go down, she did not want him to founder on her account.

The Hall lay seven miles off, and the Kennels six.   But they were not in line from Poesy.   At the cross roads you went straight on, if you were bound for the Hall : but, if you were bound for the Kennels, you turned to the left.

With Arthur moving behind her, Vivien cantered the length of the Longsden fields.   Then she pulled up, and Arthur opened a gate which gave to the Hasted road.

As they were approaching the cross roads, a dark-blue, four-wheeled dog-cart swung out of the road to the left.

The County Police.

A constable was driving : Inspector Rudkin sat by the driver's side.   A sergeant was sitting behind—with another man.

Vivien had been carefully schooled.   Ladies must always

44

ignore the executive 'on the job'. But the dog-cart had turned the corner, before she had known it was there—and she would have known her assailant a furlong away.

Hatless, dishevelled, wild-eyed, Anderson was sitting, hand-cuffed, upon the back-seat.

Vivien pulled up her mare, as the vehicle made its way by. And then she was round in a flash and had come alongside.

"Stop, Mr. Rudkin, stop."

The Inspector touched his cap and shook his head.

Vivien kept pace by his side.

"But, Mr. Rudkin, you must. It's all a mistake. It—it was only a joke, Mr. Rudkin. The huntsman meant me no harm."

The Inspector stared.

Then—

"Please go your way, my lady. I've got my duty to do."

"But I can't bear it," wailed Vivien. "You see, I know what happened."

At the Inspector's nod, the constable pulled up his horse.

Arthur's hand was on Vivien's rein.

"Come away, my lady," he said.

"Let go my rein," flashed Vivien. "I'm not a child."

"It's not for you, my lady. You don't understand."

"I do understand," cried Vivien. "They're taking the man to prison, because he blooded me. And that is my affair."

There was a pregnant silence. Even the horses were still. The clink of a stone-breaker's hammer was all the sound there was.

Vivien looked round.

"What's the matter?" she said. "Why are you all staring?"

The Inspector took a deep breath.

Then—

"I know nothing of that, my lady. This man is under arrest for the murder of Sally of the Mill."

Then the dog-cart passed on . . . and Vivien sat looking after, with sightless eyes.

Presently she turned to the groom.

" Sally's murdered ? " she said.

" Yes, my lady, that's so."

" And that man, Anderson, did it ? "

" So they say, my lady."

" And I was going to the Master to beg him off." Vivien drew in her breath. " Can you see people hung, Arthur ? I mean, I'd like to be there."

* * * * *

Lady Ursula and Miss Carson were walking upon the terrace, ready and waiting to leave at once for the lodge. As soon as Big Ben was installed, they were to be told.

A footfall, and there was Vivien.

" Oh, dear," said her aunt. And then—" You've been very quick, my darling."

Miss Carson said nothing at all. She had seen in a flash that her ward was changed. A girl had left Poesy : a woman was standing there, tapping her boot with her switch.

" Yes," said Vivien, slowly. " I never got to the Hall. You see, I ran into the police. They've—made the arrest."

Aunt and duenna stood as though turned to stone.

" Anderson murdered Sally. And then he came back and hunted . . . and killed at Peppercorn Brake." Lady Ursula felt sick of body : Miss Carson felt sick at heart. " I suppose he was Sally's lover. Perhaps he hated me so, because he knew he couldn't be mine."

" Vivien ! "

The girl raised her eyebrows.

" I've been trying to work it out : and that's the best answer, I think. But it doesn't really matter, because it can't alter things. Only, he's like the serpent. This was our Paradise . . . and now he's ruined it all." She pointed over the meadows. " The wheel's not running, you see. But

46

when it is running again and we see its splash, it will always remind us of what the serpent did. And how can I hunt again? He's ruined that, too."

Miss Carson found her voice.

"No, he hasn't, Vivien. He's done most dreadful damage —havoc's the word. But evil men have done murder ever since Cain. And yet the world has gone on and happiness still persists. For us all, this place is now poisoned—and all to do with it. But that is only a phase. We should be heartless indeed, if we could look upon this landscape and find it fair to-day. But Time will restore its beauty—for us three here. It couldn't for Anderson . . . even—if he were to live. But we are guiltless, we three. And though we are deeply shocked, so long as *we* do not spoil it, nobody else can spoil our heritage."

Tears began to trickle down Vivien's cheeks.

"Poor, poor Sally," she said. "I expect she wore my scarf for him." And then. "What fools girls are."

*   *   *   *   *

Coles Willing was a tower of strength.

"The milk is spilt, Ursula. All we can do is our best to mop it up. Take Vivien to Town at once and see she goes out and about. Don't keep the papers from her—that's no good. I'll keep an eye on things here."

"Could it have been worse, Coles?"

Coles Willing pulled at his chin.

"I really can't see that it could."

"We have been spared nothing. No circumstance of horror has been omitted from our ordeal. Sally and Big Ben were our familiar friends. The murderer was a hunt-servant whom Vivien has known for years. An utterly barbarous murder by an adulterer. The murderer daubing Vivien—his hands still red from his crime. And then that fearful encounter upon the Hasted road. . . . What have we done to deserve this?"

47

"God knows," said Coles. "I'm as distressed as you are. And I cannot acquit the Master. I don't believe in oppression; but socialistic huntsmen are out of place. When he learned of Anderson's leanings, the man should have gone. Then all this would never have happened."

"It's dreadful when you put it like that."

"Unhappily, it is true. If a man wants to be a socialist, well and good. I'll give him the wall, whenever he wants to have it. But don't ask me to employ him."

"But they're only misguided, aren't they?"

Coles Willing moved to the window and stood looking out.

"If socialism is good, why doesn't the Bible commend it? Of all the thousands of precepts in Holy Writ, there is not one commending the equal state. 'Give to the poor' —yes. 'Be kind to one another.' 'Do as you would be done by.' But 'Be ye all equal'—no. Why, then, this— startling omission?" The man swung round. "I'll tell you, Ursula.

"Socialism is unnatural, and, therefore, false. Nature is not always kind: some of her laws seem harsh: but rise against her, you cannot—she'll always win in the end. 'All men equal, and no more rich and poor.' Desirable—yes: but quite unnatural. Except by force, you never can have such a state. A may be forcibly weighted, to keep him abreast of B: but when you get back to catch-weight, as one day you will, A will leave B standing, just as he did before.

"Now that is such plain, common sense, that the socialist can see it as clearly as anyone else. Why, then, does he still persist in supporting this foolish doctrine which only pulls down A and cannot raise B?"

"I've no idea."

Coles studied his finger-nails.

"You can divide the world in many ways. There are those who are healthy, and there are those who are sick.

48

There are those who are wise, and there are those who are fools. There are also those who have, and those who have not. I have yet to see a socialist who is among those who have.

"You may say that that's natural—and so it is: but, Ursula, the point is this—that, if he came into a fortune, his socialistic tenets would melt like the summer snow.

"The socialist knows his doctrine for what it is. He knows it's false and quite unworkable. He knows you can't fight against Nature, as well as do you and I. But he is an envious man. He is jealous of those who have what he has not. Upon this he broods—and his jealousy turns to hate. He hates the aristocrat and he hates the rich, because he covets their rank and their worldly goods. Give them to him to-morrow, and he would abuse them both: but he'd never give either up, and, if anyone tried to share them, he'd stamp him under his feet.

"Well, a man like that is evil. No man can have such an outlook—and be a good man. I don't pretend that all socialists come to the gallows, but they are completely selfish: they don't care a rap for their fellows, no matter how much they protest. What did Anderson care for his wife . . . or Sally, for the matter of that?"

He stopped there, to shake his head.

"I cannot acquit the Master. A huntsman, with such an outlook! Fuel poured on the fire at every meet. Rank and riches constantly thrust before him. All that he envied always before his eyes." He shook his head again. "No good can come of such things. I think he sees it now. The Chief Constable tells me he's taking it very hard."

"Poor Sir Willoughby."

"Poor everyone," said Coles. "Still, as I said to begin with, the milk is spilt. No good crying now. And Time will wash out the stain."

"It'll take a long time, Coles."

The lawyer sighed.

49

" I'm afraid it will—in a way. They're calling it ' The Peregrine Murder '—that's just bad luck, of course ; but there you are. Whenever the village is mentioned, people will think of the crime. It'll be forgotten here—at least, it won't be thought of in two or three years. But—I hate to say it, Ursula—but I think that you would be wise to turn to Brocade."

Lady Ursula pursed her lips.

" I felt that you'd say that, Coles."

" I'm awfully sorry, my dear. But—just for a year or two. For every reason, you know. When Vivien's in Paris, Philip will probably want to bring a boy back." He shrugged his shoulders. " They're morbid imps, boys. I used to be one, myself."

* * * * *

The brougham went bowling by Willesden along the Harrow Road. Traffic was slight, and the greys were enjoying themselves. The cold was intense. Holly and Wickers were glad of their fur-lined rug.

" I think," said Vivien, " Jack Sheppard was buried here."

" Was he, my dear ? " said Miss Carson. " I don't think I ever knew that."

" Harrison Ainsworth says so. He—he was a felon, of course. But the way he escaped from Newgate was really wonderful. Philip knows it by heart."

Delicate ground, this. Vivien had stumbled upon it and must be led off.

" I think I like *The Tower of London* best. With Xit and the giants and poor little Lady Jane Grey. Still, I'd rather read Thackeray."

" So'd I," said Vivien. " *Esmond.* Shall we have Philip alone ? "

" I doubt it," said the duenna. " On an occasion like this, I think it's the thing to ask one or two of your friends."

Vivien looked out of the window.

" Oh, well," she said. " It's only ten days now."

On the twenty-first of December Harrow School would break up.

" When we reach *The King's Head*, Vivien, I'd like you to give the orders."

" To Holly and Wickers ? "

" Yes : and in the hotel. You can do it as well as I can—just as well."

" But I never do, if you're there. I never should."

" That's because you have manners, darling. But now I want it so. With Lady Ursula, no—unless she asks you to. But I am not your aunt, and you're growing up."

" You mean, I'm to do it always ? "

" When you're with me. I'll look after the tea to-day and I'll always help. But I do want you to take over."

" It doesn't seem right," said Vivien. " I mean, you're older than me. Besides—well, you're Miss Carson. I wouldn't like the servants to think I was being rude."

The duenna smiled.

" They won't, my darling. They'll only be very pleased. But think what you're going to say, before we get out."

Vivien was thinking aloud.

" We'll be there at a quarter to four, and lock-up's at six. So we'll want the brougham then. He can put the greys up for two hours. What about paying, Miss Carson ? "

" Holly will settle the bill and put it down in his book."

" I mustn't kiss Philip, must I ? "

" Leave it to him. If he thinks he can, he'll kiss you and then you can kiss him back. But I shall shake hands."

At twenty minutes to four the greys were pulled up at the inn.

As Wickers opened the door, Philip came running up and took off his hat.

" Hullo, Pip."

" Hullo, Vivvy."

Philip put up his face . . .

"How d'ye do, Miss Carson?"

"Very well, thank you, Pip. But isn't it cold?"

Vivien was speaking to the coachman.

"Be back here at six, please, Holly. That'll give you nice time to put up the greys."

"Very good, my lady. At six o'clock."

"And—and you and Wickers must have a proper tea."

"Thank you, my lady."

While Philip was admiring the greys, the women entered the house.

"They're a lovely pair, Holly."

"They are, my lord. Bit of a handful at times, when the traffic's thick: but they've enjoyed this run."

Philip made much of the truly handsome pair.

"Oh, how's your knee, Wickers? I quite forgot to ask."

"All right again, thank you, my lord: as good as new."

Philip stood back.

"You must get them in, Holly. It's cold."

"It is that, my lord," said the coachman.

"See you the week after next."

"Very happy to hear it, my lord."

"Goodbye. Goodbye, Wickers."

"Goodbye, my lord."

Miss Carson was speaking.

"Pip, allow me to say that I'm really truly thankful to see you're wearing a coat."

"We have to. It's up on the board."

"Where do we go to, darling?"

"First to my room. Woodville and Scot will be there—they're coming to tea. Then we'll go to 'Bill', and then to ——'s. I've got a room upstairs."

('Bill' is the Harrow roll-call.)

"Splendid. Woodville, I remember—a very nice ch—man. I don't think we've met Scot."

"I think you'll like him, Miss Carson. His real name's

Ross. We always call him ' Scot ', because he's mad about Scotland. When he's at home he always wears a kilt."

The three walked up the High Street, Philip on the edge of the pavement and Vivien against the wall.

The girl looked a picture in sealskin, her hands in a seal-skin muff. Miss Carson's cloak was of face-cloth, lined with fur.

Conversation was not too easy. Philip was preoccupied. He was constantly on the watch, in case some ' man ' who knew him should pass and take off his hat. On no account must he fail to return the salute.

" This is Hallam's we're coming to, and further on is Coler's. Ruthven is in his House. Here's Loriarty coming. I'll be up to him soon—he takes the Army Class."

He took off his hat, and Mr. Loriarty raised his.

" That elastic's too tight, Pip."

" No it isn't, Vivvy. I've had to knot it like that, to keep the hat on."

" But it makes a line in your hair."

" That's the bug-run," said Philip. " We've all got that. Come on, it's not far now."

Down some steps and across a dull, paved yard; by gaunt stairs and passages into a cheerless room.

" Hullo, Sheep. You know Woodville, Miss Carson— and Vivvy, too."

" How d'ye do, Mr. Woodville? It was warmer than this at Lord's."

" How d'ye do, how d'ye do? "

The boy pump-handled their arms.

" Where's Scot? "

" I don't know. He said he was coming."

" Sit down, Miss Carson. Look, Vivvy. That's mine. I bought it from Denniston Mi."

The Ares Ludovisi, framed in black oak.

" I think it's lovely, Pip."

Ross burst into the room.

" Hullo, Scot. This is Ross, Miss Carson. My sister, Vivien."

" How d'ye do, Mr. Ross? Don't tell me you all sleep here?"

" No, only Ringwood and Woodville. I'm upstairs."

" I hear a bell, Philip."

" I know. That's for ' Bill '. But we've got plenty of time."

" It's really very convenient, being so close. The men at Hallam's have very much further to go."

" Marshall's is awful, Miss Carson. It's simply miles."

" Are all the form-rooms as close?"

" Most of them are," said Ross. " But Linden's is by *The King's Head*."

" Up a passage," said Philip. He began to bubble with laughter. " A woman selling bananas came up last week. She didn't know it was a class-room. She just knocked on the door, and Linden said ' Come in '. And so we all bought bananas. She was frightfully pleased, but Linden was simply wild."

" She was Irish," said Ross, "and Linden is French. So they could not communicate."

Miss Carson began to laugh.

" Do do her, Scot."

" Och, the divil fly away wid yer, tacher : your tongue's that faulty, the bhoys shud be tachin' you."

Miss Carson and Vivien were justly overcome.

The five proceeded to Bill Yard in a hilarious mood.

" Up on the steps, Miss Carson. You stand beside the Master, but not too close."

" By God," said Rivers, " who is that lovely girl?"

(Rivers was just eighteen. He was in the Cricket Eleven, played for the School at racquets, was due at Christchurch next year.)

" Ringwood's people," said someone.

" That's right. She was on his coach," said somebody else.

Snow was beginning to fall.

Mr. Wilson, taking 'Bill', was without an overcoat. Vivien liked him at once. His air was merry and careless—devil-may-care.

" Here, sir ! Here, sir ! Here, sir ! "

The boys touched their hats and went by.

A late-comer made a great effort to reach his place. Just before he could whip into line, his name was called. " Here, sir ! " he cried boldly, six feet out of his place.

Wilson threw back his head and laughed.

Then he jerked his head to the left. Crestfallen enough, the boy passed up the steps and took his stand behind Wilson, awaiting his fate.

" That's rather hard," whispered Vivien.

" Here, sir ! Here, sir ! Here, sir ! . . ."

" Look, Miss Carson. Here's Pip."

" Woodville . . . Berriman . . . Ringwood . . ."

The roll had been called.

Wilson turned to the ladies and took off his mortar-board. Then he looked at his victim, before passing up the steps.

" Off you go, you Burgher of Calais. And don't be late again."

" Oh, thank you, sir."

Miss Carson tried not to smile.

Tea was a festive meal. A most enormous tea, in a room with a roaring fire.

Masters were approved—or disapproved. Wilson got a very good chit. Then the ' bloods ' were dealt with. Rivers of the Headmaster's was clearly popular. Ross was telling Miss Carson about his Scottish home. Vivien, Philip and Woodville were talking of horses and saddles and Woodville was exposing the art of driving a coach. (His uncle, Sir Samuel Rust, was a famous whip.)

" It's no joke to turn off a high road and in through a five-barred gate. I mean, you've nothing to spare. And if . . ."

The lock-up bell was pealing—flinging its rigorous orders into the sullen night.

Miss Carson glanced at her watch.

"It's quite all right," said Philip. "We needn't go till it stops."

Miss Carson became *distraite*: she was trying to measure the distance to the Headmaster's house.

At length, to her relief—

"P'raps we'd better be going," said Ross.

Hats were identified, overcoats were assumed.

"Thank you very much for having me . . . Goodbye, Mr. Woodville . . . Mr. Ross . . . Goodbye, Pip. See you on Tuesday week. . . ."

A clattering down the staircase. . . . The three were gone.

The walk to *The King's Head* was cold, indeed; but Wickers had seen that the foot-warmer was refilled.

"Grosvenor Square, Wickers."

"Very good, my lady."

Then the door of the brougham was shut, and Wickers was up on the box.

The greys sprang forward. . . .

* * * * *

Christmas in Grosvenor Square.

Safety bicycles for the children—to be used out of London, of course. Presents for the servants—presents for everyone. To Church on Christmas morning in Hanover Square. Lord Henry and Coles to dinner at half past seven o'clock. Revelry afterwards—snap-dragon and charades. Lord Henry and Coles stage a prize-fight—and laugh so much themselves that they have to give in and sit down. And so to bed. . . .

* * * * *

The second caller had been sped, and Philip and Vivien were at ease in the Small Saloon. This had been rendered to them; and though it was a stiff chamber, they made it their own.

The fog was coming down. An hour ago you could only just see the railings: now you could just see the pavement, but nothing more.

"Are—are we going to Poesy, Vivvy?"

Vivien shook her head.

"If you'd been there when it happened, you wouldn't want to, Pip."

"I can't understand it, Vivvy. How could Sally have done it?"

Vivien shrugged her shoulders.

"I can't answer that question, Pip. I think that beast must have fascinated her. You know, as snakes do birds."

"But—but he was married, Vivvy."

"I know. But he was a beast. It's all so dreadful, Pip. He's—ruined everything. Big Ben is dying and Sally is dead. The Master's resigned, and——"

"He hasn't!"

"Yes, he has."

"But why? It wasn't his fault."

Vivien swallowed. Philip was never to know what had happened by Peppercorn Brake.

"He felt it was, for keeping such a man on."

"But how could he know he was a beast?"

"I don't suppose he knew that. But he knew he was a socialist. And they do hate other people. Any way, he was his huntsman, and so he's resigned."

"But what are they doing about the hunt?"

"Major Hyslop is acting as Master, and Filson is doing huntsman, until they can get a new man. I tell you, Pip, that beast has spoiled everything. Miss Carson says we'll forget it; and so, I suppose, we shall. But just now—well, when you're there, you think of it all day long. Everything makes you think of it. You look out, and the wheel's not running: you see a horse, and that makes you think of

hounds : Pricket never stopped crying, until we came away. She and Sally, of course, were bosom friends. And how can we hunt—or even think of hunting ? We couldn't help thinking of him. And the moment you think of him—well, everything's spoiled."

Philip stared at the fire.

" P'raps it'll be better when he's dead. I mean, when one thinks of him then, you'll know he's been jolly well hung. I mean, that's something, Vivvy."

" It may make things better," said Vivien, doubtfully.

" It won't be for ages yet. He's got to go to Winchester, to be tried. But he can't get off. Did you see about the footprints ? "

Vivien shook her head.

" One of his boots had a bit of iron on the heel : but the other hadn't. So the prints he left were different. Besides, they fitted his boots. And then his wife was trying to burn his clothes."

" I wouldn't have burned his clothes, if I'd been her. I'd 've kept them to show to the police."

" So'd I," warmly. " And he took the paraffin with him. Took it to the mill, I mean. Moon swears he sold him that bottle the day before."

" Good. I'd like to be there, when he's sentenced to death."

" So'd I."

" I know. But I feel worse than you. You see, I'm a girl. And Sally was a girl. And he ruined Sally first. And he deserved hanging for that, for Sally was always so happy—she and Big Ben. Besides, he was married, which makes it filthier still. And then, I suppose, she told him . . ."

" Told him what ? "

" That she was going to have a baby."

" Oh," unconvincedly, " I see."

" And then the beast was frightened—you can't hide

58

things like that. Frightened. And poor little Sally must have been terrified. And that was why she told him. He'd made her have a baby, and so she turned to him. But he only thinks of himself. Sally doesn't matter. Because he's a married man, he's got to save himself. And so he kills her—and tries to burn her body, so that no one shall ever know."

"Know what?" said Philip.

"That she was going to have a baby. If they hadn't found that out, it might have been anyone. But they'd been seen together, making love."

"I see," said Philip, again without conviction.

"But the point is this, darling—that Sally was a girl like me. And so I know what she suffered, better than you. Men are different. They can't be deceived like that. And so they can't understand, as women can. That's why I hate Anderson even more than you. I hate and loathe the very sound of his name. And—and if he gets off, I'd like to kill him myself."

"He won't get off," said Philip. "Rivers says he hasn't a cur dog's chance."

*　　　*　　　*　　　*　　　*

Five days later Lord Henry kept his word.

"Ready, Pip?"

"Yes, sir."

Philip had been ready and waiting for half an hour.

The boy looked very well. His Etons were almost new, and he wore a low, white waistcoat and white bow tie.

A hansom was waiting . . .

Mount Street . . . Berkeley Square . . . Piccadilly . . . St. James's Street.

"Time you got to know the Clubs, Pip. That's White's with its famous bow-window, and, over there, is Brooks's—the corner house."

"White's and Brooks's, sir."

"That's right. And the clock at the end of the street?"

" St. James's Palace, sir."

" Pall Mall on the left at the bottom. What's on the right ? "

" I—can't remember, sir."

" Cleveland Row."

One minute later, perhaps, the doors of the hansom were opened, and host and guest got out.

Double doors swung back, and the two passed into a cheerful vestibule.

Lord Henry nodded to the porter.

" Evening, Haylett."

" Good evening, my lord."

Up the steps and into an echoing hall.

" Follow the page, Pip. He'll take your coat and hat and show you where he puts them."

Boy followed boy, first to the strangers' cloak-room, and then to the great fireside.

" Isn't it cold ? " said Philip. " I mean, outside."

" Yes, sir. It's very cold."

Lord Henry appeared.

" Come into the morning-room, Pip. If you'll excuse me, I'll have a glass of sherry, before we dine."

" Of course, sir."

As they came to a mighty sofa, a man looked up.

" Hullo, Henry. I thought you were down in Norfolk."

" Christmas in Town, Arthur. Let me introduce my nephew, Philip Ringwood—Mr. Pope."

" How d'ye do, sir ? " said Philip, shaking hands.

" God bless my soul. I knew your grandfather, Philip. That was a long time ago. We were up at Magdalen together. You going there ? "

" No, sir. I'm going to Sandhurst."

" And so to the Blues ? "

" I hope so, sir."

" Been to Drury Lane ? "

" Yes, sir. Last Friday night."

" Wasn't it good ? "

" Glorious, sir. When Dan Leno . . ."

The two of them laughed together over some memory.

" You seen it, Henry ? "

" Not yet."

" My dear fellow, you must. You'll laugh till you cry.
Go with Philip. He'll love to see it again."

" Oh, sir, I'd love to."

" That's an engagement, Pip. Vivien like to come, too ?
Matinée, I think. And if it's not over too late, we'll bring
her back here for tea."

The evening was going well.

Lord Henry finished his sherry and led the way to the
strangers' coffee-room.

The old head-waiter received them.

" Your table, my lord, is the one on the left of the fire.
Will that be too close ? "

Host and guest took their seats, and a servant presented a
card.

" Clear soup for me. And you, Pip ? "

" Clear, please."

An atmosphere of discretion distinguished a noble room.
The thick carpet made for silence : the shaded candles dispensed an intimate light—host and guest were illumined, but
nobody else : a murmur of conversation was all you heard.
Under the head-waiter's eye, the perfectly trained servants
passed to and fro, changing plates, charging glasses, offering
food.

" What will you drink, Pip ? The barley-water here is
usually very good."

" I'd love barley-water, sir."

" Barley-water for Lord Ringwood, and I'll have a pint of
champagne."

" Very good, my lord. The Bollinger ? "

" Yes, please. . . . Tell me of Harrow, Pip. Is Welldon
popular ? "

At last the cloth was drawn, to reveal the lovely rosewood lying beneath. Then ginger wafers appeared, and Philip dealt with an apple, while his great-uncle sipped his port.

Coffee was served upstairs in the splendid smoking-room. There the two spoke of horses and racing—and so of Tattersall's.

Arrangements were made to go there the following day.

The evening was approaching perfection.

As they were descending the staircase, a very old member came out of the morning-room.

" Look well at that man, Pip. If I can, I'll introduce you. Stand by the fire."

The old fellow made for the cloak-room with faltering steps. Lord Henry followed him in.

" Can I help you, General ? "

The other peered.

" Damme, it's Henry Daring. Yes, if you'd be so good. That's my coat hanging there."

The two of them talked for a little : then they passed into the hall.

" My great-nephew's with me, General. He's going into the Blues."

" I'm glad of that. Where is he ? "

Host beckoned guest.

" Philip Ringwood, General. Pip, this is General Clay."

" How d'ye do, my boy ? "

A tremulous hand was clasped.

" So you're going into the Blues. I'm glad of that. I commanded the ——s a long time ago. Ringwood— I know the name."

" You knew his grandfather, General."

" That's probably it. I've met so many people in my long life." He turned to look upon Philip. " I served with the Duke, my boy—a long time ago. And I dined with him at Walmer. He was a very great man. And always humble, except, of course, in the field. Very touching, that, Daring.

62

Very conscious of the shortcomings he never had." He
turned again to Philip. "Remember that, my boy. The
greatest man in all England : and he was very humble. So
glad you came up, Daring, and brought the boy. I'm all
right now, and my man will be by the lodge."

He tottered towards the swing doors.

As he approached, these opened : a servant was waiting
there, to guide his steps.

Lord Henry watched him out.

Then—

"Never forget that, Pip. You've shaken hands with a
man who fought at Waterloo. And always remember what
he said—you heard him say. ' The Duke was very humble.'
I cannot conceive a greater epitaph."

*   *   *   *   *

29th January, 1893.

Sir Humphrey Raynes, Q.C.
        to
The Treasury Solicitor.

Dear Forest,

            Rex v. Anderson.

*The evidence which the depositions disclose justified a committal
for trial. But if I am to obtain a conviction, I ought to have more
than that.*

What have we got?

We have :—

(a) The footprints.

(b) The bottle of paraffin.

(c) The attempt to burn the man's clothes.

*(d) That the two were seen together one evening late in Sep-
tember by Mrs. Birchup.*

*Without (d) the case would break down. The accused must
be linked with the girl, before the murder was done. Well, he is
linked—by Mrs. Birchup. But the link is not very strong, and*

counsel for the defence will go for it tooth and nail.   Dusk, two shadowy figures, no voices heard.   And if he can shake Mrs. Birchup, the man may get off.

Can you not strengthen this link.   The great probability is that the two met time and again.   Surely somebody else at some other time caught a glimpse of them.

Yours very truly,
Humphrey Raynes.

16th February, 1893.

The Treasury Solicitor
          to
Sir Humphrey Raynes, Q.C.

Dear Sir Humphrey,

Rex v. Anderson.

I think the enclosed statements should close the gap.
Yours very truly,
Allen Forest.

Enclosure No. 1.

William Lane will say :—

On the seventh of October I was returning from Blackbird to Peregrine.   I took a short cut that I know, by Moseley Copse. The footpath there has high hedges on either side.   These had not been trimmed.   As I was passing along it, I felt something touch my hand.   I stopped and took hold of it.   It felt like a piece of silk.   When I pulled it, it would not come : it was caught by the briers.   I struck a match and unhitched it.   I saw it was some dark colour—I thought it was green.   I struck another match to see it better.   I saw that it had tassels at either end.   The match was still burning, when a hand came over my shoulder and snatched it away.   It was a man's hand, and I saw the wrist.   This was tattooed.   I saw the design—crossed swords.   This told me who the man was.   I knew it was the prisoner, for I had seen this tattoo mark on his arm.   He said

64

nothing, neither did I. Then he went off down the path. I did not see him again. I said nothing about this to anyone. It was no business of mine.

I have been shown a green scarf (Exhibit 13). That is the one I found by Moseley Copse. I will swear to it anywhere. You can see the little rents made by the thorns when I pulled it.

Enclosure No. 2.

Amy Masters will say :—

The dead girl showed me a green scarf which had been given to her. That would be some time about the end of August. It was of beautiful silk and it had a tasselled fringe. I have been shown a green scarf (Exhibit 13). That is the one which the dead girl showed to me. I would know it anywhere.

Enclosure No. 3.

Detective Inspector Albert Reynolds will say :—

In the course of my duties, I went through the deceased's effects. Among them was a green scarf, which I produce (Exhibit 13). This was wrapped up in tissue paper. There are two little rents in the silk, such as might have been made by thorns.

I have examined the prisoner's wrists. On the back of the right fore-arm, close to the wrist, there is a tattoo mark. This represents crossed swords.

Sir Humphrey Rayne, Q.C.
                to
The Treasury Solicitor.

Dear Forest,
                Rex v. Anderson.
    That's more like it. I think we have him now.
                                Yours very truly,
                                Humphrey Rayne.

*　　*　　*　　*　　*

Yet another letter.

Sunday.

My darling Vivvy,
   Rivers is frightfully decent.   When I was on Boy on Wednesday, he said he'd seen me down at the racquet-court.   I said I was having lessons.   So he said he'd play with me on Friday at a quarter to twelve.   You know, he's marvellous.   He showed me all sorts of shots, and he said I wasn't too bad.   I mean, he plays for the School.   So it's really very decent of him.   He's a four-yearer, of course.   I can't play much because of Torpids, but I'm better than I was—the pro. says so.   But it's frightfully decent of him, isn't it ?   There was a fire last week, and Woodville and I got down there and helped to pump.   You have to be careful to keep your fingers clear.   One of the fireman didn't, and his hand was an awful mess.   Woodville and I took jolly good care to keep our hands away.   The barn was burned right down, but they said that he was insured.   Rivers thinks Dan Leno is frightfully good.   I told him we did, too.   I must stop now.

Your loving brother,
Pip.

*   *   *   *   *

The Assize Court was crammed.

The atmosphere was stifling, for every window was shut. His lordship would have it so.   He was a grim man, a very able lawyer, an excellent judge.

Sitting there, in his powder and scarlet, he might have belonged to the eighteenth century.   The High Sheriff, in blue and silver, sat in the stall on his right.   On his left was his pale-faced Marshal, sitting as still as death.

The gas in the globes was flaring : the time was six o'clock. But then Sir Henry Hancock sat to all hours—till two o'clock in the morning, if he felt so disposed.

Counsel looked very tired—it had been an exhausting day. But the Judge looked as fresh as paint.   Long hours seemed to sustain him—a most remarkable man.

66

The jury was listening intently to what he said. And so was everyone. The man compelled attention. No need to strain the ears. His voice was as clear as his sentences were crisp. And, except for these clean-cut accents, there was the most absolute silence. Men knew better than to cough, when he was up on the Bench.

Seated in the dock, the huntsman regarded the Judge with narrowed eyes . . .

'And this was what they called " justice ". The same old thing. One law for the rich, and another for the poor. That man had everything—rank, riches, power over other men. Clerks and servants, to bow him in and out, and a coach to bring him to Court, with a couple of flunkeys behind. He'd seen the Red Judge go by—in other days: and had spat as he passed. And what of the Sheriff, beside him? He knew the —— all right. Came out hunting one day—with two of the finest hunters that ever were seen. Two. Rich, titled, owning six thousand acres, his brougham would be waiting outside, to take him home. A footman would be there, with a rug. And another footman to open the door of his mansion—what was its name? And a valet to take off his duds —pull off his boots—well, stockings. White silk stockings —wonder how much they cost. . . . How the hell could he get justice of people like that? Jury be ——. Juries did what they were told. And now that old —— was telling them . . .'

The clear voice went steadily on.

" Mr. Moon, the grocer, was most definite. In this particular bottle, there is a flaw in the glass. It closely resembles a crack—you have seen it, gentlemen. Mr. Moon thought it *was* a crack; but when he examined it closely, he saw that it was a flaw. And so he filled the bottle out of his cask. He sold it to the accused on December the third—the day before the murder was done. The accused at once protested that the bottle was cracked: whereupon Mr. Moon showed him that the crack was no crack, but a flaw. The accused was not

67

convinced, and demanded another bottle, to take its place. But that was the last bottle; and so, against his will, the prisoner took it away.

"Now bottles are sold to all and sundry: but in this particular case there was that little argument, between grocer and customer, to stamp upon Mr. Moon's mind that it was in fact the prisoner to whom that bottle was sold.

"How then did that bottle come to be found upon the stairs of the mill? Who . . . left it there, gentlemen? We know that the contents had been used . . . to soak the clothing of this unfortunate girl. That, no one seeks to deny. But who . . . left the bottle there? We know who purchased it . . . and took it away from the shop. Can you have any reasonable doubt that the man who purchased it is the man who used its contents . . . and left it on the stairs of the mill?

"I have purposely left to the last the something dramatic evidence, given by William Lane. I will not recite it again, for Counsel for the Crown and Counsel for the Defence have, both of them, dealt with it in detail, so that you know its burden as well as do I.

"Now unless William Lane is lying—and I must confess that I can see no reason why he should lie—the hand that came over his shoulder and snatched that scarf was the hand of the accused. That does not prove that the prisoner is guilty of this murder: but it does prove, gentlemen, that the prisoner was familiar with the deceased.

"There can be no shadow of doubt that this barbarous murder was done by a man who had something to fear from the fact that this girl was with child. He desired to destroy her body, and since he could not destroy it while she was alive, he murdered her first. Then he was free to soak her clothes with his oil, in the hope that her body would burn.

"Now the only man who had something to fear from the fact that this girl was with child was the man who had got the girl in the family way.

"Who was that man?

"As a general rule, as you know, plenty of fingers are ready and waiting to point to the guilty father : but here there is only one witness who ever saw the prisoner with the deceased. Now if Mrs. Birchup's evidence stood alone, I should be bound to tell you to receive it with the greatest caution : but, as luck will have it, it does not stand alone. It is confirmed—and more than confirmed by the evidence of William Lane.

"The scarf is a pointing finger—one of those pointing fingers I mentioned just now. It points directly at the prisoner, as being surreptitiously familiar with the girl who has been destroyed.

"'*A hand came over my shoulder and snatched the scarf away.*'

"No word of explanation—much less of greeting or thanks. No word at all. Nothing spoken. *Why?*

"Was it because the man who snatched the scarf had something to hide? And, if so, what? What did he wish to hide? Was it his identity, gentlemen? And, if so, why? Why did he not wish the finder of the scarf to know who it was that had come to look for Sally Merton's scarf?

"'*Directly I saw it, I knew whose hand it was.*'"

The Judge picked up the scarf which Vivien had given to Sally one August day.

"This green silk scarf is a document in this case. And documents cannot lie. It was a treasured possession of this unfortunate girl : on that October evening, the prisoner snatched it from Lane and left him without a word : and, when the girl was dead, it was found, laid carefully up, in her chest of drawers.

"By themselves, these facts do not prove that the prisoner put her to death : but they do prove incontestably that a clandestine familiarity was existing between the two. Which puts him, automatically, among those men one of whom had a powerful motive to commit this terrible crime.

"I say 'one of whom'. . . . But was there anyone else?

69

If there was, we have not been told of him. No other finger is pointing at any other man. But this is pointing directly at the accused.

" With such an indication behind it, the other evidence against him assumes a deadly significance. Bottle, footprints, burned clothes—these fill in the pattern which this green scarf has sketched."

The Judge sat back in his stall.

" Well, gentlemen, the evidence is before you. If you have any reasonable doubt that this man committed this cruel and barbarous murder, it is your duty to find him ' not guilty ' of this charge. But such doubt must be reasonable. If, on the other hand, you have no reasonable doubt, it is your bounden duty to see that he does not escape the consequences of his crime.

" Consider your verdict."

Twenty-five minutes later, the doors of the Court were locked and Anderson was sentenced to death.

As he passed down the steps to the cells, the Judge leaned over his desk and spoke to the Clerk of Assize.

" I'll adjourn for dinner," he said. " Resume at eight o'clock."

The High Sheriff heard what he said—and felt like murder, himself.

*   *   *   *   *

Easter was four days off.

Back from Harrow that morning, Philip was sitting with Vivien, alone in the Small Saloon.

After a glance at the doors—

" Vivvy, did you see the papers ? "

Vivien nodded.

" Yes."

" But it was your scarf, Vivvy, that cooked his goose."

" I know. I'm terribly glad. I suppose I oughtn't to be ; but I can't help that. I'd wanted to see him hanged, but this

70

is better than that. I've helped to avenge Sally. And you see I was right, Pip. She wore it for him."

" Of course I said nothing about it being your scarf, but Rivers says it's the scarf that bowled him out. You've got to have a motive, you see."

" I don't know about that, Pip. But the Judge said it pointed to him. ' The pointing finger,' he called it. And I do feel better, you know. I mean, when we go to Poesy, everything will come back. But the feeling that I helped to hang him will come back, too."

" Did you see the *Daily Graphic* ? "

Vivien shook her head.

" There was a picture there of the Judge with the black cap on. I must say he looked pretty awful. How's Big Ben ? "

" Big Ben died last week."

" Oh, Vivvy, I'm terribly sorry."

" Don't be sorry, Pip. He was only half alive. That beast finished him, too. But now he and Sally are together —and happy again."

" I'll bet Anderson goes to Hell."

" Well, if he doesn't," said Vivien, " I don't see the point of Hell."

*   *   *   *   *

The journey to France was gorgeous—from Philip's point of view. Vivien would have enjoyed it, had she been coming back. Poor Miss Carson loathed it from first to last. She could not bear inefficiency in herself. She was the very worst sailor that ever was foaled.

" Vivien, dear, you won't forget what I've said. I shall be *hors de combat*, so you must attend to things. Matthews and Cummings will put all our things on board. I shall go down to the cabin, and Dalton will come with me." (Dalton was Miss Carson's maid.) " When we reach Boulogne, look out for Bidaut at once." (Bidaut was Lady Ringwood's

71

courier—a quite invaluable man.) " He will know you, of course, and you ought to know him. As soon as you see him, point him out to Matthews and tell him to do as he says. You may have to deal with the Customs—there are the keys. If you don't see me, don't worry. I shall go straight to the train."

The packet did her best—against very heavy odds. The tail-end of a gale made fun of her labouring paddles and let her go very late. Rolling to hell all the way, she reached Boulogne at last—about an hour and a quarter behind her time.

Whipped by the wind and the spray, Vivien and Philip shared the unequal fight—and ' looked a million dollars' when they arrived in port. The poor duenna emerged from her ill-smelling cabin more dead than alive.

" Is all all right, my dear ? "

" Yes, Miss Carson. Matthews and Bidaut's men are getting our things. And Bidaut is waiting to see us through the Customs. I'm so dreadfully, sorry, Miss Carson. You look so ill."

" My darling child, if I look as bad as I feel. . . . Never mind. I'll do it somehow. Which way do we go ? "

By the grace of God, sea-sickness has a short run. When the three reached the Gare du Nord, the duenna was almost herself.

There a carriage and pair was waiting. . . .

Paris was windless and warm, and her trees were in leaf. The air was alive with Spring. Everyone was talking and laughing. Cries and clatter distinguished the busy streets. The pavements seemed crammed with tables—all of them occupied.

Lady Ringwood's mansion was very discreet. Close to the Champs Elysées, it boasted a pleasant garden, behind high walls. Here an old fountain was playing by day and night.

" My darling children, you do me far more credit than I deserve."

"Mummy, Mummy! How lovely to see you again!"

"And where is my deputy?"

"I think she's gone to her room. We had a pretty rough crossing, and she was dreadfully ill."

"Poor, dear Miss Carson. She has her maid?"

"Yes. But I didn't bring Pricket."

"That is well. I have a French maid for you. Her name is Thérèse, and she will be very good. But Matthews will look after Philip. I think that's best."

"Mummy, you're prettier than ever."

Mother smiled upon daughter.

"Philip should have said that. But it is worth twice as much when it comes from you."

"Did you enjoy Budapest?"

"Budapest, my darling, is heaven on earth. I've engaged an apartment there. You must both come and stay. And the manners of the people are charming—they made me feel *gauche*. The courtesy here is assumed : but there it is natural.

"Philip, darling, you reek of the public school. You are so clearly a man. André—that's the butler—will be your slave. That's the strange thing about France. They know a man when they see one—and worship him as he deserves. But they simply cannot produce one. Their youths are beyond all words. If one of them saw you coming, he'd take to his heels. I'm talking about the *élite*. The peasants, of course, are better; but the spirit of France is poor. They don't look at things as we do. They're always talking of their honour—a most embarrassing trait. But I don't see much of them, really; and you shall see less. The Ambassador's wife is coming to luncheon to-morrow and bringing her boy and girl. The boy is at Winchester, and I think you'll both like them both. But if you don't, you must tell me, and we won't have them again."

"I love your watch, Mummy. I've never seen a watch in a bracelet before."

"Isn't it nice, darling? And it makes it so very easy to

see the time. Not that I ever bother. I always guess. I find it saves so much trouble."

'The children' shrieked with laughter. Mummy was simply glorious : she always spoke as she felt.

"And how's Aunt Ursula?"

"She's very well. She sent you her dearest love."

"She's very sweet. Her body seems to be frail, but she has a heart of oak. Always be proud of her, darlings. And Great-Uncle Henry?"

"Oh, he's full of beans," said Philip.

"Delightful phrase. So very, very English. And it exactly describes him. You know, you two are going to do me good. Tell me of Harrow, Pip."

"Oh, Harrow's all right. Rivers thinks we shall win the Match this year."

"I thought you had a friend called Woodville."

"So I have, Mummy. He shares my room. Good, old Sheep. His birthday's two days before mine. But Rivers is a four-yearer."

"And so, a Nestor. Darling boy, I do love you. But don't let Woodville go. Stick to your own age—always. Don't pick older friends, or your own age will write you off. Vivvy, you listen and smile. You're growing up. Last year you were impulsive : now you are critical."

"Yes, Mummy, I'm growing up."

Lady Ringwood smiled. Then she got to her feet and took Vivien's face in her hands.

"My little girl . . . growing up. . . . It seems to me that someone has waved a wand. Never mind—it's all to the good. We shall be the better companions—you and I."

Vivien flung her arms round her neck.

"Oh, Mummy, Mummy, you always say the right thing."

"That's living so much in Paris. They're very quick-witted, darling. One picks it up."

"It isn't. It's 'cause you're Mummy."

"Yes," said Philip, stoutly. "There's no one like you."

74

I cannot describe Lady Ringwood—Rachel, Lady Ringwood, to be precise. But Sargent painted her and captured that worldly wisdom that sat in the eyes of a child. The portrait hangs at Brocade—and can be seen to-day for the price of half a crown. (A seat in the char-à-banc from Bristol will cost you seven and six—there and back, of course. 'I'd sooner go to the pictures,' says Erny Balch. So would I, Erny. Mausoleums have never appealed to me.)

*   *   *   *   *

" Don't you think you should take her, Lady Ringwood ? "

Miss Carson knew her shortcomings. Her French was not that of France.

" No, my dear Miss Carson. That is your right. Besides, I want Madame de Vosges to make your acquaintance. I want her to see for herself how fortunate Vivien has been."

Miss Carson coloured with pleasure.

" That's very handsome, Lady Ringwood."

" It's very true."

Miss Carson braced herself.

Then—

" Lady Ringwood."

" Yes."

" So far I have said nothing to the Trustees : but, as Vivien is to stay here and—and Philip is now at school for more than two-thirds of his time, my services are no longer essential—if, indeed, they were ever that." The duenna paused, twisting her hands. " May I put it like this, Lady Ringwood. The Trustees have always shown me the greatest consideration. I should not like them, out of consideration for me, to hesitate to terminate an engagement which they no longer required."

Lady Ringwood smiled. Then—

" You dear thing," she said. She rose, passed to a table and opened a drawer. " I have here a letter for you which was sent to me to read. I was to give it to you, when you

75

came back from St. Cloud. But, since you've said what you have, I'll give it you now."

Grosvenor Square.

My dear Miss Carson,

The duty for which you were engaged is nearly done. But your interpretation of that duty has been so wide and so generous that, while you have every right to ask to be relieved, it is the Trustees' earnest hope that you will remain.

I can give no name to the functions which you will perform : all we can ask you to do is to be yourself. That is more than enough for us. In these seven years you have won our love and respect—and have been the greatest comfort to the Trustees. As for the children, I am perfectly sure it has never entered their heads that you might leave. Were you to do so, I think it would break their hearts.

So please write and tell me, my dear, that you will stay.

Lady Ringwood would like to keep you, till Vivien has settled down. After that, you and I might very well go to Brocade. I shall depend on you there, for, as you know, I seldom visit the seat. But everything must be right before Philip returns.

Yours always sincerely,
Ursula Brabant.

Miss Carson burst into tears.

" There, there," said Lady Ringwood, in tears herself. " Promise you'll never leave them."

" Never," sobbed the duenna. " I—I love them too well."

*　　*　　*　　*　　*

Madame de Vosges was very, very French.

A perfectly mannered woman of forty-five, she was most beautifully dressed and moved like a queen.

" *Bon jour, Vivienne. Bon jour, Mam'selle.* Now I shall speak my English. I trust Miladi Ringwood has a good health."

" She's very well, thank you," said Vivien.

76

"And the *Comte de Ringwood*? I trust he is full with joydom to be with his scholars again."

Not daring to trust her voice, Vivien inclined her head.

"You'll do," said Madame de Vosges, and kissed her on either cheek. "As a matter of fact, my English is very good. But I wanted to see if you knew how to behave." She turned to Miss Carson. "*Mam'selle*, my congratulations. Very few girls of her age would have suppressed a smile. . . .

"Well, here we are, my pretty. All will be strange to you —extremely strange. French people, French tongues, French ways. But you mustn't mind that. I know the English so well, and I'll make you a present of this—that they are, without exception, the finest race there is. But English, French, Italian—what you will, the man is a better man, if he spends a year in a country that is not his. You see, it broadens his mind. It shows him that, good as he is, he still has something to learn which he cannot be taught at home. You will see our failings, my dear : alas, we have many of them. But you will see also our virtues. And you are coming to me, to add what virtues we have to those which you were born with and which Mam'selle, beside you, has taught you to cultivate.

"And now I have a blow coming. . . . Within these walls, you must speak nothing but French. From the time you leave this room, for one year . . . nothing but French. There are other English girls : but I put you upon your honour, as I have put them, never to let any English pass your lips. It will be hard—for a week. But one day you will thank me for this, my discipline. . . ."

She passed to a French window and raised her voice.

"Jane, my dear." She turned to Vivien, smiling. "You see, I may break my rule : but nobody else."

A moment later, tennis-racquet in hand, a jolly-faced English girl came pelting up the steps.

"Let me introduce Miss Jane Purcell—Lady Vivien Brabant."

The girls shook hands, smiling.

" Take her with you, Jane, for a quarter of an hour."

" *Bien, Madame. Viens, Vivienne.*"

The two disappeared.

" I suggest," said Madame de Vosges, " —mark you, it is only a suggestion—that you should not see her again, till to-morrow at tea.   Come to tea to-morrow, and you shall have her alone for half an hour.   And you shall speak English together—my rule will be relaxed."

" Madame," said Miss Carson, " I think you are very wise —and very understanding."

" I don't know about that.   But it is not so very long since I was a girl myself.   Longer than in your case : but not so very long.   That is our secret, isn't it ?   Never to forget for one moment the days when we were young. . . . And now it is your turn to talk.   You must have many things you would like to say to me."

The duenna smiled.

" You have made half of them superfluous, Madame."

The other laughed.

" I am so very glad.   But I think that some remain. . . ."

" There's just . . ."

Miss Carson was driven back to Lady Ringwood's *hôtel.*

" My dear," said that lady, " we must distract ourselves. After luncheon we'll go to Claude's and consider some frocks. You will allow me to make you a present of some—and will advise me what I should choose for myself."

*   *   *   *   *

When Philip learned that Vivien would not return till her year was up, he was distinctly depressed for nearly three hours.   When Speech Day came and went, but Vivien was not to be seen, Rivers was more than annoyed.   Still, though he had noticed Philip, in the hope of meeting his sister, now that he knew him, he liked the boy for himself.   When he left at the end of the term, he told his successor to watch him.

78

'I don't know that he'll get his flannels, but one of these days he'll be worth his Sixth-Form coat. And if you can help his racquets, he ought to play for the School.' Such commendation was quite invaluable. (It was certainly thanks to Vivien that Philip played racquets for Harrow before he left. No favouritism was here: he was simply given the chance to develop his bent.)

In August Woodville spent three weeks at Brocade. The following Easter Philip visited Ross, caught his first salmon and fell in love with the kilt.

Colonel Ross was explicit.

"If you will, you've the right to wear it. Your mother's mother was a Stuart. She died before you were born, but I have the pleasure to remember her very well."

"If you'll have me again, sir," said Philip. . . .

The Colonel laughed.

"Next time you'll come properly dressed."

The boy returned from Scotland the day before Vivien was due.

Lord Henry was out of Town, Lady Ursula had a cold, and Grosvenor Square was dull after Break o' Day. Miss Carson had gone to Paris, to bring back her charge.

Lunch in Carlton House Terrace had been an ordeal, but 'billiards' with Cousin Mary had made up for that. The marker was sent away, no cues were used, and the two had a roaring time.

"But this is between us, Pip. If father knew, there'd be the most awful row. When are you going back?"

"Tuesday," said Philip. "Worse luck."

"Tell Vivvy I'm coming to see her on Wednesday next."

"All right."

"I'll bet you don't," said Mary.

"I bet I do. Next Wednesday."

"Pip, I'm going to be married."

"Oh, Cousin Mary. Why?"

" Oh, I don't know. It seems the best thing to do. But don't tell Vivvy. I want to tell her myself."

A servant entered the room.

" The brougham is here, my lord."

" Thank you," said Philip, gravely. He turned to Mary Trelone. " Come back and have tea, Cousin Mary."

The lady shook her head.

" I will when I'm married, Pip. Whenever you like."

" Good," said Philip, warmly. " You'll still be Cousin Mary ? "

The girl took his face in her hands and kissed his nose.

" Oh, Pip, I do love you," she said. And then, " Of course I shall."

Tea with Lady Ursula—feeling like Death, but gallant and very sweet.

" When d'you think they'll be here, Aunt Ursula ? "

" Heaven knows, with this weather, Pip. They ought to be here by six. But it may be much later than that. Don't wait, if you've finished, darling. Go and get on with your letter to Mrs. Ross."

Two hours had gone by, and Philip was reading the letter which he had composed.

Grosvenor Square.

Dear Mrs. Ross,

Thank you very much for having me at Break o' Day. I enjoyed myself very much indeed. There was a very nice old gentleman in my carriage. (The poor man was just forty-five.) He knew all about fishing and showed me one of his rods. Please tell Colonel Ross Aunt Ursula says I can have a kilt. My sister is coming back from Paris to-day, but Aunt Ursula thinks they'll be late because the weather's so bad.

Yours very sincerely,
Ringwood.

A lady of fashion came floating into the Small Saloon.

" Vivvy, Vivvy ! "

" Oh, Pip ! My darling Pip ! "

As a cliff falls into the sea, twelve long months crumbled
and fell away.

*   *   *   *   *

The Honble. Mary Trelone was married on the fifth of
July. The wedding was solemnized at St. Margaret's, West-
minster. The bridegroom was Sir Oliver Bleeding, whom
nobody—not even Mary—liked very much. But his income
met the demands of Mary's sire. Such demands were whimsical, for the Viscount Pursuant was rich, and Mary Trelone
was the only child that he had. But in 1894—and later than
then—fathers were funny like that. To round the tragedy,
Mary might have done so much better, had it not been generally known that she and Algy Crosswood were deeply in love :
and as Algy was very much liked, none of his compeers was
willing to wipe his eye. But Algy, a younger son, could only
just pay his mess-bills. . . .

Lord Henry did his best in the hall of the Carlton Club.

" It's a damned shame, Pursuant. I take it very ill. Why
shouldn't your gal marry Crosswood ? You know very well
you can give 'em six thousand a year."

The other drew himself up.

" My lord," he said stiffly, " be good enough to permit
me to know my business best."

" Well, you're buying trouble, Pursuant. And if, with
all your money, you can't do better than that. . . . Damn
it, man. Put up Bleeding for Brooks's. I'll lay you an even
pony he doesn't get in. But there's nothing the matter with
Crosswood."

The Viscount turned on his heel.

So Mary Trelone was married—one beautiful July day.

Vivien was one of her bridesmaids—and very lovely she
looked. The girl was just eighteen, and even the fashions
which we deplore to-day could not diminish her manifest
excellence.

Some said that she was too young—she was not to be presented until the following year. But Vivien had a poise which none of the others had, and the dignity which she displayed knocked criticism flat.

As she left her carriage—

" Coo, there's the bride," said a voice.

" Don' talk silly," said another. " She ain't come yet."

" Well, she's my money," said the first. " You won' beat 'er."

Vivien heard—and, because she was human, approved.

Four days later, to Lord's for the Eton and Harrow Match.

Vivien held a positive court. Rivers, Old Harrovian, approached and was introduced. Colonel Ross made much of the beauty. Virgil, another cousin, spent much of his time on the coach. Miss Carson had her hands full : in fact she was truly thankful to get the girl to Brocade. So much attention was more than Pallas Athene could stand. But Vivien could stand it. Admiration was not ignored : it was accepted, appraised, and put in its proper place. The maid might have been a matron of thirty-two. Her address was remarkable. What was more astonishing still, at Brocade she at once threw back, to become the adorable child she had always been.

" My bicycle, Miss Carson ! I've never ridden it yet. Can I have a man to teach me ? I must be able to ride when Pip comes back."

" Ernest shall teach you, my darling. He's very good."

After an hour's instruction—

" Look, Miss Carson, look. I'm riding alone. I don't know where Ernest is—I think I've left him behind. . . . Oh, dear, how do I stop ? Ernest, I've done it now. I can't use the brake."

Zinnias below the terrace provided a soft enough bed.

As Ernest arrived, panting, Vivien sat up with earth all over her hands.

" Just look at that ! And I was going so well. What ever

will Hardcastle say?" (Hardcastle was the head-gardener.) "Not your fault, Ernest." She lifted a glowing face. "Isn't it glorious, Miss Carson? You'll have to learn."

The duenna was looking down, smiling.

"I'm sure that Madame de Vosges would recommend gloves."

Vivien regarded her hands. Then she looked up and laughed.

"Next time—I promise. Oh, I'm so glad to be here. You know, Miss Carson, I'm getting quite fond of Brocade." She scrambled up to her feet. "Take her away, Ernest. I'll go on this afternoon. And ask the gardeners to come and put this straight."

"Very good, my lady."

Vivien left the bed and ran up the terrace steps.

"When Pip comes back, can we go to Wells for the day? I want to see the swans ring the bell. Jane Purcell says they always ring for their dinner. I'd love to see them, you know. And they've never been taught, Miss Carson—it's just been handed down."

"In Lady Ursula's absence, I venture to promise that."

"But wouldn't you like to see them?"

"That's why I'm letting you go."

Vivien threw back her head and laughed. Then she put up her face and kissed the duenna's cheek.

"France was lovely," she said. "I wouldn't have missed it for worlds. And Madame de Vosges was terribly good to me. But you're my money, you know. You always were."

The duenna stared at her charge, who smiled disarmingly back. Then the former covered her face and laughed uncontrollably.

"Darling Vivien," she wailed, "I shall always value that phrase. But I decline to believe that you got it from Madame de Vosges."

* * * * *

Philip arrived from Harrow : Lord Henry came for ten days, before his departure for Aix : Lady Ursula was expected. The fine, old mansion was coming into its own.

Walking on the terrace before dinner, Lord Henry snuffed the air.

" Nice place, this, Pip, you know.   Seems a bit big at the moment, but it's an excellent house.   By the way, my dears, I made an acquaintance to-day."

" Who was that, Uncle Henry ? "

" Well, I was in the train, when another fellow gets in. Nice-looking man : a good deal younger than me, but I felt I'd seen him before.   At Paddington Station, this was.   After a while, I gave him my name and asked his.

" ' Anthony Hinton,' he says.

" ' That's right,' said I.   ' And you're your father's son.'

" I used to know ' Punch ' Hinton years ago.   We served as Stewards together, in the days when I used to race.   And this was his boy. . . .

" Well, that doesn't matter to you ; but the long and the short of it is, he's taken the hounds.   Next season will be his first.   So he's coming to lunch here on Tuesday.   I thought you might as well know him—always a help."

' The children ' seized his arms.

" Oh, sir !   Oh, Uncle Henry, how simply marvellous ! The new Master !   How spiffing ! " (from Philip).   " Is he going to live at The Grange ? "

" No, he's bought Rosemary House—that used to belong to the Coultons—some five miles off.   His heart's right in it. I think he'll do very well."

" Did you tell him of Olgivy Bottom ? "

" I did.   I said we had two good covers—Infanta Planta- tion is very nearly as good.   I thought we might ask Rodney : just as well he should meet him here."

(Rodney was the estate-agent.)

The Master duly arrived—driving two bays in tandem, to Vivien's and Philip's delight.   To say that ' the children ' ate him is less than the truth. Captain Anthony Hinton, bachelor, aged thirty-two, clean-living, caring for nothing but horses and hounds, was one of those pleasant beings that never fail to do their company good. His sense of humour was high, and luncheon became a jolly festival. He was charming to Miss Carson, respectful to Lord Henry, familiar with Rodney, used Vivien and Philip as though they were both his age.

As he was going—

"Well, you two," he said, "you must come to lunch. I'll see my house-keeper and send you a line. And then we'll have a look at the Kennels. But I count on you for cubbing. You're just the sort that can be a lot of help."

That night 'the children' remembered him in their prayers.

* * * * *

When the visit to Wells was mooted—

"I'm coming, too," said Lord Henry. "I haven't seen Wells for years. Ursula, you and Miss Carson will take a landau. Vivien and Philip will go in the phaeton with me."

This improved the occasion beyond all words.

Such expeditions seem small enough beer to-day : in 1894 they could have been fairly compared with audit ale. The going and coming alone were precious things.

Eighteen leisurely miles of beautiful English country : this on a summer's day, when larks were losing themselves in a cloudless sky. A spirited pair of roans making light of their duty and signalizing the handsome equipage : Lord Henry driving—gray bowler and button-hole—with Vivien and Philip beside him, the former using her prettiest parasol. . . . The ancient, cathedral city, sunning her lovely self and seemingly half asleep. . . . Warm, gray stone and green turf : the incomparable West Façade—that everlasting broadcast of what old men thought meet to offer God : (no forty-hour week there, Erny : no waiting on the whistle : *amour propre* and piety brought that about. 'Piety? Gawd 'elp!' I think He probably did.) Lunch in the shadowy inn—a hilarious meal: Lady Ursula is made to drink shandy-gaff. . . . The Vicar's Close and the moat of the Bishop's Palace —complete with swans, who happily do their stuff. 'And they've never been taught, keeper?' 'Never, miss. The cygnets learn of the swans.' . . . A chance encounter with the Bishop and an invitation to tea. 'We have it in the garden this weather: I always think that excuses an inexcusable meal.' The Bishop's wife, very sweet. 'Not Eleanor Carson—the daughter of Helen Lefevre? My dear, I was bridesmaid to your mother—a very long time ago. And this is her little girl. I believe you attended my wedding. Dear me, dear me.' . . . Home through an evening so lovely it seemed unreal. . . . By wood and stream and cloth of gold for pasture, such was the magic touch of sinking sun. . . . The low of cows, the song of a nightingale. . . . Farm horses knee-deep in a horse-pond, lifting their dripping muzzles to eye the equipage. . . . An aged stone-breaker cheering as they went by, and Lord Henry raising his hat. . . . Two colts in a blowing paddock, running abreast of the phaeton on the other side of the hedge and frolicking in their freedom of bit and trace. . . . Slowly overtaking a dray on punishing Bell-wether Hill. 'Good evening, drayman. Your cattle do you credit.' 'The same to you, my lord—'s a handsome pair.' . . . The road full of sheep, and the shepherd doing his best with his foolish flock. 'Very well managed, shepherd. I'm much obliged.' A shilling passed. 'Drink the young lady's health.' 'That I will, and thank you kindly, sir.' Vivien bowed and smiled and the three men raised their hats—the courtesy of the road in 1894. . . . The comfortable cries of rooks, as the roans, within scent of their stables, sped through the spreading park. . . . The truly magnificent timber—an oak that was known as Bateman's, when James the Second was King . . . the herd of deer standing and staring—and taking to its elegant heels . . . and

86

the long South front of Brocade, less stately than cordial this evening, smiling upon the landscape it had the honour to rule.

*　　*　　*　　*　　*

The garden-party was an immense success.

Of those who order them, such functions make heavy demands : these, Lady Ursula faced—and looked them down. Except to odd visitors, the gates of Brocade had been closed for more than seven years : if they were to be flung wide, those that were bidden must find the occasion great.

It was largely a matter of staff-work. Lady Ursula was in command ; Miss Carson and Rodney were her staff-officers ; the steward, head-gardener, stud-groom instructed their respective commands.

The weather excelled itself, the gardens were looking their best, a band from London discoursed. Lady Ursula, supported by Miss Carson, put up a splendid show. Her gay and care-free demeanour argued that she was a guest : yet, she missed nothing at all and, like some army-commander in days gone by, was always where her presence was most required. Vivien and Philip did their duty, as deputy hostess and host— and found high favour, as old Lady Churt shall declare. And she knew how to behave. ' Ursula, I'm impressed. Vivien is outstanding. And it's very hard to remember that Philip is still at school. You have my congratulations upon a remarkable pair.' Rodney was always at hand, now on the lawns and now in the stable-yard, and the fact that the servants confirmed their masters' report is positive proof that the function was a notable business from first to last.

Champagne was served that night. ' I think we deserve it,' declared Lady Ursula. ' The children ' drank it, because they were drinking champagne : Lady Ursula, Miss Carson and Rodney, because it was the medicine they most required.

Ten days later—

" D'you think," said Miss Carson, " they might give a little dance ? "

"Oh, my dear," said Lady Ursula.

"It's only an idea," said Miss Carson. "Ten or fifteen couples—no more than that. And they would have to manage it all. You would approve the arrangements, and I should keep them straight. But they would have to do it. . . . What do you think?"

Lady Ursula thought.

"You're right, as usual, my dear. They ought to begin to learn. Will you, er, put it to them?"

"If you'll forgive me, I'd rather it came from you."

"Which isn't fair, my dear. But I see your point."

Vivien and Philip were ravished. The list of invitations was compiled with the greatest care. All very young people, of course—except for the Master : he simply *had* to be asked. The two made all the arrangements, and made them extremely well. And they received their guests, at the head of the stairs. Miss Carson was in the gallery, ready to urge their victims into the dance. Lady Ursula appeared later. The Master, of course, was worth his weight in gold. And Rodney was marvellous. What should have ended at midnight went on until one o'clock. Such was their entertainment, the servants would not have minded had it gone on until two.

So, for the second time, Brocade came into its own. But that is beside the point, which is that Vivien and Philip truly enjoyed the duty which they had been led to do.

*　　*　　*　　*　　*

Four interviews must be recorded.

The first took place on a gay September morning, when Autumn was in the wings, but Summer, ignoring his presence, continued to hold the stage.

"And now for the Tildens'," said Rodney, holding a gate.

"Thank you," said Philip, leaving the field for the lane.

The land-agent followed the boy, watched the gate swing to and latch, before setting his mount.

"Joss Tilden wants new pigsties—three new pigsties, he

says. To do it properly, that will cost fifteen pounds. I said all right, we'd do it : but, if we did, his rent must be raised by fifteen shillings a year. Twenty years' purchase, you see. He said that wasn't fair. Now what do you think ? "

Philip reflected. Then—

" I rather like pigs," he said.

" So do I," said Rodney.

" Well, I'd like them to be comfortable."

" They are. Though their sties are old, they're perfectly good. But the thatching is giving in."

" Can't they be re-thatched, Mr. Rodney ? "

" I offered to re-thatch them and leave the rent as it is. But Joss said he wanted new sties."

" I like thatching better than slates. Those new sties of Gallop's look awful."

" They'll tone down in time, Pip. But tell me —how d'you feel ? "

" You're sure the pigs are all right ? "

" Yes," said Rodney, laughing. " The pigs would much prefer to stay as they are."

" Well . . . If the old sties only need thatching, why does Joss Tilden want new ones ? "

" Because Gallop has got new ones. He doesn't say so, of course. But that's the truth. But Gallop's sties were worn out."

" Gallop's not paying more rent ? "

" Oh, no—because his were worn out."

" Then I don't think Joss Tilden should have them, unless he pays. And I jolly well hope he doesn't, 'cause then his sties will be thatched and the pigs'll still have their old home."

" So do I," said the land-agent. " Come on. We'll see what he says."

They cantered the length of the lane and up to the farm. . . .

After twenty minutes' discussion, in which the sties were viewed—

"Well, there you are, Joss," said Rodney. "New thatch for nothing : new sties, if you feel you must have 'em, for fifteen shillings a year. And that's a very fair offer—his lordship agrees with me."

"Ben Gallop's rent's not raised."

"Ben Gallop's sties were in a very bad way : but yours are sound. You'd better let me thatch 'em."

Joss Tilden began to laugh.

"No foolin' Mr. Rodney, my lord. When the thatcher comes, can he thatch the lean-to ? "

"Ten by six," said Rodney. "We'll throw that in."

"Thank you, sir. You won't step in, my lord ? "

"We're rather late, but I'd like to see Mrs. Tilden."

The farmer raised his voice.

"Amy, 'is lordship's 'ere."

An apple-cheeked dame came bustling, wiping her hands on her apron, eager-eyed.

"How d'ye do, Mrs. Tilden ? " Philip leaned out of his saddle and took her hand. "You've got some jolly nice pigs."

"So they should be, my lord, with all the swill they get."

A golden-haired child came running. She might have been eight. "Mary Anne, my lord. She's me sister's child."

"How d'ye do, Mary Anne ? "

"How d'ye do, boy ? "

The Tildens were scandalized.

"Say ' my lord ', you hussey."

Philip was off his horse.

"That's all right, Mary Anne." He put out his hand. "My name's Philip," he added.

Mary Anne took his hand.

"Philip what ? "

"Philip Brabant."

"I see. Lord Ringwood's got a horse, too." Philip looked at Rodney. "He's my lady's brother."

90

The land-agent put in his oar.

" This is Lord Ringwood, Mary Anne."

" He said he was Philip Brabant."

" I know. He's Lord Ringwood, too."

Mary Anne's eyes filled with tears.

" I couldn't know, could I ? " she whimpered.

" Of course you couldn't," said Philip. " And please don't cry, Mary Anne. Can I have a lump of sugar to give my horse ? "

" That you shall."

She ran off.

" Get up, Pip," said Rodney.

Tilden ran for his leather, and Philip got up.

Mary Anne came back with the sugar.

" Flat o' the 'and, me girl."

" *I* know," said Mary Anne.

Paragon having been favoured, Mercy must have some, too.

" Goodbye, Mrs. Tilden. Goodbye, Mr. Tilden."

" Goodbye, my lord."

Mary Anne dropped a curtsey. Then, with a mischievous smile—

" Goodbye, Philip," she said, and turned and ran into the house.

" There's a minx for you," gasped Tilden.

Mrs. Tilden was bereft of speech.

Rodney was shaking with laughter and Philip was laughing, too, and waving his crop.

*   *   *   *   *

The second interview took place some ten hours later. This, in my lady's chamber. Pricket was brushing her hair, before she retired.

" I wish I was a man," said Vivien.

" Oh, my lady. If you was anyone else. . . . But being what you are——"

" I don't care. I wish I was. Till I marry, I'm bound by

convention—girls can't do this and that. And when I marry, I'll have to obey my husband, more or less. I mean, he'll have the reins. And *I* want the reins, Pricket."

" I 'spect you'll have them, my lady."

" Never," said Vivien. " I'd never marry a man who'd let me have the reins."

Pricket gave up.

" They say her Grace is very cross with his lordship—the Marquess, I mean."

" For being sent down from Oxford ? I'm not surprised. He ought to be ashamed of himself."

The Marquess of Brest had kidnapped proctor and bull-dogs, had them thrust into his coach, whipped up a willing team and set his prisoners down in a desolate place, seven miles from a village upon a rainy night.

Vivien continued slowly.

" Men of his rank should never do things like that. Nobody should—it's beastly. But for him to do them is dreadful. I didn't like him, Pricket—the way he looked at me."

" At the garden-party, my lady ? How did he look ? "

" As a man looks at a horse. I almost expected him to run a hand down my legs."

" My lady ! "

" You know what I mean. Because he's bound to be Duke, he thinks he can do as he likes. I only hope he asks me. I'll put him straight."

Pricket was overcome.

After a little, she said in a very small voice—

" I'd like your ladyship to be a Duchess."

" Not at that price, Pricket. You haven't seen Mr. Rivers. He's very nice."

" And who would he be, my lady ? "

" He was at Harrow with his lordship . . . a good deal older, of course. But he has very good manners. He's at Oxford, too."

92

"You'll have many beaux, my lady."

Vivien shrugged her shoulders.

"That I don't know. I'll always love Philip best."

"Of course. But he's your brother. He'll always be there."

"Always, Pricket, thank God. And will you, too?"

"Always, my lady. I give you my solemn word."

"Don't you want to get married, Pricket?"

"Not all that, my lady. I might, some day. But only if I could stay on, like Lady Hannet's maid. She's been with her thirty years, and married for seventeen. Her husband's a page at the Palace; and so it works out very well."

"Lady Bleeding's coming next week."

"I'm glad of that, my lady. We all like her."

"And a nice mess she's made of things. How would you like Sir John to maul you about?"

"My lady!"

"It's true, and you know it, Pricket. She's simply been sold. It's bad enough to bear children, but if you don't fancy their father, their siring must be pure hell. Pricket, dear, I'm going to marry for love. And Philip will see I do it. Dukes be damned: if I like a dustman best, I'll marry him. I'm going to have some fun, Pricket, although I'm a girl."

But Pricket, who knew not Paris, had lost the power of speech.

*   *   *   *   *

The third interview took place in the Italian Garden, where Lady Ursula and Miss Carson were walking after the heat of the day.

"I believe," said the latter, "that they would both be content."

Lady Ursula reflected. Then—

"It really amounts to this—that, except for the month of December, we stay here till May."

" Well, April," said Miss Carson.

" April."

" Then we return to Town, and Vivien's presented in June."

Lady Ursula nodded.

" I see your point, my dear. And Philip would get some hunting."

" That's right. Once she's presented, you see, we needn't worry at all. Vivien is very sane. But now the position is awkward. If she wasn't so dazzling, it wouldn't matter at all. But add to that that she's not exactly old for her age, but she has far more poise than any of her contemporaries. Compare her, for instance, with——"

" The Duchess's girls ? "

" Exactly. Compared with Vivien, they don't know how to behave. And they have both been presented."

Lady Ursula nodded.

" In a word, if we go to Town, she will be paid attention which she should not receive."

" I'm sure of that. I'm equally sure that she would be none the worse ; but it would be out of order—and very worrying : and the girls who have been presented would be upset."

Lady Ursula laughed.

" I'm afraid a good many will be upset next June."

" I know : but that will be the luck of the battle : at least they won't be able to throw any stones."

" She'll create a great sensation. You know, Miss Carson, I think her Mother should present her."

" I entirely agree. But will she ? "

" I don't know. But I'm going to Paris, to see her and ask her to. Let us be honest about it—Vivien deserves the best. And Rachel can give it to her. Such a mother, presenting such a daughter will be the talk of the town. Now, if we stay here till December, shouldn't she have someone to stay ? "

94

"I think so," said Miss Carson. "There's a girl who was with her in Paris. I only saw her for a moment, but Vivien took to her and I thought she was very nice. They correspond."

"Does she hunt?"

"Happily, yes. She lives in Leicestershire."

"That would be very good."

"And Philip ought to ask Ross. They gave him a very good time."

"Later," said Lady Ursula. "They won't have much longer together—'the children', I mean. When's Philip go to Sandhurst?"

"Next year, Lady Ursula."

"Oh, dear, they are growing up."

"Isn't it dreadful?" said Miss Carson.

Lady Ursula shook her head.

The duenna changed the subject.

"Philip goes back on Thursday. D'you think we could run up to Town before people come back?"

"Of course. The inside of next week?"

"That would do very well. There are one or two things she should have. And Jane Purcell—that's the friend. She must write and suggest a date. Some time in November, perhaps?"

"After the Bleedings have gone. They're coming here on October the twenty-eighth. For a fortnight. You'll have to help me, my dear. He's not a nice man."

"Please count upon me, Lady Ursula."

"I know that I can. Lord Henry is coming down. I felt we must have a man. I'm so dreadfully sorry for Mary. She's such a dear girl."

"Why on earth did she do it, Lady Ursula?"

"Moral pressure, I think. Her father's a difficult man. And Lady Pursuant has always given way."

"And she might have been so happy, if what I hear is true."

" Of that," said Lady Ursula, " there can be no doubt. Captain Crosswood's the dearest fellow. I've hardly seen him for years, but he was so sweet to women. He used to seek out the girls whom nobody asked to dance."

* * * * *

The fourth interview took place in the stables and stable-yard, while Vivien and Philip were making much of the horses, feeding with sliced carrots the inmates of boxes and stalls.

" Shut up, Trueboy : you're greedy. You're lucky to be staying here, Vivvy."

" I know I am, Pip. I wish so much you were."

" Oh, well. . . . Any way, we'll be back after Christmas. It'll be jolly decent to have three weeks. You'll tell the Master, won't you ? "

" Yes, rather. I expect he'll arrange to draw our covers then."

" That'd be gorgeous, Vivvy."

" You know Mary's coming later. What shall she ride ? " Philip reflected. Then—

" Well, Cherry Boy and St. Martin are steady enough. Or Light Heart would suit her, I think. If she's good, I don't mind her riding Hermes."

" No, I think I'd better ride him, Pip, while you're away. And Trueboy, too. What about Sir Oliver ? "

" Crumbs," said Philip. " We don't even know if he hunts."

" In case," said Vivien. " No, it's no good, Rainbow. You've had your share."

" Oh, leave it to Akers, Vivvy. But he mustn't touch yours or mine."

Vivien nodded.

" I'll see to that. I do hate having him here."

" I know. It can't be helped. And Uncle Henry's coming."

" I'll write and tell you about it."

96

" If he hunts, I'll bet he comes off.   He's made all wrong."

This was a fact.   Sir Oliver Bleeding had not the build of a horseman.   The man was thick-set and clumsy.   His thighs were round.

" The Master knows Captain Crosswood."

" Who's Captain Crosswood ? " said Philip.

" You remember him, Pip.   He lunched at Grosvenor Square—and made us all shriek with laughter about his Second-in-Command and his new bicycle."

" O-o—h, yes," cried Philip, bubbling.   " But he was gorgeous, Vivvy.   Aunt Ursula simply cried.   He would be a friend of the Master's.   Is he coming down ? "

" I hope so.   I don't know when.   He wanted to marry Mary."

" He didn't !   Why didn't he, then ? "

" Too poor," said Vivien, shortly.

" But Lord Pursuant is rich."

" I know.   But he wouldn't allow it."

" What a beastly shame," cried Philip.   " And he'd 've been topping for a cousin.   What fun if he'd been coming, instead of—of Sir Oliver."

Vivien nodded.

" Fun . . . for everyone.   As it is . . .   Oh, well.   I hope he doesn't come while they're here."

" Why ? "

" Because I'd like the Master to bring him to dine."

" Well, can't he ? " said Philip.

" Not if Mary's here, Pip.   She'd probably faint or something."

" Did she want to marry him, too ? "

" Of course."

" Oh, God, how awful, Vivvy.   And now it's too late."

" Looks like it, Pip."

" P'raps Bleeding'll die or something."

" That sort of brute never does.   It's only people like Father who ever die young."

" I can remember him, Vivvy. Not very well."

" I'm glad you can—just. He was so glorious."

" Like Sargent's picture ? "

" Exactly."

" Frightful bad luck on Mummy, his dying like that."

" Frightful," said Vivien. " Still, she did have him for a little. But Mary will never be with the man she loves."

*   *   *   *   *

As the equipage swept to the foot of the broad flight of steps, the tall double doors were opened and Merton, the butler, emerged. He did not descend the steps, but stood to one side. As the groom was opening the landau's nearside door, Vivien, in blue and white, appeared at the head of the flight.

" Mary, Mary."

" Oh, Vivvy, darling."

The two girls met half way down.

With Vivien's arms about her, Mary, almost in tears, was trying to master her lips.

" It's all right, Mary dear. I understand."

" Don't—don't be kind to me, Vivvy."

" Aunt Ursula's in the Gray Room : I'll take you there. How d'ye do, Sir Oliver ? "

" How d'ye do ? "

" You'd like to go to the gun-room. I think my great-uncle's there. Look after Sir Oliver, Merton."

" Very good, my lady."

Almost the last thing the baronet wanted was to be with Lord Henry alone : quite the last thing that he wanted was for his wife, upon her arrival, to be alone with Vivien and Lady Ursula. First impressions were—were misleading ; and Mary had not got over that scene with the guard.

" I think," he began . . .

But Vivien and Mary were gone.

" This way, if you please, Sir Oliver."

98

The baronet entered Brocade, looking up and down the footmen who stood to the doors.

Then—

" Where can I wash ? " he demanded.

The butler inclined his head.

" I will show you, Sir Oliver."

A lavatory adjoined the gun-room—which more than deserved its name. There were certainly cases of guns there : but for that, it resembled the smoking-room of a club on a smaller scale. Leather-covered sofas and easy chairs . . . two well-found writing tables . . . ash-trays and even spittoons. . . . A rare set of sporting prints hung on the walls : *The Field*, *Ruff's Guide* and *Baily's* lay ready to hand.

Lord Henry was standing, smoking, with his back to a slow, wood fire, and *The Times* in his hands.

" Hullo, Bleeding. How are you ? "

" Oh, well enough," said the other. " And you . . . my lord ? "

" I'm very well," said Lord Henry. " Which will you have—tea, or brandy and seltzer ? "

" Brandy and seltzer, I think."

Lord Henry looked at the butler, who bowed and withdrew.

" Make yourself comfortable, Bleeding. Have a cigar ? "

" Thanks."

" Have a good run down ? "

" So so. These railway servants are getting above themselves."

Lord Henry raised his eyebrows.

" I hadn't noticed that."

" Won't take orders," said Bleeding. " I told the guard to lock the carriage, of course. And, damn it, the man refused. Grossly impertinent fellow. I told him I should report him and get him fired."

Lord Henry frowned.

" Weren't you in the slip-coach ? "

" What of that ? "

99

"This," said Lord Henry, shortly. "They mayn't lock the doors on a slip, for it's only one coach. Rest of the train, there's usually plenty of room. But the slip's only got two firsts."

"I'd paid for my seats."

"Of course. But not for the whole compartment. In any event, locking the door is purely an act of grace."

"I don't agree," said Bleeding.

When Lord Henry spoke again, he spoke from behind *The Times.*

"Well, I shouldn't report the man. I happen to be on the Board, and I know the answer you'll get."

The arrival of the brandy and seltzer covered an awkward pause.

And there you have Sir Oliver Bleeding: selfish, unjust, rude, continually giving offence, and always raging when this was given back. The scene at Paddington Station had approached the obscene. The guard had been perfectly civil, explaining that he was not allowed by the rules to lock the doors on a slip. Sir Oliver had called him a liar, had threatened and stormed. An unsympathetic crowd had begun to collect. Mary had been ready to die of shame.

Lord Henry was speaking again.

"Opening Meet's next week. Will you be out?"

"I've brought my things."

"Then have a word with Akers: he's the stud-groom."

"Thank you, I will."

"Your wife be hunting?"

"So far as I know."

"Vivien will look after her."

"What's she know about horses?"

Lord Henry stared.

"What's Vivien know? My great-niece? She's an authority, Bleeding—at eighteen years of age. Knows more about shoeing than I do. And seat and hands quite perfect. You wait and see."

Sir Oliver blew and snorted his discontent.

Had he now been in the Gray Room, this would have been magnified.

His wife was seated on the floor by Lady Ursula's side. After a flood of tears, she had herself more in hand. Lady Ursula's arm was lying about her shoulders, and Vivien was kneeling beside her, a cup of tea in her hand.

" Drink this, Mary darling : it's not too hot."

Mary beat upon the floor.

" You must not be kind to me. I can stand anything else ; but kindness breaks me down. Be short, be rude, be rough—but don't be kind."

Lady Ursula covered her eyes and Vivien went very pale.

Here was stark Tragedy.

Mary continued slowly.

" Well, here I am. Years since I saw Brocade. I used to think it was stiff, as its name suggests. But now I find it so friendly. Aunt Ursula, you must forgive me—I've come without any maid."

" My dear, what on earth does that matter ? We have a very nice girl, who will be only too pleased to wait upon you."

" Of course you have : but I shouldn't have come without one. But mine left yesterday."

(The maid in question had left because of Sir Oliver Bleeding. She was not prepared to endure the way in which he spoke to his wife. More. She had not endured it. She had told him what he was fit for, in very plain terms.)

" Vivien, you'll see to that. Hansard will look after Mary while she is here."

" I'll see her now, Aunt Ursula."

Vivien left the room, and after a word with the house-keeper, spoke to Hansard herself.

" You'd better have Pricket to help you unpack her lady-ship's things. And she will keep you straight. Oh, there you are, Pricket. Hansard is going to look after Lady

Bleeding. Help her unpack, will you? And see that she knows what to do."

" Very good, my lady."

When Vivien returned to the Gray Room, Mary was more herself. Her new self, of course. Something hard and brittle : Mary had always been soft.

" Hello, Vivvy. I hear you're on terms with the Master. You would be, of course. Will you give me something nice for the opening meet? I wish Pip was here. How is he? Let's be presented together, Vivvy dear. I've got to be —' on my marriage '. The matron and the maid."

Lady Ursula could have screamed. Vivien, still very pale, was twisting her hands.

At last they got her upstairs, with a promise to rest.

" Dinner's at eight, my dear, and you've had a tiring day."

" Not . . . more tiring . . . than usual . . ." Mary's hand went to her mouth. " There you are, you see. I tell you, you must not be kind."

Lady Ursula signed to Vivien to leave the room.

The latter fled to the suite which Miss Carson used.

" May I come in, Miss Carson? "

" Of course, my dear."

Vivien whipped into the room and shut the door. Then she burst into tears.

The duenna's arms were about her.

" Vivien, darling, what is it? "

But Vivien could only weep.

Miss Carson drew her into a chair and knelt by her side.

" My darling child, what's happened? "

" It's Mary," sobbed Vivien. " Sally was dead : but Mary's alive . . . in Hell."

" Oh, my God," said Miss Carson, under her breath. . . .

Two minutes later, perhaps, Lady Ursula entered the room.

She had come for consolation, as Vivien had. Had she not been distracted, she would have realized that she would find Vivien there. And then she realized that it was just as well.

Vivien was crying quietly; Miss Carson looked very grave.

"I don't know what Vivien's told you, but Mary is much upset. I'm afraid she's very unhappy. I may be wrong there, for, when a girl first comes home—and we are her relatives—her emotions are sometimes misleading. I mean to say, it may not be as bad as we think. But even if it is, there is nothing that we can do. Let us all remember that. It is terribly sad—and most unfortunate. But we can do nothing about it. Only her parents can possibly interfere. Sir Oliver Bleeding and Mary are man and wife. If they are unhappy together, so far as we are concerned, it cannot be helped. Together, they are our guests. And we must do our best to make their visit pleasant in every way. Mary will probably talk. Well, let her talk, poor girl: it will do her good. But we can take no action, for they are both our guests."

"But, Aunt Ursula, Mary's in torment."

"My dear, she broke down."

"But I saw her before. I saw her out on the steps. She looks like a ghost. We can't stand still and not help. It's like watching a dog that's run over and doing nothing at all."

Lady Ursula steeled herself.

"My darling Vivien, I don't have to tell you that I am easily moved. I feel things terribly. But for us to step out of our ground would not only do no good, but would be in the worst of taste. Her husband would have the gravest cause for complaint. I can write to Lady Pursuant—and that I shall do. But no one of us three in this room must interfere. We can listen and sympathize: but we may do no more. I'm much afraid that Mary has made a mistake —the greatest mistake a woman can ever make. But she has made it, my darling; and no one but she or her parents can hope to put it right." Lady Ursula passed to a sofa. "Oh, dear, I'm so tired. I'm afraid I'm not meant for these things."

Miss Carson and Vivien succoured the virtual head of their

house. Such succour was richly deserved. To rise to such an occasion had cost Lady Ursula dear. As she had said, she was not meant for such things. Her head was splitting : she dreaded the sight of food : but nothing short of a stroke would have made her miss dinner that night.

The meal passed off much better than she had dared hope. Mary, looking like death, had accepted Lord Henry's arm and had actually kept the ball rolling better than anyone else. Her sprightliness was that of the priests of Baal : she was gashing herself with knives—to make Convention sport. Sullenly, Bleeding watched her, saying hardly a word. Lord Henry, shrewd as you make 'em, was smiling at her sallies and watching her, too. ' Near breaking-point,' he decided : ' but putting up a wonderful show.' Vivien was perfectly natural, doing her best with Bleeding, playing up to Mary, as though there were nothing wrong. Lady Ursula and Miss Carson were, seemingly, quite themselves.

Tea was served, as usual, at ten o'clock. Then Lord Henry took Bleeding to the gun-room, and Mary retired. . . .

The next morning she rode with Vivien. All their talk was of Paris and days gone by. Flashes of the old Mary appeared once or twice, but the haggard look in her eyes was always there. That day and the next and the next she was never with Bleeding alone—and seldom with him at all. She simply avoided contact. That Bleeding resented her action was painfully clear. Nobody knew what passed between them of nights ; but Miss Carson had the impression that he was biding his time. Lord Henry groaned in secret —with him, a little of Bleeding went much too far : but the shooting was a resource : both men shot very well, but Bleeding was always cross—cursing the dogs or his loader and laying down the law to the party at lunch.

Then came the Opening Meet. This was at Pie-crust Corner, a short two miles from Brocade. Lady Ursula and Miss Carson attended in a landau. Lord Henry, who had given up hunting, drove a dog-cart himself. Vivien hacked

to the meet, and her guests with her.   Both girls looked very
well.   Their beautifully fitting habits, their boots, their top-
hats, the perfect condition of their mounts served to set off
the excellence of their style.   Mounted on Regency Buck, a
magnificent brown, Vivien was truly excelling : the horse
seemed proud to bear her and eager to do her bidding, whatever it was.   That horses believed in Vivien there can be
no doubt.   And Mary looked her best in the saddle, as some
women do.   Her husband's turn-out was good, but he did
not fit into the saddle, looked out of place.   Horses were
never happy between his legs : his hand and his heel were
heavy, but it was more than that ; they felt his inherent ill
will.

"Captain Hinton, the Master—my cousin, Lady Bleeding,
Sir Oliver Bleeding."

Courtesies were exchanged.

Vivien moved to the hounds.

"Good morning, Mr. Berry."

The huntsman raised his cap.

"Good morning to you, my lady.   I think it should be
a good day."

"Promises well, Mr. Berry."   Hounds came up to her,
smiling.   "Well, Challenger, boy.   And Ranger."

"They know your ladyship's voice."

Vivien returned to the Bleedings.   The Marquess of Brest
came up and was introduced.   And others came also.   Vivien
rode up to the Duchess, to pay her respects.   'My dear, you
do your house credit.'   Vivien coloured and bowed.   Lord
Henry was very cheerful.   'A very nice field—not too big.
Wish I were coming with you.   If he should make for
Pelham, look out for The Wryneck, Vivvy : its banks are
not too sound.   Who's with you ?   Arthur and Thomas ?
Oh, they're all right.'

Hounds were moving off . . .

It was some fifty minutes later that, for the first time that
she could remember, Vivien felt the definite stab of fear.

A great dog fox had left the capital lying of Moleskin Wood and now was heading for Pelham, just as Lord Henry had said.

Well, that was all right. Fine country, and little plough. Vivien knew how to go—but Mary was going like hell.

Hounds, a field ahead, were running mute : if they were setting the pace, the pace was hot. But Mary, on Light Heart, was breaking every rule.

Light Heart, a beautiful fencer, was jumping like a stag ; but Mary was riding like a fool—an irresponsible fool, who thinks his pluck is in question. She was going at everything, bald-headed. No collecting Light Heart, no picking of places—nothing. In a word, Lady Bleeding was out to break her neck.

The Master was with his hounds. Well away, to the right, the huntsman was riding hard. The rest of the field was coming, but Vivien and Mary were more than a meadow ahead. Mary was leading Vivien by nearly a hundred yards. As she came to a post and rails, she looked round and waved. But Light Heart carried her over with four good inches to spare.

There was, of course, nothing to be done. Vivien could pray for a check, but that was all she could do.

Had she known it, no check was coming.

The fox was tiring : his only chance, he knew, was the earth at Bellingham Gorse. He had meant to give hounds an outing—no more than that : he had meant to slip to the left by Crosby Gate : but hedgers at work had spoiled that, and he had had to go on. And now it was going to be a very near thing. View was what he feared. After the Wryneck, yes : they'd be bound to view him then, with only three furlongs to go. But, if they viewed him before, then hounds would make their effort, and he would be done.

The Wryneck was coming now, and Mary was going all out. Vivien felt rather sick.

As she cleared a stone wall, she saw the fox leave the water
106

and start to climb. . . . Hounds were crossing now, and the Master was collecting his horse. . . . And then he took to the water and crossed as his hounds had crossed. The Wryneck was not to be jumped, but it could be swum.

Mary was coming up. . . . My God, she was going to jump it. The Master hadn't tried, and Uncle Henry had said that its banks . . . Light Heart could never do it—not even had Mary been riding, instead of being borne. It was too much, too late, too dreadful. . . .

Vivien checked Regency Buck and bore to her left. Her eyes upon Light Heart, she heard herself whimpering ' Christ ! '

Light Heart gathered himself . . .

My God, he was over . . . No, he was down; and Mary . . . No, by God, he was up. He had pecked and was up, and Mary was back in her seat. Slowly enough, he was climbing to Bellingham Gorse. . . .

Vivien made for a bridge three furlongs away.

The Master was looking at Mary.

" I should get down," he said quietly. " You've asked a lot of that horse."

Feeling very small, Mary slid down to the ground.

Vivien came cantering up.

" He's beaten us," said the Master. " He's won a very good race and I'm going to let him lie."

" Content," said Vivien. " You ought to go home and change."

" P'raps you're right," said Hinton, smiling.

The huntsman came up, and Arthur, and three or four of the field.

Arthur was down and had taken charge of Light Heart.

Vivien looked at Mary.

" Would you mind riding Sandown back ? "

" Of course not, Vivvy."

" Then Arthur can bring him in gently. Here's Thomas coming. Change her ladyship's saddle, Arthur, and you bring Light Heart home."

" Very good, my lady."

Mary made much of Light Heart—kissed his nose.

" Sorry, old fellow," she whispered. " It wasn't fair to you. And you returned good for evil."

Bleeding was not to be seen. He had had words at a gate and, being left to himself, had made for the lanes.

Vivien and Mary rode home, with William behind.

" You must try to forgive me, Vivvy."

" Oh, Mary, there's nothing to forgive."

" Yes, there is. You can ride your own hunters like that, but not other people's. To tell you the truth, I forgot. I—I think I was very excited."

Vivien looked straight ahead.

" I—I think you were, too."

Mary lowered her voice.

" Did anyone see, except you?"

" I don't think so. I don't know about the Master."

" I don't know, either," said Mary. " But he looks a decent man. I mean, if a girl . . ." She broke off there, to jerk out a bitter laugh. " I should have said ' a woman ' : I keep on forgetting that I'm no longer a girl."

Vivien could have burst into tears.

*   *   *   *   *

" And so, you see, I've only myself to thank. What did it matter, being a rich, old maid? But I wanted some fun, Vivvy. And it seemed that, unless I married, I shouldn't have any fun. I stared at the state, Vivvy, the married state. I should have stared at the man : but, as I couldn't have Algy, I didn't care who it was. That's where I went wrong, Vivvy. And now that brute's my husband—can do with me what he likes. Somewhere in the Bible it says, ' And all these things shall be added unto you.' So they have been, Vivvy. Riches, servants, a title—for what that's worth. And I'd swap the lot for the life of a working girl. Hunger, poverty, work . . . washing and lighting fires. I'd take it all, Vivvy, and thank God every day. But now it's too late. . . .

" Oh, Vivvy, for God's sake, be careful, when your time comes. Be very, very careful. Think what marriage means and look damned hard at the man. Don't marry, unless you love him—unless you're sure that you love him . . . with all your heart. Not that you'd make the blunder that I have made. You'd never do that. There can't be two such beasts ; and, if there were, you're not such a drivelling fool. So you're safe to that extent. But, if you're to be happy, Vivvy, either love your husband, or never marry at all. Learn of me, Vivvy. I rather liked life once. But now, my dear, my only hope is in death."

" Mary, Mary."

" What else ? Even a woman of the town can pick and choose. But I can't pick and choose. I don't even get paid. I have to ask him for every penny I want. I can't even tip Hansard. I'll have to ask him for that—and he'll give me half-a-crown. Oh, my God, I shouldn't talk like this to you, Vivvy. I know it's wrong. But I've got to talk to someone, or I shall go mad."

" Oh, Mary, if I could help you ! "

" You can't. Nobody can. I've tied myself to this revolting creature, and only Death can ever undo the knot. He's like a venomous toad that everyone has to hate— because—he—is—hateful, Vivvy. You know it as well as I. I can only suppose I was mad. But I'd give the rest of my life to be back as I was."

Vivien was weeping quietly. To see Mary strip her soul was a fearful thing.

The two girls were sitting on either side of the fire. This was burning brightly in Vivien's agreeable bedroom, upon the first floor of Brocade. It was half past eleven o'clock, and Pricket had been dismissed. Sir Oliver was in London. To everybody's relief, he had had to go up for a night, to see his solicitors.

"But can't you leave him, Mary?"

"Where can I go? I can't go home—they'd only send me back. And I've no money, Vivvy. I'd sell my jewels, but I don't know how to do it. I'd disappear, if I could— I'd go to France: but you must have money for that and you must know where to go. And he'd be sure to find me, for I don't know how to lie low."

"Can't you stay here?"

"He wouldn't let me, Vivvy. Not without him. When we leave here, we're going home—to Carlton House Terrace, I mean. But that's of no use to me. Mamma's as weak as water, and Papa will take his part. Dear Eldridge will be sympathetic, but what can she do?" (Eldridge had been Mary's nurse and now was acting as Lady Pursuant's maid.) "And then we're to go to Godfreys, to settle in." Mary shuddered. "That's what frightens me, Vivvy. Deep in the country . . . no friends . . . just alone with him. No one will come to see us, because they hate him so. And he's so cruel, Vivvy—I mean, to horses and dogs . . . To human beings, too: but they can fend for themselves. I can't, because I'm his wife: but all others can."

Vivien was twisting her fingers.

"You must tell Aunt Ursula, Mary."

The other shook her head.

"She can do nothing but bid me go to Mamma. I know she'd help if she could—she's always been sweet to me. But how can she interfere? Her hands are tied, Vivvy. Everyone's hands are tied, except Papa's. And he'll do nothing, Vivvy, because he approved the match."

"But it seems so awful, Mary. I mean, we all love you so."

Mary stared at the fire.

"And it is what it seems," she said slowly. "In France, you know, if a dog kills a chicken, they tie the dead bird to his neck. I don't know whether it works; but they say it cures him for good. He can't get away from the dead thing, and, after a day or two, he'll never look at a chicken so long

110

as he lives. Well, Oliver's tied to me. Do what I will, I can't get away from him. He's revolting, Vivvy, because he's alive. And he's bound about my neck for the rest of my life."

"I can come and stay with you, Mary."

Mary rose to her feet.

"I know you would. But I'd never ask you, darling. I—couldn't subject my friends to such an ordeal." She cupped her face in her hands. "I've done very wrong in talking to you like this. But it's been an immense relief. Unfair to you, of course. But I can't help that. You see, I'm like Dives, Vivvy—Dives in Hell. And you've dipped your finger in water and cooled my tongue." She threw a glance round the room. "I shall remember this, Vivvy, when things are very bad. I shall remember this evening and comfort myself by saying 'Vivvy would understand.'"

*   *   *   *   *

Four days had gone by, and the very difficult visit was nearly over and done. In the privacy of her bedroom, 'Only three more days,' murmured Lady Ursula. Not even to Miss Carson, would she have breathed such words. 'Not long now,' Miss Carson said to herself. Lord Henry said nothing, but eyed the calendar. He had carried more weight than the others and carried it very well. He found Bleeding's presence offensive—had come to hate the very sight of the man. Vivien said nothing, either, but, of her simplicity, prayed.

It was a hunting day—the last before Mary went. Bleeding was not going out, but Vivien and Mary were. The meet was at Hilton Crony, some six miles off: the horses had been sent on, and Vivien and Mary were using the ralli-car.

Of this decision, Bleeding had disapproved.

"Why can't you take a carriage?"

"Oh, I don't know," said Vivien. "A carriage means such a fuss."

"Who's going to drive you?"

" I am," said Vivien, quietly.

Bleeding looked very black.

Lord Henry raised his eyebrows.

" A ralli-car's nippy, Bleeding. You ought to get Mary one."

" I don't approve of women driving themselves about."

The next morning he had stood on the steps watching the girls' departure with beady eyes. Too late now, but he ought to have said he'd hunt. Then they'd 've had to have a carriage, instead of —— about like a couple of bookies' ——. Fast, he called it : that's what this young bitch was. Fast. Damned bad company for Mary. Wished he'd never come to the blasted house. Her cousins, the Brabants. Well, let them keep their distance. And that old snob, Lord Henry. Just because he was a Gentleman-at-Arms. . . . So he stood, louring, pulling a coarse lower lip.

The old snob appeared.

" Well, my dears. All tight and sound ? 'Member me to Hinton, and mind you have a good day."

The two smiled and cried their thanks.

Then Vivien nodded her head, and the groom stood back from the mare, to whip to his seat behind.

Mary looked back and waved. Lord Henry waved back. . . .

The girls were hardly mounted, when hounds arrived.

The village was all excitement—for once in a way the hub of its universe. Carriages, dog-carts, gigs : Norfolk jackets and bicycles : scarlet and rat-catcher : hunters, cobs, second horsemen, farmers and grooms.

With one consent, Vivien and Mary preferred to keep to themselves, sitting still in the mouth of a lane that led to the village green.

Hounds went by them, with Berry, full of goodwill. His quick, gray eye caught Vivien. Off came his cap.

" 'Morning, my lady. Happy to see you out."

" Good morning, Mr. Berry."

Termagant turned and came smiling, with Dulcet behind.

"Good lass, Termagant. Well, Dulcet."

The Master appeared, riding with Algy Crosswood and laughing at what he said.

Seeing Termagant leaving the lane, he looked to his right. Then he checked his horse and lifted his cap.

"Good morning. Algy! Let me introduce Captain Crosswood—Lady Bleeding, Lady Vivien Brabant."

Crosswood took off his hat.

"Oh, but we're—old friends," he said.

Vivien was looking at Mary.

Pale as death, she looked upon Crosswood and loved him, for Vivien to see.

Vivien looked at Crosswood. The man was smiling somehow, but his fingers were gripping his crop as though he would squeeze it to pulp.

With a hand to her throat—

"Yes, we're—old friends," said Mary. "Well, Algy, what's Ireland like?"

With a visible effort—

"Well enough, but you can't beat England, Mary. I have to come back for a breather now and again."

After a word with Vivien, Hinton passed on; and Crosswood raised his hat and followed behind.

Mary sat very still. Then she looked at Vivien.

"Spared nothing, Vivvy, you see. But that's the way of Satire: he knows how to use the whip. I've got to be thankful that Oliver wasn't here."

"Are you sure you're all right?" said Vivien, anxiously. "I mean, you know I don't care——"

"Of course I'm all right," said Mary—and forced out a laugh. "'What's Hecuba to him . . . or he to Hecuba?'"

Some sixty minutes had passed.

Vivien was holding Trueboy. She had marked Crosswood's mount, and her quick eye had told her that the latter was not to be pushed. And so she was holding Trueboy, while Mary, on Lovelace, and others were going ahead.

113

The game she was playing was a very difficult game. Watching and waiting, she played it extremely well. Fortune, of course, gave her chances : she never missed one. And at last she had her reward. She and Algy Crosswood had a high-hedged field to themselves.

Quick as a flash—

" Captain Crosswood, I'm dreadfully sorry—I've dropped my crop."

Crosswood pulled up, smiling.

And then he was off his horse and had picked the thing up. As he handed it to her, Vivien shot a glance round. Then—

" Listen," she said. " It's the only chance I'll have. I don't know how much you love Mary, but Mary loves you. And she's in hell, Captain Crosswood. Ten days ago she tried to break her neck." Crosswood went very white. " Nothing would matter, if she could get out of hell. Nothing. She envies scullery-maids, because they're free—and when I say free, I mean they're not tied to her husband, day and night. I'm telling you this, because I've got to do something. I can't sit still and watch her agony. . . . On Friday they're going to stay at Carlton House Terrace—I think for ten days. If you want to write to Mary, you can trust her old nurse. Write to Miss Eldridge, care of Lady Pursuant. She'll give her the note inside." She shot another look round. " And now I must go. But don't forget—Mary's in hell : and when you're in hell—well, anything upon earth is better than that."

With that, she took her crop, put Trueboy at a gap in a hedge and was gone, like the wind.

A check, two miles further on, allowed her to take her place.

*   *   *   *   *

As luck would have it, Crosswood had just been left three thousand pounds.

Six days later a Mr. and Mrs. Boughton arrived at a private

hotel in the *Rue St. Honoré*. They spent the next day shopping, buying a lady's clothes. Mr. Boughton was in great form, chaffing the *midinettes* and making Mrs. Boughton laugh very much.

The plain truth is that Crosswood had taken the plunge —the very deuce of a plunge in 1894. He had sent in his papers and had resigned from his Clubs. In a word, he had done the best he could. And London was very pleased. He had to be written off, but London was very pleased. Lord Elmham sent him a line.

White's Club.

Dear Algy,

My stables at Chantilly. You're just the man. Nice house, very pleasant surroundings. Seventeen at the moment, two mares in foal. Six hundred a year any good? Think it over, old fellow. I'd like you to have the job. All of us here are with you. You shouldn't have taken your name off, you silly fool.

Yours ever,
Victor.

And Lady Ringwood wrote.

My dearest Mary,

Bring Captain Crosswood to lunch on Tuesday next. This time we shall be alone, for I want to talk. After that—well, Paris loves a romance, and you will be personae gratae *wherever you go. Dearest child, I want to see you so much.*

Yours affectionately,
Rachel Ringwood.

PS. So very much better, you know. And so appropriate.

And Mary wrote to Vivien.

My darling Vivien,

' Between us two there is a great gulf fixed.' But you can't be as happy on your side as I am on mine. And I owe it all to

you. *God bless and keep you, darling, all your days. Oh, God bless you, Vivvy, I love you so. I am so very happy. We are so very happy. And you've done that. Oh, Vivvy, Vivvy, I am so very happy. Tell Light Heart that for me —I'd like him to know.*

Your loving
Mary.

His solicitors wrote to Sir Oliver.

Lincoln's Inn Fields,
November, 1894.

Sir,

The Honble. Lady Bleeding.

We desire to put upon record the advice we ventured to tender yesterday.

In our opinion, you will be well advised to allow us to institute divorce proceedings against your wife.

The thing is done. Nothing can be gained by recrimination; and, in our considered opinion, the only dignified course is for you to file your petition without delay.

So you will command sympathy.

If you persist in demanding that we shall endeavour to embarrass the guilty parties, we can only respectfully suggest that you seek the assistance of a firm of solicitors other than ourselves.

We are, Sir,
Your most obedient servants,
Lundy and Pulbrook.

Upon reading this missive, Sir Oliver wept with rage.

Part Two

'PRESENT MIRTH HATH PRESENT LAUGHTER'

Philip was 'standing at ease' by the door of a suite. This was in Buckingham Palace. In June 1897, Royalty—monarchs excepted—had come to pay its respects: since it was accorded all honour, officers of the Household Brigade were posted without its rooms. So Philip, in all his glory, was on parade.

His helmet increased his stature—and added years to his age. Beneath his polished cuirass, his tunic fitted like a glove. His white buck-skin breeches, 'leathers', were skintight. His jack-boots were immaculate. His spurs were of solid gold.

A rustle, and he sprang to attention: his sloped sword came to 'the carry': his eyes looked straight before him, not moving at all. People passed by the living statue, as if, indeed, the soldier were carved out of stone. Not till the rustle had faded, did Philip relax.

It was a boring procedure, this sentinelship. All you could do was to think.

Philip thought.

Vivvy's marriage last year was working out devilish well. It hadn't made any difference, except, of course, that she wasn't at Grosvenor Square. But Charles Street was very close. And Hubert was very decent—liked her to do as she pleased. (Captain Hubert de Guesclin, of the Grenadier Guards: late of Eton and the R.M.C. Sandhurst: now of Charles Street, W., and Fairing Over, in the County of Berkshire: Clubs, Bachelors', Guards', White's. Five years older than Vivien, gentle and easy-going, a very giant of a man: handsome, witty, immensely popular: apparently without effort, leading a very full life.) And Fairing Over

was topping—Vivvy loved it. And Hubert loved Poesy. . . .
There was nothing like Poesy, of course. Brocade was all
right and awfully good for hunting. But Poesy . . . Still,
London was good—very good. Funny how he'd always
disliked it. Well, not exactly disliked it, but wanted to get
away. And Vivvy loved it now. And London ' loved her
back '. Old Lady Tallis had said that, and it was perfectly
true. London did love Vivvy. And she was awfully happy,
yet just the same. My God, at the Juliots' ball, in that gold
dress she'd looked like something out of the picture-books.
And Virgil had said, ' She's one of those mortals the high
gods used to fall for. I dine out on being her cousin three
times a week.' Of course, what with his duty and her
engagements . . . but she and Hubert were coming to Poesy
later, and then they would be together all the time. He
wished he could tell her about Sunday. He'd told her he'd
seen her, of course. Jolly decent of her to get up and wait
at the corner, just to see him ride by. And she hadn't the
faintest idea that Dolly was standing beside her, *to watch
him, too*. He'd never dreamed that either of them would
be there. And there they were, standing together . . . and
Vivvy was talking to Dolly, who looked so pleased. Neither
knew who the other was, unless Vivvy had said. She might
have, of course : but Dolly would hold her tongue. Poor
Dolly, of Clarges Street. It didn't seem fair. She—she
gave so much ; and he could do nothing in return. Nothing.
He wasn't allowed to. Just as she wasn't allowed to know
him outside. She probably didn't care, but it didn't seem
right. Stenning had told him plainly—' Never forget,
Ringwood, that Clarges Street's off the map. It simply
doesn't exist. If you should meet someone you've seen
there, you've never seen them before. All the girls are
very well treated—we see to that.' All the same, he didn't
like it—it didn't seem fair. And Dolly loved to hear about
the dances and balls. Oh, hell, he supposed that was life :
but it didn't seem fair. Never mind. The Rufford House

ball was to-night—that ought to be good.   Aunt Ursula was actually going.   She and he and the Master—he was great fun.   Nice to have him staying at Grosvenor Square.   Vivvy had a party, of course : but Ross and his sister were coming, before going on.   Ildico Ross, with the cold, clean-cut features and raven hair.   ' She diminishes me,' said Vivvy, which wasn't true.   Still, he knew what she meant.   There was about Ildico something that looked you down.   Not that she put on airs, but the air was there.   She and Vivvy together. . . .   ' Kings' daughters ', Virgil had called them— he always knew how to put it better than anyone else.   He was very decent, Virgil.   He'd been so nice to Mummy two years ago.   Called himself her tame cat.   Pity she wasn't here now ; but, though she never showed it, Miss Carson said it had been the deuce of a strain.   Not in those words, of course.   It must have been awful, lunching at Marlborough House : but she'd gone through with it somehow, and the Princess had come to see her the following day. (The fourth Earl of Ringwood had been *persona grata* with H.R.H. Four days before he died, Rachel and he had dined with the Prince and Princess.   And Ringwood had a bad chill.   He would, of course, have cancelled any other engagement. Doing his humble duty had probably cost him his life.) But she'd come for Vivvy's wedding and promised to come for his.   She was in Budapest, and Mary and Algy Cross-wood were staying with her.   Pity they couldn't come back ; but they were happy all right, and Mary had had a baby six months ago.   Philip, called after him.   And their place at Chantilly was gorgeous—and what a job !   Uncle Henry had lunched with them and was awfully pleased.   Good old Uncle Henry. . . .   But he was getting on.   Although he wouldn't admit it, that fall had shaken him up.   H.R.H. had been very nice . . . sent round to inquire every morning for several days.   And came to see him, himself.   Showed what he thought of him.   Aunt Ursula seemed younger : Uncle Henry said it suited her, getting about.   Last year at Lord's she'd actually mounted the coach. Funny she'd never married—that night at Covent Garden she'd looked immense. So'd Miss Carson, by Jove. Stunning. She must have been able to marry heaps of times. Jolly good thing she hadn't—for Vivvy and him. There was no one like Miss Carson—she understood and she knew. She'd got the telephone for Grosvenor Square. And he'd rung up from the Club the first day they'd had it in—and asked for Aunt Ursula. And at first she'd nearly died, and then she wouldn't stop talking . . . kept on saying, ' But, Pip, that can't be you.' And now Miss Carson was seeing about the electric light. Of course, she was marvellous. What ever would she say about Dolly ? And Clarges Street ? (Philip reflected, frowning.) She wouldn't say it was wrong. She never said that. But she'd probably show you a side which hadn't occurred to you. After all, it wasn't quite fair. Dolly ought to have married and had a home. And now . . . She was all right, of course—would be all right for some years. Say, six years. And after six years . . . what then ? Stenning had said they were well treated—' We see to that.' Yes, but when they left Clarges Street, who saw to that then ? Supposing . . .

Philip was biting his lip. . . . Then his eye-brows went up.

Oh, well. . . . He supposed that was life. ' The oldest profession in the world.' And so it had always been life, and always would be. Even if he didn't go, the others would. So it wouldn't make any difference . . .

He was at Harrow again, and Miss Carson's steady gray eyes were smiling at his.

" I know it'll make no difference. Just because you stop, it'll make no difference at all. The rest will go on—chucking a stone in at the open window, as they go by . . . and then taking to their heels. As you say, it's become a custom. But that is a custom, Pip, to which the Earl of Ringwood should not subscribe. It'll make no difference to ' Nosey ', unfortunate man. But it will make a difference to you. Your self-respect will be served. If others like to do it, that's their affair. But, because you were born Lord Ringwood, you have no choice. *Noblesse oblige.*"

Standing at ease in the corridor, Philip wrote Clarges Street off.

* * * * *

Sixteen hours later, perhaps, Lady Vivien de Guesclin returned from the Rufford House ball.

It had been a most brilliant function, and most enjoyable. People had been very nice—they always were. The supper dances had been the greatest fun. George Forest had taken her in, and Pip and Hubert and Virgil and Ildico Ross had all contrived to join them for half an hour. And the Duke had been very charming. Ildico had, of course, been in great demand : but she had danced twice with Pip and had, she would swear, been glad to dance with him. Pip always seemed pleased to dance with everyone. And so he was. That was his blessed nature. Plenty of time, of course : but so far Ildico had come nearest to filling the role.

Followed by Hubert, Vivien entered the hall—and stopped in her tracks.

" Pricket," she said, " I told you to go to bed."

" I know, my lady," said Pricket, taking her cloak.

" Is Merry ill ? "

" No, my lady."

" Then why don't you do as I tell you ? "

" I did lie down, my lady."

" With one ear open. What is the good of that ? This is the third night running you've waited up. If you go on like this, I shall have to give up going out."

" Think of that, Pricket," said Hubert. He picked his wife up in his arms. " If, because of you, your mistress declines to go out—well, you'll be lynched, Pricket. A posse of angry swains . . ."

A soft palm covered his mouth.

"You may do me to-night, Pricket : but don't you dare come near me before mid-day. Merry will call me at nine and will see me up. Is that understood ? "

"Very good, my lady "—meekly.

Hubert stepped to the staircase, and Pricket fell in behind. Vivien called over her shoulder.

"Good night, Connel."

The night-footman's voice replied.

"Good night, my lady : good night, sir."

"Good night."

Arrived upstairs, Hubert set his wife down, kissed her nose and made for the room next door.

Pricket took charge. . . .

The change was made in silence. Not till her lady was sitting before her table, did Pricket open her mouth.

"Your ladyship enjoyed it ? "

"Every minute, Pricket. It was a lovely ball. Lady Charlotte was the best to-night—yes, she beat me, Pricket. It was a glorious frock. Blue and silver, with . . . I'll have to go to Paris, Pricket. They have the line. Mrs. Ronnie Quaritch looked terribly well. She was wearing the Poseley diamonds—a most magnificent set. Lady Gorget was very striking—that lovely hair. Of course it's made for emeralds. But she was awfully sweet—came up and called me ' Vivien ' and said the nicest things. The Prince and Princess came in for half an hour. . . . Yes, we were summoned, Pricket— I'm sure that'll do you good. And now I've got something for you—I suppose that's why you stayed up. They're coming to Fairing Over one afternoon."

"Oh, my lady."

"Yes. The Princess said she'd heard how lovely it was, and might they come down one day for an hour or two. I said we should be honoured. And she said, ' That'll be lovely ' and turned to the Prince. ' Bertie, we're going to Fairing Over one afternoon.' And the Prince laughed and said, ' Splendid, my dear. Tell George to arrange it with

Lady Vivien.' That's Sir George ——, who's one of his equerries."

" Oh, my lady. How—how wonderful. How will they come ? "

" Oh, special train. They'll clear the line for them, and they'll be down at Birdcage in half an hour. But I hope they give us a chance. Everything new, you know. New cups and plates and linen. . . . And then who they want to be there. You'll have to look after Her Royal Highness' maid. She'll come down in the morning and tell you what she wants. And a valet and coachman and footman . . ."

There was a little silence. Pricket was overwhelmed.

At length—

" And his lordship, my lady ? "

" Had a great time. Danced twice with Miss Ildico."

" She's a lovely young lady," said Pricket; " and nice as nice." She hesitated. " If she were a year or two younger . . ."

" I know," said Vivien, " I know. But his lordship will always be very young for his age. So if we're to stick to that rule, the girl that he should marry is now about ten. And we can't wait all that time."

" That's very true, my lady. But Miss Ildico's less than a year."

Vivien raised her eye-brows.

" I don't know that that matters, really. She's the best so far, Pricket. Quiet, intelligent, poise—she's a very exceptional girl. He's got to love her, of course : but, if he did, she'd make him a wonderful wife."

" I understand, my lady, that in Scotland she wears the kilt."

Vivien began to laugh.

" In that case, he'd better go up there. If his lordship sees her in a kilt, it'll be all over."

" Oh, I hope not, my lady."

" Don't be silly, Pricket. You know what men are. And now that's enough for to-night. Leave a note for

Merry to call me at nine. If I see you before mid-day, I'll send you away for a month."

* * * * *

Three letters shall speak for themselves.

Poesy,
16th July, 1897.

My dearest Rachel,
You will see, from the address, that I have thrown in my hand. I am perfectly well, but I cannot go on any more. Eleanor is staying in Town till the end of July. How Vivien and Philip do it, I cannot tell : needless to say, they do four times as much as I. But they enjoy every minute and never look tired.

Vivien continues to have a succès fou. *I know she has told you all about the royal visit to Fairing Over, but she certainly has not said how very lovely she looked and how superbly she managed everything. I think T.R.H. were truly charmed. Of course, upon such occasions, Hubert's a tower of strength. His address is always perfect, and I think the Prince is very fond of him. It was a most lovely afternoon, and tea on the great lawn was unforgettable. The Princess spoke so very sweetly of you. She charged me to give you her ' dear love', when I wrote. So there you are.*

After Goodwood comes Cowes. Then V. and H. will withdraw to Fairing Over for two or three weeks. Pip will visit them, after which all three will come here.

Pip was not at the party—he could not get away. But he seems to manage to go everywhere in Town. And he is persona grata *wherever he goes. He always looks so nice and he has a most charming way. What d'you think Uncle Henry told me the other day ? He happened to be in Bond Street, and there was a poor, old lady who wanted to cross the road : but she was afraid of the traffic and didn't know enough to walk along to where it was being held up. Uncle Henry said it was pathetic*

126

and he was just going to help, when a very young well-dressed man came up, took off his hat and offered the old lady his arm. Rachel, it was Pip. And he took her across so nicely and spoke for a moment or two before taking his leave. Uncle Henry said he never felt so proud. After all, it was a good deal for a boy of nineteen to do.

You've got two darling children, and that's the truth.

And now for a matter that's giving us some concern—Eleanor and me, I mean. You'll remember Andrew Ross : he was at Harrow with Philip, and Philip has stayed with him. Very nice people. But you won't remember his sister, because you never saw her. If you had seen her, you would remember her. She is enchanting. Very lovely, very quiet, very dignified. All the makings of a great lady. Vivien is very fond of her ; and the two girls and Pip and Hubert and Andrew seem to be together a lot. They're asked to the same places all the time. I think there's no doubt that Ildico is attracted to Pip. That is natural enough, for Pip is most attractive. And I think that Pip is looking at Ildico. That's equally natural. But he must not think of marriage until he is twenty-one. If only she was three years younger—she's eighteen. As it is, she is, to my mind, too old for him. I think the difference in ages should never be less than five years. Mercifully, the Colonel will not have a married subaltern : and as Pip is devoted to his Regiment, that may be the end of it. But I am not easy. What upsets us both is that Ildico seems ideal. And yet he's too young to marry, and she is too old for him. Nothing, of course, can be done, unless he should move. I hope and pray he won't and that the thing will fade out. Yet, I have—we have—this dreadful feeling that she is the girl for him. I tell you all this, my dear Rachel, because it is right you should know. But you can do nothing, either. It is a distracting business. Of course, if they cared to wait for two or three years. . . . She would be always, in my opinion, four years too old : but she is, in all other respects, so exactly right. Conceive a young queen, Rachel. Well, that is what the girl is. She is, I suppose, a throw-back. The blood *of the Kings of Scotland runs in her veins.   I don't know what to say.   Of course there are plenty of others coming on.   But none, I fancy, will come up to Ildico.*

Your loving sister,
Ursula.

Budapest.

My dearest Ursula,

Pip is much too young.   But if Ildico is the girl you and Vivvy say she is, you need have no fear.   She will wait for him.   And nothing could be better than that, for, though they are not engaged, she will be in his background all the time, as the knights' ladies were in the days of old.   I agree that it's a pity there's only one year's difference in their ages, but one cannot have everything, and Pip, whoever he marries, will always be younger than his wife.

Vivvy is certainly having a splendid time.   I am sure she does all things well.   I can't help feeling she should have a baby soon.   I mean . . .

Break o' Day,
17th August.

My dear Pip,

I said I would write to you within the week, and so I am doing. I preferred to write, because I wanted to think it over and decide —not what I wanted to say, for I knew what that was, but how best to put my reply.

You asked me to be your wife.   If you had been five—no, three years older, I would have said yes.   I would like you to know that.   But, as it is, my dear, I'm going to say no.   I don't know what people do in cases like this, and I don't really care, for I know how I feel about it and I know I am right.   Any sort of engagement would be a great mistake, because you and I are the kind that honours engagements no matter what they cost : yet, in the next three years, one or both of us might see someone that we liked better.   We might, Pip—either of us.   So let us go our ways, not forgetting Tuesday last, but remembering that

128

we would not be the first two that have taken a liking to each other and later married elsewhere.

I see I have never thanked you for the honour you did me, Pip. I am very sensible of that.

Yours affectionately,
Ildico.

*　　*　　*　　*　　*

The Adjutant looked up.

" Yes, Ringwood ? "

" I've just had a message, sir, to say that my great-uncle's . . . been taken very ill."

" Lord Henry ? I'm devilish sorry. Too few of him left. Well, cut along."

" There's the shoeing, sir : but Mortimer's said he'll take over, if you're content."

" Of course. Get back when you can. Here. Wait a minute. You'd better take my hansom."

" Thank you very much, sir."

" That's all right."

Albany Street . . . Harley Street . . . Davies Street . . . Berkeley Square . . . and the fog coming down.

And, at last, the quiet room, with the blinds half drawn.

" Who's that ? "

" It's me, sir. Pip."

" Good boy. I'm—not too well."

" I know, sir. They said——"

" They didn't tell you the truth. I'm going out."

" Perhaps, sir——"

" There's no ' perhaps ' this time. This is death."

There was a little silence.

Then—

" I've had a good life, Pip. Seventy-five, and hardly a day in bed. I was a page at Her Majesty's coronation— that's a long time ago. And she was gay in the old days— you wouldn't think that. God bless my soul, I've seen so many changes. And you'll see many more. When I was your age, Pip . . ."

Here a terrible bout of coughing had its way, and a nurse whipped out of the shadows, to minister to its victim as best she could. Philip watched her at work with horrified eyes.

At last all was quiet again, but Lord Henry lay like her dead that the sea had given up. And the nurse, herself, was uncertain. She had her fingers upon the fine, old wrist.

Then the eyelids flickered, and she withdrew.

The assault had been repulsed, but it had cost the defender extremely dear.

"You there, Pip?" whispered Lord Henry.

"Yes, sir."

"Good boy. Couldn't be sure. It's getting dark. Listen to me, Pip—I haven't got long. . . . You're very young, but you've got the right instincts, just as your father had. And that is everything. But I've the experience. I ought to know my world and I think I do. Don't retire till they make you Captain : you'll always regret it if you do. But don't go on after that—Brocade and Poesy will take up all your time. Don't dismiss the agents, but run them yourself. If you feel like it, marry : but don't unless you're sure. I have never married, and I'm all right. See Coles about Eleanor Carson. She deserves the best and must be provided for. And now I'm going to surprise you. You must look after Vivvy . . . all your life. That's really de Guesclin's job : but he may fall down. So you be ready— always. . . . I don't think there's anything else. And now you talk for a bit. What was the shoeing course like? I did one . . . a—long—time—ago. . . ."

Philip heard himself talking about his shoeing course. . . .

After a minute or two, the nurse slipped out of the background, stooped for a moment and then spoke quietly enough.

"His Lordship's asleep," she whispered.

Philip, who had been kneeling, sat back on his heels.

130

The door was opened a little. At once the nurse was there.

After a whispered parley, Coles stole into the room.

He nodded to Philip, passed to the bed and stooped to peer at the patient.

Then he looked at the nurse.

" Asleep ? "

" I think it's a coma, sir."

Coles pursed his lips and nodded.

" The doctor coming back ? "

The nurse looked at her watch.

" Any moment now, sir."

Ten minutes dragged on their way.

Then the door was opened and the doctor came in.

He glanced at the quiet form and then at the nurse. Then he passed to the fire and held his hand to the blaze. . . .

With his fingers about the wrist—

" Not long now," he said quietly. " He's going out."

Coles caught Philip's eye and jerked his head at the door.

As they gained the landing—

" Nothing to be done, Pip. I don't think he'll speak again."

Together, they waited downstairs. . . .

Twenty minutes later the doctor looked into the room.

" I'm afraid it's all over," he said. " Slipped out as he was when you saw him. His breathing just stopped. Please forgive my not waiting. I've got a very bad case in Berkeley Square."

" That's quite all right, doctor," said Coles.

As the door closed—

" He—was—so—splendid," said Philip, and burst into tears.

*   *   *   *   *

Eleanor Carson was visiting Lincoln's Inn Fields.

Coles Willing rose to receive her.

" Good morning. So glad to see you. Please sit down."
Miss Carson did as he said.

" Now, first, I want your advice. One of the Trustees,
Lord Henry, is now no more. Who do you think should
replace him ? "

" Oh, Mr. Willing, I've no idea at all."

" That's natural enough. But, you see, now that he's gone,
things will very largely be in my hands. I mean, Ursula does
as I say."

" Of course."

" That means that I to-day am virtually sole Trustee.
Well, that's all wrong, Miss Carson, in an affair like this.
There's a very great fortune involved, there are three estab-
lishments and Pip does not come of age for more than a year."

" Will the Trust end then ? "

" Oh, no. The Trust goes on. He'll have control of
more money—more say in things : but the Trust goes on.
And it's a great mistake to have only one man in charge. I
mean, we're all mortal, you know. And if I was run
over to-night. . . ." Miss Carson shuddered. " Exactly.
Ursula couldn't take charge. She's a perfect sleeping Trustee,
but she couldn't take charge."

" No, there you're quite right, Mr. Willing. She simply
couldn't do it. No woman could."

" Well, there you are. Now what is in my mind is to
appoint two Trustees in Lord Henry's place. One my junior
partner, a very nice man, and the other—Pip."

Miss Carson started.

" Pip ! "

Coles Willing nodded.

" Pip. He'll have to learn, of course. And he'll lean on
Defoe—that's my junior partner. But he is eligible, and it
wouldn't be a bad introduction to the duties he ought to do
when he comes of age. You see, he has great possessions,
and he should learn what that means. It means great responsibilities. For one thing only, between Poesy, Brocade

and Grosvenor Square we employ more than one hundred souls. The fortunes of all of those are bound up with ours. I'm not talking of the tenants, you know; the servants alone. They've got to be cared for, watched over, kept up to the bit and pensioned, when they grow old. We've taken them on, and, if they do their duty, we've got to look after them. It's right and proper, Miss Carson: it's always been done. Well, if Pip becomes a Trustee, he will get an insight into these things. As things are, he takes too much for granted. That isn't his fault. But now the time is coming when he should know where he stands—and where all those people stand who are dependent on him."

"I quite agree with you there. Indeed, you've opened my eyes. I'm afraid I've taken a very great deal for granted."

"Why shouldn't you? I mean, it's not your affair. But three of the clerks in this office do nothing else but attend to the Ringwood Trust. And I've only shown you one facet. There's Vivien's share, and the tenants, the upkeep of the estates: there's Rachel and Ursula. . . . Of course, it's decentralized: the land-agents and the stewards render their accounts and make their reports: but it's a little realm— which has to be administered, cared for, looked after and made to pay dividends in kind."

"It's a very good realm," said Miss Carson.

"I think it is. In any event, it's a very happy realm. High and low are content—and proud to belong to it. Times are changing, of course: but this is Nature's system, and I, for one, shall be sorry to see it go."

"Will it ever go, Mr. Willing?"

"Yes. And after untold misery, it will come back. False prophets will arise—men with the gift of the gab. Envious men, who, because they weren't born Lord Ringwood, desire to bring him down. And so they will strike at his roots— infect with the poison of envy the very tenants and servants he treats so well. . . . They're a clever lot of blackguards.

133

You see, there's no antidote to envy. . . . But that's by the way. Do you agree that Pip should be a Trustee?"

"I think it's awfully wise. Mr. Defoe will help him?"

"That's the idea. Put them in together, and together they'll find their feet." Here Coles Willing rose and began to pace up and down. "And now there's another thing. We can't regularize your position, for it is unique. I don't know how to describe it, and that's the truth. You're rather like a clock, to which all of us always refer, because we know that we can count upon it and it will always be right."

Miss Carson began to laugh.

"That's very complimentary, and I wish it was true. Nowadays, Mr. Willing, I'm often out of my depth."

"If you are, it never appears. The clock keeps perfect time." He fingered his chin. "The point I'm approaching is this. We cannot dispense with the clock. If the clock were taken away, we should all feel lost. All. I don't think you know how much I depend upon you. As long as you're there, Miss Carson, I know that, whatever happens, all will be very well."

Coming from Coles Willing, this was a compliment, indeed. Miss Carson was embarrassed—and quite unable to reply. Willing proceeded slowly.

"Words are all very well: they are not enough for us. We have a sense of security. We want our—our clock to feel that she has one, too. And so a Trust has been formed . . . I advisedly use the past tense. A Trust has been formed, and a Deed has been executed. In a word, Miss Carson, it's all over. A sum has been settled upon you, which will bring you in just about six hundred a year." Miss Carson gasped. "The capital, you cannot touch, but you can leave it by Will. You see, we want you to feel that you are secure, that, no matter what may befall, you have a private income which nothing can touch."

Miss Carson got to her feet.

"Mr. Willing, I can't possibly accept such generosity.

134

From the day I came, I have been used with the greatest kindness. My duties have been made pleasures, year after year. Then, again, I have saved some money. There is no reason on earth——"

"My dear," said Coles, " it's all over. The thing is done. You have no say in the matter—none of us has any say. I've a copy of the Deed here, for you to take and keep. But nothing you can say can undo it. But, if you could, I'm sure you wouldn't undo it—if only because, that you should be so secured was Lord Henry's dying wish."

Miss Carson stared. Then she sat down again, with the tears running down her cheeks.

* * * * *

The straw was down in Charles Street. It made a considerable difference. The horses' hoofs were silenced; and the iron tire that met it lost its sting. Hubert had favoured tan, but had been converted to straw. So straw had been laid in Charles Street outside the de Guesclins' house. But Vivien was past caring. She had been in labour for seventeen hours.

Lady Ringwood was there—downstairs, and Miss Carson and Lady Ursula. The first-born was the first born in 1898. Hubert—and who shall blame him ?—was in St. James's Street. These women . . . As Virgil put it later, ' Childbirth resembles a ship-wreck—women and children first.'

"She's timed it well," said Lady Ringwood.

"My dear," said Lady Ursula. . . .

Miss Carson smiled.

"If she has, I don't know that you can blame her. For Vivien to miss the season would be extremely hard."

"She's set on Poesy ? "

Lady Ursula nodded.

" The seat means so much to her that I think she'll be better there than anywhere else."

Philip's head came round the door.

" May I come in ? "

" Of course, darling," said his mother.

Philip came in.

" Is Vivvy all right ? "

" Perfectly, darling. It shouldn't be very long now."

" I had to come," said Philip. " I mean . . ."

" Hush."

A cry like that of a cat rang out from above.

" My God," said Philip, and his mother began to laugh.

" That's your nephew, Pip. I don't think such a noise could be made by a niece."

Lady Ursula, all of a twitter, moved half-way to the door.

Philip looked at Miss Carson.

" A nurse will come down," she said.

Perhaps five minutes went by.

Then a nurse flitted down the great staircase and into the hall.

As Philip swung open the door, she looked into the room.

" Sir Arthur's compliments, my lady, and it's a handsome boy."

A chorus of delighted exclamation greeted her words.

Then—

" Is Hubert with her ? " said Philip.

Miss Carson stepped into the breach.

" He couldn't stand it, Pip, and went off to White's. Will you go and ring him up ? "

Lady Ringwood had rung the bell.

As Philip left the room, the butler himself appeared.

" Champagne, please, Welling. Lady Vivien has a fine son." The butler bowed, beaming. " Serve something below stairs, for all must drink his health."

" With very great pleasure, my lady."

The butler withdrew.

Philip was on the telephone.

" Is that you, Hubert ? Vivvy's got a boy."

" Very well done," said the distant voice in reply. " I'll be round forthwith."

*   *   *   *   *

The day after the baby had been christened, Lady Ringwood returned to France. Philip escorted his mother . . . to Paris in April—and 1898.

Philip preferred London—perhaps because London was his. London was real : but Paris was like a play. Everybody was acting : the crowds were crowds of the stage. The absurd importance of officials ; the clamour of discordant voices, unnecessarily raised ; the complete lack of reserve ; the fantastic mask of politeness which never slipped ; the language of gesticulation—the exaggerated shrug, the violence of extended fingers, the spread-out arms, the features transfigured—these things belonged to farce : you paid to see them in London, and laughed like anything. But here it was life—a very preposterous life, but life all the same. Still, it was all very gay. It had been cold in London, but here it was nice and warm : and people were sitting and strolling as though they had nothing to do. And when they laughed, they laughed uncontrollably—and passers-by joined in and were told the jest : and then they laughed, too, like madmen, till you had to laugh yourself. And then, because you were laughing, they clapped you upon the back and laughed the more.

Sitting back in the brougham—

" Fun, isn't it, Pip ? " said Lady Ringwood.

" Yes, it is fun, Mummy. I can't help liking it all. But it doesn't seem real."

" I know. But, in fact, it is. Intensely real. The French behave as they feel—when they're off parade. And if you're nice to them, they'll carry you shoulder high. And by nice, I mean sympathetic. Nothing else counts in France. Laugh and cry with them, and you can't go wrong."

" And when they're on parade ? "

" Then they are playing a part. French polish is very well named. The Frenchman on parade is overlaid with veneer. His compliments are exquisite—and utterly valueless. But it's very entertaining. Living here as much as I have, I've got deeper down. Touch the roots of the French, and you'll find that the lower classes are honest souls. Take the servants, for instance : I really can count on them."

The home-coming shewed forth this truth. The pride and delight with which the lady was received were unmistakable. That she was an exceptional mistress, I quite admit. For all that, true devotion looked out of her servants' eyes.

This devotion was extended to Philip, partly because he was Philip, partly because he was Lady Ringwood's son.

And Rachel looked after him.

Two young attachés came to lunch the next day : before they left, an evening had been arranged. Then came Mary and Algy—to luncheon, of course—and to take Philip out of Paris for twenty-four hours.

" Darling Pip," cried Mary, and kissed him on either cheek. " You'd never have known me, would you ? I'm actually getting fat."

" Of course I would, Cousin Mary. But I've never seen you look so happy and well."

" That's me," said Algy Crosswood. " I've done it, all by myself. Pip, my lad, I'll show you a string to-morrow that will lift up your heart."

" I want to see my godson."

" You shall see him and hear him ; and if you want to please him, you'll take him into the stables and put him up on a horse. That's what he really likes. One of these days he'll win the National."

Mary looked at her hostess.

" Cousin Rachel, you must forgive him. Horses are Algy's life."

Lady Ringwood was smiling.

138

" Not all of it, I think. May I drive down to luncheon to-morrow and bring Pip back ? "

" Of course. We'd love to have you. But tell me more of Vivvy."

" You must ask Pip. I saw her at a bad time."

" Vivvy," said Philip, " is dazzling. There's no other word. And yet she's just the same as she always was. She'd rather be at Poesy most of the time. She can't, of course : but—well, wash out the London Season and ninety per cent of the girls would burst into tears : but Vivvy wouldn't, although she's such a success."

Algy put in his oar.

" That's because she's a sense of values."

" I think," said Lady Ringwood, " you're right as far as you go. She has a sense of values. But if she were to write down the values she set upon things, I'm not at all sure that they would agree with the books. Never mind. She's wonderfully well—and goes to Poesy next week."

" I expected she would. And the son and heir ? "

Lady Ringwood smiled again.

" What d'you think ? Vivvy does all things well."

*   *   *   *   *

A very select establishment, far from Montmartre. No brass or plush or marble, but the very hell of a band, all wearing Harlequin's dress. Shaded lights and elegant tables and chairs, fine glass and fine napery, beautifully dressed women and well-groomed men—and all the abandon of a Decameron night.

Philip was quite overcome. The two attachés watched him amusedly.

After a little.

" I've been to Montmartre," said Philip, " but . . ."

" Montmartre is a circus," said Marchmont. " This is a masque." A *maître d'hôtel* was bowing. " Good evening,

139

Reynard. This is Monsieur le Comte de Ringwood. Please know him again."

Reynard bowed again.

"*Parfaitement*, Monsieur Marchmont. Welcome, *Monsieur le Comte.*"

"Thank you," said Philip, smiling. "I'm very glad to be here."

"I hope that milord will come often. Paris will always be Paris; but *Cerigo* is unique. A table, Monsieur Marchmont?"

"If you please. That one away from the band."

Philip took his place, as a man in a dream.

Montmartre was good, but vulgar. No doubt about that. It was intensely amusing to let oneself go. But one did pay a certain price. To be frank, the company was mixed. It was sometimes extremely low. All were friends, of course: still, to rub shoulders with bullies . . . But that was Montmartre. You cannot make a silk purse out of a sow's ear. Montmartre was the sow's ear: *Cerigo* was the silk purse. People let themselves go, but knew how to behave. Propriety was mocked, but not outraged. Abandon sat at the board, but she ate delicately. Every being there was in full evening dress, and every single woman was tightly masked.

"Are they *grandes cocottes*?" said Philip.

Marchmont shook his head.

"Not even that, Ringwood. Everyone here is gentle— by marriage, if not by birth. They are the wives or daughters of the *élite*. You see, marriage in France is made. Love doesn't come into the matter. It doesn't always in England; but never in France. Hence, *Cerigo*. No unmarried girl comes here, of course. . . . Don't ask me how they arrange it, because I don't know: but there's no one here that you couldn't introduce to your sister in ordinary life."

With his words, two ladies approached,—one took her seat on the table, after the way of Montmartre. Conversation, half French, half English, was soon in full swing. Champagne appeared. Presently one of the women slipped away, to return with a third—a very attractive girl, with auburn hair.

"She is for you, Monsieur." The new-comer took her seat on the arm of Philip's chair. "She has a weakness for soldiers."

"But that is quite true," said the other, playing with Philip's hair. "Are you in the Guards, my pretty?"

"I'm in the Blues," said Philip. "The Horse Guards."

The girl took his head in her hands and kissed his nose.

"But I have seen them, *mignon*. They ride through the streets. And they wear the plumed helmet and breastplate and great thigh boots."

"That's right. I wear them, too."

"Darling! My name is Claude. And yours?"

"Philip."

"Come and dance with me, Philip, and tell me everything." They took the floor. "Have you a sweetheart, Philip?"

"Well, no."

"That means that you have a sweetheart, but she does not know."

Philip laughed.

"Any way, I can't marry yet. If I did I'd have to retire."

"And give up your plumed helmet? Oh, no, you must not do that. Soldiers should never marry : they should have friends. And are you long in Paris?"

"Only another four days : I have to get back."

"To ride through the streets?"

"And other things. I have to look after my troop—they're terribly good."

"And proud of their officer."

"I don't know about that. They help me a lot on parade. My sergeant's marvellous. I'm very lucky to have a troop at my age."

"Which is?"

"I'll be twenty this year."

"Where were you at school ? At—at Eton ?"

"No, I was at Harrow."

"H-h-harrow. I do not know that. Yes, I do. They strive with Eton, don't they ? In London. And everyone goes."

"That's right. At cricket, at Lord's."

"I remember now. But I have not been to that. To Ascot—yes. I liked that very much. But I do wish more of your ladies would dress over here. They are so lovely, you know—far better than us. But we have the *couturiers*. So sometimes we look better, although we are not so good."

"I think you'd be hard to beat."

Claude threw her arms round his neck.

"No, go on dancing, *mignon*. That's the best of this place. One can do as one feels."

Something shaken, Philip continued to dance.

"And call me ' Claude ', please. I like to be called by name."

"All right, Claude."

"And now I am tired of dancing. Come and sit down. No, not at the table, darling. I've something private to say." Claude led him to a settee, and they took their seats. "Now put your arm about me and pretend to make love."

Philip did as she said.

"Now, Philip, listen to me. When I was in London last autumn, I went to some very good parties. And then, at one of these, I met a man that I knew. I mean, I had met him here. And he recognized this ring. You see ; it is rather unusual. And perhaps he would have known me—for other things ; although, of course, he had never seen my face."

"I think," said Philip, " that I should know you again—Claude."

"Sweet heart ! " Claude ruffled his hair. "Any way, he knew me. Let us say it was my perfume. . . . He never said so, of course : but I knew that he knew. And when I

142

was dancing with him, I told him so. . . . You have no *Cerigo* in London, but matters can be arranged. And so we were able to meet upon different terms. . . . Now, Philip, listen to me. It is really very important that I should see him again. *Mais, très, très important, chéri.* You see, it is now essential that I should bear a son. There is a great title involved. But I do not love my husband—nobody could. But *his* son—Hubert's son—would be worth carrying. . . . You understand, darling, that on this I have set my heart. And when a woman sets her heart on a certain man—well, unless he is the father, the birth will fail. Your son would be good—very good. But his would be a king. And I am very sure that he will do this for me—if only he knows, Philip. In fact, he has said he will. But I do not want to write to his Club, and my husband is pressing me hard. So there is no time to lose. Now will you help me, Philip? He is in the Grenadier Guards."

As a man in a dream—

"He's over seas," said Philip. "I know him quite well. And he's just been sent to Egypt."

As though to stifle an outburst, Claude clapped her hands to her mouth.

After a moment—

"There now!" she cried. "If that is not too provoking! You will understand, my sweet, I had set my heart upon him. And he said he would always do it, provided I sent him word!"

"I'm very sorry," said Philip.

"Oh, well," said Claude. She shrugged her beautiful shoulders. "*Tant pis.*" She drained a glass of champagne. "Come and dance, my pretty, and I shall forget. One comes to *Cerigo* to forget. That is what it is for. But it is very provoking. . . . You see, I want a good son, for the title is very old."

As they took the floor—

"You might have a daughter," said Philip.

143

"Never," said Claude. "Never—if you have the right man. And now be nice to me, *mignon*, because I desire to forget."

Somehow or other Philip excused himself.

"Claude, if Hubert were here, you would not think about me."

"But Hubert is not here, darling."

"I know. I say, if he was. I do not like playing second best."

"Pah, you are unsympathetic. I have been frank—I have told you how I am placed. Or are you thinking always of somebody else? Very well. I do not like playing second best, either. . . ."

Sitting, half-dressed, on his bed, Philip had much to think of that beautiful April morning. Uncle Henry was perfectly right—how on earth had he known? Hubert had let Vivvy down. Hardly married a year, and he had let her down. No one would ever know, but that was what he had done. And if he had done it once, he would do it again. Philip had no doubt at all that, could he have given the message, Hubert would have contrived to do as Claude wished. And Vivvy loved him so—had just borne him a splendid son. And Vivvy was so excelling : Claude didn't count beside her. Old French title be damned—a nice way to keep it going. If *Cerigo* was anything to go by, half the bearings in France should include the bend sinister. Of course, these French. . . . But could anything have been more brazen ? Or more outrageous ? Claude knew Hubert was married —she must, of course, have met Vivvy—and she was married herself. What did that matter ? Nothing. Hubert suited her, and that was enough. But we were not like that. Once we had passed our word . . . Philip's hand flew to his mouth. 'We were not like that.' Apparently Hubert was.

*   *   *   *   *

Miss Carson and Vivien were strolling on Poesy's terrace

towards mid-day. A few yards away, Philip Hubert de Guesclin was fast asleep.

"I'm sorry," said Vivien, "that Ildico wouldn't come. I think it's because of Pip. She doesn't want to stay in his house." Miss Carson held her peace and presently Vivien went on. "I'm sure she's in love with him."

"I'm sure," said Miss Carson, "she's very scrupulous."

Vivien nodded.

"That's right. She knows he's too young. I only hope she doesn't think she's too old."

"I confess I wish she were younger."

"She is so admirable," said Vivien, "that her age doesn't really matter. If I were a man, I should be mad about her. And it isn't as if she was older—she's actually younger than Pip."

"I know, I know. But Ildico's old for her age, and Pip is young for his."

"I can't help that," said Vivien. "She is the girl for Pip. And I think she'll wait for him. The danger is that he may not wait for her. I mean, he's a very good catch."

"He is, indeed," said Miss Carson. "Still, Pip's no fool, and he's very fond of his regiment."

"Oh, yes. He won't marry yet : but he might get tied up. He doesn't see it, of course. He simply thinks that everyone's awfully nice. But I see it all right—in the season. Half the mothers in London are after Pip. And what can I do, Miss Carson? Nothing at all. What he wants is a mistress, to whom he's entirely devoted—rather older than him. She'd do him a lot of good and keep him warm."

"Really, Vivien ! "

Miss Carson was scandalized.

"Oh, I know. It's all wrong, of course. But I do love Pip so much that I couldn't bear to see him make a mistake. Ildico is his woman. And she will marry Pip, provided he isn't caught in the next three years."

In a very small voice—

" Would she marry him, if he'd had a—a mistress ? "

" Oh, yes. Before marriage doesn't matter. After—yes. Once a man's plighted his troth, for him to look elsewhere is the unforgivable sin."

" I see," said Miss Carson, humbly.

Non docent, sed discunt.

Vivien looked at her sharply. Then she put up her face and kissed the duenna's cheek.

" Darling, I love to shock you. But you know quiet, honestly, you're very hard to shock. Aunt Ursula would have fainted about two minutes ago. . . . What is the truth ? I'm worldly, and I love Pip. If I wasn't worldly, I should not have married, but should have kept house for him. And then I'd have seen that he waited for Ildico."

" Which is absurd," said Miss Carson. " In fact, it's absurd to worry. If Pip was like some I could mention, you might have cause for alarm. But Pip is level-headed—and has ideals. I'm not at all sure that he'll dance so much this season. I think this Trustee business will take a lot of his time."

" What could be better ? " said Vivien. " Trusteeship shall be his mistress. We'll urge him into her arms. Or can't you allow that metaphor ? "

" I think," said Miss Carson, " I think it's extremely good."

* * * * *

Grosvenor Square,
April, 1898.

My dear Ildico,

I am so sorry you couldn't come to Poesy : I know Vivvy would have loved to have you. But I do hope you're coming to London soon. I took Mummy back to Paris after the christening, but I was glad to get back. Paris is gay, all right, but it's

146

frightfully false.   I don't quite know how to explain it, but you know Paris and so you'll know what I mean.   Mummy and I went to Versailles one day and saw the Trianons.   And I stayed one night with Cousin Mary and Algy—the Crosswoods, you know.   Their little boy's my godson, and he's a splendid chap. He's not even two yet, but he's simply mad about horses.   Every day he's taken into the stables and put up on a horse : and there he sits and crows, as pleased as Punch.   And the horses simply love him.   I'm off on a course next week—a musketry course. So think of me at Hythe.   But I'll be back before June.   Rather fun, I've just been elected to White's.   It's strange going into a Club as a member for the first time.   You feel quite nervous, and the older members all stare.   I say, let's have a party to go to The Oaks.   You and Vivvy and Miss Carson and Andrew and Hubert and me.   Write and say yes, and I'll arrange everything.   Poesy's looking gorgeous—it really is.   I'm going to Brocade on Friday, just for two nights.   You see, I'm a Trustee now and I have to look after things.   Of course, I don't do much really, because I can't.   I don't know enough.   But I'm beginning to learn.   Defoe is Trustee with me, and he's terribly good.   He's a lawyer, of course, and explains everything. Cousin Coles is really in charge, and there's an old clerk, called Allen, who's helped for fifty years.   He's terribly old now, but he knows every little detail about the estates.   And he is so nice to me, Ildico.   I asked him when he was last at Brocade.   D'you know he'd never been there.   Or to Poesy, either.   But he knew them both better than I do.   And then he said, very humbly, he'd often looked at the outside of Grosvenor Square.   You know, I nearly cried.   But he gets a fortnight in August, so he's going to spend one week at Brocade and one at Poesy.   After all, it's only right—he's done so much for us.   What's your best salmon so far ?   And how are Andrew and Colonel and Mrs. Ross. Please give them my love.   You will come up, won't you ?   I want to see you so much.

Yours affectionately,

Pip.

Break o' Day,
May, 1898.

My dear Pip,

We are coming to London at the end of the month and will be very glad to join your party for The Oaks. I think you will now be at Hythe. Musketry sounds very old-fashioned, but Father says it means you will be a rifle-expert. And shoeing, too. I am very glad you are making yourself so good a soldier. You do not sound as if you enjoyed your time in Paris very much. I always found the French rather false; but then the Scots are a downright lot and make few allowances. I think we're about as blunt as the French are polite. But we do mean what we say. I told Angus, my gillie, that I'd had a letter from you. ' Will you answer ? ' says he. I said that of course I should. ' There's no of course about it—you'll please yourself : but give the young man my respects.' Now that's a great compliment, Pip : but I can't hear a French retainer talking like that. I know that everyone here will be glad to see you again : so one day you must come back. I am so glad your Cousin Mary is so happy at Chantilly. I have never met her, of course, but I know all about her and I think there is a lot to be said for the quiet life she and her husband lead together. I mean, they would never have led such a life in England, even if they had been married in the first place : yet it is the life which a man and his wife were really meant to live. I am so glad you are a Trustee and are doing so well. You do not say that you are, but that I know. When you retire from The Blues, I think you will become a country gentleman and I think that will suit you very well. Brocade and Poesy will take up all your time—as two such fine places should. And you'll be a J.P. and, one day, Lord Lieutenant and things like that. Break o' Day is small by comparison, but Father's life is always full. But you mustn't take your duties too seriously yet, for you've got your cousin and Defoe and two good land-agents. I mean, there's plenty of time, and I think it must be fun to be a man-about-Town. Please write from Hythe and tell me about your course. Father speaks of The School of Musketry, but

*I don't know what that means. Do you live in barracks? I
suppose so. And have you your servant with you? The Spring
here is very lovely—you only saw the beginning, but now it is
in full flush. All the trees in new leaf and the forests and glens
are grand. Robert's Water is a picture, and all the banks are
alive with the speech of burns. Still, I'm looking forward to
London and I'll like to be dancing again. When I told Angus
I was going to The Oaks, he said that horse-racing was a wile
of the devil. But the next day, after a lot of hesitation, he
produced five shillings and asked me to put it on a good horse
for him. 'The laddie,' he said (that's you) 'will be knowing
trainers and such like, and their counsel will be good.' 'Angus,'
I said, 'sometimes the best bets go wrong.' 'I rely upon your
prudence, Miss Ildico.' We're simple serpents in Scotland.
Any way, two of the latter are coming to London soon and one
will be very glad, Pip, to see you again. Both, really, of course.
The family send their love.*

Yours affectionately,
Ildico.

*   *   *   *   *

Mr. and Mrs. Bullen's shop in Shepherd's Market was
shabby and unpretentious, but it was eminently respectable.
It might, I suppose, have been called a newspaper shop:
papers, tobacco and matches were certainly sold: but Bullen's
purveyed other things which no other shop in Mayfair seemed
inclined to supply. Back-studs which never gave in, exceptional boot-laces, buttons which would not break, a certain
special boot-polish, made from an old receipt, a wonderful
paste for strops and excellent cleaning pads; beautiful rubbers,
too, and many another trifle, to warm a valet's heart. So
Bullen's was very well known to the menservants of Mayfair.
And Mrs. Bullen had been a lady's maid. Fat, and cheerful
and honest, she would engage to dispose of second-hand
clothes. And excellent prices she got for ladies' discarded
gowns. Ten per cent commission—that was the way she

worked. But you had to be known to the lady . . . Mrs.
Albert Bullen was very particular. She was also a kindly
soul and always welcomed Miss Bullen, her husband's niece.
Miss Bullen was lady's maid to the Countess of Frome.
Indeed, after two or three years, Miss Bullen came to be
used as the daughter of the house and was, as such, encouraged
to bring her friends to Bullen's whenever she pleased. The
arrangement worked very well. The Bullens were childless
and made more money than they could conveniently spend :
Miss Bullen and her cronies were glad to have somewhere to
go ; the comfortable back-parlour in Shepherd's Market
became the meeting-place of a highly exclusive Club. The
refreshments were copious and always above reproach. Mr.
and Mrs. Bullen knew how to live.

One wet afternoon in July three members were there,
relaxing, drinking tea and discussing the fashionable world.

" In course, he's spoiled her," said Miss Pittock. " Before
she was married, she was as nice as nice : now—well, Miss
Mason's leaving . . . says she can't stand 'er tongue. An'
what was she before—I ask you. Youngest of seven children,
an' 'ad to make 'er own bed."

" You don't say," breathed Miss Pricket.

" 'S fact," said Miss Bullen, helping herself to plum cake.
" Lived in Lowndes Square—some'ow : if 'er people 'ad
'ad any sense, they'd 've lived in Surbiton."

" They married off three," said Miss Pittock.

" They'd 've married off five, if they'd lived in Surbiton.
An' they'd all of been 'appier. No scrapin' an' pinchin' at
'ome, to keep appearances up. They wouldn' 'ave married
nobs, but they'd of done very well. An' made their 'usbans
'appy. Look at Sir Giles . . . spoils 'is little darling, an'
can' call his soul his own. That's what you get for keepin'
appearances up. Father an' mother paupers, an' children
soured. Pity, too, 'cause she's a beauty, she is. Neck a
shade long, perhaps, but that's 'er only fault. But give me
'er little cousin."

" I think Mrs. Stere's lovely : an' such a very sweet manner to everyone."

" So she 'as, Miss Pricket. Sweet as 'oney, an' just about as good. Come out of a country rectory four years ago. Never put on a silk stocking until she was Mrs. Stere. But she's not spoiled. Ole Lady Stere was that wild—she wouldn' attend the wedding nor see the bride. An' now she eats out of 'er 'and. That's 'cause she's nice an' gentle : she broke the old gorgon down. But you got the prize, me dear. You got the champion belt. I like my old Luv-a-Duck, and if anyone spoke against 'er, I'd scratch 'er eyes : but Lady Vivien's got the lot of 'em beat."

" That's right," said Miss Pittock, thickly, because her mouth was full. " And all of 'em know it, too." By a superhuman effort, she cleared the way for speech. " Not that they mind, because they like 'er too much. 'Er grace was sayin' as much the other night." (Her Grace was the Duchess of Eythorne, aged thirty-six.) " ' Pittock,' she says, ' I'm not too bad myself, but Lady Vivien de Guesclin's the best I've seen. I'm glad she's dressin' in Paris. She only wanted that.' "

" I'm glad, too," said Miss Pricket. " She does deserve the best."

" Clocs be snookered," said Miss Bullen. " She don't need any cloes. Nor jools, neither. I wish you two could of seen 'er at ours las' Toosday night. I was up in the ball-room gallery, all mixed up with the band : but, except that the oboe pinched me, I got safe home." Scandalized squeals approved the reminiscence. " There they was, all swarmin' into the ball-room, an' Luv-a-Duck an' 'is lordship beamin' all over their faces an' sayin' the proper things. An' I know 'er shoes was too tight an' 'e was out of sorts. . . . But they're true blue, an' nobody would of guessed. And 'e 'ad 'is Garter sash and Luv-a-Duck was wearin' 'er rubies—you never see such stones. Well, there they was, all of 'em pourin' in an' lookin' their best—tiaras and chokers and bracelets an'

151

the gentlemen wearin' their orders, Lady Peruke in 'er emeralds an' Mrs. Lace in her pearls an' Lady Roche lookin' lovely in black an' gold. . . . An' then Lady Vivien comes in. . . . No tiara, no necklace : only a star in her hair an' that plain gold dress. . . . An' everyone turns an' looks—at 'er an' the Captain be'ind. I give you me word, she looked that lovely it made me catch me breath. An' then I wanted to cry. An' the oboe says, ' Gawd,' 'e says, ' does 'alf the kingdom go with 'er ? She's out of the story-books.' An' then they're all round about 'er—the ladies laughin' an' talkin' an' holdin' on to her hands, an' the gentlemen bowin' an' smilin' an' payin' 'er compliments. And she so quiet an' gentle an' smilin' jus' right. . . . Cor, you ought to of seen 'er. . . . An' there I was with the tears runnin' down me cheeks. Jus' sort of caught me some'ow—I 'ad to cry. . . . An' then the Prince an' Princess, an' Luv-a-Duck an' 'is lordship escortin' them in—a sort o' lane they made, an' all the ladies curtsyin' as they went by. An' the nex' thing, there's Lady Vivien in front of them both. . . . A lovely curtsy she made, an' the Princess looks so pleased an' you could see 'er talking about her frock—touched it, she did an' made Lady Vivien turn round. . . . Oh, dearie me, Miss Pricket, you got a mistress there that nobody won't forget. I can 'ear the old jossers in their Clubs in forty years' time. ' Ah, yes,' they'll say, ' but you oughter of seen the Lady Vivien de Guesclin.' That's what they'll say, Miss Pricket, an' will they be right ? Oh, an' then I saw 'is lordship, 'er brother —'e looks so nice an' so 'appy, did your 'eart good. 'E danced with that nice Miss Ross, an' they made a lovely pair : an' 'er brother was there an' was makin' everyone laugh.— ' The Merry Andrew ' they call 'im, old Luv-a-Duck says."

" That's right," said Miss Pricket. " An' does he deserve the name ? Life an' soul of a party, that's what he is. An' such a nice gentleman, too."

" It was very nice seein' it all—I wish you two could of been there—and then the Prince an' Princess : just like

152

a picture it was, to see them come in : an' they 'ave such
lovely manners—the way she bowed . . . gracious—that's
the word : they were gracious. . . . All the same, you
know, I'd sooner of been lookin' on than down on the floor.
Not my idear of amusement—nothin' easy about it, can't let
yourself go."

"It's 'ow you're born," said Miss Pittock. "They're bred
to that sort of thing an' that's what they like. Same with
their suppers. Quail in aspic—an' you can 'ave it for me.
I'd rather 'ave crab an' stout at *The Eyre Arms.*"

"So would I," said Miss Bullen. "Give me another cup,
dearie : I've ate too much. And do they get tired ? When
it was over on Toosday, my old Luv-a-Duck could 'ardly
stand up. An' yet she was that 'appy—God bless 'er 'eart.
'Bullen,' she says, 'it's been a big success. I reely think
people enjoyed it.' 'My lady,' I says, 'it's been the ball o'
the season, if you ask me.' Then I told 'er 'ow I'd been
watchin', an', bless my soul, I couldn' get 'er to bed. 'Ad
I seen this an' that ? An' 'ow did that look ? And was
many ladies sitting out ? An' did 'er dress look all right ?
She's game, my old Luv-a-Duck is. She's not too strong,
an' 'is lordship's getting on. But that don' count with them
—they got their duty to do. An' do they do it, Miss Pricket ?
Many a time I've asked 'er to give up this or that, because I
knew she was tired an' needed a rest. 'No, Bullen,' she says,
'for what it's worth,' she says, 'we must play our parts.
Look at his lordship—he's much more tired than me. I
often wish we were Mr. and Mrs. Frome : but there it is.
People look up to us because of our rank : and so we must
do our best to deserve their regard.' "

"Ah," said Miss Pittock, darkly, "not all of them 'as those
ideas. You've heard what they're sayin' about the Marquess
of Brest ? "

"I've 'eard enough," said Miss Bullen. "An' 'e's a dis-
grace to 'is name. Nice sort o' Duke 'e'll make. I don'
wan' to know what 'e's done, but I did 'ear the nex' thing

'e done, his Grace would send him away. Out to Australia, they said, an' pay 'im so much a month." Here the door was opened, and Mrs. Bullen came in. " Auntie, dear, we've missed you. Sit down, an' I'll take your shoes off. Make 'er some fresh tea, Miss Pricket—she's been a good Auntie to me."

" Nonsense," said Mrs. Bullen—and did as Miss Bullen said.

* * * * *

Six care-free months slid by—for Philip, a lively pageant of duty, Goodwood, Cowes, three weeks at Poesy, long week-ends at Brocade, lawn-tennis at Fairing Over, a fortnight at Break o' Day, an engineering course, dinners at the Club with Defoe, the Gaiety Theatre and suppers at the Savoy. If he played, he knew how to work. Lieut. the Earl of Ringwood could be relied upon. His Colonel was very pleased. So was Coles Willing. Pip was making a conscientious Trustee.

If Vivien's season had been short, it had been all glorious. She was the rage of London—in 1898. The attention she was paid was extraordinary : Royalty, statesmen, ambassadors —all fell for Vivien de Guesclin, a lady of high degree. A century before, she would have been a toast. With it all, she was simple as ever, quiet and pleasant in her life, enjoying this to the full, but never assuming the honours so thick upon her. In fact, she was glad to leave Cowes, and flew to Fairing Over and Philip Hubert, her son. Except for a short three weeks, she passed the rest of the year in the countryside. This meant seeing less of her brother : but, though she loved the high lights, the country was in her blood. As a child, she had eyes to see—to read the gorgeous document the shires unrolled : the precious beauty of old England, a thing so exquisite and rare that neither brush nor pen has ever snared its quality. Old men remember it : but all their memories cannot present a picture of that lovely scene. The half was atmosphere. The quiet content, the

154

rich, leisurely progress of horse and foot, the honesty of toil, the pride of man and master in the fruits of the earth, the old tradition of husbandry—these things were part and parcel of the hills and dales, the streams and meadows, the woods and lanes and villages which made that Arcady. For that is what it was. ('Wouldn' suit me,' says Erny—Erny Balch. 'Of course it wouldn't, Erny. You'd find it dull. But, then, you'd never see it. You'd have to walk from the station . . . seven miles.' 'Me walk seven—Oh, be yer age,' says Erny. 'That's what I'm doing, Erny—being my age.') I think, perhaps, it figures in the portfolio of Time. Greek temples are there, and Venice, as it was, and old Japan. And if these things have been chosen, why not the English scene ? For lump the three together, and that was worth more than they. It was the very field of Nature and of Husbandry : there these two met and kissed and settled down, and there they lived together, each magnifying the other : there never was so perfect a relation. The miller loved his water and the woodman his trees : the ploughman loved his furrow, and the roadman his ways : the herdsman loved his pastures, and the shepherd his down. Few could write their own names, but they had learning of another sort. They knew the ways of the wind, and the midwives of the clouds told them when rain would fall : they were free of the seasons' plans ; and the frosts of winter would send their running footmen to warn them of their approach : the birds told them their secrets ; and the prophecy of the day-spring was in their mouths. Of such was their understanding with Nature herself, a finer fable than any that Aesop wrote. Little wonder that their domain was the kingdom of earth.

So Vivien stayed in the country—mostly at Fairing Over, but visiting Poesy and hunting for three weeks from Brocade.

*   *   *   *   *

Two days before Christmas, Vivien was doing up parcels and checking lists. Miranda de Guesclin was helping her sister-in-law. 'Mira' was very charming and sat at Vivien's feet. All this, at Fairing Over . . . in Vivien's boudoir, a pleasant first-floor chamber, private enough. All servants must knock before they entered that room.

Philip was helping, too, clumsily wrapping gifts. And Cousin Virgil was sitting beside the fire, writing to Lady Ringwood, now in the South of France.

> *Fairing Over,*
> *Christmas, 1898.*
>
> *My dear Rachel,*
> *I wish you were here at this moment, in Vivvy's private room. It would warm your heart. For here are brother and sister, as always two beautiful children, wrapping the gifts she has bought to delight less fortunate eyes. The attractive apartment is something between a woollen-draper's shop and a parcels' office. I never knew there were so many deserving souls. There probably aren't. But Vivvy's bounty falls on the just and on the unjust. . . .*

Philip was very happy. This was just like old times, checking the lists with Vivvy and helping Vivvy to do the parcels up. And Mira was splendid—and laughing all the time.

"There you are," said Vivien. "That's Mrs. Pelmet's shawl. I knew I'd got it somewhere. Cross her off, Mira— I think she's over the page. Wait a minute . . . Here's her card. Thread the ribbon through it and give it to Pip. Where's Amy Bostock's brooch? I had it just now."

> *. . . 'For beauty lives with kindness.' You know, she is Silvia. In spite of her succès fou, she is as natural as the day. Hubert has gone to Birdcage, to meet the guests—you may remember the Oakhams, a charming pair—and Mrs. Ronnie Quaritch, whom everyone loves. I do not feel like a guest or behave like one. I think I'm taken for granted. What more can any man ask? So that is our little party, including, of course, Miranda, a laughing nymph. . . .*

156

Here a knock fell upon the door.

" Come in."

A footman entered, bearing a telegram.

" Open it, Pip, will you ? And see what it says."

" The boy is waiting, my lady."

" Very well. When I'm ready, I'll ring."

" Very good, my lady."

The man withdrew.

Philip was frowning upon the flimsy sheet.

Vivien looked over his shoulder.

Just back from Monte Carlo house not ready at Melton can
we spend Christmas with you.
*   Connie Welham, Hotel Cecil.*

Vivien glanced at the address.

Captain de Guesclin, Fairing Over, Berks.

Philip produced the envelope.

On this, *De Guesclin* was written, and nothing more.

Vivien had met the Welhams, who were among Hubert's
friends. They were a hard-riding pair. The lady was most
attractive. They certainly went about, but Welham lifted
his elbow and Mrs. Welham's frocks could be seen a great
way off.

" Write the answer, Pip. There's a pad over there."

Philip passed to a table and picked up a pen.

Vivien dictated clearly.

" *Mrs. Welham, Hotel Cecil, Strand, London.*
*   Regret house full.*
*   Vivien de Guesclin.*

" Got that ? Ring, will you, darling ? And copy the
answer on to the foot of the form. What were we doing,
Mira ? Oh, I know. Old Humphrey's blanket. That's it,
over there. Don't bother to wrap it up. Just tie a ribbon
round it. Here's his card."

157

The footman re-entered the room, and the telegram was dispatched.

. . . My lady has just put her foot down. She has stamped presumption out. Quietly, firmly and most effectively. That affords me infinite pleasure—as it will you. Vivien is a great lady. I wish so much you would come back and be a great lady here. You have the knack, Rachel. Still, I know how you feel, and I do not blame you at all. But we miss you terribly. It is right that you should know that. . . .

Virgil did not add what he knew in his heart—that the 'presumption' was not so much Connie Welham's as that of Hubert himself. The business had been arranged before ever the Welhams went South. Connie suited Hubert down to the socks : he had meant to force her entry in Vivien's teeth. What Virgil did not suspect was that Vivien was sure of this the moment she read the wire.

* * * * *

Lady Oakham and Mrs. Quaritch took the laudau : Sir Charles and Hubert, the dog-cart, which Hubert had driven to Birdcage, to meet the train. Well ' rugged up ', the men were as warm as toast.

" By God, this is good," said Oakham, snuffing the evening air. " These trains, you know, are stuffy. Nice of you to meet us, old boy : and nicer still to have us for Christmas. Devilish dull season, if you can't keep it with friends."

" It's going to be simple," said Hubert. " Good cheer and all that, you know ; but very quiet."

" Simple," said Charles Oakham. " That's what Christmas should be. Church in the morning, an' jolly old dames beaming as you come out. Stroll round the stables in the afternoon ; an' fun an' games in the evening in the traditional way. Fun for everyone, Hubert—simple fun. Happiness. I'll lay a bucket of brandy that Vivien sees to that."

" Yes," said Hubert. " Vivvy wouldn't sit down on

Christmas night, if she didn't know all our people had had their fill."

"That's the style," said Oakham. "What damned good lamps you've got."

"It's a new reflector," said Hubert. "Shows you a bit of the road."

The roan was on her way home, and the six miles soon went by. Six shadowy miles of hard, high road, and lane and sudden corner; of elms rising from hedgerows and over-hanging oaks; of rise, when the men leaned forward, and the groom trotted by their side; of fall, carefully taken, for Hubert was a good whip; of pricked ears, steaming nostrils and the soft slap of hoofs. . . . Slow through the village of Fairing, past light seeping through curtains and the glow from the doorway of *The Crown* and a burst of jolly laughter thrust-ing into the night; past the windows of the church, six pale lancets peering out of the darkness, declaring a practice of sorts for the coming festival. And then, at last, Fairing Over, and Vivien standing against the glow of the hall, and the roan, impatient for her stable, resenting the check. . . .

"Just a minute, my beauty. Stand still. . . . Better lead her round, William. She may not let you get up."

"Very good, sir."

"Well, Vivien, m'dear."

"Well, Charles. How nice to see you again."

"Most charming of you to have us. Hullo, Pip, how are you? And Coleton, too. The compliments of the season!"

"The same to you, sir."

Hubert appeared.

"Come to the library, Charles, and have a whiskey and soda. There's plenty of time—we dine at half past eight."

"Suit me well. Can you mount me on Boxing Day? I've brought my things."

"You shall pick your hunter to-morrow."

"That's the style."

Five hours had gone by.

Pricket had been dismissed, and Vivien was sitting, reading beside her fire.

" May I come in ? " said Hubert, opening a door.

" Of course, darling."

Hubert came in, buff envelope in hand.

" I see you . . . answered this wire."

" That's right," said Vivien. " I did."

" Considering that it was addressed to me, I think I should have been consulted."

" Listen, Hubert," said Vivien. " If you choose to hobnob with a drunkard and his notorious wife, that is your affair : but you cannot subject Sir Charles and Lady Oakham, Mrs. Quaritch, your sister, the Earl of Ringwood, Virgil Coleton and Lady Vivien de Guesclin to that indignity."

Before such a broadside, Hubert broke down.

A hand went up to his head.

" I'm sorry, m'dear."

" That's all right, old fellow : but please don't do it again."

" Do what, Vivvy ? "

" Allow such a woman to make a fool of you."

So Vivvy knew. Talk about instinct. These women . . .

" It's so damned difficult, Vivvy."

" They make it so, my darling. That is their policy. Connie Welham knows that she's put herself out of court. Her only chance is to force an entry back. She's only one card to play—and that isn't in the pack. She can make things difficult for people who do know how to behave. It's not a card that decent people play. Algy and Mary don't play it, though God knows I'd welcome them. But they would rather die than play such a dirty card."

" You're perfectly right," said Hubert. " You always are."

" No," said Vivien, " I make a lot of mistakes. But it's easier being a woman. Women are very much quicker : they don't have to play for time. Then, again, you're very good-natured. But you do see, my darling, that it was a put-up job ? "

160

" Oh, yes, I see that now. Does—does anyone know ? "

" Only Pip. He opened the wire. Virgil may have heard me dictate the reply."

Hubert nodded. Then he stepped to his wife and folded her in his arms.

" You're damned good to me, Vivvy."

" I don't know about that. I think I'm damned good *for* you. You've got a soft spot for women—that I know. But try to remember this—that the woman who plays upon that is poaching on my preserves. If I can't fill your life——"

Hubert smothered the sentence there and then.

So Christmas at Fairing Over was kept with peace and goodwill. The New Year was greeted at Poesy. Lady Ursula, Miss Carson and Coles subscribed to the pleasant rite. The play may have been less lively, but Vivien and Philip were at the top of their bent. Brother and sister were closer than they had been for two years. And Hubert ran third.

*   *   *   *   *

The Duchess lay back on her pillows and looked at the Duke.

" I trust," she said, " that Monsieur is satisfied with his heir."

The Duke raised his eyebrows.

" He is the first son of mine to be born with a twisted leg."

" Is that so ? How—very unfortunate."

The Duke shrugged his shoulders.

" It will be—for him. That he is your son, Madame, there can, of course, be no doubt."

" Unhappily, none," said the Duchess. " Do you suggest that he does not belong to you ? "

" Speculation is idle, Madame. The fact remains that he will bear my name. He will be the first Duc de Sevignac to be deformed."

" Monsieur is charming. Allow me to make him a present.

The father I wanted was not available; and so—the child is yours."

"I trust the world will think so. But whether it does or no, you and I will know that you are a faithful wife. Which, after all, is the great thing."

"Monsieur overrates our understanding."

"Possibly," said the Duke, rising. "At any rate, I shall not incommode you again. By the way, I think country air would be good for your little son. Brouilly is at his disposal from this time on. And, of course, at yours. This house has been sold."

The Duchess started up.

"What on earth d'you mean?"

"What I say. This house has been sold. With possession, one month from to-day. So you will have plenty of time."

"And where do I live?"

The Duke inclined his head.

"The maternal instinct, Madame, will indicate that. And now you will please excuse me."

With that, he withdrew.

Her underlip caught in her teeth, Claude continued to stare at the tall double doors.

Brouilly was a show place. It was also three hundred miles from Paris and nearly twenty-two from the nearest town. During a heat-wave the *château* was agreeably cool.

As, at length, she lay back on her pillows—

"Hubert," she said, "whoever sent you to Egypt has much to answer for."

*   *   *   *   *

"Well, what d'you think?" said Defoe.

Philip looked out of the window at Lincoln's Inn Fields.

"We must have a celebration at Poesy, too. I quite see that Brocade comes first; but I won't leave Poesy out."

"Well and good. Will August do for Brocade?"

162

" The first week in August—yes."

" And for Poesy ? "

Philip shrugged his shoulders.

" What about the end of the month ? "

" Shall we say the last week ? "

" That'll do. But it must be just as good, on a smaller scale."

Philip was coming of age. Such occasions were handsomely marked in 1899. At Brocade oxen would be roasted and bonfires lit. And a great marquee in the park would shelter the many liegemen that Ringwood had. (' What's a liegeman ? ' says Erny Balch. ' Hush, Erny. Don't use that word. If you look it up, you'll see *Obs.* put against it. That used to mean *Obsolete* : now it means *Obscene*.') No expense would be spared. Tenants and servants, their wives and sons and daughters were to be royally entertained. A roundabout and fireworks would play their part. And a houseparty would assemble, and there would be a ball. The celebration at Poesy would be more intimate. The marquee, the oxen and fireworks would all be there. Oh, and the roundabout. But there would be no ball, and the houseparty would be a strictly ' family ' affair.

" Old Allen must come," said Philip. " On that, I insist."

" To which ? " said Defoe.

" Give him his choice, Dennis."

" I think you should invite him to one."

" All right. I expect he'd like Brocade best. And you'll be at both."

" I will, if you want me, Pip."

" Of course I do. Besides, you ought to be there."

" I don't know about that. Never mind. The first and the last week in August. And this is May. Nice time to fix things up. Will you tell Lady Ursula ? I suppose Lady Ringwood won't come."

Philip shook his head.

" I haven't the heart to ask her. It hurts her too much."

163

"I understand."

Coles Willing opened the door, and then came into the room.

"Hullo, you two. And what are you hatching now?"

Defoe was up on his feet.

"Twenty-first celebrations, sir."

"God bless my soul, Pip. I remember drinking your health when you were born. Next thing we know you'll be married. You'll have to think about that. We must have an heir."

"When I've got my promotion, Cousin Coles."

"P'raps you're right. I saw your Colonel last week, and he's very pleased with you."

"I don't think he is," said Pip. "He told me off on Tuesday."

"'Whom the Lord loveth, He chasteneth.' What had you done?"

Philip began to laugh.

"I nearly fell off on parade. I was riding a charger of Herring's—rather a moody horse. You see, Herring wants him cast; but he's too good for that. So I said, 'Let me try him.' And we very nearly got through. But right at the last, he got fractious and started to dance."

"What did the Colonel say?"

"That the Horse Guards' Parade was neither a circus nor a manège, and the next time I used it as either, he'd cast me for riding-school."

"Quite right," said Coles, laughing. "What's your next course? Equitation?"

Philip shook his head.

"Signalling, I hope. That's always useful, you know. Of course these courses don't make you a specialist. But you don't feel quite so helpless. If anything were to happen, you would be able, at least, to pull your weight."

Coles nodded, rubbing his nose.

"Yes, I see that," he said slowly. "I see what you mean."

164

In fact he saw more.   He saw that, if war did break out,
Philip would stand a good chance of being sent over seas.

*   *   *   *   *

The Oxford of 1899 was, *mutatis mutandis,* the Oxford of
Verdant Green.   The mail-coach no longer ' took up and set
down ' at *The Mitre* : but the stations kept their distance,
and only the horse-drawn tram conducted a fitful correspondence between the railways and the inn.   The Oxford of
1899 was wholly unspoiled : and since, in spite of the havoc
of progress, she is still the fairest city to be seen to-day, it
may be believed that in 1899 she was all glorious.   From her
appearance, her spirit and her manners, there issued continually an incomparable quality : this was not rare—it was
unique.   It was of the nature of a fragrance. . . .

In 1899, Oxford was a merry monastery, peopled by
reverend fathers and irreverent sons.   Andrew Ross, of
Christchurch, made the most of his membership.   He 'fleeted
the time carelessly, as they did in the golden world ' : so did
others ; but, old for his age, Ross sucked his gorgeous orange
drier than most.   His acquaintance was wide ; but, had he
known no one at all, he would have been happy as the day
was long.   The lad was no pedant, but he had eyes to see.

After all, Tradition is but a garment—a mantle old places
wear.   It is gradually woven and embroidered throughout the
centuries, until it can wrap a city from head to foot.   Nothing
can hasten the process, the secret of which Time holds : but,
with the finished article, nothing can ever compare.   Unhappily, Tradition is at the mercy of commercial man : but
in 1899 Oxford's mantle dazzled the dullest eye.   No stuff in
all the world was so exquisite : no embroidery was ever so
varied and so rich.   Her very stones cried out ; her many
gates lifted their lovely heads.   And over this precious garment, Oxford was wearing the chasuble of youth.   The lawn
lent to the mantle a sweet humanity, catching the smile upon
Tradition's face, to call back Time and make a miracle.

165

Young men subscribed to customs, ancient before their ancestors were born. This, as a matter of course. Antiquity knew no dust—in 1899. There was nothing common or unclean in Oxford then; only old, mellow walls rang with the lively din : only the equipage distinguished time-honoured ways : and the servants were jealous servants, each setting store by his master and swearing by the college to which he belonged.

Andrew had eyes to read this splendid document, had ears to hear the vivid echoes of a sumptuous past, had nerves to feel the tug of Magdalen's Tower, of Charles the Second's elms, of Oxford's mid-night chimes—the most harmonious argument that ever was. Happy, indeed, the youth can roll such comfortable wine upon his tongue : of such is the privilege of manhood : but Andrew had louted to Tradition from childhood on.

He was gay and popular, a poor but valiant horseman, quite a good whip. Unable to read music, he played by ear—to the great content of his fellows, some of whom hired pianos for him to use. Taking the History School, he attended very few lectures and made his tutor laugh. ' But why go to Mr. Rogers ? You're taking History, not Law.' ' He lectures in Queen's College hall, sir.' ' What if he does ? ' ' It's a noble chamber, sir, not noticed enough in the books. Sitting still there for an hour, one can measure its quality.' ' Get out, Anthony à Wood.'

It was Andrew who was hailed by a tourist, who was surveying Tom Quad and spitting now and again upon the flags. It was Andrew who informed him that admission to the Senior Common Room was by ticket—price two guineas, procurable at the door—and that Friday was Ladies' Night. He also showed him the Senior Common Room's door. The tourist spat upon the threshold, and Andrew hardened his heart. ' Five minutes to eight, for eight. Don't knock : just go straight in. The Bursar will give you your tickets and show you the Ladies' room.' The tourist duly arrived, money

166

in hand, and since he and his fearful wife were accustomed to
having their way, the scene which ensued was unforgettable.
In the end, the proctors were summoned. Andrew was
dining out.

Commemoration was perfect, in 1899. Chaperoned by a
cousin, Ildico Ross came up, stayed at *The Mitre* and gloried
in all she saw. The Cher was a lively dream : evensong at
Magdalen, a vision : the ball which she attended, not of this
world. As brother and sister strolled out one of the dances,
the chimes of Oxford stole upon the lilt of a valse, while
the moon, not yet to be seen, was lighting an order of pin-
nacles, standing against the sky. ' It's unbelievable, Andrew.
Things like this don't happen. One day we shall look back
. . . and know that we were enchanted—for half a week.'

Then Oxford fell asleep, and Andrew followed his sister
back to Town.

*   *   *   *   *

A day or two later an announcement appeared in *The Times*.
*The Duchess de Sevignac has arrived in London and is staying
at Claridge's Hotel.*

Claude had come to London in something approaching
despair. Brouilly had proved too awful. Her neighbours
had proved even worse. All were poverty-stricken, main-
taining a sordid state. They knew neither how to dress, nor
how to live. They swarmed about her, as beggars about a
tourist, bringing their brats to Brouilly, magnifying her son
with fulsome prophecy and commending the vices of Brouilly,
till Claude could have screamed. Her personal comfort had
simply ceased to exist. There were no bathrooms at Brouilly ;
there was no central-heating, of course no electric light. The
principal rooms faced north, and the atmosphere of the house
was that of the tomb. After six frightful weeks, Claude had
returned to Paris, more dead than alive. But Paris, without
her own house, was not what it had been. She stayed in the
Place Vendôme, but her friends had written her off when

her house was sold. After a month of chagrin, the diet of Dead Sea apples began to pall : and so she had come to London, where, more than once before, she had had a very good time.

After two or three days, invitations began to arrive.

The ball at Westmorland House was a very splendid affair. And Claude looked very striking in black and gold.

" Look at that hair," said Andrew, dancing with Ildico. " I wonder who she is. I've never seen her before."

" French," said his sister. " They do know how to dress."

" Confess she's striking," said Andrew.

" Indeed, I will. I find her most attractive. And you always had a weakness for auburn hair."

" Good thing not everyone has."

" I am content," said Ildico, tilting her chin.

She might well be that : her magnificent blue-black hair was a lovely sight.

Her Excellency was speaking to Claude.

" Madame, let me present——"

" Oh, but we've met," cried Vivien. She put out her hand. " How d'ye do, Madame ? Have you come back to England to teach us how to dress ? You remember my husband ? "

" But of course." Claude nodded to Hubert. " And now how are you, my dear ? I have been very busy, having a son."

" Oh, isn't it a business ? " said Vivien.

" Never again," said Claude. " No, I have said to my husband, ' This is too much.' And our doctors are very bad. My figure, of course, is ruined."

" No one would know it, Madame."

" You are very polite. But that is my dressmaker's fault. *Oui, Monsieur, avec plaisir*." She handed her programme to Hubert. " I think there are one or two left."

" Hullo, Pip," cried Vivien, catching his arm. " Madame, my brother, Lord Ringwood—la Duchesse de Sevignac."
168

Philip bowed.

" How d'ye do, Madame."

" Very well, thank you, Monsieur."

" May I have the pleasure ? "

" Of course—if my programme permits."

Philip wrote down his name for an extra and handed the programme back.

" Are you here for long, Madame ? "

" A month, perhaps. Paris is dull."

Ildico and Andrew arrived—and were introduced.

" *Enchanté, Madame*," said Andrew. " And will you dance with a Scot ? "

" I think so," said Claude. " I have always heard that the Scots were trustworthy."

" Allow me to prove it," said Andrew, writing his name.

Philip carried Ildico off.

" Are they engaged ? " whispered Claude.

Vivien shook her head.

" Oh, no. But she's a great friend. Her brother was at Harrow with Philip, and they have gone on."

" Who is he engaged to, then ? "

" To his Regiment, Madame. My brother is a good soldier and puts his profession first."

" Perhaps. But men will be men. I think he is in love with Miss Ross."

Vivien shrugged her shoulders—and smiled.

Twenty minutes later Hubert was dancing with Claude.

" Oh, Hubert, my god," she breathed, " and I never knew you were back."

" Steady, sweet," murmured Hubert. " Back from where ? "

" From Egypt, of course."

" Egypt ? " said Hubert, frowning. " Why should I go to Egypt ? "

A cold, iron cage seemed to be suddenly clamped about Claude's heart.

Somehow—somehow she answered.

"I was told you'd been sent to Egypt . . . more than a year ago."

Hubert shook his head.

"Who told you I'd gone over seas?"

"I—I don't know," said Claude, faintly. "Can we sit down?"

Hubert led her out of the ball-room, set her down on a sofa and sought for champagne.

As always, the wine restored her. . . .

After some light conversation—

"Listen," said Claude. "I heard you'd been sent to Egypt; and so . . . I gave in. My son was born last winter. He has a twisted leg."

There was a pregnant silence.

Then—

"Oh, well," said Hubert. And then, "Who told you that lie?"

"I—I don't know his name," said Claude. "I happened to meet him—somewhere. Of course, I ought to have written : but I believed what he said. And you were here all the time."

"I haven't been out of England since '96."

"Mother of God," breathed Claude. . . .

Here Andrew arrived to claim her.

As Hubert bowed and withdrew—

"Mr. Ross, I am going to ask a very great favour of you."

"Consider it granted, Madame."

"That is what women like. Well, here it is. My ankle is growing tired—I sprained it six weeks ago. And I have no one with me. Instead of dancing with me, will you send for my carriage and take me to my hotel?"

"Of course. But I am so sorry. Are you sure . . .?"

"Yes, yes. I am quite all right. But I fear to go on in case I should—go lame. Is that right?"

"Your Scotch, Madame, is impeccable."

170

"Is that a compliment?"

Andrew drew himself up.

"The highest that a Scotsman can pay. And now I shall order your carriage. And when I have given the order, I shall come back."

"Let us meet in the hall, please. You will be returning, but I must slip away."

Claude made the most of the drive. By the time they had come to Claridge's, Andrew, who knew no wrong, was the Duchess's slave.

As he put her gloved hand to his lips—

"Luncheon, to-morrow, then—at a quarter to one."

"With great pleasure, Madame. Good night."

"*Bon soir, Monsieur, et merci—merci mille fois.*"

Philip was dancing with Ildico.

"What's the matter, Pip?"

"Nothing," said Philip. "This coming-of-age business is looming up. I wish you'd come and support me."

"Very nice of you, Pip, but I'm needed at Break o' Day."

"Oh, well. I suppose I shall get through somehow. Just in time, I hope."

"What d'you mean—just in time?"

"Major Hardinge thinks there's going to be war."

For the second time that evening, a woman's heart felt cold.

"You mean with the Boers?"

"Yes. I mean, if they won't give way. . . ."

"They won't send the Household Brigade."

"They might. Or, if they don't, one or two of us might be detached. And if we are, my musketry course might help."

"Don't try and turn this into the Waterloo Ball."

"I'm not. But if it comes off, you must give me a favour to wear."

"You can't appear on parade with a glove in your hat."

"I could wear one of these in my pocket."

"Don't be mediæval, Pip. By the way, Andrew's attracted. He finds Madame de Sevignac a very paragon."

" He doesn't "—incredulously.

" He does, indeed. He worships auburn hair. And you must admit that she is very attractive."

" Yes, I 'spect she is," said Philip. And then, " She's completely French."

" How d'you know? Have you ever met her before? "

" I met her in Paris once. She wouldn't remember me."

" Why's she completely French? "

Philip shrugged his shoulders.

" The usual thing. She isn't seen with the Duke."

" Scots lassies don't understand such talk as that."

Ildico's broad Scots always broke Philip down. The two were laughing so much that the dance had to go by the board. . . .

Philip was dancing with Vivien before the evening was out.

" Vivvy, listen. This is between you and me."

" Understood. Go on, darling."

" Do you like Madame de Sevignac? "

Vivien nodded.

" I think she's charming, Pip."

" Have you asked her to Fairing Over? "

Vivien opened her eyes.

" Not yet. I'd meant to ask her. She's all alone."

" I've met her before, Vivvy. Don't ask her to stay."

There was a little silence.

Then—

" Thank you, Pip," said Vivien. And then, " There's no one like you."

*   *   *   *   *

From Eleanor Carson's Diary.

July 16th, 1899.

At Fairing Over.

I had the very great honour of being presented to Their Royal Highnesses The Prince and Princess of Wales. No one could

172

have been more gracious, more charming, more natural. They used me like a great lady. . . . I cannot write any more. My heart is too full.

Let me elaborate that entry.

" Let's sit down," said His Royal Highness.

Miss Carson and he sat down.

" Did you bring up these children—the Brabants, I mean ? "

" I was their governess, sir."

" In the absence of Lady Ringwood, you took charge ? "

" More or less, sir. Lady Ursula was usually there."

" Oh, yes. A very sweet lady. . . . I hope you're proud, Miss Carson. They have the most perfect manners I've ever seen."

" The stock, sir, was very good."

" There I agree. But children are bred, Miss Carson ; while men and women are made."

" I know. But they were responsive. They made my duty a pleasure day after day."

" Let us say that the combination has proved a great success."

" I'm glad you think so, sir."

" I do, indeed. Upon this youth of England so much depends. Example is going to count as never before. And Lord Ringwood and Lady Vivien will always set an example. You've seen to that."

" Your Royal Highness is very gracious—and very generous, too."

" No. I've said nothing but the truth." The Prince looked pleasedly round—at stately timber and aged, emerald turf. " What a charming place this is. And not too far from Town. When the automobile comes in. . . . There's the Princess with the baby." At sixteen months Philip Hubert de Guesclin was no respecter of persons. . . . " Come and deliver her, Miss Carson. If we don't take some action, the baby will tire her out."

Together, they crossed the sward.

" Pick-a-back, Huffy," said Miss Carson.

The child came running : Miss Carson swung him up.

" Oh, thank you so much," said the Princess. " What tyrants all children are."

" This is Miss Carson, my dear. She brought Lady Vivien up."

" Oh, isn't that nice ? How proud you must be, Miss Carson."

" You are very kind, Ma'am. My task was easy enough."

" That was because she loved you. I mean, that's everything."

Miss Carson tried and failed to make a reply.

So the three strolled together over the time-honoured lawns ; the future King and Queen commending the pleasant place, and the governess silent beside them, with the little child on her back.

*   *   *   *   *

Philip was worried.

To his immense relief, Claude seemed to have written him off. She might not have recognized him. She certainly treated him as though they had never met. He did what he could to avoid her—naturally. But he had to dance with her twice and she was at more than one party to which he went. Yet, never by word or deed did she give the slightest sign that she had met him before. Philip decided that Claude knew how to behave. Yet, she must know by now that he had put a spoke in her wheel. Of course she had spoken to Hubert ; and Hubert, of course, had told her that she had been told a lie—that he had been ready and waiting to do as she had desired. Of course she realized now why Philip had spoiled her game—that it was, in fact, Hubert's wife's brother whom she had requested to be her go-between. That would, of course, absolve him. All the same, with women . . . Philip decided more firmly that Claude knew how to

174

behave. And Hubert . . . Hubert gave no sign, either. His manner showed no alteration of any kind. Possibly Claude had not named him as her informant. After all, she must see that he had had to choose between his own sister and her. Still, with women . . . with French women . . . Philip thought kindly of Claude. She—had her faults: but she knew how to behave. Perhaps he shouldn't have turned her down as he did. And yet he had to do that. He couldn't take Hubert's place, when Hubert was ready and waiting to take it himself. . . .

But it was none of these things that worried the Earl of Ringwood. What did concern his lordship was Claude's most clear fascination of Andrew Ross.

Andrew was crazy about her—of that there could be no doubt. It was a preposterous connection. Andrew was scrupulous, witty and very popular : but he had not those things that appealed to Claude. Yet, Claude accepted his homage—and asked for more. She gave him favours which far more attractive men had not even sought. Had he known what Philip knew, he would have left for Scotland without a word. No thought of a liaison entered his head : but, had Claude been a widow, he would have pressed his suit. His was a romantic attachment—which made many people smile, Hubert pull his moustache, Vivien open her eyes and Philip frown.

Ildico, too, was uneasy.

" Madame de Sevignac, Pip, has Andrew in thrall."

" I know. I wish she hadn't. At least, he can't marry her."

" He can be very unhappy."

" I know. I'm afraid he will be. But what can anyone do ? "

" Nothing," said Ildico. " He will hear nothing against her—not that there is anything, except that she's French."

" That should be enough," said Philip.

" I know. But Andrew, Pip, has never been in France.

He takes her at her face value—that's very high. That her demeanour is perfect, you must admit."

" I suppose it is. I—don't like her very much."

Ildico knew in that moment that Philip and Claude had clashed.

" You must confess, Pip, that she is most attractive."

" Oh, yes. There's no doubt about that. At a party she's rather fun. But she is essentially French."

" And so false ? You're very unkind. And she's perfectly charming to me. But why she should have picked on Andrew, I can't conceive. You or Hubert, for instance, are very much more in her line."

" I'm sure I'm not," said Philip. " Hubert may be, perhaps. And she hasn't picked on Andrew. He's picked on her."

Ildico bubbled with laughter.

" Oh, Pip. Be always as simple. Never mind. Have you written your speech."

" Not yet. But that won't take long. It's going to be very short. Ildico, why won't you come ? After Vivvy, I want you—more than anyone else."

Ildico steadied her voice.

" Scotland calls me, my dear. I should have been gone before."

*   *   *   *   *

Charing Cross Station was cool—at half past eight in the morning that July day. The boat-train was ready and waiting —to leave at nine o'clock. At five and twenty to nine, Claude, escorted by Andrew, took her place. A carriage had been reserved. When the two had taken their seats, the door was locked.

The Duchess addressed her courier—

" Return at ten minutes to nine, to let this gentleman out."

" It is understood, *Madame la Duchesse*."

Claude regarded Andrew.

176

"This is our last talk, my dear. I wished to arrive early, that we might converse in peace."

"But you will return, Madame. If not, I shall come to Paris, to pay my respects."

"Perhaps, I don't know. You have been very sweet to me. And now I have something to tell you—let us say that I have a communication to make."

"You sound very grave," said Andrew.

"I feel very grave," said Claude. "Three times I have tried to tell you, and each time my courage has failed. But now I am going away, and the chance may not come again. You see, to tell you the truth will involve myself: you will learn something about me that no one must know. Yet, if I do not tell you, a terrible wrong may be done to somebody else. And so I must do my duty—and sacrifice myself."

The small, gloved hands were twisting each other's fingers. Andrew stared from them to the beautiful face.

"You see, my dear, it concerns your beautiful sister."

Andrew started.

"My sister? Ildico?"

"Your sister, Ildico—that very exquisite girl. I think that she loves Lord Ringwood: I think that Lord Ringwood loves her."

"Yes," said Andrew, wide-eyed. "I rather think you're right. I know no more than you, but I've half an idea they're waiting. I mean, if he married just yet, he'd have to leave the Blues."

"No doubt you are right. But I am sure that I am: I know the signs. *But he must not marry her*, Andrew."

His mouth a little open, Andrew was frowning on Claude. Presently he swallowed, and then he spoke.

"Must not marry my sister?"

Claude shook her lovely head.

"Why must not Lord Ringwood marry my sister, Madame?"

Her underlip caught in her teeth, Claude stared out of the window.

"Can you not guess?" she said. "Must I tell you right out?"

The man was up on his feet and as white as a sheet.

"How should I guess?" he said hoarsely.

The Duchess shrugged her shoulders.

"Very well," she said. "It seems I must cut my throat. Lord Ringwood is the father of my son . . . and my son is —not very well. . . . Oh, do not look at me so. I know I am all to blame. One night in Paris, last year . . . I was beside myself and I lost my head. It was not his fault at all. And it is not, of course, his fault that the child is sick. These old families sometimes—you know what I mean. But how could I see your sister . . . ? He does not know, of course. I think he has no idea. He may not have recognized me. . . ."

As the train steamed out of the station, Claude sat back in her seat and wrinkled her nose.

"*Mon dieu*, these Scotsmen," she said. "I do not know what they are made for, unless it is to be clowns. Still, I have paid my debt. Claude must not have Hubert, so Philip will not have Ildico. I wish he could know I had done it: but that will never enter his head. And the clown will hold his tongue. Hubert will probably get it. He will add up two and two and he will arrive. I think he suspects already. I am sure that he wished me to stay at Fairing Over. And this absurd friendship with Ross has made him think. Ah, well. I feel better now. I think I will go to Deauville after all. Antoine is sure to be there, and will make me laugh."

*　　*　　*　　*　　*

From Eleanor Carson's Diary.

August 27th, 1899.

At Poesy.

One of the happiest days I ever spent. ' The children ' came into their own. The love and esteem in which they are held was

178

overwhelming. Philip insisted on Vivien's sharing it all. He made the most charming speech. He wrote it entirely himself and spoke without notes, but Mr. Defoe had his script and has lent it to me.

. . . Before very long, I hope to be able to spend much time at Poesy. As you know, my military duties prevent that now : but later on I shall be freer, and then I shall be at Poesy—not for odd days and weeks, but for months at a time. Once I knew every face here, but now there are some I don't know. I don't like that. I want to know you all and I want you all to know me. I want you all to feel that I am available. I shan't be really happy until I can sit at home on a winter's night and think of every one of you doing the same—until I am able to picture the home each one of you keeps, and so to assure myself that you are warm, as I am, and have the food and comfort that you deserve. When I was a little boy, you made me very happy year after year : now that I am grown up, it is my great desire to do the same by you. . . .

When he sat down, the outburst of good will was most moving. Lady Ursula was deeply affected—as, indeed, were we all. A truly wonderful day.

*　　*　　*　　*　　*

Cape Town,
November, *1899*.

My darling Vivvy,

I still can't get over my luck. To think that I'm actually here ! But we'll let that go. We landed yesterday, and I was very busy all day helping to off-load our ship. The horses stood the trip well, but seemed very glad to land. As I told you, it was no joke getting some of them on, but they all came off like lambs. But, of course, they'll take some time to harden up. Everyone is terribly nice to us here. We shan't be moving just yet, but, I think, as soon as we can. I don't know whether we shall go for Ladysmith or Kimberley : the latest news is that both are holding out well. I ran into Sheep's elder brother this morning. He's on the Staff and is going back to-morrow. He says the Boers are all mounted infantry and that their ponies stand up to anything. They have no uniform and some of their leaders actually wear top-hats. This, of course,—I mean the 'no uniform'—is very much in their favour, for unless you catch them red-handed, you have to let them go. He says it's a new style of warfare and, once we're used to it, they won't stand a chance. Whenever we can get at them, they go to bits. Has Hubert sailed yet? And how is Huffy? You know Cousin Coles has got my Power of Attorney. I know Dennis Defoe was thinking of joining up. Try and stop him, if you can. I mean, after all, it's my job : but it isn't his. And it is so much more important that he should look after things. My love to everyone. I must stop now.

Your loving
Pip.

Charles Street,
November, 1899.

My darling, darling Pip,

I know you will write when you can, but I'm hungry for news. I cannot bear your being so far away. I'm trying to do all the things you'd do if you were here. I don't mean I'm going to stables in Albany Street, but I've been to Brocade and I'm going to Poesy. Just to look round, you know : for we know what to look for. Everyone at Brocade is terribly proud : you see, you represent them. Other places claim sons and nephews : but they are represented by the head of their house. In Town all is just the same. Charity concerts, of course : but life is just the same. Aunt Ursula is at Poesy : Miss Carson at Grosvenor Square. That is largely my fault, but I will not let her go. We lunch or dine together on three days out of four. Huffy is in great form—thinks London very good fun. Hubert is chafing. I doubt if he will get out before the end of the year. Ildico wrote last week. It seems that Andrew has taken things very hard. She says she can do nothing with him.

I fear the Duchess has much to answer for. What fools men are—some men. But, of course, she is very attractive. You can't get away from that. To-morrow night we're dining at Marlborough House. I'll write and tell you about it. On Tuesday we dined with the Scropes. Lady S. was especially nice and spoke so sweetly of you. But everybody does that. To-night we go to the play, but I forget what. I suppose one must do these things, when all one's thoughts are thousands of miles away. Oh, Pip, my very darling, you will take care. Don't forget I pray for you every night.

Your loving
Vivvy.

PS. I'm going to have a baby again. I hope it's a girl.

South Africa,
December, 1899.

My darling Vivvy,
   It was awfully nice of you to wire. There really wasn't much in it and I don't think I deserve the D.S.O. In fact, I'm sure I don't. I mean, after all, it was the purest luck. You want to know what happened—well, here you are. I was out on patrol with ten other ranks. We left at half past four and had gone about six miles when we came to the mouth of a donga or old river-bed. It must have been full once, but now there's hardly a trace of the water left. A little brook running down. I saw at once that horses had gone that way —probably the night before : they'd gone up the donga, the sides of which were quite high. So I got off and went up one of the sides, looking over into the donga now and again. After about half a mile, there was the camp. No sentries, as far as I saw. About seventy Boers. Some were waking up and stretching themselves, and some natives were cooking breakfast. Their ponies were roughly tethered and looked pretty poor. Well, I got back to the patrol and we drew arms and rode straight up the donga and into the camp. The Boers were all simply staggered, and I shouted that no one must move. One man

181

did, and I fired and hit his arm. I had to do that, of course : and nobody moved again. Then I called for the corporal, for I thought it was a corporal's command. A big man came forward and said he was a field-cornet. I told him that his cornetcy was covered from either side of the gorge and that my squadron-leader had sent me to say that he must either surrender or be wiped out. Well, it came off, Vivvy. You see, there was bush above, so he couldn't see that there wasn't a squadron there, and, if one had been there, then he could have been wiped out. I told him to tell his men to fall in without their arms and that he would ride with me, while they followed on foot. When he protested, I said that those were the orders which I had received. I left three men behind in charge of the camp and rode off with the field-cornet, leading his men on foot. My other five men were behind and beside the column. When we got to the mouth of the donga, the field-cornet looked round and back, but my N.C.O. and the others played up and saved the game. They shouted and waved as if to others who were lying on the top of the cliffs and they kept the column moving with drawn swords. Fortunately the ground wasn't flat, so there might have been a squadron coming along in rear : but the field-cornet wasn't satisfied and kept on looking behind. And then I had a great piece of luck. We'd covered about three miles, when I saw C squadron ahead, a little way to the left. I just turned and looked at my N.C.O. and he was off in a flash. Five minutes later, there were two troops behind us and one either side, and Rankin rode up, grinning, to take my place. I had to go and report to Major Dawes. ' But where's your squadron ? ' said the field-cornet. ' I'm sorry,' I said, ' I'm afraid I made that up.' He cursed for a minute and then he began to cry. I was dreadfully sorry for him—I really was. When I told Major Dawes what had happened, he laughed so much that he nearly fell off his horse. Then he sent off two troops, to bring in the ponies and arms. And so we got back to camp. And about a week later I got a wire from the C. in C. saying ' Heartiest congratulations on your D.S.O.' Everyone was terribly nice

*about it, and Major le Hay had the ribbon taken off one of his
tunics and sewn on mine. But I feel uncomfortable, Vivvy,
because it was only luck. Apparently, this particular field-
cornet was wanted, but I didn't know that. However, there it
is. I think they'll give two D.C.M.s to the men. They jolly
well deserve it. No time for more now. Take care of yourself,
Vivvy darling.*

Your loving

Pip.

*PS. The first time I was under fire I was frightened to
death. I was out on patrol and we ran into some Boers and
had to get out. There wasn't much danger really, for we were
going all out and it's really very hard to hit a man who is moving
fast. In fact not one of us was touched. But it was all round
us, and I didn't like it a bit. What I really want you to know
is that I found myself saying, ' Oh, Vivvy, Vivvy.'*

*Cape Town,
March, 1900.*

My dear Ildico,
    *I'm mending fast now, and they don't think my arm will be
stiff. I was very lucky not to lose it. Isn't the news wonderful ?
Bobs is a marvellous general, you must admit. They're terribly
good to me here and I've had lots of visitors. Mrs. Ronnie
Quaritch is nursing out here—it seemed so strange to see her
in nurse's dress ; and so is Lady Roche—you know he was killed.
And Sheep was passing through and came to see me and quite
a lot of fellows I used to know. Major le Hay came to see me
—he's on his way home. He was wounded at Chitral, you
know. That's where he got his D.S.O. And the wound has
been giving trouble and now he can't go on. (Incidentally, he's
taking this letter.) He's awfully nice. It's very hot here now
and I wish I could go to Poesy for the week-end. Dennis
Defoe is very good about writing and tells me everything.
Cousin Coles has my Power of Attorney, so that's all right :
but Mr. Leith wants to retire as soon as I'm back, and, as he*

183

has no assistant, I think I shall have to, too. We'll find someone else, of course, but he won't know Poesy. I hate the idea in some ways, but now that I'm Captain, I think I must make the break. I mean, if I do stay on, I cannot really look after the estates. I'd have liked to p.s.c. but I've got to choose. And if war breaks out again, I can always go back. It's not the same thing, of course : but Poesy and Brocade must come first. I mean, the Regiment can spare me, but P. and B. can't. And so, when this show is over, I shall retire. And when I do retire, will you marry me, Ildico ? I'll be three years older then—I've got your letter before me : three years, you said. I don't know about you, darling, but I've never seen anyone else. And I love you the same as ever and always shall. And it would be so wonderful. We won't announce it at once, if you'd rather not : but I'd like to know.

Your loving

Pip.

PS. St. James has just been in. He says that as soon as I'm fit, I'm to go to the staff. I'd rather stay with the Regiment, but of course it's all experience—rather like taking a course.

PPS. I suppose you couldn't send me a wire.

Six weeks later Philip received a wire.

Captain the Earl of Ringwood D.S.O.

Yes.

Ildico.

*   *   *   *   *

" And why," said Ildico, " may I not marry Philip ? "

" You must take my word for it, Dicky, and put it out of your head."

Brother and sister were standing above the glen. The world about them was lovely. A morning shower had drenched it, and now the sun was flaming out of a cloudless sky. The vivid turf, the peerless green of the trees, the

184

sparkle of Robert's Water, the leisurely way of an eagle—and, far below, Break o' Day, set like a precious jewel on a woman's breast. . . . Of such were their surroundings. But Ildico's heart felt cold. She probably scented danger : there was, indeed, about her much of Artemis : and Artemis' senses must have been very fine. That her kilt remembered the goddess, there can be no doubt. Her virgin beauty, too : but, most of all, I think her royal air. Her dignity was outstanding. But now, though she did not show it, her heart felt cold.

"Andrew," said his sister, "you are a perfect fool. You speak as one forbidding a cake to a child. And who are you, my dear, to forbid me my cake ? "

"You cannot marry him, Dicky."

"May I know why ? "

": He is not fit for you."

"I see. And if I think that Lord Ringwood is fit to marry me, that is beside the point ? "

"I'm afraid it is, Dicky. You'll have to write him off."

The girl expired.

"Are you trying to tell me, Andrew, that Pip has already a wife ? "

"No."

"Or fifty mistresses ? "

Andrew shook his head.

"Yet you know of a just impediment ? "

"Yes, I do."

"In that case, please declare it."

"I have declared it to father. He quite agrees with me."

Ildico's heart felt colder. Her father was her liege-lord.

"Very well. I will speak with father. He will have the courage to give the slander a name."

"It is no slander, Dicky."

Ildico looked at her brother and looked him down.

"I think the less of you, Andrew. The time will come when you will think the less of yourself."

Five hours and a half had gone by, and father and daughter were seated beside the glow of the hearth.

"I do not believe it, father."

"I do not like to believe it," said Colonel Ross. "But Andrew is very sure. In any event, it is so grave a matter that 'non-proven' will not do. Before we can go any further, this ghost must be laid."

"Who was Andrew's informant?"

"He may not say. I do not see that that matters. Be his informant a scullion, this report is so serious that it must be disproved."

"Father, be fair—to us both. We cannot make bricks without straw. Andrew has heard a rumour. How can we prove it false unless we know whence it comes? It is all very well for Andrew to make this dreadful statement—prefer this shocking charge. Any man can do that about his fellow, if he is so inclined. But charges must be supported. It is easy enough for Andrew to say that his lips are sealed. That is not the way of justice, and never was. It would be laughed to scorn in the puniest court of law. . . . Myself, I have no doubt that this is a wicked lie. I did not know that Pip had an enemy—he is so frank and gentle with all the world. But this report proves that he has. It has been wilfully made, to—to break our hearts."

"My darling, I trust you are right. And, if you are, be sure that the ghost will be laid. But . . . laid it must be, my dear. Our blood is better than Philip's, though he is a lord and we are commoners. And—and I cannot suffer my daughter to risk the blood in her veins."

"Then, father, Andrew must speak. He has said too much or too little. No man can make such a statement and then retire. Where should we be—where would society be, if idle statements like this were quietly accepted until they could be disproved?"

"I know, I know. But Andrew is not feather-brained. He is your loving brother: he has been a close friend of

Ringwood's for several years. I know he would dance at your wedding with all his heart. If, then, he feels constrained to dash your hopes——"

"Father, father."

"My darling child, I would spare you, if I could. But this report is such that, before you marry Ringwood, it must be shown to be false."

Ildico braced herself.

"I am of age, father."

"I know. But you are Ildico Ross. To your ancient house, to the children whom you may bear, you owe the confutation of this report."

There was a little silence.

Then——

"What shall I do to compass this confutation?"

Colonel Ross stood up.

"I am going to London," he said. "Sir John Forsyth, the Judge, is a very old friend. You may remember him here, a year or two back. I shall lay the case before him and see what he says."

"Please take me with you—and Andrew."

"I must take Andrew, of course. I had not meant you to come."

"It might be as well, father. And, after all, I am very deeply concerned."

"Very well, my dear. Make some excuse to your mother and come with us."

*   *   *   *   *

Sir John, a Common Lawyer, was now a Lord Justice of Appeal. By his most just promotion, the Queen's Bench Division had lost a valuable Judge. He was very shrewd and kindly and seemed to see farther than most men into the heart of a case. He was a widower.

He acceded, without hesitation, to Colonel Ross's request, and saw the Colonel and Andrew one Tuesday afternoon.

187

When they had said their say—

"I must think this over," he said. "Please dine with me on Thursday, at 44 Rutland Gate. And bring your daughter with you. Let us say eight o'clock."

Of the three guests, Ildico was the calmest, the most at ease. Nobody would have dreamed that she had so much at stake. The Judge saw and approved.

He greeted her very kindly and spoke at once to the point.

"If you please, my dear, you will take the head of the table."

"I shall be honoured, Sir John."

"One thing more. Please take your coffee with us. In other words, don't withdraw. Discussion about a table has always appealed to me. We can all see one another, and we shall be at ease."

"I can ask nothing better, Sir John."

"Then that's all right. Now tell me of Break o' Day."

At last the cloth was drawn and coffee was served. Then the servants withdrew, and the door was shut.

The Judge looked round.

"I have," he said, "considered this grave affair : and I entirely agree that such a report as this must be shown to be false. Myself, I believe it is false. But it must be shown to be false—beyond all reasonable doubt.

"The position is delicate. A report of another nature could be submitted to Lord Ringwood or to Lord Ringwood's friends. But this report is venomous : submission would spread the poison—a quite unthinkable thing.

"Very well. What do we do ?

"First of all, we consider the facts.

"As I understand, Lord Ringwood has always appeared to enjoy the best of health. So has Lady Vivien de Guesclin, and so has her son. Their mother is very healthy : so is their aunt—so far as we know, of course. But I rather think that, if there was anything wrong, it would have got about.

"Secondly, Andrew states that no one, except his informant, has ever suggested to him that there was a Ringwood taint.

188

Indeed, he says quite frankly that, until he was thus informed, no such idea had ever entered his head.

"Well, that is all we have, except the informant's statement that Lord Ringwood has had a child and that child is diseased."

The Judge paused there, to take up his cup and drink. Then he sat back in his chair.

"In my considered opinion, Andrew's informant is Ringwood's enemy . . . and has selected this very cunning method of doing him infinite harm. It is extremely cunning : it is insidious." The Judge's eyes were on Andrew. "And that is one reason why I am perfectly sure that Andrew's informant was a woman—a woman who was aware that Lord Ringwood was attached to Miss Ross. . . . What she has against Ringwood, I do not know. She knows and Ringwood knows. Possibly, others may know. But I have no doubt at all that my deduction is true. This report smells of vengeance. It is exactly the blow that a wicked woman would strike. Was it a woman, Andrew, who told you this thing ? "

White to the lips, staring upon his dessert-plate, Andrew replied.

"Yes, sir."

"As being Ildico's brother, she warned you off ? "

"Yes."

The Judge addressed Colonel Ross.

"It's a thousand to one," he said, "that Ringwood had turned her down."

"He hadn't," cried Andrew, furiously.

"Oh, she was the victim, was she ? "

"I never said that."

"Have you seen the child ? "

"No."

Once again the Judge addressed Colonel Ross.

"Andrew's been used," he said. "No doubt about that. By an evil-disposed lady, whose name he will not divulge."

Ildico laughed.

" Try the *Duchesse de Sevignac*."

Andrew clapped his hands to his face.

" Thank you, my dear," said the Judge.   " That's why I wanted you here."

" A Frenchwoman," snapped the Colonel.   " Andrew, you should be ashamed."

" It's true," flamed Andrew.   " She tore herself in pieces, for Ildico's sake."

" Oh, well," said the Judge. . . .   And then, " Who else in London knows this—this Magdalen, who sacrifices herself to expose an English Earl ? "

Ildico laughed again.

" What about Captain de Guesclin ?   He's a man of the world and he's Philip's brother-in-law."

Andrew started to his feet.

" You can't possibly tell him," he cried.   " I mean, you can't mention her name.   You've dragged it out of me, but, at least, that's between these walls.   You can't dishonour me by——"

" And what of Philip ? " flashed his sister.   " His name can be dishonoured, his love thrown back in his face—because the light-o'-love who told you this infamous lie——"

" Ildico," cried the Colonel.

" I'm sorry, father.   I beg your pardon, Sir John.   But it is so clear to me that Andrew's been fooled."

" To me, too," said the Judge.   " But we've got to be sure.   Captain de Guesclin may be able to help.   As Ringwood's brother-in-law, he's an excellent choice ; for he must keep his counsel, because of his wife.   Can you get hold of him, Arthur ? "

" I will," said the Colonel.   " Andrew, what are his Clubs ? "

Pale as death—

" The Guards' and White's," said Andrew.   " The Marlborough, too, I think."

The Judge nodded.

" Bring him here when you can get him. I'm always home by six. Don't tell him what it's about. Say it's a personal matter of great importance to you."

*   *   *   *   *

Hubert looked round.

Three pairs of eyes were regarding him steadily.

" Could we clear the Court ? " he said. " I've something to say for the Judge's ear alone."

At a nod from his lordship, Colonel Ross and Andrew left the room.

Hubert said his piece.

" Well, there you are," he concluded. " She wouldn't say who told her that I had gone over seas. Of course, I see now it was Pip. I ought to have guessed. He took Lady Ringwood to Paris just about then. Of course, he told her a lie —to spoil her game : but, as Vivvy's brother, he couldn't do anything else. But she didn't see it that way—Claude is completely amoral. To her way of thinking, he'd served her a dirty turn. And so she tried to get back."

The Judge was nodding his head.

" I wasn't far out," he said. " But I thought that he'd turned her down."

" I've no doubt he did," said Hubert.

" Good God."

" That's the Frenchwoman, sir. I couldn't understand why she bothered with Andrew Ross. I mean, he's not her style. But now it's perfectly clear. He was Ildico's brother, and Pip very plainly had eyes for nobody else. Incidentally, sir, she gave me to understand that the Duke had fathered her son : and she never said he was sick : he had a twisted leg."

" Well, I'm much obliged," said the Judge. " Arthur Ross is a very old friend of mine, and Ildico—what a girl ! —is the light of his eyes. And now you've laid the ghost."

" I'm thankful you called me in. Pip's the most charming

191

fellow I've ever known. And Ildico will make him a perfect wife." Hubert considered his port. "I'm afraid I come rather badly out of it all."

"Few men would have been so honest. Of course I shall keep your counsel."

"What shall you tell them, sir?"

The Judge looked down his nose.

"I shall say that you happen to know that she bore the Earl of Ringwood a violent grudge. They'll probably think he'd rejected her advances."

"As I say, I've no doubt he had. But that's by the way."

"Well, that is what I shall say—a violent grudge. That from what you know of her, she would stick at nothing to gain revenge." Hubert nodded. "May I say that she said that her son was her husband's child? Apart from anything else, such a communication will show the class of woman to which she belongs."

"Yes, sir, you may."

"And that she volunteered that he had a twisted leg?"

"That's right."

"Well, let's have them in," said the Judge, and got to his feet.

* * * * *

So a sinister bid for vengeance was brought to naught. Still, Claude achieved something which would, if she had known it, have warmed her heart. To gain her wicked end, she had suffered a fool. It was the fool that paid. Relations with father and sister were never the same. Andrew had gone a-whoring after false gods : and, as a result, had let the family down. Before two months were out, he had sailed for Canada.

Philip never knew what had happened—how very nearly a woman had spoiled his life : for, but for Hubert's revelation, Colonel Ross would have witheld his consent. In those days, the taint was dreaded as nothing else. To gain revenge,

Claude had committed the unforgivable sin. She had laid Philip under suspicion—and that of something so dreadful that it could never be whispered, in case it was overheard. Such suspicions are very hard to allay. Other women had done the same thing. Some, who played their cards well, were paid large sums of money—instead of being arrested and charged with blackmail : for, had they been so charged, the world would have said that where there is smoke there is fire. The man who made that proverb has much to answer for.

*   *   *   *   *

Charles Street,
June, 1900.

My darling Pip,
I am so very, very glad. Ildico is the only girl I have seen that I should like you to marry. You are absolutely right for each other and I am perfectly certain that you will both be terribly happy. I think you are quite right not to announce it yet. When you come back will do. But I will tell Aunt Ursula and Miss Carson and Cousin Coles. I am writing to Ildico and asking her to come and stay with me at once. At Fairing Over, of course—I'm only up here for two or three days. I would have liked to have had my baby at Poesy, but Hubert made me promise to have it in Town. The idea is better doctors, in case of accidents. But, as soon as I can, I shall go to Poesy, as I know you would like me to. If I can, I'll get Ildico to come with me—I should like that, and I know you would. Pip, darling, you're both very lucky. I am so happy and thankful I don't know what to do. Hubert sailed last week. I'm really sorry for him—he's had a rotten time. Too useful here, you know. I decline to worry. I know you'll both come back. God bless you, Pip darling.

Your loving
Vivvy.

193

My dearest Vivvy,

I shall always keep your letter. I know what Pip means to you and I do not believe there is another sister in the world who, loving her brother as you do, would have written so handsomely. And now I want to say this. I have loved Pip from the day I saw him first. And if love can make a good wife, then I shall make him one all our days. I don't know that it can, but I hope so. But I have never seen a brother and sister so close as you two are : and I would rather die to-morrow than do anything to disturb so perfect a relation. Will you please believe that? Of course I shall take my place, as you will wish me to do. But it will only mean that Pip will now have two women, instead of one. Of course I will come to you at once. I shall be with you on Friday—on the heels of this letter, indeed. And I shall sit at your feet, so that, when Pip and I are married, I may make the better wife. You call him 'our darling boy'. That is how I shall always regard him —yours and mine.

Your loving
Ildico.

PS. So far as Andrew is concerned, that wretched Duchesse de Sevignac has much to answer for. Life has lost its savour for him, and I think he will emigrate.

Lincoln's Inn,
June, 1900.

My dear Pip,

Vivien tells me, sub rosa, *that you are engaged to be married to Ildico Ross. This I am delighted to hear. Nothing could be better. I have only met her three or four times, but they were quite enough to make me hope that one day she would be your wife. She is exactly right. She is exactly what your wife should be. I am quite sure that you will both 'live happily ever after'. I hope very much that your marriage will not be* long delayed. I assume that, when this business is over, you will retire. Myself, I don't think it should be so very long now. Defoe is writing himself. The estates go on very well, but will be all the better for the presence of their master.

Believe me, my dear Pip,
Your affectionate cousin,
Coles Willing.

Charles Street,
August, 1900.

My darling Pip,

You have a lovely niece. Vivvy did not have a very bad time and is mending fast. We hope to go to Poesy three weeks from to-day. You see, I am making free with your seat. But Vivvy wants me, and I know that that would be quite enough for you. We talk about you nearly all the time. The niece is to be called Rachel Ursula. I get on very well with Miss Carson. She is as sweet a woman as ever I knew, and wonderful company. London is quiet—for London, and I rather like it so. Sometimes I lunch with Miss Carson at Grosvenor Square. I did so on Wednesday, when Mr. Willing was there. He was perfectly charming to me. One of the lords in waiting has told him that the Queen is beginning to fail. Prince Alfred's death has shaken her very much. He says that it is only her will that keeps her going. Her mind is still perfectly clear, but her body is giving in. One thing Mr. Willing repeated stuck in my mind. ' Her Majesty gives the lie to the saying that No man is a hero to his valet. Only her personal attendants know what a heroine she is.' He happened to mention that the old clerk, Allen, was ill. He said he was much afraid he would never come back. So I asked him for his address, and Miss Carson and I went to see him in Kilburn, yesterday afternoon. I thought you'd like us to. Pip, darling, he was dying. You couldn't mistake the fact. So I told him that we were engaged. And he was so sweet—he blessed me . . . very humbly, just as they used to do. And then he said very quietly, ' Now I can

195

die in peace.' In fact, he died this morning—a good and faithful servant has entered into his rest. We are sending flowers in your name. This is a dreadful letter—I'm so ashamed. Andrew likes Canada well and is making many friends. I think he will settle down in Vancouver, B.C. I forgot to tell you that the Princess had insisted to Vivvy that someone must write and tell her as soon as the baby was born. So Lady Ursula was to do it, and then she forgot. So Vivvy said I must do it—and Her Royal Highness's most humble and obedient servant, Ildico Ross, accordingly informed the Princess that all was well. I will write again, my darling, almost at once. I am very impatient, Pip, to see you again. I hope and believe that it will not be very long now.

Your loving
Ildico.

Lincoln's Inn Fields,
March, 1901.

My dear General,

I gather from Begbie that, though the war may drag on, it is unlikely that there will be any more major engagements.

In these circumstances, I venture to draw your attention to the case of Captain the Earl of Ringwood, D.S.O., of the Horse Guards Blue. Lord Ringwood, who is nearly twenty-three, is now serving on the Staff of General —— He was awarded the D.S.O. in 1899 and was more or less severely wounded some six weeks later.

I am writing as one of the Trustees of 'The Ringwood Trust'. This is a Trust of considerable importance and includes the administration of an establishment in London and two estates in the country. Lord Ringwood's absence for eighteen months, on active service, has not so far embarrassed the administration : but his continued absence will do so. Changes are taking place, and the master should now be here. Though he would still have his military duties to do, it would mean a great deal to the

Trustees to have him within call and in touch with his many responsibilities.

He has no idea that I am writing to you and must never know that I have done so : but, unless his presence in the field is still required, and unless his place cannot be properly taken by another, I should be greatly obliged if he could be returned to home duty. You will, of course, scrutinize his report as a soldier. Lord Ringwood's duty to his country must come first. But, if you see no good reason why he should not now be relieved, I can assure you that his return to England at this juncture will be of very great value to ' The Ringwood Trust', and will be a source of great satisfaction to

Yours very sincerely,
Coles Willing.

PS. Not for anything, would I stand in his way if he has any chance of further distinction. But I gathered from Begbie that those days were over and that it was now a case of spreading nets and blocking escape-routes.

War Office,
March, 1901.

My dear Willing,
Very glad you wrote to me. —— is coming home in June and I see no reason why Lord Ringwood should not accompany him. The boy has done very well and heartily deserves to be relieved. I am, accordingly, arranging this.

Yours very sincerely,
——

*   *   *   *   *

Poesy in September, and a King on the throne of England, once again.

Lady Ursula and Miss Carson had retired, and Vivien and Philip were sitting in the Great Hall.

"Your bachelor days are nearly over, Pip."

" I know. I've been awfully happy. I do believe I'm going to be happier still."

" I'm sure of that. You're marrying at just the right time. As for Ildico—well, it's rather like doing a puzzle, and she's the missing piece. I mean, she exactly fits."

" I never looked at it that way."

" Why should you, darling? You loved her, and that was enough. But I've looked further than that. There was you and me and our house. Whoever you chose would not only be your wife, but she would have charge of my brother and be the Countess of Ringwood and mistress of Poesy and Brocade. Well, Ildico's made for those things. I've had an eye out for years, but I've never seen anyone else to compare with her."

" I'm terribly glad, Vivvy. I don't know why I'm so lucky, but there you are. I'll wait for the Coronation and then retire : the war will be over by then. I'll be sorry, of course, but I must. With Leith and Rodney gone, I'll have my hands full. And old Allen's a serious loss. Dennis says he misses him terribly."

Vivien nodded.

" That I can well believe. And he was such a dear old man. We saw to his grave-stone, of course : but I thought you might like a panel over the pew."

" Why not ? " said Philip. " He gave his life to the Trust. What did you put on the stone ? "

" ' Well done, good and faithful servant.' "

" I am so glad."

There was a little silence, while Vivien stitched at her tapestry and Philip stared at the fire.

Presently Philip rose and lighted a cigarette.

" Vivvy," he said.

" Yes, Pip."

" There's something I've got to tell you. I can't bear doing it, Vivvy ; but it's better that I should tell you than —than somebody else."

198

Vivien's needle stopped.

"Go on, Pip."

"When I came through Cape Town, Hubert was there on leave."

"I see," said Vivien, slowly. "Who was he living with?"

Her brother bit his lip.

Then—

"Mrs. Welham, Vivvy."

Vivien sat very still, not seeming to breathe.

At length—

"This isn't rumour, Vivvy. I know it for a fact."

"I see. So, of course, do others."

"Yes, I'm afraid they do."

There was another silence.

Then Vivien buried her needle and pitched her tapestry down.

She took a deep breath.

"It's the devil, isn't it, Pip?"

"I'm so frightfully sorry, Vivvy."

"I know you are, darling. It can't be helped. Hubert's the best in the world; but an unscrupulous woman can do what she likes with him. Of course he loves me best. I know that perfectly. But other women can command him at any time. And one of these days he'll fall down."

"But it's such a damned shame," cried Philip. "The damnedest shame."

His sister shrugged her shoulders.

"In every other respect, he's all that I could desire."

"But—you're so wonderful, Vivvy. And you make him such a marvellous wife."

"I'm not too bad, I know. But women are Hubert's failing, and there we are. It's a very grievous failing; and, if the woman is married, extremely dangerous. What he needs is the hell of a shock. That might cure him—might. The burnt child dreads the fire." Vivien got to her feet, stepped to her brother's side and took his face in her hands.

" Don't look so grim, Pip darling. Things like this hit hard, but they don't bring you down. And, then, I've always got you."

*   *   *   *   *

Alone in her bedroom, Vivien considered her case. Divorce was out of the question. For one thing, she could not obtain it, for Hubert had never been cruel. But, could she obtain it, she might as well cut her throat. What was more to the point, she did not desire a divorce. If, upon Hubert's return, she denied him her bed, he would only turn to that of somebody else. Yet, to share her husband was bitter indeed. To reason with him was futile. The man could not help himself. He was born polygamic. For all that, she could not pretend that Hubert counted as he had counted once. For one thing alone, she despised him. Hubert had broken the troth which he had plighted—in Vivien's eyes, as we know, the unforgivable sin. In equity, that released her : but not in law. Besides, she had no desire to be unfaithful to him.

" Our days are numbered," she whispered. " I must play up and go on for as long as I can. But one day the crash will come. I don't know how it will come, but I know it will. And then I shall have to withdraw. Thank God for Poesy. And Pip. And Ildico. Oh, Hubert, Hubert, why ever must you be such a blasted fool ? "

*   *   *   *   *

Four sober months went by. Then the Court put off its mourning, and the curtain rose upon the cordial splendour of the Edwardian age. The scene was memorable. The Court, so long a legend, became an entity. His Britannic Majesty commanded the world's respect, inspired the utmost devotion, induced goodwill. His people worshipped him— and followed his handsome bent. For every honest man, only the very best was ever good enough : the finest meat

200

was served in cabmen's shelters : high and low found life a good thing : the King himself called the tune, and his subjects were happy subjects, going cheerfully about their business and doing their simple duty with proud content . . . ' against the envy of less happier lands '. (' Relax,' says Erny Balch. ' You can' fool me. That bit about the cabmen. . . .' ' Sorry, Erny, but this is where I *know*. The best from Smithfield went to the cabmen's shelter. The second-best went to ——'s. I've eaten at both. And the cabmen's shelter had it—every time.') In every walk of life, duty and pleasure ran in double-harness, so that the coach they drew bowled cheerily down the years : abundance was there for all that would pull their weight : and men and women were kind, one to another.

Philip and Ildico Ross were married in May. Lady Ringwood was present. ' Sheep ' Woodville was Philip's best man. The Duke and Duchess of Eythorne lent them their Devonshire seat—for a very short honeymoon. When that was over and done, they repaired to Grosvenor Square. In September, Philip retired and retained his rank. Vivien and Hubert were still the best of friends : but the silk of the wedding-garment was wearing thin.

Vivien, now twenty-six, had attained that acknowledged pre-eminence which is extremely rare. She was, as Virgil had said, the Silvia of her time. ' For *Vivien* is excelling.' She made no effort whatever : the girl was always herself, apparently quite unconscious of the sensation she caused. She spent much time out of Town : but that made no difference at all : when she returned, there was the place waiting, for her to fill. The de Guesclins were frequently ' commanded ' : they stayed at Windsor for Ascot : the King drove to Fairing Over as soon as he had a car. Vivien took it all as it came : nothing could turn her head : she was invulnerable. At Covent Garden all eyes were upon her box : when she drove in the Park, people ran to the rails to see her go by : Her Majesty came to tea, and the scarlet of

Royalty waited in Charles Street, outside. To say that Vivien enjoyed it is nothing at all : she loved every minute of her superb success : but, when the Season was over, she turned a radiant face to the countryside. During the Season, Hubert did more than support her : he was her lord and partner in all she did. The man was always just right, taking the head of his table with easy confidence, squiring his beautiful wife with affectionate pride, receiving the royal favour with humble dignity. It was when they were off parade that the wedding-garment began to show signs of wear.

Without a house-party, Hubert was very soon bored. He loved his tweeds and his Melton : but, when he came home of an evening, he liked to find the house full. Against her inclination, Vivien met him halfway. They visited country houses, filled Fairing Over with guests. But half-way was not enough. Hubert tired of Poesy after three days, and Vivien watched his departure with an uneasy frown : out of one of those goings the crash would come.

* * * * *

On Trafalgar Day in 1902, Philip brought his Countess home to Brocade. Years of tradition had made such occasions great. The agent had been at the station, and all the principal servants had been in the hall. The steward had bowed their allegiance.

" Welcome home, my lady. Welcome, my lord."

" Thank you," said Ildico, smiling. " Let's see if I get my names right. You're Mr. Warwick, aren't you ? "

" That's quite right, my lady."

" And this is Mrs. Shawcross. How d'ye do ? "

The housekeeper bowed and smiled.

" Very well, thank you, my lady."

The groom of the chambers, the butler, the chef, the sergeant-footman, the first and second housemaids—all were duly presented and charmingly used.

Then Ildico gave her first order.

202

" Mrs. Shawcross."

" My lady."

" My maid's behind with the luggage. Her name is Winter, and she's a very good girl. I'm sure you'll look after her."

" Certainly, my lady."

" And now will you show me my bedroom ? And then I'll come down to tea."

Breakfast, the following morning, was laid in the Small Saloon.

Ildico looked about her.

" I like this chamber, Pip."

" So do I, my sweet. It's not too large."

" Unlike the menu. ' Porridge, sole, kidneys, eggs, bacon, York Ham, cold pheasant, muffins.' Pip, d'you want a fat wife ? "

" You must talk to the chef," said Philip. " And I should begin with sole. It's terribly good."

" Porridge," said Ildico. " No, let me help myself. What are we doing this morning ? "

" I'm showing you over your house : and this afternoon I'm taking you round the estate."

" Riding ? "

" Unless, my sweet, you'd rather go in a gig."

" No, I'd sooner ride. Put me on something safe that won't give me away."

" You silly girl," said Philip. " No one would know that you hadn't hunted for years."

" Liar," said his wife. " Never mind. Don't go and eat too much. I want to see over Brocade."

Half an hour later they entered the library.

This was a magnificent chamber, eighty feet long. Five great windows looked South, and the pleasant, autumn sunshine was slanting into the room. The comfortable walls of leather, the mighty, old-rose carpet and the curtains to match, the heavily carved tables and leather chairs, the three great fires burning—these things preserved the stately, spacious atmosphere of bygone days.

"It's not enough used," said Philip. "It's really a splendid room."

"Let's remedy that, darling. Let's make it our sitting-room from October to May. Here we can do as we please and be undisturbed. This atmosphere is invulnerable. The fireplace right at the end will give us a chance. We shall sit about that, of course. With flowers and cretonne covers. . . . We'd have to change some furniture. What d'you think ? "

"I think it's a brilliant idea."

"You know. Just you and me and Vivvy—off parade."

"Gorgeous," said Philip. "Our room."

"D'you mind if I work it out ? "

"I'd love you to."

And so on.

Withdrawing-rooms, gallery, ball-room ; suites and the many bedrooms, kitchens and offices ; still-room, dairy and laundry—all were visited. When sherry was served before luncheon, the two were most glad to sit down.

"Well, my darling ? "

Ildico drank her sherry and crossed her legs.

" 'Behold, the half was not told me.' Brocade is a notable house. I've several suggestions to make, but not to-day. Before I do that, I must study the various rooms. But there are three things, my darling, which I can say right off. First, we should have two lifts, and, possibly, three. Secondly, I should consider installing electric light. And thirdly, central heating. I'm speaking, of course, at random. The cost will be very high. And there may be other objections, that I don't see. But, with those three improvements, Brocade would be not only a stately home, but a very livable house."

Philip looked at his lady over the rim of his glass.

"It's just about time that I married Ildico Ross."

" 'Ildico Ross.' I've almost forgotten the name. I've

become the Countess of Ringwood, heart and soul. Was I really that plain Scots lassie, Ildico Ross ? "

Ildico Ross or Lady Ringwood, the girl was capable. Her eye was very quick and she had a practical brain. While others approached a problem, she attacked it. She wrote for text-books on turbines and electricity. When Defoe's engineers arrived, they were deeply impressed. One of their private reports shall speak for itself.

' I hope and believe that we shall get the order : but her ladyship will be hard to satisfy. She is by no means capricious : but she is most intelligent and knows exactly what she requires. She asked very many questions, but never an idle one : and I must honestly confess that it was a privilege to deal with a customer so quick and understanding.'

(Within the year, Brocade had two lifts, had been furnished with central heating and was one of the few great houses lit by electric light.)

Still, many can deal with bricks and mortar who cannot deal with the stubborn heart of man. Ildico's sternest test took place exactly five weeks from the day she entered Brocade.

" You wished to see me, my lady ? "

" That's right, Mrs. Shawcross. Sit down."

" I prefer to stand, my lady."

" As you please," said Ildico, seated on the arm of a chair. " It's nearly seven years, Mrs. Shawcross, since you became the housekeeper of Brocade."

" It will be seven years next March, my lady."

Ildico leaned forward.

" I hope it will be fourteen years in seven years' time."

The housekeeper stared, coloured, looked round uncertainly, subsided on to a sofa and put a hand to her eyes.

Ildico was by her side.

" There, there, Mrs. Shawcross. Will you please believe that I understand ? That every time I think of you, I feel so grateful to you for all you've done. For his lordship's sake, you have discharged a very difficult duty in the most faithful of ways. You have had no recognition. Your efforts have been taken for granted for year after year. Yet you have never faltered, but gone straight on, giving the best that was in you to the House of Ringwood. That was your duty, as you saw it. That is the way I hope you will always see it. That is the way I see my duty—and I have only just come.

"Of course our position is delicate. As the Countess, I am your mistress, and I should do very wrong if I forfeited that estate, because it is his lordship who has promoted me. So I mustn't shrink from it—you wouldn't wish me to. What is more to the point, you wouldn't respect me, if I did. But please believe that I shall never assert my authority : those who do that are the people who have small minds. Believe, instead, that when I give an order, I have considered it first. But please remember, too, that when I give an order, it must be carried out."

The housekeeper's head went down.

"Yes, we both know what I mean. The servants' hour for rising is half past five. I gave you two orders. One was to advance that hour to six o'clock : the other was that every servant on duty after ten at night was not to return to duty for eight clear hours."

"It's very difficult, my lady."

"It means some re-arrangement—possibly, extra staff. I'll go into it with you whenever you please. But the staff deserves these concessions, and you will please see that they have them without delay."

Mrs. Shawcross clasped her hands.

"In a house like Brocade, my lady, I have to keep a tight rein."

"I know. You're perfectly right. Discipline's everything. But it is the unnecessary order that makes men and women chafe. Times have changed, Mrs. Shawcross : and six o'clock is early enough to-day. You know as well as I that the work will be perfectly done. Give them another

206

half hour, and the work will be cheerfully done. A willing heart goes all the way, you know."

"I—expect your ladyship's right. I was brought up very strict."

"I'm sure I'm right, for this is an easier age. If any difficulty arises, come to me. Let's meet it together, Mrs. Shawcross. Always remember that you can teach me so much ; and that one day, when you retire, I shall be left to work it out all alone. So I do depend upon you to teach me to care for Brocade, when that day comes. But I'm more in touch than you with manners and modes to-day, and, if I have any ideas, I shall bring them to you.

"Please always remember three things. One is, I'm a soldier's daughter, and I was ' brought up very strict '. Until I was ten, I had a cold bath every morning and I had to be out, rain or fine, by eight o'clock."

"That's very severe on a girl."

"Severe or no, those were my orders, Mrs. Shawcross, and they were carried out. The second thing is that I am now the Countess, and when I give an order, that's got to be carried out. The third thing is that I never have and never shall give an order of any consequence, except through you ; so that if you think it's a bad one, you've got to tell me so."

The housekeeper burst into tears. Ildico comforted her.

"I know you meant to give notice. When you know me better, I don't think you'll feel like that. I've only one idea, and it's just the same as yours. To keep his lordship's house as it should be kept. If we can't do that together, nobody can."

Three weeks later, Ildico caught a chill and was ordered to bed. In Winter's teeth, Mrs. Shawcross nursed her, herself.

The steward was very easy : but he was a man. That is hardly fair, for Ildico was beloved. The stud-groom swore by his lady. As for the tenants, they looked upon her and loved her—and that was that. Winter was Scotch. She told her beautiful mistress where she got off—and would have died for her, as a matter of course.

* * * * *

June, 1903, and an early dinner for four in Grosvenor Square.

" Did you take the barouche ? " said Philip.

" By your lordship's order, I did."

" Good," said Philip, smiling. " I'll bet you carried it off."

" I did my best," said his wife.

" She looked the part," said Miss Carson. " I went to the Park myself, to see her go by."

" You didn't, Miss Carson ! "

" Why not, my dear ? I wanted to see for myself. May I say that I had my reward ? " Ildico coloured with pleasure. " Pip, it's her equipage."

According, no doubt, to custom, with the exception of Royalty, only the peeress ever affected the barouche : but by no means every peeress could ' wear ' so splendid a setting. Properly appointed, it was a magnificent sight. Clad in black, the servants wore knee-breeches, the footman going powdered, the coachman in curls : the horses were superfine. Such pomp became ludicrous, if the occupant was not renowned or had no air. Ildico was not renowned, but she had an air. A very beautiful girl, she knew how to keep her state.

" I felt very small," said the Countess.

" Then you covered it up very well."

" I wish I'd known," said Defoe. " I've never been bowed to by somebody in a barouche."

" The barouche," said Ildico, " is a pomp and a vanity. As such, I thoroughly enjoyed it and, whenever the weather's set fair, I shall use it again."

" Hurray," cried the men.

" Of course it attracts attention. And all the time I kept thinking, ' Here I am, a cynosure, because of this equipage. If all these people could see me asprawl in a kilt. . . .' "

" If they could, you'd be mobbed," said Defoe.

" So you would," said Philip.

" I should like Angus' ruling on that. Pip, my darling, I think we must have him up. He'd simply love the barouche. He wouldn't say so, of course. He'd probably say it was a wile of the devil. But in his heart he'd love it. And the fight between head and heart would do me good."

" I wish you would have him," said Miss Carson. " I'm sure I should like Angus. His strictures upon the Season would be invaluable."

" Wire to-morrow," said Pip. He turned to Defoe. " Angus is Ildico's gillie—the perfect, primitive man. London will fascinate him and command his great contempt."

Ildico nodded.

" That saying is very true."

" A sane point of view," said Defoe. " We should all be at Poesy."

" No, we shouldn't," said Miss Carson. " Men and women to-day must play their parts. One of their duties towards their neighbours is to honour Convention. Very few men have the right to be unconventional. A great poet has ; or, perhaps, a scientist. But they give a *quid pro quo*."

" You should have been a lawyer," said Defoe. " Of course you're perfectly right. In nine cases out of ten, the man who is unconventional is being purely selfish. Provided that they are decent, man should observe the habits and customs of his class."

" He's right," cried Ildico. " But customs change. Old customs are sometimes harsh : but courage in the right people can alter them. Vivvy has courage and standing. And Vivvy has asked the Crosswoods to come and stay."

" Good for Vivvy," cried Philip. " My God, I'm glad."

" To Fairing Over, in August. ' Little by little,' she says : and she's perfectly right. Next year, they can come to Charles Street."

" Let's have them to Poesy, darling."

"Why not?" said Ildico.

"As a matter of fact," said Defoe, "I think the country will suit them, but not the Town. Convention has compelled them to lead an excellent life : a charming and natural life : a better life than that Convention lays down. They're all in all to each other, and Crosswood has his job. They'll come to Fairing Over, to stake their claim : but I very much doubt if they will return for the flesh-pots."

"I think you're right," said Miss Carson. "Convention has her laws : but they're not impeccable. Algy and Mary Crosswood were forced by Convention to live an unconventional life. By now they have proved its value. And so they have won the right to laugh in Convention's face. 'You turned us out,' they'll say. 'Just try and whistle us back.' "

"Theirs is a good life," said Philip, wistfully.

"The best," said Ildico. "But you and I can't lead it. We've got to conform."

Philip fingered his chin.

"For less than twopence," he said, "I'd wash the Season out."

"So would I," said his wife, "and you know that's true. But the Earl and Countess of Ringwood can't do that."

Miss Carson nodded.

"Ildico's right," she said. "You've got to go on. Duty goes with the birthright. After all, there are compensations. The play we are going to see is quite a good play."

Defoe began to laugh.

"Galley-slaves," he said. "Tied by a silver chain to a golden oar. And yet I most truly believe that both of you would be happier out of Town. Even, perhaps, at Chantilly. Still, your sentence is quite a light one—and lightens that of your friends."

Ildico lifted her glass.

"I looks to Dennis," she said.

"And I to Pip," said Miss Carson, "because he knows his duty and does it so very well."

Philip raised his glass.

"And I to Ildico."

His wife inclined her head.

"Thank you, my lord." Again she raised her glass. "And now let's drink to Angus. He'll put us where we belong."

*   *   *   *   *

The gorgeous years slid by: the gorgeous years of plenty and content: the gorgeous years of comfort and security; of faith and hope and charity—three virgins, undefiled; of loyalty and mutual kindliness: brimming with happy days, the years slid by, while envy, hatred and malice bowed their abominable heads. (Nobody knew the sands were running out . . . the golden sands. . . . Nobody knew that a neighbour was biding his time, waiting to ease his hatred, waiting to blast the beauty of the English way. Jealousy knows no law. The *Hymn of Hate* was the anthem of the greatest explosion of class-hatred the world has ever seen. Such was the occasion of the first world war—class-hatred and nothing else. The poisonous cad of Europe hated the peer.)

The motor-car 'arrived'—that pleasant playfellow, that carpet whose black magic was to corrode the English country-side. The old, leisurely ways began to fade. . . .

The House of Brabant prospered. Vivien de Guesclin's name became a household world. 'Look. There's Lady Vivien . . . Oh, if Lady Vivien's going . . . Ask Lady Vivien . . . I'm afraid Lady Vivien's gone. . . .' Hubert delighted in the car. Vivien's electric brougham just climbed St. James's Street. Huffy had spent one term at Summer Fields. His sister, chubby, big-eyed, supported a governess. Philip, now a J.P., was a country gentleman. No estates were better cared for than Poesy and Brocade. Ildico, lovelier than ever, was the perfect chatelaine. Their son, the Viscount Haven, was a most excellent child: Angus, appointed his retainer, treated him as less than an equal and worshipped him as more than a god. But his mother had had a rough passage : Sir William hoped that she would not have to take it again. Husband and wife passed the Season in Town : when that was over, like Vivien, they gloried in their release : occasional visits were paid to Break o' Day, but Poesy and Brocade made up their life. During a royal progress, Their Majesties stayed at Brocade. . . .

From Eleanor Carson's Diary.

July, 1906.

At Brocade.

The King's Postmaster and his staff arrived this morning, and an equerry and four servants soon after lunch. If Ildico was nervous, she gave no sign. Pip was the same as ever— quiet, imperturbable, sure. At a quarter past five the royal car was signalled, and they repaired to the steps. Their Majesties looked tired, and the King had his hat in his hand. Pip and Ildico received them perfectly. The house-party was in the hall, but Their Majesties passed straight through, the equerry backing before them, and entered the lift. The Queen did not reappear for nearly an hour, but the King was changed and down by a quarter to six. He would not sit on the terrace, but strolled on the lawn with Pip and Ildico. Then some of the house-party were summoned. Everything went like clockwork. Dinner was served at small tables—everything used by Their Majesties new, of course. His own sergeant-footman stood behind the King. Her Majesty was charming to me. For some remarkable reason, she knew me at once. ' Come, Miss Carson,' she cried, ' and sit and talk to me.' The next morning they went to Church, as, of course, did everyone else. It was, really, most affecting. The Vicar received them with tears running down his face, and half the older villagers were similarly moved. I admit that I wept, myself. Sir ——, the junior equerry, told me that, such was their reception at ——, almost everyone broke down. ' Hardened,' he said, ' as I am, I was in tears myself, and the chauffeurs were crying—they couldn't help themselves.' . . .

(' Wot did they want to cry for ? ' says Erny Balch. ' I
can't answer that question, Erny. I mean, I can't put it in
words that you'd understand. Let's say that their hearts
were too full.' ' But wot they got to cry about ? ' ' Sorry,
Erny. I'll have to leave it there.')

. . . *To see those two great people, the greatest in all the
world, going so naturally to Church and smiling so gently upon
the simple souls who had gathered in the churchyard, to pay their
respects, was moving, indeed. At luncheon the Vicar told the
King of old Baldrick, who had been bed-ridden for years and had
tried and failed to get up, to see Their Majesties. His Majesty
had a car out immediately after tea and went with Pip and the
Vicar to see the old man. When he came back, he drove slowly
round the park. Then he came back to the house and sent for me.
I suppose Her Majesty had reminded him. I cannot write of
this ; but, as once before, he used me like a great lady. . . .
Early on Monday morning, they took their leave. . . . And
the Queen kissed Ildico.*

*   *   *   *   *

And then, just eighteen months later, came the crash.
As Hubert was leaving the Marlborough, after an early
lunch, a clerk came up to him and lifted his hat.
" Major de Guesclin, sir ? "
" That's right," said Hubert, " and what can I do for you ? "
The clerk drew out of his pocket a legal document.
" I'm afraid I must serve you with this, sir. It's a Petition
for Divorce. Will—will you give me a receipt ? "
His brain racing, Hubert folded the sheets and put them
away, unread.
" Can't we dispense with that ? "
" Yes, if you like, sir. I have—to make the request."
Hubert nodded abruptly.
" All right."

213

The clerk raised his hat and turned, to make his way back to a cab on the opposite side of the street.

Hubert's eyes followed the youth, to meet the narrowed gaze of the man he had wronged.

"God damn all women," he murmured, between his teeth.

Then he turned on his heel and began to walk down Pall Mall.

Bitterly cold as it was, there was sweat on his face.

Realizing this, he stopped a passing cab, and told the driver to take him to Bedford Row.

Once in the cab, he took his handkerchief out and wiped his face and his throat. He did not read the Petition : he knew what it said. That damned week-end at Melton, six weeks ago. . . . Somebody'd tried the door . . . Kate had said he was wrong, but he knew he was right. . . . And then they'd waited and watched . . . to see him come out of her room. . . . Of course he'd been mad to touch her —with a jealous husband like James. But she would have it : and when he'd shaken his head, she'd given him one of her looks. . . .

"God damn all women," he cried, and his driver looked round. . . .

The de Guesclins' family solicitor saw him almost at once.

"Why, Hubert, my boy . . ."

"Look at that," said Hubert, and gave him the death-warrant.

The other adjusted his glasses . . .

Then he recoiled, staring.

"Good God, Hubert ! Not you ? "

"I assume that it bears my name."

The other read through the Petition. Then he returned to his table and took his seat.

When he spoke, he spoke with an effort.

"Whether it's true or false, we can't deal with this. I mean, we don't do divorce, and we don't know the ropes.

You must go to——" He stopped there, to look very hard at his man. "Is there anything in it, Hubert? I'm not asking you to confess: but have you been indiscreet?"

"I'm afraid I have."

The other nodded.

"You must go to Roach and Roach. I'll speak to Frederick Lacey. I know him well, and he is a first-class man."

"Shall I go straight on? I'd like to get it over."

The other regarded his palms.

"I fear you won't get it over in half an hour. Things like this entail many interviews." The lawyer got to his feet. "Come and sit in the waiting-room. I'll telephone to Lacey and see what he says."

Hubert obeyed.

After a long three minutes, the lawyer reappeared.

"Lacey's full up. Appointment after appointment. However, at my request, he'll see you at half past six. It's a great concession, Hubert: but then we're very old friends."

Hubert bit his lip.

"He can't possibly see me before? I mean . . ."

"Lacey, Hubert, is a very eminent man. He's a very nice house in Brook Street, and I happen to know that he dines at eight o'clock. To see you at half past six will mean that he's late for dinner: his wife and his guests will have to sit down without him, because he has stayed to help you. Of course, if you can wait till to-morrow . . ."

"God in heaven, no. I've got to know where I stand."

"Then we'll let the appointment be. I'm sorry I can't help you, but there it is. Divorce is not in our line. I'm simply not qualified, Hubert, to give you advice. You have my very best wishes—that you know. I confess that it's shaken me up, for you have so much to lose. And I've known you since you were born. . . . Never mind. By handing you over to Lacey, I've done my best."

Hubert put out his hand.

" I know you have, Mr. Winslow. I'm only devilish sorry to let you down. There's something the matter with me." The lawyer laid a hand on his shoulder.

" That's all right, my dear fellow. What ever happens, I'll always do what I can. And Lacey's very clever. He may be able to arrange it. But please don't do it again."

" Again, my God," said Hubert. " Just let me get clear of this . . ."

For two hours he walked the streets. Then he drove to White's and rang up his house.

Everything was cursedly awkward. The Gordons were dining at Charles Street . . . and Lady Mary and Virgil . . . and going on . . .

" Tell her ladyship that I am detained on business. I may be late, but she's not to wait for me."

Hubert had a very stiff drink and set out for Bandbox Lane. . . .

" How d'ye do, Major de Guesclin ? "

" How d'ye do ? "

" Sit down, please. May I see the document ? "

Hubert handed it over, glad enough to be rid of the loathsome thing. The other read it through. Then he looked up.

" Sir James Furlick. I take it you know the man."

" Yes. The Second Life Guards."

" What sort of fellow is he ? "

" I don't know him very well. I think he's all right. I'm bound to say he's a very jealous man."

" He has that reputation ? "

" Yes. He's not particularly attractive."

" And his wife ? "

" Oh, she's extremely attractive. Hadn't a bean."

" That's why she married him ? "

Hubert shrugged his shoulders.

" Some people have that idea."

" Of such a marriage, jealousy's often born."

" Yes."

216

" I'm not asking for guidance : I want your opinion—that's all. Do you think we can do anything with him ? "

Remembering the face in the taxi, Hubert steeled himself.

" I don't think so."

" You think that such a man will be out for blood ? "

" Yes."

Lacey nodded.

" I see. Well, I shall try and stop this. I'll see his solicitors to-morrow and put forth all my strength. It may come off. If it doesn't come off, I take it that you will defend ? "

Hubert put a hand to his head.

" I must," he said. " She'll fight it, tooth and nail."

" That's what I wanted to know. You haven't heard from her ? "

" Not yet."

" Well, you probably will. If you do, don't talk. Just give her my name and address."

" Very well."

" I've said that I'll try and stop it. I can't make bricks without straw. I'm sorry to have to ask you—but do you know anything to Sir James Furlick's discredit ? I don't care how slight is the rumour : I don't care what it may be. I don't care how distasteful this question is . . . because upon the answer your fortune may depend. Please bear that in mind. Upon this answer, your fortune may depend."

Hubert sat very still.

Then—

" He wouldn't be in ' The Tins ', if there was anything bad. There was a question once . . . about some bet. I don't know the rights. But he refused to pay up. And some people said he should have. But I think he had a case. I can't pretend that the fellow's popular. If he put up, I don't think White's would have him. That's probably why he doesn't."

Quick as a flash—

" Has his name ever been down ? "

" As a matter of fact, it has. But it was put back."

" That's what I want," said Lacey.

" You can't use that."

" Yes, I can—*out of court*. Please realize this. I've got to do my best to make him retire. The only way to do that is to show him what he may expect if he goes on. And it's you or him, you know."

" I can't help that. The fellow's within his rights. If he'll call it off, well and good. But I can't say, ' If you don't, I'm going to blacken your name.' "

Lacey regarded his nails.

" I know how you feel," he said. " It's dirty work. I don't want to do it : and if you tell me not to, it won't be done. But don't lose sight of two things. The first is this —that, unless I can stop these proceedings, your—race—is—run. You can defend, of course. But, short of an alibi—unless you can prove, for instance, that you were not in the house . . . that on the date in question you were, say, the guest of Lord Ringwood a hundred miles away—whether you win or lose, your race will be run. Innocently enough, the Press will see to that. Well, that's one thing. The second is —Lady Furlick. Whether she wins or loses, her race will be run, too. And if she loses—well, all she can *count* upon is two pounds ten a week."

" Good God ! "

" So you see, Major de Guesclin, how very much depends upon my being able to snuff it out. If I can't snuff it out, I can't ; but, unless you tell me not to, I'm going to try : and the only way I can do it is by showing Sir James the whip. Of course it's a dirty whip. That can't be helped. It won't be used in Court, because, for one thing, it wouldn't do any good : but he is not to know that."

" It smacks of blackmail," said Hubert.

" It does rather," said Lacey. " But there we are. Of course if you have an alibi——"

218

" I haven't."

" Then it's your only chance."

The conference came to an end at a quarter to eight.

Hubert felt soiled ; Lacey felt very tired : Vivien, in Charles Street, felt uneasy—something was wrong.

*   *   *   *   *

His guests were already at dinner, when Hubert came into the house.

To the servant who took his coat—

" Tell her ladyship I've come in and have gone up to dress."

" Very good, sir."

As Hubert came to the staircase, his valet was by his side.

" Excuse me, sir.   There's a message from Lady Furlick— ' Would you please ring her up the moment that you came in ? ' "

Hubert put a hand to his head.   The man was trying to think.   Was it better to get it over, or—

The thresh of the telephone-bell cut his uncertainty short.

" I rather expect that's her, sir.   She's rung up twice."

" All right," said Hubert, heavily.   " Put her through." He made for the library.   " Oh, and bring me a brandy and soda—up to my room."

" Is that you, Hubert ? "

" Yes, Kate."

" My God, I've been trying to get you since four o'clock. Hubert, I've——"

" I know," said Hubert.   " So've I."

" Oh, my God."

" Listen, Kate.   The first thing to-morrow morning——"

" Damn to-morrow morning.   We've got to do something now."

" I've already done all I can.   Until to-morrow, we can do nothing more.   At half past——"

" What have you done ? "

" I can't tell you here. The first thing to-morrow——"

" D'you want to make me scream? For more than four hours I've been trying to run you to earth. I've tried your Clubs and——"

" Christ ! " said Hubert.

" Well, what d'you expect? I've got to see you at once."

" Listen, Kate. To meet is the very thing we must not do. Surely you can see that. In a lawyer's office—yes : but not outside."

" But it mustn't come to that, Hubert."

" I hope it won't. I tell you, I've done my best. If you want to help, you'll do what I'm trying to tell you."

" What is that? "

" Have you got a pencil? . . . Then write this number down. . . . Got that? . . . Ring that number to-morrow at half past nine and say you want to speak to Mr. Lacey."

" Lacey? "

" Lacey."

" What then? "

" Well, he's a solicitor. He'll——"

" I don't *want* a solicitor, Hubert. This has got to be stopped without going to law. Some friend of yours must see J. and tell him to call it off. Why don't you get hold of Pip Ringwood? "

Hubert's blood ran cold.

" That's out of the question, Kate—you must take it from me. I'm doing all I can. If you want to help us both, you'll cover up. That's what I'm trying to do and why I must go. For God's sake do as I say, and I think that all will be well. And now goodbye."

Hubert put the receiver back and wiped the sweat from his face. . . .

Twenty minutes later, he took his seat at his table, bathed and changed.

" I'm very sorry," he said. " A friend of mine is in trouble. I've been trying to get him out."

It seemed best to go on—to the Empire . . . and later to the Savoy . . .

When he got home, Hubert felt very tired.

The slip on his chest of drawers was the last straw.

10–15 p.m. Lady Furlick would like to speak to Major de Guesclin directly he comes in. It does not matter how late.

As he laid it down, he heard from the floor below, the thresh of the telephone-bell.

*   *   *   *   *

Lacey did his utmost : Furlick's solicitors went as far as they dared ; but Sir James was adamant—because, of course, he wished to be rid of his wife : and Lady Furlick's frenzy finished what chance there was. And so appearances were entered—there was nothing else to be done. In due course, answers were filed. And then the case was set down—and the Press declared the fact.

*   *   *   *   *

Ildico never forgot the day when the news came in Brocade, and a bone in the ground : all hunting had stopped.

A letter for Philip from Vivien came by the breakfast post.

Charles Street,
February, 1908.

My darling Pip,

Remember our talk at Poesy, when you were back from S.A. ? About Hubert, I mean. Well, now the worst has happened, as, one day, I knew it would. He has been cited as co-respondent by Sir James Furlick—Furlick v. Furlick and de Guesclin. You'll see it in the paper to-morrow.

Your loving
Vivvy.

As Philip read the words, Ildico saw the blood drain out of his face.

She flew to his side.

221

" Pip, my darling, what is it ? "

Philip gave her the letter without a word.

Ildico read it through, put a hand to her head and swayed.

Philip caught her : together they passed to a sofa two or three paces away.

" Sorry. I'm all right now. What do we do, Pip ? "

" I must go to Vivvy at once."

" We'll both go to Grosvenor Square."

" All right. Will you see Warwick ? I'll get on to Foden and ask them to halt the express."

" Wires to the steward and Dennis ? "

" Yes, if you please."

" What shall we tell them here ? That Vivvy's not very well ? "

" Yes, that'll do."

All the way to London, they hammered vainly upon the cold iron of fact.

' Hubert has been cited as co-respondent.'

Philip drove straight to Charles Street : Ildico to Grosvenor Square. There Dennis Defoe and Virgil Coleton were waiting.

" No lunch ? " said Defoe.

Ildico shook her head.

" I thought as much. Sandwiches and sherry are in the library."

The three repaired there at once.

As the door closed behind them—

" Can anything be done ? "

" Nothing," said Virgil. " As soon as Hubert told Vivien, she got into touch with Dennis, who'll tell you the rest."

Dennis Defoe shrugged his shoulders.

" There's little enough to tell. Hubert had been to see Lacey of Roach and Roach. Quite the best man for the job. I got into touch with him and asked what I could do. He'd already been to see Fyfields', Furlick's solicitors. They were sympathetic, but held out little hope. He asked if Coles

222

could approach Furlick's C.O. I said I'd see Coles at once. Coles was sick, but when I told him the news, he left his bed. He went straight off to the Colonel, who promised to see Furlick and do what he could. He was as good as his word, but Furlick wouldn't give way. While all this was going on, Lady Furlick was tearing everything up—talking right and left, ceaselessly ringing up Hubert, making scenes at Lacey's and generally doing her worst. And now the balloon's gone up."

Ildico bit her lip.

" This is the end ? " she said.

" Of Hubert and Vivien—yes."

" Whichever way it goes ? "

" From what Lacey tells me—yes."

Tears began to trickle down Ildico's cheeks. . . .

Philip appeared two hours later.

" Miss Carson's with her," he said. " But she'd like to see you. Fairing Over, to-morrow—she only waited for us. She's perfectly calm and simply wonderful."

On the following day, the Ringwoods returned to Brocade.

*　　*　　*　　*　　*

' The way of transgressors is hard.' Hubert was spared nothing. All his life he had taken the line of least resistance : now he was forced to fight a sordid, losing battle under the banner of bad form. To defend the case was the last thing he wanted to do : but Lady Furlick insisted—and how could he let her down ?

The crash was complete. Some people would, of course, have sought to carry things off. Not so the de Guesclins. Such a course never entered their heads. From the moment the case was set down, they knew that, as Lacey had put it, their race was run. Could they have done so, they would have retired then and there. What turned the iron in their souls was that they *had* to keep going until the case was heard. This, again, of course, for Lady Furlick's sake.

Six months of misery.

The case was heard in July. I need hardly say that it was a *cause célèbre*. I need hardly add that Sir James obtained his divorce.

Hubert sent in his papers, resigned from all his Clubs. About that there was no question. The man could do nothing else—in 1908. After a talk with Vivien, Charles Street was put up for sale. Then Hubert went abroad, and Vivien sat at Poesy, thankful for many mercies, far more sorry for Hubert than for herself, talking hardly at all, but thinking, for some strange reason, of Sally of the Mill.

*　　*　　*　　*　　*

From Eleanor Carson's Diary.

7th August, 1908.

Poesy.

I see it is nearly three weeks since I wrote down anything. I feel as though I had been hit over the heart. Everything is over now ; and one day, I suppose, this hideous nightmare will fade. Darling Vivien is simply wonderful. From first to last—and I have been with her constantly—she has never said a word against Hubert, although he has wrecked her life. Indeed, she is always saying, ' It isn't so bad for me : but it'll break Hubert's heart. You see, he's lost everything that matters—Regiment, Clubs, his Town and country life.' When I said, ' He's got his friends.' ' Thousands,' she said. ' I should think more people like Hubert than any man in the world. But he won't let them touch him : they are his friends, and he's not going to let them down. I think you know that I begged him to stay with me. But he only said very quietly, " I've done enough harm." ' I cannot think what she will do : I don't think she knows herself. She is going to visit her Mother, in Paris, next month. After that, I suppose, Fairing Over. Pip and Ildico are coming on Tuesday next. They would have come before, but she wanted to be alone. Poor Lady Ursula is shattered—but carries on.

224

*For the first time she looks an old lady. I daresay I do, too.
I feel one any way.*

Divorce has become so common that it bears no longer the
stigma that once it did : but in 1908 to have figured in the
Divorce Court meant, not, perhaps, social extinction, but a
definite degradation—a stern reduction in rank. A great
many doors were closed, as a matter of course. What was
almost worse, there were flung open other doors, through
which the de Guesclins would sooner have died than pass.
Vivien was so much beloved that, she could, I firmly believe,
have weathered the storm. But nothing on earth would
have ever induced her to try. She never would have accepted
the loyalty she could have had. And everyone knew as
much, because they knew her.

A note from the Duchess of Brooch shall speak for itself.

My very dear Vivien,
*It does not seem long to me since I saw you first—at Brocade,
with your hair down your back. It was clear to me then that,
when the time came, you would have an immense success. Well,
you have had it, my dear : I cannot remember a more outstanding
triumph or one that lasted so long. And now that particular
triumph is over and done. I am grieved at the way in which it
was brought to an end : but nothing can ever dim it, and you
may be proud of the memory all your life. You will know,
better than I, how you should use the years which lie before you.
All I know is that you will use them well. But don't do as
Rachel has done. We couldn't bear that.*

Yours always affectionately,
Harriet B.

*   *   *   *   *

Three years had gone by, and another King had been
crowned.

Hubert was still over seas. Never leaving Europe, he

passed from town to town, avoiding those places to which old friends might resort. The motor-car was his stand-by : he played much golf : his acquaintance became very wide ; and he never touched a woman, except in the dance.

He wrote to Vivien humbly from time to time.

Quite early on—

> . . . *If ever you want to divorce me, you've only to say the word. I've found out all about it. This is desertion, you see, so you've got your case. You shouldn't have married me, Vivvy : I'm not up to your standard, and never was* . . .

Nothing that Vivien could say would bring him back.

> . . . *Sorry, my darling, but I have done enough harm. The least I can do is to keep out of the picture. Besides* . . .

'Besides.' No Regiment, no Clubs, no entrée. Vivien knew what he meant.

She herself had kept out of the picture for three full years, seldom visiting London, sometimes visiting Paris, but making her home in the country for months on end. She was, of course, free of Poesy and Brocade, but seldom visited either if Philip and Ildico were there. Lady Vivien of Fairing Over . . . devoting herself to her children, boy and girl. 'Huffy' was now at Harrow—with Hubert's consent : he was to follow his uncle into the Blues. Rachel Ursula—'Sully'— eleven years old, had all her mother's looks and much of her charm. And since it was clear that ' the children ' were growing up, Vivien decided to enter the picture again.

I cannot pretend that it did not cost her dear : but Vivien never shrank from the duty she had to do.

In August a garden-party was held at Brocade. And Vivien was there. It was her first appearance since 1908.

She need have had no fear. Old friends crowded about her, speaking their hearts.

The Duchess of Brooch embraced her and made her sit by her side.

226

"My dearest girl, this gives an old woman great pleasure. How wise you are and how very well you have done. Will you come to lunch at the Castle?"

"I will, if you ask me, Duchess."

"That's the style. Tell me your secret, Vivien. How did you know the moment at which to come back?"

"I shall never come back, Duchess. I've only picked up my bit."

"Don't make me want to cry. Let's gossip, instead. Now that his Uncle's dead, the vulgar German thinks he has nothing to fear. I didn't like his manner, when he was over this year. The fellow was condescending—made my blood boil. Edward Grey is charming and conscientious : we need a Palmerston, who was neither. Winston continues to be unpopular : but he isn't afraid of talking about sows' cars, while everybody else talks about silk purses. I saw the Queen Mother in June, and she brought your name up. She spoke of you, Vivien, most sweetly. . . . Well, come to lunch on Tuesday—I'll speak to Ildico."

Half an hour later—

"You don't remember me, Lady Vivien."

Vivien surveyed a very good-looking man.

"Yes, I do," she said. "The Eton and Harrow match."

"Well done, indeed," said Rivers. "I was at Oxford then. I knew your brother at Harrow : he brought me up to the coach."

"A long time ago. I've never seen you since."

"I've been over seas. I was in the Indian Civil. I liked the Army better and made the change."

Vivien raised her eyebrows.

"But you came home on leave."

"Very seldom. You see, I came in late and I had to make up for lost time. In fact, you're talking to a ranker."

"I give you best. It must have been a hard row to hoe."

"It was, rather. But I'm Captain and Adjutant now, and I love the life."

" Why did you change over ? "

" The Boer War finished me. I naturally wanted to go, but I ' couldn't be spared '. I wasn't prepared to let that happen again."

" D'you think it would have happened again ? "

" Yes."

" How do you come to be here ? "

" I'm staying with Hinton, your Master. And Lady Ringwood said he could bring me along."

" Where is he ? I'd like to see him. He remembers me when my hair was down my back."

" So do I," said Rivers.

" Oh, no. I had my hair up at the Eton and Harrow match."

" I remember you at Harrow. That's where I saw you first."

" I never met you."

" Oh, no. But I saw you there. You were on the steps of Bill Yard, and snow was beginning to fall."

" That's right. It was bitterly cold. And the master——"

" Whose name was Wilson."

" Oh, I give up," said Vivien. . . .

Cubbing in late September. Rivers and Vivien were out.

" I'm going back on Friday."

" Back to India, you mean ? "

" That's right, Lady Vivien. I don't know how you're placed. But I've been in love with you for nineteen years, and I think I should be a fool if I didn't tell you so. Please don't think I'm presuming : I know my place. But I've got a job to do. I can't stay here and see what my lady does."

Vivien sat very still.

" Is this a proposal of marriage ? "

" It would be, if you were free."

" I see. How many times have you seen me ? "

" Seven times," said Rivers, " and five of them here. But once was enough."

228

"I see. Well, I'll give you this. I've never forgotten you. I may forget you yet. I shall never divorce my husband, and I am fancy-free. But since we are such old friends, I think you may write to me. . . ."

"Thank you very much," said Rivers—and meant what he said.

* * * * *

That night, in her room—

"I like him, Pricket," said Vivien. "Years ago in this room I told you so. You don't remember that."

"I can't say I do, my lady."

"Nevertheless, I did. I liked the look of him then and I like him now. He's quiet and dignified : and he never presumes. And you must admit he's faithful. What about nineteen years ? "

"If you would be happy, my lady."

"It hasn't got so far. I'm badly placed, Pricket. I've every right to be free : and yet, you know, I can't let the Major down."

"But he won't come back, my lady."

"I know. It's very awkward. I'm not in the market, and yet I'm not a wife. Don't think I'm in love with Captain Rivers, because I'm not. But I like him—very much. And he has opened my eyes. He's rammed home my position— which is that I am in balk. Well, what do we do about it ? I'm damned if I know."

"It isn't fair," cried Pricket. "You're half a saint, my lady, an' always were. You 'ave behaved most perfect. Everything taken away, an' you've never so much as kicked. And here you are, a widow. That's what you are. A widow. It isn't right, my lady. If Captain Rivers suits you . . . I don't know about these things, but it isn't fair or right that you should go on like this."

"It'd mean leaving Fairing Over."

"A lot I'd care. I never did like the place. Poesy or Brocade, I feel at 'ome."

"I can't cut the Major out."

"You can, if you like—to-morrow."

"I know. But I can't do that. He's—paid enough."

"Think of yourself, my lady."

"I think I'm beginning to, Pricket. Don't rush me. I know best."

*　　*　　*　　*　　*

Vivien wrote to Hubert that autumn.

> . . . *I'm not at all sure that I can go on like this. Frankly, it isn't natural. If you will come back, we'll take up our life again. Of course, it will have to be a different life. But it shouldn't be too bad. Things are easier now. I'm going about a little, and people are terribly nice. I'm sure they'd be glad to see you. Of course, it can't be the same—I can't pretend that. But we can live quietly together, if that's any use to you. . . . I shouldn't write like this, if I shouldn't be very happy to have you back . . .*

An answer came from Vienna.

> . . . *I'm better out of the way. If I came back, I should only cramp your style. If you want a divorce, it's yours. Just go to Defoe . . .*

After a lot of thought, Vivien went to Defoe.

"You are in order, Vivien. Hubert declines to return. You can have a divorce to-morrow, if you wish."

"Must the—the other business be raked up?"

Defoe raised his eyebrows.

"It will have to be proved."

"What do you mean by that?"

"It will have to be mentioned in Court. Evidence must

be given that he was the co-respondent when Furlick obtained his decree."

" And I should have to appear ? "

" Yes."

" The Press would get hold of it ? "

" Yes. They'd probably splash it. They wouldn't have much to splash."

" They'd splash the old business ? "

" I'm bound to say they might."

" That's all right, Dennis. I come to you for the truth."

" May I offer you my opinion ? "

" Of course."

" Then I should do it, Vivien. I know it would be an ordeal. But it would be very short. I quite agree that memories would be jogged. The Clubs would talk about it —for two or three days. And then the little sensation would fade and die. And please remember this. Everyone knows your history : and everyone who sees you remembers what's gone before. They don't have to read the papers, to be reminded that Hubert smashed your life. So the fact that you are doing the natural thing will make no difference at all. You go to the theatre, and people see you there. ' There's Lady Vivien de Guesclin. She's never divorced him, has she ? I wonder why.' Don't think I'm being brutal. I want you to face the facts. Nothing can touch the position you'll always have. And in divorcing Hubert, you're doing the natural thing."

Vivien nodded.

" Thank you very much. I'll try to see it that way."

" Well, think it well over, Vivien. You've been more than fair to Hubert. Be fair to yourself."

" I will—and I'll let you know."

But, though she heard from Rivers and wrote in reply, she could not bring herself to seek a divorce. She had no religious scruples : she just disliked the idea.

*   *   *   *   *

Three more years went by, and the sands ran out. The golden bowl was broken, the silver cord was loosed—and all to serve the envy of a less happier land. Few knew that these things had happened, that very soon the mourners would go about the streets. The English may be forgiven. Not for ninety-nine years had they had cause to consider a European war. And then, with the bound of a beast, the terror was at their throat. They were, of course, elated. Danger will always elate the Englishman. Whether they lived or died meant nothing to them. They knew that, whatever befell, England would live. Misfortune was nothing at all. It didn't count. Little wonder that Fate recoiled. . . .

But there were other things they did not know. They did not know that the way of English life had come to an end . . . that, ere the war was over, English would look English up and down. That exercise had always been reserved for foreigners.

It came upon us in the twinkling of an eye. One day Hubert was at Como . . . the next at Paris . . . the next at Buckingham Gate . . .

Nobody knew it was the end . . . the end of Merrie England. . . . If I may borrow from one far greater than I, ' Tipperary ' was the national anthem of a *fait accompli*.

* * * * *

Somewhere in France.
November, 1914.

My darling Vivvy,
I've never loved you so much. This is the real thing. I'm up to my knees in mud, but I don't care a damn. This is the real thing. South Africa was a Bank Holiday. This is it. I've found my metier *at last. I never was so happy in all my life. The men are wonderful. And, being wonderful, we always win. If anything ever goes wrong, they always send for us. And we've never failed them yet. We're right on top, Vivvy. We've*

232

got the Boche where he belongs. He knows that, and we know it. It may take a little time, but we've won the war. I don't care how long it goes on—we've won the war. And, by God, this is the life. Doing something worth doing. Smashing the swine that meant to get us down. I tell you, we've learned them, Vivvy. They don't like us. They're ten to one, all right; but they can't get through. St. George for Merrie England. Honestly, Vivvy, it is the most glorious life. Rough, hard, savage. I haven't had my clothes off for thirteen days. I think I'm lousy, Vivvy. But it's the real thing. The thing that men were made for. The thing that I was made for, any way. Beating the Hun.

God bless you, darling,

Hubert.

December, 1914.

Dear Lady Vivien,

Your husband died gloriously. There is no other word. He and his splendid company fought to the death. God knows what it cost the Germans to gain that piece of ground. But, when at last they had gained it, they had not the strength to go on. So the situation was saved. Major de Guesclin is the most fearful loss. He was so debonair. His gaiety was infectious: nobody could be gloomy when he was about. His confidence lifted you up. When the Brigadier heard he was killed, he put his head in his hands. ' He was worth a battalion,' he said— and so he was. I think he will be awarded the Victoria Cross. No man deserved it better. Few men so well.

With my deepest sympathy,

Believe me, dear Lady Vivien,

Yours very sincerely,

———

The citation set all hearts throbbing.

By his magnificent death, Hubert de Guesclin wiped his escutcheon clean.

No man dared to remember that he had once put a foot

wrong : all men thanked their God upon every remembrance of such a warrior.

So Vivien had her reward.

His Majesty wrote to the widow in his own hand. The past was blotted out. A gentleman of England had died in the great tradition ; and the honourable name of de Guesclin would live for evermore.

Part Three

'WHAT'S TO COME IS STILL UNSURE'

THE WAR was over and done: eighteen months had gone by since the last shot was fired. People were still 'letting go'. After all, it had been a famous victory.

Lady Vivien de Guesclin was forty-four. No one would have believed this. She looked a young thirty-five. For her children's sake, she now had a house in South Street, at which, again for their sake, she spent more time than she liked. But Sully was twenty and Huffy was twenty-two. The latter had seen active service for eighteen fearful months, had gained the M.C., had been severely wounded a week before fighting stopped. The former cared for her brother more than for anyone else. The two were always together and, in post-war London, were having the time of their lives. Their mother watched them contentedly. Lady Vivien de Guesclin had had her day.

Colonel the Earl of Ringwood had spent four years in the field. And that, in France. He had done very well—that splendid type of soldier on whom all men may count. Tireless, resolute, cheerful, from general to trooper, he never let any man down. He richly deserved his C.B. and the bar to his D.S.O. Constantly in the front line, for some astounding reason he never received a scratch: but his splendid constitution had been undermined: overwork, exposure and strain had seen to that. To Vivien's and Ildico's distress, he looked a man of fifty, although he was forty-two. The Viscount Haven was at Harrow: to his father's delight, his cricket was very good. One more year, and he would be seen at Lord's.

Rachel, Countess of Ringwood, was killed, so to speak, in action, towards the end of the war: a bomb had been dropped on the hospital which she controlled. The news of her death was the end of her sister-in-law. Coles Willing was dead, too. The leases were falling in. Only Miss Carson remained, moving between the great houses, as and when she was desired.

The pound was not worth a sovereign : expenses, however, were higher than they had ever been. Vivien was all right—so far : for she had Hubert's fortune as well as her own. But Philip was badly placed. Brocade and Poesy ate money. He flatly refused to raise rents or dismiss any staff. ' It isn't their fault, Dennis.' And wages and pensions were raised, while the income fell. After deep reflection, Grosvenor Square had been sold, and the staff absorbed or pensioned. A flat in Arlington Street served Philip's and Ildico's turn.

Rodney had returned to Brocade ' for the duration of the war ' : he had been invaluable : but, when the war was over, he had again retired. Philip, more tired than his agent, had taken over his job. Leith's nephew was dealing with Poesy ; but he was not like Leith.

In February, 1921, Philip, then at Brocade, contracted a chill. . . . Three days later, a notice appeared in *The Times*. ' The Earl of Ringwood is lying seriously ill with pneumonia at his Somersetshire seat.'

After ten frightening days, the weary specialist smiled.

" It's all right, now, Lady Ringwood. He's in the straight. You can take rooms at Brighton and say that he will arrive one month from to-day."

Ildico was past speaking. Vivien replied.

" Let's all have a glass of sherry." She poured the wine. " My sister-in-law and I would like to drink your health. You see, we owe you rather more than our lives."

" Thank you very much," said Landon. " But the nurses and the patient have done as much as I. Never mind. He's going to get well. But this I am bound to say—that from now on he must take care. It's a rotten thing to say of a

238

man of forty-two. No man likes 'taking care of himself' And it's very hard to begin at forty-two. But his constitution was undermined by the War. He'll never regain the resistance he used to have. Let me give you an example—unless the weather's set fair, he must never hunt. That is because, if ever he should get wet, he must immediately change. If you hunt, you can't do that. I'm very sorry indeed to issue orders like this : but I shouldn't be doing my duty, unless I did. To be perfectly honest, I'd like him to winter abroad." Ildico bit her lip. "Well, that isn't an order. I don't say he's got to—yet. But another go like this, and he'll *have* to winter abroad if he wants to survive. But, honestly, if he doesn't, there will be many days when he must be confined to the house. I'll write all this down, of course. The point is—you needn't worry. Lord Ringwood's going to get well. He's going to be as well as ever he was. But from now on, he's got to take care."

So the expenses mounted. Not fit to go out in all weathers, Philip was forced to have agents at Poesy and Brocade. The fact hit him hard. He had always meant to run the estates himself.

* * * * *

Rivers had behaved very well.

Although he had written to Vivien, not once had he asked her to meet him throughout the war. And now at last he wrote from the 'In and Out'.

> *Naval and Military Club,*
> *Piccadilly,*
> *April, 1921.*

My dear Lady Vivien,

When I read your husband's citation, I knew that I must retire. For no man could dare to pretend to such a throne. I felt as everyone felt—that a king among men had fallen . . . and kings can do no wrong. That is how I feel now. Still,

239

I should love to see you. Perhaps we could be friends. After twenty-one years' service, five of them in the ranks, I have retired. Times are changing, you know : and I shall be too old, when the next war comes. And so I have made the break. May I suggest, very humbly, that I should give you lunch at the Ritz? Any day, of course. If you would rather not, I shall quite understand.

Yours very sincerely,
John Elvin Rivers.
Lt.-Col.

South Street.
Mayfair.

Dear Colonel Rivers,
  I can do better than that. Come and lunch here on Friday and we can talk. I think it's natural that I should feel much as you do. I think that is all the more reason why we should be friends.

Yours very sincerely,
Vivien de Guesclin.

So, twenty-eight years and more from the day he had found her so lovely, Rivers lunched *tête-à-tête* with the lady he loved.

Coffee was served in a pleasant drawing-room.

The two had much to talk of ; many things had happened since they had met at Brocade.

At last—

"I sometimes wonder," said Vivien, "if any woman has ever found herself in such a strange position as mine to-day. I was the injured party, and I had every right to put my husband away and marry again. I didn't choose to do that. By his death, he sets me free—and binds me far more surely than I was bound before. For six long years he dared not fly his flag : now it's my privilege to fly it : de Guesclin's a name that the world would be proud to bear. How on earth can I put it off? I couldn't look my son in the face."

240

"I entirely agree," said Rivers. "Others have won the V.C.; but the show your husband put up—well, it ranks with Agincourt."

Vivien began to laugh.

"It's really rather funny," she said. "Hubert clasping about me a girdle of chastity. Of course, you never knew him. He was the most splendid fellow. He really was. The most attractive man I have ever seen. But women could play with him. That was his only fault."

"No decent woman did."

"No. No decent woman. But I'm not throwing stones. He was immensely attractive : and there are women who cannot help themselves. Any way, all of this is beside the point. I can accept no addresses, because I march under a banner I cannot desert."

Rivers nodded.

"I quite see that," he said. And then—"I take it we can be friends."

"Of course we can," said Vivien. "I'd like to be friends with you. So long as you are content to be nothing more. . . ."

"Half a loaf," said Rivers. "Now will you lunch at the *Ritz* ?"

"Whenever you please. Have you called on Lady Ringwood ?"

"Not yet, I'm afraid. They've given up Grosvenor Square."

"Yes, they've got a flat now—in Arlington Street. The point is this. Pip and his wife and I—and one or two more, form a sort of coterie. I think it might suit you. We see a good deal of each other. I'm ready to put you up."

"That's very handsome," said Rivers. "I'd like to belong."

"Well, go and leave a card. I'll pave the way."

Rivers was readily accepted. When all was said and done, he was a most charming man. More. Before the war, his family place had been sold, and all he had was a suite in the *Albany* : yet he was country-bred. Before the year was out, he was helping Vivien and Philip to run their three estates.

* * * * *

By 1922 the post-war world was getting into its stride. Life was very much changed. Standards were lower, and money was everything. The gap between rich and poor was far more pronounced. In thousands of cases wishes had become horses and beggars rode. *Amour propre* was not encouraged : ' the constant service of the antique world ' was derided : the age of false values was in. All ranks were demanding a luxury never before conceived : entertainment took pride of place : extravagance knew no law.

Lady Caserne's parties were a sign of the times : the frantic endeavours to obtain invitations to these were unbelievable : that they were very good parties, I cannot deny : Sir George was a millionaire, and Lady Caserne ' knew her onions '—and more than that : she had been Mrs. Connie Welham. . . .

Fine ladies were clad by contract : some paid Paris *couturiers* ten thousand pounds a year : in return, they were perfectly dressed ; their furs were their own affair.

Drunkenness in public was pardoned : Clubs became much less exclusive : divorce was nothing accounted : the young attended dances to which they had not been asked : elderly craftsmen saw themselves begging their bread.

Philip, shocked and bewildered, held to the old way of life and came less and less to Town : Vivien, neither shocked nor bewildered, kept very much to herself, regretting the onset of manners to which she could not subscribe. After all, there was nothing to be done.

* * * * *

It was two o'clock in the morning, and Vivien, safe in bed, was regarding the ' golden girl ' who sat on its foot.

" And Huffy ? "

" He went on with the Cockburns. They'll probably finish up at a coffee-stall."

Vivien smiled.

" I used to think I could go."

" Darling Mummy, we started where you left off."

" That's right. I think you did."

" They call it progress," said Sully, and swung her legs off the floor and under the quilt. " I love having you to come back to."

" That's not progress," said Vivien. " That's reaction."

Her daughter shook her fair head.

" No, it's just you. Are you tired, or can I talk ? "

Vivien glanced at her clock.

" I'm not tired, but I want you to get to bed. Let's say a quarter of an hour."

" That'll do. I—want to be married, Mummy."

Vivien's heart missed a beat.

" Oh, Sully ! Must you, darling ? "

" Yes," said Sully, slowly. " I think I must."

" All right," said Vivien, quietly. " Who is the man ? "

" Ballachulish."

Vivien felt ready to faint. The Marquess of Ballachulish had only one fault—he was impossible. Young, rich, well-bred, he looked like a Greek god. He was, without doubt, the handsomest man in Town. When he rode, he seemed to be part of his horse. Virgil called him ' The Statue '—and that, I think, is as near as I can get. He had no sense of humour—had never been seen to smile. Not that he was a dummy : he certainly said very little, but, then, there are silent men. But when Ballachulish spoke, what he said was not to the point. . . . He had received his Commission in 1912, but, to his fury, had never been sent over seas : no one who knew him would have him : the man was not safe.

More of instinct than anything else—

" I'd never have thought," said Vivien, " that you would choose him."

To condemn the man would be fatal : the only chance was to make him cut his own throat.

" I know. But I—love him, Mummy."

" Then that's all right."

" People don't understand him, Mummy. He's inarticulate."

" I'm sure you can loosen his tongue. And Scotland's all right."

" We shan't be there all the time."

" Of course you won't. And I'm sure he'll make a good husband. But you are so gay, my sweet : and he is—rather serious."

" That's how he's born, darling."

" I know. It's a very good fault. But I don't want to see you damped down."

" If I pipe, I think he'll respond."

" He'd be a strange man if he didn't. Ring him up to-morrow and tell him to come to lunch."

" You're very sweet to me, Mummy."

" Don't be silly, my darling. I'm doing the normal thing."

Vivien was out the next morning, before her daughter was up.

The first call she made was on Philip and Ildico.

When she told them the news—

" God Almighty," said Philip. And then, " She must be mad."

" Put it that way if you like—she's sorry for him."

" Everyone's sorry for him. I'm sorry for him, myself. But his brain has adhesions. Sully can't possibly marry a man like that."

" She won't," said Vivien. " We've got to show him up."

" And how ? " said Ildico.

" By being ourselves," said Vivien. " You're coming to lunch. And I'm going to collect Virgil. A family party is natural. And by his reactions to us, Ballachulish himself will open Sully's eyes. If we say a word against him, she'll stick

244

in her toes. The only chance we've got is for her to see him in the setting to which she belongs."

"But, Vivien darling, she can have no idea. She's only seen him in Town. I've seen him at Gorm." Ildico drew in her breath. "Gorm itself would silence the most frivolous tongue. The place is a fortress—as it has always been. Compared with Gorm, Elsinore was a night-club. But Ballachulish doesn't see that. Gorm, to him, is perfection. Seventeen Dukes of Tulse have stalked on those ramparts and lain in those ancient rooms. And that is enough for him. At Gorm, he's at home—and he does as his fathers did. His air is that of a mediæval sovereign: he never addresses a servant—he looks or points. Sully could never stand it—nobody could. I mean, Gorm by itself is frightening: I was there for lunch and it made me feel ill. But add Ballachulish to it . . . The man's not normal, Vivvy."

Vivien nodded.

"If you ask me, I think he's mad. Not fit to be certified, but mad. But we've got to be careful. Pity's harder to deal with than love itself. So just forget him to-day, and be yourselves."

Virgil Coleton was strolling opposite Friary Court.

As he sank back on the cushions by Vivien's side—

"I can't remember when you've sent out an S.O.S. Which is it, Huffy or Sully?"

"Sully desires to marry Ballachulish."

Virgil closed his eyes and fingered his chin.

"I see. *Pitié a l'amour*: rather like *café au lait*. What will these dear little rogues be thinking of next? And if you venture to say, ' D'you think you're wise?' I suppose it'll be all over. And so we elders and betters—and make no mistake about that—have got to put on an act . . . which will demonstrate to Sully the suicidal nature of the action she proposes to take. I mean, if she must be a wardress, Colney Hatch is more convenient than Gorm. And she would get afternoons off."

" You said ' an act '," said Vivien.

" Discourse," said Virgil.

" A family lunch," said Vivien, " at one o'clock to-day. Ballachulish is coming. And Pip and Ildico. So Sully will see him against a background of us. If that doesn't open her eyes . . ."

" If the child is normal, it will. But don't forget that Pity is blinder than Love."

" There are times when I hate you," said Vivien.

" Sorry, my sweet. I'll do my very best. But these young things enrage me. Sully's adorable. I'd give my life for Sully any day of the week. But when she behaves like this, I could let her go hang. I mean it's such damned nonsense. ' Reformation of the Sawdust King.' Who wants to reform a robot? Who's such a fool as to try? Of course I'll come to lunch, and I'll do my best : but I'm very cross with Sully for worrying you."

Vivien took his arm and held it close.

" I believe I should have married you, Virgil, a good many years ago."

" I'm sure you should have," said Virgil. " And I'll tell you another thing—no daughter of ours would have looked at Ballachulish."

" Ah, my dear," said Vivien : " but perhaps no Ballachulish would have looked at a daughter of ours."

Virgil smiled and nodded.

" There's something in that."

" But what about luncheon ? " said Vivien.

" If we are ourselves, Ballachulish will cut his own throat. He's bad enough touching bottom : but when he's out of his depth, he—well, he takes precedence."

" Good God," said Vivien.

" I've seen him do it, my dear. But we mustn't be too hearty. You see what I mean. Nothing forced. For if we are, the child will take his side and say he was weighted out."

" I depend upon you," said Vivien.

246

"That's easy," said Virgil: "but you're his hostess and you've got to call the tune."

"No, we shouldn't have married," said Vivien. "No woman can stand a husband who's always right."

For more than thirty years, Virgil, old for his age, had been a man about Town. It follows that he had acquired a very considerable knowledge of manners and modes. Let us say that he 'knew his stuff'. Dowagers, débutantes, die-hards and *nouveaux riches*—he could assess them more surely than almost anyone else. He knew them all. He knew their virtues and failings: he knew their outlooks on life: he could deal with them as he pleased, because he knew the cards they were going to play. He could have reduced Ballachulish within two minutes of time. But such a display would have done more harm than good. If Sully was to be saved, Ballachulish had got to reduce himself.

Of course the dice were loaded: but Vivien's luncheon-party was not to the Marquess's taste. Manners were much too easy. When Ringwood addressed the butler, he called him by name: Lady Ringwood and Sully were sparring, as if they had been the same age: Lady Vivien was talking of 'pink champagne'. Only Virgil Coleton seemed to know how to behave. . . .

Virgil was very skilful. He toned affability down and, when opportunity offered, took Ballachulish's side. Sully could have embraced him for helping her lover out. And then, for no reason, her lover was 'scrapping with' Virgil and, what was a hundred times worse, was looking at Virgil as lords used to look at commoners two hundred years ago. She had, of course, no idea that Virgil had led her lover out of his depth. . . . So Ballachulish became the heir to the dukedom of Tulse. His superiority complex became most marked. He was rude to Philip, off-hand with Ildico. He was coldly civil to Vivien. Virgil, he simply ignored. A squirming Sully was ready to die of shame. . . . Suddenly she became angry. Who was this half-baked Scotsman to

247

treat her family so? Her mother, her uncle, her aunt and Cousin Virgil. . . . What was his father's record, compared with theirs? The Duke of Tulse was a skin-flint—that was his title to fame. But her father's title to fame was rather better than that. Hubert de Guesclin, V.C. And he had died in France . . . but neither the Duke nor the Marquess had ever been over seas. . . . And what of Colonel Lord Ringwood, D.S.O. and bar . . .? Sully began to wonder what sort of a fool she had been.

Ballachulish might have been trusted to drive the nail home. Before he had tasted his coffee, he said he was playing polo and had to be gone. Stiffly, he took his leave.

Then he turned to Sully.

"You'll come with me?"

"No," said Sully. "I—can't."

"A man's game," said Ballachulish. . . .

Sully gave him two minutes' law and fled to her room.

As the door closed behind her—

"What did I say?" said Virgil. "Your daughter is cured."

"No doubt about that," said Vivien. "Well, thank you all very much. It's been a most unpleasant experience; but I know you don't mind that, because Sully is saved."

"Not unpleasant," said Ildico. "Illuminating. ' The study of mankind is man.' "

"I entirely agree," said Virgil. "It interested me very much. I imagine it's in-breeding. The man's a border-line case."

"To you, the glory," said Philip. "I never saw a hand so beautifully played."

"Easy enough," said Virgil. "I'd stacked the pack."

Ildico had to be gone. She had an appointment in Sloane Street at three o'clock. Virgil left with her . . .

The butler was speaking.

"Your ladyship would like a taxi?"

Ildico stared.

248

" Isn't the car outside ? "

The butler started. Then—

" The—the Marquess took it, my lady."

Ildico put a hand to her head.

" But I don't understand," she said.

" The Marquess took it, my lady : to drive to Hurlingham."

" The Marquess of Ballachulish took my car ? "

" I'm afraid so, my lady. Peters, I think, assumed . . ."

" Of course he did," said Virgil. " Summon a taxi, Bateman. And tell Peters to go to Sloane Street, as soon as he reappears."

" Very good, sir."

Virgil turned to Ildico, still looking something dazed.

" The Parthian shaft," he said. " I must tell Pip and Vivien." He whipped upstairs, opened the drawing-room door and put in his head. " The Most Honourable Marquess," he said, " has taken Ildico's Rolls. Told Peters to drive to Hurlingham. Peters, of course, complied. So Ildico's taking a taxi to go to Sloane Street."

Vivien and Philip began to shriek with laughter.

* * * * *

Six weeks later, Sully became engaged to Captain Enderby-Lowe, the second son of Lord Fastnet, a bosom friend of Huffy's and a most charming man. The two were married at Fairing—quietly enough, for September was nearly out. But Summer hung on for them. It was the daintiest wedding Miss Carson had ever seen.

And then, within the year, Huffy must have his bite.

A brilliant July morning—and the South Street telephone went.

" Is that you, Mummy ? Will you be in to tea ? "

" I shall, my darling. But tea ? You're sure you're well ? "

" I'm bringing someone to see you. Could you be ' not-at-home ' to anyone else ? "

Vivien's heart sank.

" I could and will," she said. " Somewhere about half past four ? "

" That'll be fine, Mummy darling."

" Goodbye, my sweet."

Vivien sat back and stared at the telephone.

" Oh, hell and all angels," she murmured. " Huffy's going to produce an impossible future wife. What is the matter with these babies ? We never did things like this."

She picked the receiver up . . .

Mrs. Enderby-Lowe was out.

Vivien rang up Virgil.

" Yes, my dear ? "

" I want to get hold of Blue Boy. Could you locate him, Virgil, and tell him to ring me up ? "

Virgil groaned.

" The telephone," he said, " is the most bestial invention of a most bestial bunch. I hate it more every day. Never mind. I'll do my best. Shall I try his tailor's first ? "

" I'm terribly sorry, dear. But, old as I am, I decline to ring up a man's Club."

" Thank God for that. ' How far that little candle throws his beams ! ' Will any time do ? "

" As long as it's before four."

" I think, perhaps, I'd better try the hairdresser's first. All right, Silvia. Poor old Dobbin will do the best he can."

Enderby-Lowe rang up at a quarter to one.

" You want me, Lady Vivien ? "

" Yes, Blue Boy, I do. Listen. Who's Huffy fallen for ? "

There was a long silence.

At length—

" Are you there ? " said Vivien.

" Yes, I'm here all right," said Blue Boy.

" Then what's the trouble, my dear ? I mean you're telling no tales. He's bringing the lady to tea at half past four."

" Oh, my God," said Blue Boy.

250

" As bad as that, is it ? Well, be a sport and put me out of my pain. Besides, if I am forearmed, I'll have a better chance of breaking it up."

" Have you seen *Let Go*, Lady Vivien ? "

" Three times," said Vivien. " Once with you and Huffy, once——"

" So you did. Well, I don't know, but Huffy's been taking the leading lady about."

" Not Orley Mantlet ? "

" That's right."

" But, Blue Boy——"

" I know. I think he's bewitched. But there you are."

" D'you mean to say she's coming this afternoon ? "

" If Huffy's bringing someone, I can't think of anyone else."

" Oh, my God," said Vivien.

" I'm most dreadfully sorry, Lady Vivien."

" Dear Blue Boy, that's all right. I wanted to know. And now let's go and have lunch. I'm going to have a cocktail."

" So'm I. I'll drink your health."

" Thank you, darling. Don't forget dinner to-morrow."

" Not likely," said Blue Boy. " Goodbye."

After lunch, Vivien rang up Defoe.

" I want you to help me, Dennis. The thing is this . . ."
The lawyer listened intently. Vivien was one of those women who know their own minds.

At length—

" I'll do my best," he said.

Twenty minutes later, he telephoned back . . .

At three, Vivien took the car and went for a drive. She took care to be back by four. Except to ' Master Huffy ', she was not at home. At five and twenty to five Huffy appeared.

" Meet Miss Mantlet, Mummy. She's more than a friend."

" How d'ye do, Miss Mantlet? You have my great admiration—have had my great admiration for more than a year."

Miss Mantlet sighed and sat down.

" You're much too good, Lady Vivien. When all is said and done, I only play up."

" Not everybody does that. You've made a big success."

" I do think they like me."

" I've been to see you three times, and I'm hard to please."

" That's very sweet, Lady Vivien."

" It's the plain truth, Miss Mantlet. You know as well as I do you make *Let Go*."

" I don't know about that. But I think I have got off. And, as I tell Huffy, now that I have got off, it's madness not to go on."

Vivien looked from her guest to her son—and back again.

" Not go on—when you've scored your first success ? That would not be madness : that would be suicide."

" That's what I say," said Miss Mantlet.

Vivien looked at Huffy.

" But why," she said, " why shouldn't Miss Mantlet go on ? "

Huffy looked down and away.

" We were thinking of getting married."

" What if you were ? " said Vivien.

" Well, I want Orley to chuck it. But she says no."

" I entirely agree with Miss Mantlet. Why should she throw away the great position she's made. For she has made it, Huffy. Off her own bat. She's done more than you or I could ever have done. Miss Mantlet bestrides her profession. That is a great achievement. What right have you to demand that she should throw such handsome winnings away ? "

Huffy fingered his chin.

" If you put it like that," he said. " But if she's to stay——"

" Of course I put it like that. You have no shadow of right to demand such a sacrifice. Miss Mantlet has made her way. Have you made yours ? Can you fill a house, as she can ? D'you earn two hundred a week ? "

252

" Good lord, no, Mummy. But——"

" If you go on as you are going, you may be sitting at The Horse Guards before very long. I'm ready to swear that Miss Mantlet won't ask you to wash that out."

" I shouldn't dream of it, Huffy."

" Exactly," said Vivien.   " Huffy, my dear, you must learn to live and let live."

" Of course," said Huffy, " of course. But what I mean is this. Say Gorgeous asks for me—there's just a chance. Well, in the ordinary way, I'll be through at half past five. But Orley starts in at seven. Damn it, I'll never see her."

" That is the price," said Vivien, " of having a famous wife. Besides, you'll have Sundays together."

Orley was frowning upon an exquisite palm.

" I shouldn't expect," she said, " to work all the time."

" Of course you wouldn't," said Vivien.   " Leading ladies don't have to. They go very much as they please.   Perhaps I should say they go as their agents suggest."

Orley looked at her sharply.

" My agent, Lady Vivien, takes his orders from me."

" Which is why he's your agent, my dear. All the same, you listen to him. You'd be a fool if you didn't. If he says, ' Sign this contract ', you have one hell of a think before you turn it down."

" I'll give you that. What's this to do with our marriage ? "

" Nothing at all," said Vivien.   " All I'm trying to do is to plead your case. Huffy wants you to withdraw, and I don't see why you should. You don't ask him to withdraw, though he stands to lose very little, compared with you. I mean, you're just beginning—where many people leave off."

Miss Mantlet was frowning. The conversation was not according to plan. She took out a gold cigarette-case. . . .

" I'm sorry," said Vivien.   " I should have asked you to smoke."

Huffy lighted the cigarette.

" People in my position don't work all the time."

"Why should they?" said Vivien. "And Huffy can work his leave to fit in with yours. Where were you thinking of living?"

Orley Mantlet regarded her.

"Then you don't object to Huffy marrying me?"

Vivien raised her eyebrows.

"I don't quite see why I should. You and Huffy have probably worked things out. Your lives will be rather different, but that may be all to the good. You won't get bored with each other, as so many couples do."

"Why should our lives be different?"

"You won't keep the same hours: you won't have the same friends. I mean that goes without saying. I don't count those things objections. In fact, I'm not at all certain——"

"Why shouldn't we have the same friends?"

"I don't know why you shouldn't. I simply don't think you will. His friends will keep his hours, and yours will keep yours. Such people seldom meet."

"He's kept mine all right for some time."

"He's had a great incentive, my dear."

"But his friends will have no incentive?"

"Hardly the same one."

"And so they'll leave me alone?"

"I'm perfectly sure they won't. But they are accustomed to keeping certain hours. They can dine with you on Sundays—I'm sure they will."

"I'm sure they won't. On Sundays I'm out of Town."

Huffy left his seat, made his way to a window and stood looking out. If Orley noticed his movement, she gave no sign.

"I think," said Vivien, quietly, "I think that's very wise. Huffy and I both love the country best. If you're not too far, with a car you could get down on Saturday nights. Would you have a flat in Town?"

"I like a house better."

" So do I. But a flat is easier to leave."

" I don't see what difference it makes. The staff will have to be there."

" That's very true. Where were you thinking of living ? "

" Oh, Mayfair somewhere. I can't live West of Hyde Park Corner, you know."

" No, I see that. Well, Charles Street is very nice. I used to live there, and I like it better than this. But the houses are rather big. Perhaps Curzon Street would be better."

" I'd thought of Curzon Street. Some of the smaller houses are simply divine."

Miss Mantlet had been in one. In fact she had spent some nights there, two years ago. The owner, a Jew, was absent. His son was her host. It was thanks to her residence there that she ' got her chance '.

" D'you know the Levels ? " Miss Mantlet shook her head. " Well, they've a very nice house there—not too big. They're thinking of giving it up. Shall I put in a word ? "

" That's very sweet of you, Lady Vivien."

" Not at all. I think it would do very well. Three bedrooms, each with its bathroom."

" That's the style."

" I'll ring up Lady Level, and see what she says. Of course I know nothing of dates. Is it true you're going to America ? "

Huffy swung round, staring, and Orley sat very still.

Her innermost secret was out. Less than a week ago she had signed the American contract . . . to lead *Let Go* in New York . . . and open one month before Christmas. . . . She had meant to tell Huffy when she was Mrs. de Guesclin. . . . It had been a term of the contract that no one should know until October the first.

" What if I am ? "

She spat the words, rather than spoke them.

"Nothing at all. You've got to follow your star. But——"

"What's this about America?" said Huffy.

Orley was looking at Vivien with narrowed eyes.

"This," she said slowly, speaking between her teeth. "That my mother knows her place. She doesn't bribe lawyers' touts to divulge their clients' secrets. She doesn't come into meals, unless she's asked."

Huffy, white to the lips, stepped to the door.

"I'll see you out," he said.

Miss Mantlet rose to her feet.

"I had an idea," she said, "I was your affianced wife."

"You're not now," said Huffy. "Go to Court and be damned. I'll fight the case."

"You rotten bastard," spat Orley. She turned to Lady Vivien. "You can have your darling back. You're two of a kind. I thought I could stick you—somehow. I find I can't."

"That'll do," said Huffy.

Miss Mantlet forced out a laugh. Then she swept out of the room. . . .

Five minutes later, perhaps, Huffy returned.

"I'm frightfully sorry, Mummy. Hullo, what's this?"

"It's a double brandy," said Vivien. "I've got one, too. I don't care what Bateman thinks. I need a restorative."

"I'm frightfully sorry, Mummy. I never dreamed . . ."

"Why should you, darling? And don't apologize. This is what I am for. But please don't do it again. Let the stage marry the stage. 'Stick to your own kind'—it's got to be a damned good marriage to prove that precept wrong. If Defoe hadn't known Mr. Lacey . . . who happened to know the day the contract was signed . . ."

"We were to have been married in September."

"Just nice time. Mrs. Hubert de Guesclin would have gone very well in New York. It's what's called 'box-office', darling. And you're quite nice to come back to

256

—you're scrupulously clean in the house. Never mind. Let's have a party. Let's dine at Claridge's and go to a music-hall."

* * * * *

Another seven years fled on their way. Time seemed to have joined the rush which life had become.

The December day was raw, and a keen North wind was whipping the Mendip Hills. Philip, to his discontent, was confined to the house. Ildico was shopping in Wells.

" Don't wait for me, darling. I must go and see Mrs. Bishop. She'll probably give me tea."

" That's all right : but don't be too late. It's going to get colder this evening."

" I won't, old fellow. Promise you won't go out."

" Oh, no, I'll stay put," said Philip.

He worked in the library, checking estate accounts and making unsavoury notes on a writing-pad.

Presently he wrote to Defoe.

> *Brocade,*
> *December, 1930.*

My dear Dennis,
I think we should have a talk. Could you manage next week-end? I mean things are looking serious—even to me. Our personal expenditure is slight : I really don't think we can cut it down any more. But, if we're to live at Brocade, we must keep appearances up. We've cut out balls and house-parties as you know : but we must entertain a little, if only for the look of the thing. In a word, you can't pig it here—at least, I won't.

It's very worrying. Just as well I had to give up hunting—I couldn't afford it now. I've been looking at the old books. The stable account in 1904 shows an expenditure of over three thousand pounds. What on earth would it be to-day? At least, cars have saved us that. All the same, things don't look too good . . .

Somebody knocked on a leaf of the tall double-doors.
" Come in."

A tall, white-haired man entered the room.

For a moment Philip stared. Then he leapt to his feet.

" Good heavens, it's Mr. Filcher." He moved down the chamber to greet him. " I am so glad to see you. I haven't seen you for years."

Mr. Filcher took and bowed over the outstretched hand.

" Thank you, my lord. It's a pleasure to be here again. My nephew's laid up, and he didn't like the idea of his partner doing Brocade. And so he sent round for me." He laughed. " He sent me round his list, but I haven't looked at it yet. For forty-five years I wound the clocks in this house—and never missed a week. They're like old friends, my lord. Ah, there's the Vulliamy."

" I'm sure they know you, Mr. Filcher."

" You know, my lord, I sometimes think they do. It's more than sixty years since I got to know clocks. They're whimsical things, you know. You can't get away from that. They'll do their best for this man, but not for that."

" They want understanding," said Philip.

" That's very true. Of course, my ear is trained ; but, when I listen, a clock will tell me whether it's well or ill. And, if it's sick, it will tell me the nature of its illness." He stepped to the tall-case clock, and stood by its side. After a moment or two—" All's well there," he added. " A lovely pulse." He glanced at his pocket-watch and then at the silver dial. " Six seconds fast. That's nothing. Clocks like to play with Time. As like as not, next week, he'll be six seconds slow."

The butler entered the room, to set the tea-table out.

" Bring a second cup, Vickers. Mr. Filcher will take his tea with me."

" Very good, my lord."

Mr. Filcher bowed.

" Your lordship is very kind, but——"

258

" Please have it with me, Mr. Filcher.   I'm all alone, and
I do like talking to you."

Half an hour later, the old man rose to his feet.

" I've talked too much, my lord ; but it's been a great
pleasure, remembering other days.   My trade is dying.
Time-keeping doesn't count with people to-day. ' Near
enough ' is the watchword : but that's never done for me.
Nor for my father before me.   ' Near enough ' was a saying
we never knew."

Philip got to his feet.

" Please come again, Mr. Filcher, whenever you can.   I've
enjoyed your visit immensely.   I'm much younger than you,
but we feel the same about things. ' Near enough ' was
never my motto.   It never will be my motto.   I can only
do things one way, and that is as they should be done.   How
did you come, and how are you going back ? "

Mr. Filcher consulted his watch.

" I came by train, my lord.   I shall——"

" And walked from the station.   That was most good of
you.   How long will you take to finish ? "

" Half an hour, my lord."

" Very good.   In half an hour a car will be waiting.   So
you will be able to catch the five fifty-five."

" Your lordship is much too kind.   I'm perfectly able to
walk."

" I know you are.   But why on earth should you, Mr.
Filcher ?   If Brocade can't look after its friends. . . .   And
please come again one day."

" That I will, my lord.   I've had such a happy time."

Philip returned to his letter.

*. . . I've just had another nudge.   Filcher and Son, of Wells,
have always wound the clocks at Brocade.   Before the war we
paid ten shillings a week : now we pay a pound, and, considering
the time that a man is away from the shop, I think that's fair.
But it's fifty-two pounds a year.   Well, we can cut it out—I*

*can wind the clocks myself. But, if we do, it'll hit the firm very
hard. They're good, old-fashioned people and nowadays they're
having an uphill fight : so fifty-two pounds a year, on which
they can count, means a lot to them. What are we to do,
Dennis ? . . .*

*　　*　　*　　*　　*

Three months later Virgil felt very tired.

He had visited the Wallace Collection and had spent two
agreeable hours admiring the arts and the crafts of other
days. And now he was walking up Bond Street, on his
unobtrusive way to one of his Clubs.

The tall, distinguished figure attracted little attention.
Now and again a passing man or woman would give him
a second look. But most of them passed him by, as one of
the old brigade. There was no mistaking that. Nobody
knew that he was a connoisseur. Nobody knew—or, if they
had known, would have cared how high his judgment was
rated, where the fine arts were concerned. Directors,
curators, dealers—all of them knew Virgil Coleton, and
knew him well. Christie's and Sotheby's held him in great
respect. When the Trustees were uncertain, Virgil Coleton's
advice was frequently sought. And the French believed in
him. More than one ' understanding ' was due to his tact.

He was, of course, perfectly dressed ; and he moved with
a soldierly bearing at sixty-one.

And now, without any warning, he felt very tired.

Virgil had lived in London for nearly forty years. Nearly
forty. Perhaps I should eat my words and say thirty-five.
The war years he spent out of Town. In fact, he spent
them in France.

The day after war was declared, Virgil Coleton enlisted
—at forty-four : a very drastic movement, for a fastidious
man. Less than two months later he landed in France. He
suffered everything. Mud and filth and hard labour, such as
no peace-time navvy had ever conceived : blood and iron and

260

exhaustion beyond the belief of man : all the merciless cruelty dealt by the mailed fist. What it cost the dilettante, nobody ever knew. The fact remains that he was invaluable. All ranks swore by ' Coalton ' for more than four years. Danger lost its stature, when he was by. ' That man,' said one C.O. —and he saw five out—' has made many subalterns.' The saying was true. His disregard of doom forced others up to the bit. He refused to accept a Commission : he never went sick : he seldom applied for leave—if ever he did, he spent his time in Paris : he never set foot in England, until the job was done. And then, one fine May morning, he reappeared in his Clubs. . . .

Only Dennis Defoe and his doctor knew where the man had been. And they had been sworn to secrecy. Everyone else supposed that he had been doing a Secret Service job. Once he was recognized—by a member of Brooks's, in Ypres. (' By God, it's Virgil Coleton.' ' I'd be very grateful, sir, if you would keep this to yourself.' ' But, man, what a terrible waste. The Staff will jump at you.' ' I'm quite all right, sir, really '—and Virgil winked. ' Oh, it's—like that, is it ? Right-oh. Your secret's safe, old man, but I give you best.')

He never spoke of the War—he who had known it far better than any one of his friends : so far as he was concerned, the four grim volumes were closed : but the years had left their mark. Let us say it was delayed action. Any way, twelve years later, Virgil felt very tired.

And then, as he entered Old Bond Street, he suddenly felt more than tired. One of his legs was trembling, and he seemed to be short of breath.

He managed to stop a taxi and tell the driver to take him to Cleveland Row . . .

" Is that Lady Vivien ? "

" Who's that ? "

" Oh, this is Sanders, my lady. Mr. Coleton's took very bad."

261

" Oh, dear. Have you called a doctor ? "

" Yes, my lady. He's sending two nurses in."

" I'll be round in ten minutes, Sanders."

Vivien rang for the butler.

" The car immediately, Bateman : tell Pricket to bring my furs."

" It's a bitter evening, my lady."

" That can't be helped. Ring up Captain de Guesclin and Mr. Defoe. Tell them that Mr. Coleton is very seriously ill."

" Very good, my lady."

John Street . . . Berkeley Street . . . St. James's Street . . . the traffic storming and scudding . . . pedestrians hunching their shoulders against the whip of the wind . . . a flurry of snow, to usher an ugly night . . .

Sanders, clearly frightened, taking her ladyship's coat . . .

" And the doctor's report, Sanders ? "

" He spoke of collapse, my lady. He gave it no other name."

Vivien pursed her lips . . .

" Why, Virgil, dear."

" Ah, Vivvy, I suppose this is Sanders' doing."

" He naturally rang me up."

" I—don't like giving trouble. Some—nurses are on the way."

Vivien was kneeling by his side.

" Pain, dear ? "

" I—can't dignify it with that name. Say discomfort. A—sort of catch in the breath. I think—I'm going out, darling."

" Virgil, Virgil."

" I—may be wrong. First time I've ever died, so—I can't be sure. But—I think this must be it."

Vivien began to weep—there was death in his face.

" I've—always counted on you."

" I'm—so glad. Listen, darling. Huffy's looking at

262

Marion Swathe. She'll do him very well. The Swathes are charming people—I—don't have to tell you that. If—it comes off, my beauty, I hope . . . you'll marry Jack Rivers. . . . He'll—never let you down. Give up South Street and go abroad for a year. Sort—of Indian Summer . . . you owe it to yourself."

"Live, and I'll marry you, Virgil."

"No, darling. I'm no good. I've—been in love with you for forty years : but I couldn't—fill the role. But Rivers can."

"Faithful unto death."

"I hope so. But—that's your fault."

"Virgil, darling, you're not just letting go ? "

"No, my sweet. I—don't value life very much, but— I'd go on if I could. But something's gone wrong—with my works. . . . I—can't make—the requisite effort. I —don't know why."

There was a little silence.

"Can I do anything, darling ? "

"No more than—you're doing, my sweet. . . . Wait— there was something else. . . . I can't remember. . . . Oh, yes. Tell Pip to—make over Brocade. . . . Offer it to the nation. . . . He—can't keep it up."

"You advise that, darling ? "

"Yes—before it's too late. I mean—others will do it. They can't take them all."

"I'm sure you're right. And I'm sure he'll do as you say. Oh, Virgil, Virgil, ever since I was small, I've always felt you were there."

"That's been—my privilege."

"I missed you so in the War. You—just disappeared."

"I—was busy, darling."

A nurse stole into the room, and Vivien got to her feet.

"I'll come back, darling," she whispered. She turned to the nurse. "I'll leave him to you now ; but I'd like to look in for a moment before I go."

263

" May I come and call you, my lady ? "

" If you please."

As the door closed—

" That's—a very great lady, nurse."

" I know. I saw her once—before the war. I never thought I'd speak to her face to face. And now don't talk for a moment : I want to take your pulse."

In the hall of the flat Vivien was speaking to the doctor.

" I'm a cousin of his. His servant rang me up."

" I think you're Lady Vivien de Guesclin."

" That's right. He tells me he's dying."

" I'm afraid it's touch and go."

" You think in your heart that he's right ? "

The doctor braced himself.

" I'm rather afraid he is. The thoroughbred doesn't break down : it drops in its tracks. I've always known this might happen. To tell you the truth, I thought it would happen before."

" I never knew he was ailing."

" Nor he was. But at forty-four he enlisted and did four years in the ranks." Vivien caught her breath. " Four years in France, Lady Vivien. That's his secret, you know. You mustn't give me away. Among my patients, I've a Field-Marshal and three Generals : but I'm very much prouder to be his doctor than theirs." He looked at the bedroom door. " There lies a man."

Tears were slowly trickling down Vivien's cheeks.

" And nobody knew."

" Very few. But you mustn't give me away. This is, of course, the result. Few men of his age and manners would have survived so long."

" My God, what it must have cost him ! "

" I think it's appraised in heaven. We can't appraise it here."

" I'd . . . like to say goodbye."

264

"So you shall, Lady Vivien. I won't be long."

Vivien sat down in the hall.

Five minutes later, perhaps, the doctor was back.

"Would you like to see him now? He's rather weaker. I don't think he'll last the night."

"Shall I stay?"

"I don't think I should. I think he'll slip into a coma any time now."

Vivien stole into the room and the nurse stole out.

"Virgil, darling."

The tired eyes opened.

"Ah, Vivvy."

"Just to say good night, beloved."

"You're—very sweet."

"I'll be round first thing in the morning. They want you to rest."

"I—want to rest, too."

Vivien stooped to kiss the parted lips.

"Good night, my very darling."

The man was past speaking, save with his eyes. . . .

Two and a half hours later, a gentleman of England went to his long home.

When the private funeral was over, Dennis Defoe drove back with Vivien to South Street.

Neither spoke until the end of the drive—from Golder's Green.

Then Defoe cleared his throat.

"He's left you his flat as it stands. His money goes to poor friends he made in the War. And here's a sealed letter for you. I don't know what it contains, and I don't know how much you know, but I can tell you this—'This was the noblest Roman of them all.'"

My darling Vivvy,

Cleveland Row to you. When you give up South Street, you must have a pied à terre.

*The enclosed testimonials, you will please keep to yourself.
God bless and keep you always, my darling girl.*

V.

The coarse envelope was grimy.

*Mr. V. Coalton,
c/o Coutt's Bank,
Strand,
London.*

Vivien drew out the sheet.

*105 George Street Below,
Wigan.*

5–11–22

*Dear Sarge,
You tole me to write. Well, I got a good job an married and
got a kid. Nothin the matter with life as far as I know.
But every twenty-second I drinks a pint to you. Twenty-
second of October Pashendale. Ever forget that chum? I
never will. Nor Dock nor Nobby neither. When our bloke
screams retire an you up an shoots him dead. An then we goes
on an takes the —— shellole an stays there nineteen ours an
then that —— Soskin gets the V.C. An you done it all. An
when I gets back to the base an tells ole George, that's the secon
time he says. He done it at Lose. Saved the —— line.
Killed four jerries himself and the blood running down is face.
And then he turns on us Gaw dammit you —— he says wot
are you waiting for? Can't you put a lot of slowbellies where
they belong. Slowbellies, I ask you. We ad to laugh. An so
we comes again an —— well chews them up. An then our
bloke clocks in an says well done me lads and gets his V.C.
Botson, his name was. Botson V.C. I don't think. An
Coalton done it all. Thats twice. Well so long, chum. But
you know you tole me to write. So heres hoping . . .*

Joe Murdock.

And, still in its tissue paper, the D.C.M.

*　　*　　*　　*　　*

From Eleanor Carson's Diary.

South Street.
2nd June, 1931.

Vivien's baby boy was married to-day. A most attractive wedding—everyone seemed to be there. A Guard of Honour by the Blues. The crowds were great. The groom so like his father—a man standing out among men : the bride so gentle and winning—I am quite sure she will make him a splendid wife. Huffy must have been proud of his supporters. Vivien looked perfectly lovely and most absurdly young—her gray-gold hair is really beautiful. Pip so very distinguished, but sadly old for his age : his dear hair more white than gray. Ildico still beautiful, but fragile—I didn't like that. Havey, Huffy's best man, a most striking boy—with his mother's beautiful features and Pip's quick charm. Sully and Blue Boy—a most attractive pair. Huffy and Marion were so sweet to me. But that seems to be my portion. . . . Still, this marriage has shown me that I am clean out of date. It will be the last of my functions. After all, I am getting on, and things have moved so fast in the last thirty years. The old days seem like a dream. How London has changed. When I come up—very seldom—I feel quite lost. The traffic moves so fast. There was always just as much, but the pace has immensely increased. Some things, of course, are the same ; but many landmarks are gone. Park Lane looks quite different. And all these blocks of flats, which I think a great mistake. I mean, they must make for congestion—five hundred people living where fifty used to live. And Bond Street is very much changed. I'm very glad that to-morrow I'm leaving Town. It is too much for me now. I feel overpowered and I notice the motor fumes. They must be bad for people, breathing them all day long. I suppose it is all progress, but I cannot help looking back to the quieter, more leisurely days. That is, of course, old age.

I had no chance of speaking to Pip or Vivien about my plans. And so I shall have to write. I can go on no longer settling down

*in their houses for months at a time. It is all wrong. As long
as I was of use, it was all very well. But now they don't call
upon me, as they used to do. That is because I'm too old.
'We can't worry her.' The little house at Peregrine will do
very well. I should like to die near Poesy, where I have spent
so many happy days. Strange how we have all always turned
to Poesy as a haven—dearest Ursula, Vivien, Pip and I. I
am quite excited to think that this time to-morrow I shall be
there again.* . . .

* * * * *

It was on the following morning that Rivers rang up.
Vivien answered him.

"Yes, I am feeling rather lost. You know. The
pageant is over : but I'm not mad about the look of my
shelf."

"You may have a shelf, my dear, in twenty years' time.
Till then—well, let's call it a niche."

"You should have been a *couturier*. Never mind. I
don't like the look of my niche."

"Will you come and dine with me—and let the world
slip ? "

"I'd love to. Take me to the *Dorchester*, Jack. I'd like
to dance."

"What time shall I call for my lady ? "

"Let's say a quarter past eight."

Vivien and Rivers made a most striking pair.

The man stood out of the ruck. Tall, quiet, distinguished,
he was observed and respected wherever he went. There was
no mistaking his trade. His clean-cut features, his iron-gray
hair and moustache—above all, his level gaze declared the
perfect officer of a forgotten age. Vivien, moving before
him, diminished all other women, as she had always done.
Her beauty was still outstanding : her natural dignity bestrode,
like some Colossus, the gaping company. She wore but one

268

jewel, where others wore five or six : but the lift of her lovely
chin was worth all the diamonds that lighten the Place
Vendôme. And they are for sale—or were.

As she enjoyed her melon—

" Will Brocade be rendered to Cæsar ? "

" No doubt about that. Cæsar is going to play. Pip's
being absurdly generous : but, when the deal has gone
through, it'll save him six thousand a year. ' Nobody must
suffer.' That is his one idea. And nobody will. They'll
flourish at his expense. Still, the weight will be taken. And,
bitter blow as it is, he'll very soon feel the relief."

" I am so very thankful. To watch him striving and
struggling wrung my heart. You know that I'm selling
South Street."

" I didn't know it. I thought, perhaps, you would."

" Well, now that the children are done for, why should
I keep it on ? Cleveland Row will suit me down to the
ground."

" And Fairing Over ? "

" I shall make that over to Huffy. He loves the place.
And he should have a country home."

Rivers nodded.

" That's right."

" And I can go down when I please. And Poesy's always
there. We're not a bad crowd, you know. We can use
each other's houses, and nobody minds."

" I've noticed that. I sometimes think it's because your
name is Vivien. All the same, no place of your own ?
Cleveland Row is only a *pied à terre*."

" Perhaps. But it's most attractive."

" From my point of view, it's ideal. But it's small for
you."

" If I was there all the time. But, now that I'm free, I've
a whim to travel, my dear. To have a look at Europe—
before it comes to an end."

" How very—provident."

"I'll have to take someone with me. I can't go alone."

"You'll take me with you," said Rivers. "If you take anyone else, I'll follow and break their neck."

Vivien began to laugh.

"You're eighteenth century. That's why I like you so. All right. We'll go together, just you and I. See all the places we ought to have seen before. But you'll have to marry me first."

"Oh, my darling. D'you mean it?"

"Yes, my blessed, I do. Whenever you like."

"Oh, Vivvy."

"I mean it, you faithful man. We're going to have a good time. I'll shed my years and be a bride again. *Soyons communs* and do the Italian Lakes. And then I want to see Dresden."

Rivers got to his feet.

"Come and dance," he said. "I ought to be pretty good—I'm treading on air."

*   *   *   *   *

Pricket refused to be comforted.

"Everythin' 's goin'," she wailed. "Brocade's gone, an' South Street: an' now it's my turn."

"Listen, Pricket dearest. I can't take you. You've never been abroad in your life. Whenever I've been to France, I've always left you at home."

"But this is different, my lady."

"It isn't different, my dear. I must have someone with me who knows the ropes."

"It isn't right," sobbed Pricket. "I've always been your maid."

"You always will be, Pricket. No one on earth could ever take your place. But the Continent's off your beat. You simply couldn't cope: and because you couldn't cope, you would be miserable. I value your devotion: I value

270

it higher than anything that I know. But I know where you get off, and I'm not such a fool as to let you go out of your ground."

"If you put it like that, my lady."

"I do. You must trust my judgment. I'd love to have you about me : but I know it would be a mistake. You couldn't deal with the Customs and things like that : I should have to look after you, because you'd be out of your depth. And that would worry you stiff—you know it would. So take your holiday and come back to Cleveland Row. Get it all ready for me—you know what I like. You see, I count upon you."

"Very good, my lady."

"And I'll write to you all the time and tell you how I get on. And, when I get back, I'll be so happy to see you and have you about me again. Do believe me, Arabella—I'll have to start calling you that."

"Oh, my lady."

"Well, why not, Arabella? We've come to love one another, you and I."

Pricket dissolved into tears.

"There's no one like you, my lady."

"That isn't true, but I love to hear you say it. Tell me, d'you think I'm wise to marry again? "

"Of course you are, my lady. I wish you done it before. He's a gentleman, Colonel Rivers. He won't never let you down."

"And where is our country home? We can't spend all our time in Cleveland Row."

"You can for me, my lady."

"Faithful Arabella, I know I can. And now here's a precious secret, which you must keep to yourself. I'm to have Poesy's dower-house."

"Oh, my lady, how lovely."

"It's going to be ideal. Lord and Lady Ringwood will be at Poesy. I've told you they're leaving Brocade. And we shall be at the dower-house. You know, I can't help feeling that's going to be fun."

"It's going to be perfect, my lady. Poesy's where we belong."

*   *   *   *   *

Touring the Continent in comfort, Lady Vivien Rivers was having a glorious time. Never before had she led so care-free a life. Rivers delighted to help her to go as she pleased. For once in a way, Duty was off duty; and Pleasure, unembarrassed, issued agreeable orders night after night.

"Let's stay here, darling, instead of going on. The bed-rooms are quite all right, and they'd love it so. And I want to stroll through the village under the stars and stand on that old, old bridge and hear the lisp of the water, rising out of the dark : and so on, into the meadows to smell the hay."

"Consider it done, my sweet. And I'll catch you a trout for dinner—I like the look of that stream."

And so it came to pass that on a summer evening four strangers were moving beside an Austrian water—master and man, intent on the catching of fish, and mistress and maid behind them, talking of this and of that, as women will : a jolly pilgrimage, that Vivien often remembered, when far more important occasions failed to report.

Of such was her wedding tour. Over and over again they were 'off the map' : the almanac lost its sting : often enough, Vivien could not have named the day of the week.

Florence.
September, 1931.

My darling Pip,
Next year you and Ildico simply must do this. The change and the freedom would give you a new lease of life. You've been so loyal, darling : but, now that you don't have to worry about Brocade, there is no reason at all why you and she shouldn't
272

*spend some months abroad. I am enjoying every minute of it
all, and Jack is so charming that I feel half my age. He's
given me a marvellous camera—German, of course—and I use
it just like a school-girl, photographing all sorts of childish things :
lunch by the wayside, a yoke of oxen, the launch we used at
Como—and then I can hardly wait to see the results. Darling,
we four must do this together next year. It is perfection. The
servants, I think, enjoy it as much as we. They certainly seem
very happy. Mold is the soul of efficiency and Louise is an
excellent maid : she takes charge at the Customs, and the
luggage and cars are simply wafted through. Last night we
ran into the Cromlecs. Blanche was most awfully nice—about
everything. When I spoke of my ' Indian Summer ', she said,
' Not Indian, darling. You see, your life and summer are
synonymous terms.' I think that was a very sweet thing
to say.*

Well, darling, I must stop now and go and dress.

My dearest love to you both.

*Your loving
Vivvy.*

She did not repeat what Lady Cromlec had said to Rivers
—and Rivers had reported to her. ' Vivien's the only
woman that I have ever known, to whom no other woman
ever grudged anything.' And if that is not a compliment, I
do not know what is.

*   *   *   *   *

The re-arrangement was over.

Poesy now was the Earl of Ringwood's seat : nine months
of the year, he spent there, as against three in Town. *The
Dower House, Poesy,* was the Rivers' address : now and again
they stayed in Cleveland Row. Philip and Rivers, between
them, ran the estate. Miss Carson was installed in The
Shrubbery, Peregrine. Huffy enjoyed Fairing Over, and

made an excellent squire. A little house in Green Street suited Sully and Blue Boy down to the ground. Lord Haven, now in the Regiment, lived at his parents' flat.

The family was united as never before. The older generation now lived cheek by jowl. The younger clung together, as brothers and sisters and cousins seldom do. But Havey was everyone's darling, and Huffy and Sully had always been very close. What was unusual indeed was that the two generations delighted to mix. But Ildico was everyone's darling, and Philip and Vivien were an exceptional pair. Though they were over fifty, their hearts were young. The nine were constantly meeting. Havey, Sully and Blue Boy visited Fairing Over whenever they pleased. Marion de Guesclin frequently stayed at Green Street : Huffy at Arlington Street or Cleveland Row. At Poesy, all were at home —and that is the truth.

Vivien's proposal was honoured in 1933. Travelling together, the Ringwoods, Vivien and Rivers spent three handsome months exploring the Continent. Things were not quite so good, for the shadow which the German was casting was rather more clearly defined. Still, it was very pleasant, and Philip recaptured his boyhood, proving the Pyrenees.

They floated back one evening, after a day in the mountains to warm the high gods' hearts. Lunch four thousand feet up in the shade of a whispering beech : Ildico dancing a reel on a mountain lawn : Rivers falling into a pool—and Mold returning with trousers bought at a village store : Vivien making friends with a kid—to be routed and made to run by a jealous goat : Philip laughing as he had not laughed for years. . . .

As the four entered their hotel, Sully, Huffy and Havey rose up in a loving wave.

"Just for two nights, darlings : Havey's got to get back : but we felt we must come and see how you were all getting on."

274

(With Ildico's cardigan above them, Jack Rivers' local trousers went very well indeed.)

In those days children paid parents few such compliments.

*   *   *   *   *

Another year tore by—and some men saw the lightning playing upon the hills. Alarmed, they peered at the wall, to see the familiar writing taking shape. Immeasurably shocked, they caught their fellows' arms and bade them look. But their fellows shook them off and swore there was nothing there.

A man who had been a soldier determined to do what he could. . . .

" I feel damned nervous," said Philip.

" My darling," said Ildico, " if you were not nervous, then I should be alarmed. The moment you're up, you'll be as right as rain."

" It's not my line, my sweet; and they'll simply loathe what I say."

" What's that to do with you ? Ahab, if you remember, loathed what Micaiah said. She threw back her head and quoted. 'Is there not here a prophet of the Lord besides, that we might enquire of him ? And the King of Israel said There is yet one man by whom we may enquire of the Lord : but I hate him : for he never prophesied good unto me, but always evil.' "

" Comfortable words, my darling : but I'm no orator."

" That's why they'll listen to you—because they know that you are a dutiful man."

So the Earl and Countess of Ringwood came to the House of Lords.

At half past five Philip rose to his feet.

" . . . For manifest reasons, I seldom address this House . . . I should be failing in my duty if I did not at least make your lordships free—not so much of my opinion as of the evidence of my eyes and ears. In the past months we have witnessed

275

Germany's return to power. She has defied the orders of her conquerors. . . . More than four years of service in the field in the last war and seven months in Germany thereafter went to the making of the witness your lordships are hearing now . . . three harsh and bitter facts. First, the German is prepared to wage war with merciless ferocity and to use the utmost inhumanity to gain his ends . . . Thirdly, his one idea is to expunge the memory of his late defeat by a victory so overwhelming that the campaigns of the Great War will not be worth setting down in the history books. Of such is the stuff, my lords, of which the Germans are made. It is not the stuff of which fellow-creatures are made. . . . Though my military duties came long ago to an end, the duty of a Briton to his country is something no man can lay down. . . . I am not seeking to sway this venerable House. I am seeking to direct its attention to facts which speak for themselves. I cannot pretend that they are savoury facts. I think it likely that they are highly inconvenient. But I tell your lordships this—that, unsavoury and inconvenient as they are, if their clear message is ignored, the day will come when they will seem eminently desirable beside the stark brutality of their successors. . . . If Germany's ambition is not halted, her right hand will teach us terrible things. . . ."

As husband and wife drove home—

"My sweet," said Ildico, "you were most awfully good. You see, you were so patently honest."

"I only wish I could feel that I'd done some good."

"I think you must have, Pip. I mean, it shook me. Any way, your conscience is clear."

Philip sighed.

"For what it's worth, my sweet. At least, I've done what I can."

Four letters—three from divines—appeared in the Press, denouncing his lordship's words. A labour leader went further. 'The belted earl who boasts of his war crimes in one breath and traduces the honesty of a great and friendly power in the next, has rammed home the obvious truth that the sooner the hereditary legislator is confined to the acres which his great-grandfather enclosed and the sullen subservience of his unfortunate serfs, the better.'

*   *   *   *   *

A room in the London Clinic in May, 1935.

"I'm not so young," said Sully. "If anything should go wrong . . ."

"My darling child," said Vivien. "What's thirty-five?"

"Quite a lot for the first, Mummy. You know it as well as I. But please don't think I'm afraid, because I'm not."

"No, my darling, I know you're not afraid."

"It's only Blue Boy, darling. He's fond of me. And if anything did go wrong, it'd shake him up. But I think you could—tide him over . . ."

"Sully, my sweet."

"It's just in case, Mummy. I'll tell you the line to take. Tell him he's got to keep going for England's sake. That very soon now he'll be wanted as never before. As father was. He'll see the point all right. And he'll go for his duty bald-headed. . . . And that'll see him through."

"Understood, my darling. That's what I'll do. I hope and believe the occasion will not arise. But if it should— well, you can count upon me. I find it strange you should be so certain of war. We never saw ours coming."

"I know. But we can see this. That's why we gather rosebuds. They'll be in short supply before very long. We shall win, of course. We always do. But the price will be high, Mummy. I'm only a parrot, of course. But I hear the others talking, and what they say seems sense. Which will it be, Mummy? I want a girl."

"Why a girl, my darling?"

"Well, whichever it is, it can't bear father's name. So

277

I'd like it to bear yours. I mean, it can't be a de Guesclin.
So let it be a Vivien—that's just as good."

" Sully, Sully."

" We both feel that. You're a tradition, darling. It
ought to be carried on. Shall I get well at Poesy, as you
did ? "

" Ildico hopes you will, and so do I."

" Good for us both, I think. The Brabant atmosphere.
There's something in it, you know. A peace that the world
can't give. You've always had it, Mummy. Uncle Philip
hasn't : but he was born at Brocade. And I like to think
I've got it, because you took me there as soon as you could.
And I'd like my baby to have it. . . ."

" Why do you say, Sully darling, that I have that peace ? "

" Because it stands out, Mummy. That's why you're still
so young. Some people stay young, because they're placid
brutes and don't feel things. They belong to the idiot class.
They're not idiotic, of course : but they belong to that class.
The idiot is young at eighty, because he's invulnerable. The
heaven falls—and he laughs and plays with the bits. They're
not as bad as that : but when the heaven falls, their appetite's
just as good—because they don't feel things. Now you feel
things intensely, and always have. And yet, in spite of it all,
you've always kept your youth. I mean, I know about
father, and how your life was smashed. Smashed into tiny
pieces. Most women would have gone white. You never
even went gray. If you wept, I never saw you. You picked
up your bit and went on. And then he redeemed everything
—wrote his name in letters of gold on England's heart. And
all the trumpets sounded for him, as they'd never sounded
before. I wish I'd been there to hear them . . . as he came
out of the river, upon the other side. But it put you in
balk all right—*for seventeen years*. But you never faltered,
Mummy. You went straight on. And you were as young
as you looked. . . . I think your name's written somewhere
. . . in letters of more than gold. . . . And I think more

than trumpets will sound . . . when you come to the other side . . ."

Thirty-six hours later Sully was delivered of a girl. It was not an easy business, but there was no harm done. Three weeks later the two proceeded to Poesy. In Peregrine's little church her god-parents did their duty and gave Miss Enderby-Lowe her grandmother's famous name. But they were much too late. She had become Blue Girl before she was two days old.

* * * * *

On a muggy November Monday, seated upon the club kerb, the Earl of Ringwood regarded his son and heir. This, in Arlington Street. Ildico was not too well : at this particular moment, she was in Harley Street.

" Tell me from the beginning."

" Well, sir, I think you know that I very seldom play cards. I suppose I was born lucky. Any way, if I do, I always win. And that's why I've cut them out. I mean, it can be—awkward. But two nights ago, at Fairing Over, I let myself be persuaded to take a hand."

" Who was at Fairing Over ? "

" Huffy and Marion, of course. Sully and Blue Boy, Random of the Twelfth Lancers, Anna Lafone, George and Diana Worsley, Rosemary Phelips and this fellow, Choosely-Jones. He's in the Ninth D.G.s. Random brought him from Farnham—I'd never met him before."

" I see. Go on, Havey."

" After dinner they started poker : Rosemary and I sat out. At about eleven o'clock the girls went up, and then they called to me to come into the game.

" At first I refused. Then Choosely-Jones said something or other to Random, and Random laughed. I don't know what he said, but I knew it was about me. So I said, ' Right, I'll come in.' And so I did."

" You thought you'd learn them ? "

" Er, yes, sir."

" I don't blame you at all. I should have done the same."

" Well, I won, as I always do. The cards just fell for me. After a quarter'f an hour I'd won three hundred pounds.

" Well, sir, you know how it is. When you're winning like that, you've simply got to go on. *You* can't call the halt."

Philip nodded.

" I caught Huffy's eye, and twice he suggested that we had done enough. But Choosely-Jones wouldn't have it. He wanted to get me down.

" And then I picked up four aces—just picked them up. I mean they were dealt me, sir. . . ."

" Well, everyone chucked in his hand, except Choosely-Jones and myself. But he was out for blood. So we went on. At last I said I'd see him, and he put down four Kings. Then I did a silly thing. Instead of showing my hand, I pitched it on to the pile and said ' Good enough '. I didn't want his money.

" And then he put a foot wrong. He picked my hand up —a thing he'd no right to do. And when he saw the four aces, I think he saw red. I mean, he knew what I'd done —that I'd let him off. And that got him under the ribs. . . .

" ' I suppose your nerve failed you,' he said.

" I didn't answer him, but got up to get a drink. But Blue Boy let fly.

" ' What d'you mean by that, Choosely-Jones ? '

" ' What d'you think I mean ? '

" ' I don't know. That's why I'm asking you.'

" ' Honest players don't chuck away four aces.'

" There was the most dreadful silence I've ever known.

" Then Huffy spoke.

" ' You'd better withdraw that, Choosely-Jones.'

" ' I'm damned if I will.'

" ' Then take up your money,' says Huffy, ' and leave the house.'

280

" Well, then, sir, they all got going. . . . I can't be sure what was said. But Random seemed to be backing Choosely-Jones, and I heard something said about Clubs. And the money was left on the table, and Huffy saw the two out."

" What is the man suggesting ? "

" I think he suggests I'm a sharper, but that when it came to the point, I lost my nerve."

" You seem to have behaved very well."

Havey shrugged his shoulders.

" The whole thing was so stupid, sir."

" I agree. It's beneath contempt. But it's also most distasteful. Why have you come to me ? "

" Well, sir, Blue Boy says that the man's going to write to my Clubs."

" He must be mad," said Philip.

Havey shrugged his shoulders again.

" Perhaps he won't," he said. " But if he does, sir . . ."

" You'll have to sue him for libel. No doubt about that. Is Random running with him ? "

" I think Random owes him money."

" My God," said Philip, rising. " Who is this blasted man ? "

" I really don't know, sir—except that he's pretty rich. He was quite all right until this happened, you know. Rosemary'd met him before : but I think he knows her better than she knows him."

" I see. Well, I shall hear at once, if he writes to the Clubs. So we'd better forget about it, until he does. If he does, you must issue a writ and have it out."

" I'm most awfully sorry, sir."

" It's not your fault, my dear boy. It's just ' one of those things '."

*   *   *   *   *

Defoe advised that Forsyth, the son of the Judge, should deal with the case.

Forsyth saw Viscount Haven and issued a writ. Then he asked to see Huffy and Blue Boy.

"What's behind this, Major de Guesclin?"

"A lady, as usual, Mr. Forsyth. Choosely-Jones has fallen for Rosemary Phelips. And Rosemary Phelips likes my cousin best."

"I see. That was evident, I suppose, at dinner?"

"I think it was pretty plain. And then they sat out together, while we were all playing cards."

"Quite so. Now tell me this. Before the evening in question, had you ever played cards with your cousin?"

"Once or twice."

"Was he lucky?"

"Fantastically so. He's got a poker face: but it was the cards that did it. He was unbeatable. Same with back-gammon. You never saw such throws. That's why he won't play."

Blue Boy put in his oar.

"I played him once at back-gammon—no one can cheat at that. Five games on end, we played; and he won the lot, hands down. And I'm a pretty good player—far better than him. I mean, he makes the wrong moves: but his throws always pull him through."

Forsyth nodded.

"Will you say that in Court?"

"With pleasure."

"Good. Now let's go back to the poker on that unfortunate night. This fellow pretends to believe that Viscount Haven was cheating: that, somehow or other, he had furnished himself with four aces, which only a straight flush can beat—and the odds against a straight flush are half a million to one."

"Six hundred and fifty thousand—I've seen it once. Against being dealt it, of course. But neither asked for a card."

"Very well. He then pretends to believe that, when the

282

moment came to declare this winning hand, Lord Haven lost his nerve—that is to say he feared that some or all present would know that such luck was too good to be true."

The soldiers nodded.

" That's right."

" Now I'm going to be brutal.   Observing the four aces, could a stranger be pardoned for wondering whether Lord Haven was cheating or no ? "

" No," said Huffy, " he couldn't.   Blue Boy or I might pass for confidence blokes.   But Havey—no.   We're carthy, Enderby-Lowe and I : but Havey's ethereal."

" I know what you mean, but leave his demeanour out. Suppose it hadn't been Haven, but somebody else."

" If it hadn't been Haven and hadn't been in my house, the man might well have been pardoned for thinking that something was wrong."

" I'm going to be brutal again.   We all know that Viscount Haven would rather die than cheat.   Who happened to deal that hand ? "

" I did," said Blue Boy.

" Who shuffled the pack ? "

" I imagine Haven did—he was on my left."

" Could a card-sharper have stacked it ? "

Blue Boy shook his head.

" I've always heard they're slim, but no man born of woman could have done that.   He'd got to find four aces, and then he'd got to place them in such a way that they would be dealt to him.   And how could he know how I was going to deal ?   And five of us looking on. . . .   The thing's impossible.   His only way would be to have the cards in his sleeve."

" And change them with four he'd been dealt ? "

" That's right.   And what if somebody else had picked up an honest ace ?   Oh, no.   When you look at it closely, the thing's absurd.   One man can be fleeced at poker, when all the others are crooks.   Two wrong 'uns might do it

283

together, using a special pack. But one man could never get home."

"Well, I'm much obliged," said Forsyth, and got to his feet. "We shall win, hands down, of course. But it's a rotten business."

"You're telling me," said Huffy. "But Choosely-Jones will curse the day he began. There's a lot of feeling already, and when the meeting's over, he'll have to clear out."

"Serve him right," said Forsyth. . . .

*　　*　　*　　*　　*

It was by no means surprising that all who knew Philip Haven should deeply resent the suggestion that he had been cheating at cards. His quiet, gentle personality, his something shy demeanour created a pleasant impression, wherever he went. He had his father's bearing, his mother's beautiful features and raven hair. His address was admirable ; his behaviour to men and women, above reproach. He was by no means ethereal, as Huffy had said that he was : but when he had used the word, Forsyth had known what he meant. The purest blood of Scotland ran in the young man's veins : sometimes, rarely enough, such blood will declare itself. Centuries of clean living, hard lodging and simple fare, of implicit obedience and constant discipline, of little speech, of suffering wind and weather without a thought—perhaps these things are refining elements. Be that as it may, a delicate quality, seldom seen in a man, distinguished the Ringwoods' child. As his furious squadron-leader declared with an oath, ' Anyone else—but not Havey. You might as well charge the Pope with passing a dud half-crown.'

For all that, the fuse had been lighted, and in about six months the dump would go up. Choosely-Jones, it was said, would have liked to withdraw : but his victim had to go on. The name of Viscount Haven had to be cleared.

It was a hard business. The sympathy shown to the Ringwoods was very marked, and much was made of Haven,

284

wherever he went : the ugly fact remained that millions of
people to whom the names Haven and Ringwood meant
nothing at all, would presently link those names with a charge
of cheating at poker. . . .

Alone with Vivien, Ildico burst into tears.

" Oh, Vivvy, we were so happy—and now this dreadful
thing. What have we done to deserve it—my Havey, least
of all ? I never bore him for this. And he's taking it hard,
Vivvy. And so is Pip. They never say a word, but we're
all playing up. The waiting, of course, is too awful.
Forsyth is hoping for May—that's six months off. Hoping . . . I suppose we can, all of us, stand it . . . and Pip
shouldn't be in Town. But how can we leave Havey
now ? "

Vivien did what she could. But you cannot reduce hard
facts.

It was two nights later that Rosemary Phelips spoke out.
This, at a private dance in her father's house.

" Why d'you avoid me, Havey ? "

" I don't avoid you. I'm just not rushing you, sweet."

" Why don't you rush me ? The—process appealed to
me."

" When twelve true men have said that my hands are
clean——"

" Don't be a fool, Havey. What do I care what twelve
true men may say ? "

" I know you don't : but I do. When they have delivered
their verdict, if you are still about, the, er, process will be
resumed."

" I see. Can I count on that ? "

" Yes, Rosemary."

" I'm much obliged. I can have the honour of accepting
a man who has been acquitted, but not the honour of accepting a man who's been charged."

" Men who are charged don't propose."

" So that people may say, ' She waited to see which way

285

the verdict went.' I won't have that, Havey. Our engagement's announced at once, or not at all."

" But, darling——"

" I love you and you love me. If you like to announce that fact, I shall swell with pride. But you've got to announce it now."

" But, Rosemary, sweet, your people——"

" Will put their arms round your neck. And we must be married quickly. I want to be your wife when you go to Court."

" Oh, my darling."

He held the girl to his heart.

" It's perfectly natural, my blessed. If I were in trouble you'd want to comfort me."

The engagement was received with rapture. That is not too strong a word. Congratulations poured in. The two were fêted right and left. Ildico wept for joy—in Philip's arms. Jokes began to be cracked about the ordeal to come.

*   *   *   *   *

Mr. Tristram, K.C., sat down and Sir Joshua Belling rose.

" You have said, Lord Haven, that you very seldom play cards. Why did you play upon this particular night ? "

" I didn't want to."

" That wasn't what I asked you. Why did you play ? "

" Because I thought, if I didn't, my refusal would be misconstrued."

" As what ? "

" As reluctance to risk my money."

" I see. You were reluctant to play, but you were still more reluctant to be thought reluctant to risk your money ? "

" Yes."

" You knew you would win ? "

" I can't say I knew, but I had no doubt that I should."

" No doubt at all ? "

" None."

286

"Betting on a certainty, Lord Haven?"

"It really amounts to that."

"Not usually done, I believe?"

"That's why I don't do it."

Counsel leaned forward.

"But you did—on this occasion?"

"Yes."

"To some purpose, Lord Haven?"

The witness shrugged his shoulders.

"I certainly won."

"Hand over fist, Lord Haven?"

"That's perfectly true."

"Finding that that was happening, why didn't you stop?"

"When you're winning, you can't withdraw."

"But it was money for nothing, as you well knew."

"It was in a way. But anyone will tell you I couldn't do anything else."

"I want *you* to tell me, Lord Haven."

"I couldn't do anything else."

"I see. You'd won three hundred pounds in a quarter'f an hour. That's twenty pounds a minute. Not too bad, Lord Haven? I mean, at that rate, you don't have to play very often . . . to make what you want?"

"I don't have to play at all. I've as much as I need."

"I put it to you that every now and then you decide to augment your income."

"You're quite wrong," said Haven.

"And that when that occasion arises, you turn to cards."

"I assure you I don't."

"D'you mean to say you weren't glad of three hundred pounds?"

"As a matter of fact, I gave the money away. I can show you the cheque."

A rustle ran round the court. That the witness had won that trick was perfectly clear.

Sir Joshua changed his ground.

" Tell me this, Lord Haven.   In the last round that night you held an unbeatable hand.   Or very nearly so.   Only a straight flush could have got it down.   Why did you throw it in ? "   The witness hesitated.   " Come along, answer me, sir."

" I didn't want to take the defendant's money."

" You had already taken his money ? "

" I know.   I didn't want to take any more."

" Why ? "

" I don't quite know.   I didn't like him very much, and he obviously didn't like me.   Well, you don't like taking money off someone like that."

" So you were prepared to present him with a hundred and twenty pounds ? "

" Thereabouts."

" Because you didn't like him ? "

" That was about what he had already lost."

" Listen, Lord Haven.   You didn't like the defendant and you were pretty sure that he didn't like you.   You had him at your mercy—in a fight which was forced upon you, against your will.   Do you ask the Court to believe that, instead of laying him out, you preferred to present him with a hundred and twenty pounds ? "

" I suppose it sounds very silly, but that was how I felt.   I didn't want his money—and that's the truth."

" I think that before that round you shuffled the pack ? "

" That's right."

" And then—you had four aces ? "

" That's perfectly true."

" And threw them away ? "

" Yes."

Sir Joshua regarded his palms.   Then he looked up at the witness.

" Winning hands are sometimes—acquired ? "

" I think that's common knowledge."

" If that hand was not acquired, why did you throw it

away ? I mean, your conscience was clear. You had been dealt four aces. It was half a million to one that he didn't hold a straight flush. Therefore, holding four aces, an honest man could go on till the cows came home. You had three hundred pounds to play with, and he was rich. Why didn't you put your opponent where he belonged ? "

" As far as I can tell you, my reasons were three. I didn't want the man's money : I felt that it wasn't quite fair, because I always win : and I wanted to end the game."

Counsel leaned forward again.

" I suggest that you lost your nerve."

" I'm afraid your suggestion is wrong."

" Isn't what you did precisely what a sharper would have done ? "

" No. Having got so far, a sharper would have gone on."

" Is that so, Lord Haven ? "

" Yes, it is. Sharpers don't lose their nerve. It's their stock in trade."

" How do you know, Lord Haven ? "

" Common sense."

Again the tell-tale rustle ran round the court. Sir Joshua girded his loins.

" You admit that you sat down to play, though you knew you were going to win."

" I didn't say that. I said that I had no doubt."

" What is the difference ? "

" This. People who know, know. People who have no doubt, are sometimes wrong."

" You weren't wrong, were you ? "

" No. My astonishing luck still held."

" You won three hundred pounds in a quarter'f an hour ? "

" That's perfectly right."

" And you still went on ? "

" I'd every right to do so. It was the luck of the game."

" And then you threw in your hand ? "

" Yes, for private reasons. I'd every right to do that."

289

" ' Private reasons,' Lord Haven ? "

Haven leaned forward.

" Which never would have been known, if Mr. Choosely-Jones hadn't done what he'd no right to do, and picked up my hand."

" What d'you mean, ' no right ' ? "

" What I say. He had no shadow of right to look at the hand I'd thrown in ? "

" Who says so ? "

Sir Joshua's junior ventured to pull his gown.

" I say so," said Haven. " It's one of the rules of the game."

Sir Joshua leaned back, fuming.

" What d'you want ? " he growled.

" It's perfectly true, sir. The defendant had no right to touch his cards."

" Why the devil wasn't I told ? "

He turned again to the witness.

" If rules were observed," he rasped, " no sharper would ever be caught."

" You may be right," said Haven. " I wouldn't know."

There was more than a ripple of laughter, and the K.C. sat down.

To all intents and purposes, that was the end of the case. Huffy and Blue Boy simply rammed certainty home.

George Worsley got the laugh of the day.

Tristram put only two questions.

" You were there, Sir George, and saw and heard what occurred ? "

" Yes—for my sins."

" Lord Haven was accused of cheating. What do you say ? "

" Lot of dam nonsense. He couldn' cheat if he tried. An' I know what I'm saying. Fin' the lady with me, an' I'll make you think."

The roar of laughter might have been heard in the Strand.

Even the Judge broke down and covered his face.
At length he looked up.
" Any questions, Sir Joshua ? "
The K.C. rose to the occasion.
" Not on your life, my lord."
It is not too much to say that the charge was laughed out of Court.
The defendant consented to judgment.   Before the month was out, a famous Charity received five thousand pounds.
Forsyth was more relieved than anyone else.   He had seen good cases go wrong.   Still, it had been very trying for all concerned.   Though the issue had been most happy, the affliction had left its mark.

*　　　*　　　*　　　*　　　*

Philip, Huffy and Rivers were sitting over the port in Cleveland Row.
" This Spanish business," said Philip.
Huffy, fresh from Biarritz, considered his finger-tips.
" We ran into Colonel Agueira in the Bar Basque.   He asked to be remembered to you, sir."   Philip inclined his head.   " He's very much upset about the B.B.C."
" I'm damned if I blame him," said Rivers.   " ' Rebels.' You don't rebel against Communism : you try and stamp it out."
" That's what he said," said Huffy.   " He's not mad about Franco, but he will throw up his hat for any man who stands for law and order.   I'm sure I should do the same."
" If the Communists win," said Philip, " you can wipe the whole Peninsula off the map."
" That's what Agueira says.   I did my best, of course. But he's very sore."
" Did you get as far as the bridge ? "
Huffy took a deep breath.
" I'm ashamed to say I did.   The roads round Behobie were simply swarming with cars.   One peasant, up on the
291

hill, had actually built a stand—ten francs a seat. And a man had a telescope there—a squint at a franc a time."

"To see men killed," said Philip. "You know that's what Virgil said. I well remember his saying, 'They'll run char-à-bancs to the next war.'"

"He wasn't far out," said Huffy. "So we retired. Next day the police intervened, and the stand was closed : but I saw it, myself. Two or three days later, I went over alone. There's a sort of park in Hendaye, beside the river's bank. I got there about three o'clock. An old gardener saw my glasses. 'Siesta, Monsieur,' he said. 'They won't start again till five.' But they did, all right. I saw the attack on Irun."

"Well done ?" said Rivers.

"I thought so. Not knowing the terrain, I really couldn't be sure. So much dead ground, you know."

"Is it true the French are sending the Communists help ?"

"Agueira gave me chapter and verse."

"That'll let others in."

"He's much afraid it will. And Franco will have to have them. I mean, if you're up against it, you don't look gift guns in the mouth."

"And by this abuse of Franco, we're playing into their hands ?"

"Exactly, sir. I mean, the day may come when we'd be rather glad of a friendly Spain. It'll take a lot to drive them into the opposite camp. But the Spaniards are very proud— I don't have to tell you that. And they don't like being insulted."

Rivers sighed.

"Fortune favours the Boche. A chance to get a footing in Spain, and the most glorious try-out an army ever had."

He looked at Philip, and Philip got to his feet.

As he helped to put out the candles—

"I wish I could see more sunshine—at home and abroad. I mean, there's no denying the clouds are low."

292

" You're telling me, sir," said Huffy.

As they entered the drawing-room—

" At last," said Vivien. " Come on, you Regency Bucks.
We're going to see a film."

" The national anodyne," said Rivers, and everyone
laughed.

*　　*　　*　　*　　*

Another Coronation was over and done : another London
Season had very near run its course : and Ildico, resting
at Poesy, had no energy left.

The truth was this—that, for some time now, her battery
had been discharging faster than it could charge. And now
her battery was charging even more slowly. . . . Her
attendance at the Abbey had cost her extremely dear : the
effort had been almost beyond her, but nothing would have
kept her away. His Majesty must be supported. . . .

These things were manifest. Nobody said anything—
but everyone knew . . . that the Countess of Ringwood was
failing. Philip knew it, and Vivien. Whenever Havey left
her, he never was easy until he saw her again. Huffy and
Sully, too, were deeply concerned : Ildico was very much
more than their aunt ; she had been their second mother for
thirty years.

And now her fifty-eighth birthday was twenty days off.

It was Sully who had had the idea.

Among Ildico's treasured possessions were nine of the
' Cries of London '—Wheatley's famous ' Cries '. The
plates, bequeathed by an aunt, had always hung in her room.
But there were only nine. More than once, in the past, she
and Philip had sought to complete the set : but the right
ones were hard to come by, and after a while, the project
had been forgotten. Besides, they were so expensive . . .

And now five of Wheatley's ' Cries ' were coming into
the sale-room. What is more to the point, these five included
the four which Ildico did not possess.

It was Sully's quick eye that had seen the casual announcement : it was she that had rung up Havey and asked him to check her belief. Then she had visited Christie's and asked for 'a line' on the price which the five would make. The answer shook her. 'It's hard to say, madam. I think, perhaps, between four and five hundred pounds.'

But Sully was not to be beaten. The family was approached. Finally, Philip was told. So it was presently arranged that Sully should bid for the 'Cries' and should go to five hundred pounds. Philip himself would contribute one half of the purchase price, Vivien one quarter, 'the children', between them, the rest.

"We've got to have them," said Sully. "Aunt Ildico's not too good, and I can think of nothing she'd like so much."

The sale was on Wednesday.

On Tuesday Havey rang up.

"I can't be there, Sully darling : I can't get away. But Mummy's got to have them. If you must, go to six hundred, and that's my show."

"All right, Havey. I will."

Then Vivien rang up.

"Sully darling, we've got to have those 'Cries'. You can add another hundred for me, in case of accidents."

"Good for you, Mummy. I will."

Then Philip rang up from Poesy.

"That you, Sully ? Look here. We've got to have those plates. Anything over five hundred is my affair."

"Give me a limit, Uncle Pip."

"All right. Twelve hundred. We ought to get them for that."

* * * * *

Christie's Great Rooms were not crowded, but they were comfortably full. The silence was silvern : that is to say, it was not absolute. It was the silence of Christie's—a rare, subterranean murmur of whispers, of turning of pages, of

294

shifting of feet. This made a sounding-board for the auctioneer's voice. The crisp, clear speech—faultless, incredibly rapid, ruled the roast. Rich men hang upon those accents. Their word is law. Ten thousand pounds will change hands on the tap of a finger-nail. No witnesses, documents, signing. Nothing like that. Christie's hammer has fallen, and that is enough. A has agreed to pay B ten thousand pounds. Big business is at its best in Christie's Great Rooms.

Sully nodded.

"Five hundred. Five hundred pounds. . . . And ten."

The auctioneer was looking at Sully.

Sully nodded again.

"Five hundred and twenty. . . . Thirty."

Sully's clear voice rang out.

"Five hundred and fifty."

"Five hundred and fifty, thank you. Five hundred and fifty pounds. Any advance on five hundred and fifty pounds?"

The hammer fell, and the auctioneer glanced at his clerk.

"Mrs. Enderby-Lowe."

"Well done, old girl," breathed Blue Boy. "An' how do we get the stuff?"

"Huffy says you go and speak to the clerk."

"What, up to the holy of holies?"

"Go round behind. It's all right."

Blue Boy tip-toed round.

"Er, I'm Captain Enderby-Lowe. My wife's——"

"That's all right, sir. Give me your card, if you have one, and then you can take them away."

"Thank you very much."

"Tell one of the men, and he'll put them into your car."

Two minutes later, five of the 'Cries of London' passed down the famous stair.

Two suit-cases were waiting, with blankets inside. . . .

"Astonishin' chow," said Blue Boy, mopping his face. "Talk about shop-lifting. An' what do they lose a year ? "

"They don't lose a halfpenny, darling. They know we're all right. It's their job. And now let's get back. The others are coming later to see the spoil : and I want to clean them first."

Five days later, four cars stood on Poesy's apron, one lying behind the other, against the green of the turf. One was a Bentley, one was a twenty-five Rolls, one was a Sports Delage, and one was the Rivers' M.G. Two or three were gathered together, because it was Ildico's birthday, and Ildico was beloved.

The luncheon was festive. Ildico, gay as ever, seemed her old self. From the opposite end of the table, Pip watched her tenderly. Huffy proposed her health and made an excellent speech. 'We look upon her as a sister—not as an aunt. A mischievous, elder sister. She used to inveigle me under the raspberry nets. And lie down behind me, when the head-gardener came by. And Mummy once said to me, " You're as bad as Ildico." I've always treasured that saying. I used to think, Well, if I'm no worse than that. . . .' In a word, it was a famous occasion, which nobody ever forgot.

They left the table and entered the drawing-room. The 'Cries' were ranged on a sofa; in front of them lay a card.

From Pip, Vivien, Havey, Huffy—and Sully, who brought it off. With their love.

Ildico caught her breath and went down on her knees. Every plate she scanned : then she looked up and round.

" Oh, my darlings," she said. She picked up the card and held it close to her heart. " To love and be loved—what more can anyone ask ? "

296

From Eleanor Carson's Diary.

Peregrine,
3rd August, 1937.

Ildico's birthday. They asked me to lunch, but I said I would come to tea. I never remember subscribing to so much happiness. Ildico was radiant. And all the others so happy, because she was—Ildico. She looked so fragile, yet not more than forty-five. I suppose there are families as charming : yet, to be honest, I find it hard to believe. Marion, Rosemary, Blue Boy—no ' in law' about them : they seem to be part of the stock. And Pip and Vivien so happy, to see such others sharing their heritage. For Poesy is their home. And what a present they gave her! By the merest chance, I seem to have chosen well, for I brought her Farington's Diary*—and that, of course, deals with Wheatley. But I know that she reads a lot, when she cannot sleep : and Farington's very restful, with his talk of painters and pictures and exquisite days in a leisurely countryside. They all made much of me, and I told them of Pip and Vivien when they were very small. Colonel Rivers was very charming. I well remember the day, on which, as he tells me, he saw Vivien first. That was at Bill, at Harrow. She and I drove down on a very cold day. ' From that moment,' he said, ' I never looked at anyone else.' Well, he has his reward. Her hair is more gray than golden : but her face is as young as ever—or so it seems to me. Pip's thick hair is snow-white. The war did that. And Brocade. And he worries, as soldiers must, about things to come. Huffy, just like his father; Havey, just like his mother ; Sully, her mother's daughter, the sweetest girl. And the others, so very attractive. I have subscribed to-day to a conversation piece—a very rare piece of work, the like of which few people have ever seen. The cynosure, Ildico. The most perfect thing of all was Vivien's love and respect for her brother's wife.*

*   *   *   *   *

Ildico died in her sleep on New Year's Eve.

Ten days later, Philip and Vivien left for the South of France. The Raeburns owned a villa not very far from Antibes. This, they put at Philip's disposal. 'It's very quiet; and the servants know how to behave.'

*   *   *   *   *

The November day was mild, and the sunshine was almost warm.

" We should be hunting," said Rivers. " But now, you know, it's an effort to turn oneself out. There's always so much to see to. And—let me be perfectly frank—I'm getting old."

" At sixty-four, darling," said Vivien. " Don't be absurd."

Nearly a year had gone by, and husband and wife were strolling arm in arm. The flags behind the Dower House made a fine quarter-deck.

" This Munich business," said Rivers, " has made me think."

" Don't be original, darling."

Rivers laughed.

" I don't mean the way you do. I'm old enough to be selfish. I'm thinking of us. I mean, the family."

" What then ? " said his wife.

" Well, it's coming, of course. I think we both know that. For better or worse, the day has been postponed. And, when it comes—well, you and Pip and I can only sit still. After a while, I might get a job of sorts : but Pip isn't fit—he can't do anything. The boys will go at once ; and, after a bit, the girls."

" Oh, Jack."

" It's no good blinking these things. I'm trying to look ahead. Between us all, we have six residences. Poesy, this, Fairing Over, Arlington Street, Green Street and Cleveland Row. When the time comes, we shan't need six, and, what is more to the point, we couldn't keep them up."

"Huffy will give Fairing Over to the Red Cross. He was all ready to do it, if Munich hadn't come off."

"I think that's a good idea. Well, that leaves five. I think we should be well advised to make it three. I know I'm on delicate ground : but it's better to take off your coat than to have it torn off your back."

"Indubitably," said Vivien.

"I think we older three should muck in at Cleveland Row. You and Pip and I. We must have somewhere in Town, and I don't think Pip would mind, if you'd be content."

"What d'you think, my darling ? "

"Well and good. The younger generation could do with Arlington Street. They won't be on leave together. There'll never be more than four there ; and, usually, only two. Green Street, if they prefer it, but Arlington Street is a flat. And service won't be too easy."

"I think that's very prudent."

"So we come to the country. In the first place, you must remember there'll be evacuees. Pip, alone at Poesy, 's bound to take them in. Bound ? He'll throw open his doors. But . . ." Vivien bit her lip. "Exactly. Poesy will be ruined—irretrievably ruined. Possibly, if it was stripped. . . . But there won't be time to strip it.

"Now the children simply must have a country home— to which they can always resort, to forget the war. And Poesy is ideal, for it ministers to the mind. Besides, it *is* their home. If then we give up the Dower House and go to live with Pip . . ."

"That's right," said Vivien, nodding. "Evacuees to the Dower House, and Poesy for us all."

"You do agree ? " said Rivers. "I mean, I'm the outsider. I can't suggest such a thing, except to you. But I do feel that we should be ready."

Vivien put it to Philip, who warmly agreed. Together, they put it to ' the children ', who found the proposals good. Marion mourned the prospect of leaving Fairing Over : Sully

299

wept at the thought of losing her pretty house: but each accepted her fate. After all, if their husbands were gone . . .

So plans were drawn up against the coming storm.

Philip, of course, was delighted that Vivien should share his home. The move from the Dower House was actually made in June. And Philip slept in August at Cleveland Row.

And then, on September the third, the gates of Janus were opened. Once again, the German beast was enlarged.

Not even the wisest perceived the full extent of that catastrophe. They knew that England would have her back to the wall. It never entered their heads that, after the War had been won, the wall would give way.

*   *   *   *   *

Blue Boy was killed in France at the end of May.

A terrified Vivien opened the telegram. Sully, who had been ailing, was having breakfast in bed.

" Oh, Pip, I'm afraid to tell her."

Philip set his teeth.

" She'll stand it all right, Vivvy. She's one of us."

Leaden-footed, Vivien passed upstairs.

As she entered the sun-decked bedroom—

" Hullo, Mummy." Vivien tried to speak. " Oh, my God, it's Blue Boy."

The telegram passed.

Sully read it through. Then she folded it slowly and laid it down on the table beside her bed.

" Could you take the tray, Mummy? I—don't want any more." Vivien did as she asked. " You'll have to look after Blue Girl. I'm going to get a job."

With that, she turned on her face.

Vivien knelt beside her, still trying to speak.

*   *   *   *   *

The next to go was Jack Rivers.

A local command in the Home Guard became him well.

300

Dutiful, quiet, efficient, he was admired and respected by all his men.

One night he was first on the spot, when a German bomber had crashed and burst into flames. There was only one survivor, who was unhurt. He was munching chocolate— and calmly watching another, whose clothes were on fire, screaming and rolling to try and put out the flames. Rivers tore off his greatcoat and wrapped it about the victim. . . .

When the Guard arrived—

" Carry this fellow to Anstey's, to wait for an ambulance. The other will go to Headquarters under most strict arrest. He may have water to drink, but nothing else. He is unfit to bear the name of man."

It was a bitter night, and short of his greatcoat, Rivers caught a bad chill. This he disregarded—he had had chills before. Besides, he must set an example. Set an example, he did : but it cost him his life.

*　　*　　*　　*　　*

After winning the D.S.O. twice, Huffy died of wounds on the way to England from France. This was in the summer of 1942. For more than six months there had been a price on his head. This looked as if the rumour was true—that he had killed more Germans than any man alive. He was his father's son. After all, Commando warfare would have been down Hubert's street.

He died without issue : Marion's baby, a boy, had been prematurely born.

Vivien took his death quietly, but, less than three weeks later, her hair was white.

Marion wrote to her—Marion, now of ' The Wrens '.

Liverpool.

Thank you, darling. Unless you'd like to have me, I don't think I'll ask for leave. It's better to keep going—one has less time to think. The trouble will be when it's over. I don't like

301

the look of the future very much. And I think it's quite a good thing that our baby died. Those who would have loved him have been spared this agony. Our blessed, blessed Huffy. He was ours, wasn't he, darling? I think I made him happy, and of course he worshipped you.

Well, here we go.

Marion.

*   *   *   *   *

Badly wounded in Italy, Havey returned to England in 1943. Rosemary, now in the Service, was doing most vital work. For this, she had a flair : and so, could seldom be spared. But the two snatched some days at Poesy more than once. Lord Haven was fit for duty the following March. He saw to that himself—and landed in France in June. But he shared a week-end with his wife at the end of May. This, in Arlington Street.

Let us look over their shoulders. . . .

Serge brushing serge, fair hair touching the dark, the two were poring together over a plan. This was the plan of the Dower House, Poesy. That was to be their home, when the war was done. Having been grossly abused, the place had been handed back.

Lord Haven's pencil was moving.

" That's the best room, my sweet. It was the drawing-room. I think we should make it our room—let's say ' the library '. It faces south and west, and it's terribly comfortable. The bay snares all the sun. God knows what service we'll get : but, with that at our disposal, we won't want anything else. And it has a door into the garden. . . ."

" What more can we ask, darling ? "

" That's how I feel. Well, there's the dining-room. That has a door to the back ; so that service, if we can get it, will be—well, very well served. Just in and out : that's all they'll have to do."

" All *I* shall have to do."

302

"I'll help you, my beauty. Bread and cheese for lunch ; and bacon and eggs at night. That's good enough for me."

"Damn it, my lord, I'll do you better than that."

The two laughed heartily : and kissed while they were laughing. . . .

Lord Haven resumed his prediction.

"Now there's the other room—I think we'll call it 'the parlour'. That's where we receive our friends . . . and give them Daddy's sherry : he's still got forty dozen—God bless Brocade. He stuck to the cellars, thank God. Well, that's the parlour—we'll put the show stuff in there, as they always do. Mummy's 'Cries', of course, must go in the library. Would you mind if we had nothing else? Just Mummy's 'Cries'?"

Rosemary flung an arm round her husband's neck.

"Oh, Havey. I love you so."

"I don't know why. Never mind. Now up the stairs. There are two staircases—see? One goes up from the hall, just outside the library door. That'll be ours—our staircase. And it leads straight up to our suite, above the library. It's not a very big suite, but it's awfully snug. So we shall have our own little maisonette—sitting-room, bedroom and bath-room, all cut off. The other suite is reserved for Philip Brabant and Philip Brabant's nurse. There are three other rooms and a bathroom : day-nursery and any odd guest."

"You'll want a dressing-room."

"That's right. Well, I can have that one. It's just across the landing. That still leaves a bedroom and bath for anyone coming to stay."

"Darling, it's going to be heaven."

"It's going to be very simple and devilish quiet. No junkets in Town, no frills—we shan't have the money for that. Just a man and his wife and their baby making out."

"Oh, Havey, my very darling, what more could I want?"

Lord Haven held his wife close.

"Well, let's look forward to that. Next time you go to

303

Poesy, go and check up. Daddy's having the place put in order—that I know. The damage is slight, really—it's mostly dirt. Aunt Vivien's stuff is stored and she says we can take what we like. And then we can pick up things. I think it'll be rather fun. Letting the world slip, darling. Our little baby kingdom, all to ourselves. . . ."

" Oh, Havey, Havey, my darling. . . ."

" And you'll take care of yourself, my precious girl? Swear you'll withdraw in August—if not before."

" I swear I will. I'll go to Mother first, and then to Poesy."

" That's right, my sweet. It shouldn't be very long now."

*   *   *   *   *

Nearly four months had gone by, and Poesy's Summer was handing over to Autumn—a gentle transfer, always pleasantly made.

Blue Girl, now nine years old, was standing, talking to Pulse, who had worked in Poesy's gardens for fifty years. Philip and Vivien were watching the two from the terrace, and smiling to see their childhood brought up to date.

" 'Member old Dewlap, Vivvy? Who used to keep the paths. We used to talk to him. He remembered the coaches perfectly well."

" That's right. And his father had been a post-boy. My darling, we're getting old."

" Blue Girl's in the tradition. If her hair was down her back, she might be you."

There was much in what Philip said. The child made a striking picture, just as Vivien had done. The picture, of course, was different. The thick, short, golden curls, the white shirt and Jodhpur trousers were strongly suggesting a page of the Middle Ages, as painted by one of the Masters of other days.

Old Pulse had all her attention, leaning upon his spade.

" Go on, please, Pulse."

" Well, 'is man never put the chain on—the chain wot went round a spoke. An' when Rory whips up his cattle, the wheel whips out of the skid-pan, an' there you are. There's the dray running free at the top of Pitchfork Hill, an' Rory up on his box an' his unicorn trottin' out. Course 'e knew in a moment the wheel was free, an' 'e took a turn on his brake that almost bent the rods : but the dray was heavy-laden. . . .

" The wheelers tried to hold it, but all in vain. An' so 'e springs 'is cattle. . . .

" Very few men would 'a done it : but Rory were a fine waggoner—so he were. 'Is only chance was to get them goin' so fast that they still 'ad a pull on the dray. Course, the brake helped 'im a little. . . .

" Any way, 'e springs them, an' down they goes, like thunder, down Pitchfork Hill. I'll never forget it, Miss Vivien, as long as I live. I was a lad then, and I just come roun' the bend. Gawd, wot a sight. The unicorn at full gallop, Rory up on 'is box a-lashin' them right an' left, and the mighty dray behind them swaying from side to side. . . .

" Run for the bank, I did—and stayed there whiles they went by. Like a roarin' whirlwind it was—the three great horses full stretch, with their ears laid back, Rory bracin' himself an' a leanin' over 'is splash-board, crackin' 'is whip, an' the dray a roarin' an' rumblin' an' makin' a noise like the sea. . . . 'Ow 'e took that bend, I shall never know. Sheer, lovely drivin', I think. An' if one of the 'orses 'ad stumbled, that would 'a been the end. But Rory held them up.

" Right down Pitchfork Hill and over the bridge : an' 'e pulls them up just short of Allison's farm. . . .

" When I got up, Rory was down in the road and makin' much of 'is team—an' 'is man on 'is back in the gutter— Rory 'ad laid 'im out. Talkin' to 'is 'orses, 'e was, just as though they was 'is children, with the tears runnin' down his cheeks. . . .

" After a while, he picked me up and drove on to Peregrine. An' there 'e give each of 'is beauties a quart of ale."

" Gave his horses beer ? "

" Yes, indeed, Miss Vivien. It done them good. 'E drenched them out of a bottle. An' then 'e 'ad one 'imself.

" Ah, I've seen many things, but I never see anythin' greater than Rory springin' 'is unicorn down Pitchfork Hill. 'Twas a wonderful sight, Miss Vivien. An' no other man could of done it—that I'll swear. But Rory was a fine waggoner, an' when 'e called on 'is cattle, they did as he said."

" I'd have loved to see it, Pulse. What happened. . . ."

A footfall upon the terrace, and there was a telegram.

Vivien's heart turned over.

Philip opened it, read it and put it away.

" My God," breathed Vivien. " Not Havey ? "

Philip nodded. He dared not trust his voice.

Vivien caught his arm.

" Oh, Pip, Pip, my darling."

Philip surveyed the landscape with stony eyes.

After a long minute—

" I don't matter," he said. " It's no worse for me than for you or for Nobby Clark. But Germany's had her way. What was left of the flower of England is being cut off. Most of it went in my war. And now the rest has gone. Centuries went to its making, and now the trees have been felled. A very few will survive, but what can they do ? They will be utterly swamped by lesser men."

Vivien strove to master her lips.

" Let's go in, Pip darling. Let's go and sit down."

Philip braced himself. Then he turned with her, and made for the house.

" I wish," said Blue Girl, " I wish they had drays now. And unicorns. Why are they harder to drive than a four-in-hand ? "

306

" Well, you see," said Pulse . . .

*   *   *   *   *

Three days later, a letter from Havey arrived.

Monday.

My dear Daddy,
 *I went for a stroll this evening, as it was getting dusk—out of
a meadow and into a little wood. Up a grass-grown cart-track,
not very wide. I was thinking of Rosemary—I am so thankful
she's going to have a child. And then I turned, to go back, and
there was Mummy standing full in my path. About six paces
away. I can't say how she was dressed, but she looked exactly
the same and was smiling her lovely smile. She was looking
me full in the face, but she never spoke. I just cried out,
' Mummy ! ' And then she opened her arms and stretched
them out to me. But when I got there, she was gone. Well,
Daddy, I think that's a pointer, and that's why I'm writing
this note. Of course you'll never get it, unless I'm right. I've
always been so proud to be your son.*
Your loving
Havey.

From Eleanor Carson's Diary.

September, 1944.

Peregrine.
 *I hardly know how to write the terrible words. Havey was
killed by a sniper on Tuesday last. Havey—Viscount Haven,
Pip and Ildico's boy. So now they are all gone—our glorious
company. Blue Boy, Huffy and Havey. And Havey was
the rarest of them all. I feel there is nothing left. God knows
that I am no snob : but all my life I have had the privilege of
observing the spirit and manners of the nobility and gentry.
Blue Boy, Huffy and Havey were beautifully bred. As a direct
result, they had the finest instincts. Not one of them could have*

307

done a shady or shabby thing : noblesse oblige saw to that. Each one inspired and commanded his fellows' love and respect. Can anyone say that the world is not the poorer? As I heard Mr. Willing say in 1916, 'As well destroy the best of our thoroughbred stock, and then expect us to hold our own on the turf.' And, once destroyed, how can it be replaced? It can't : so it never will be. The thing is done. The old order is changing —has changed, before my eyes. For years I have been a relic. Very soon Vivien and Pip will be relics, too. Unthinkable, that : but true. And the truth is preposterous. Is a portrait by Reynolds a relic? No. It's a masterpiece. And it will be a masterpiece for so long as this world goes on. And Vivien's a masterpiece . . . and so is Pip. Yes, but they're thoroughbreds. And thoroughbreds will be relics in five years' time. I'm sorry to be so bitter, but when I see Vulgarity strutting in clothes which, but for its betters, it wouldn't know how to put on. . . . My pen is running away. It is no good writing such things. Better to remember the old days, when men and women were happy, whatever their rank. They loved one another then.

That was nearly the last of the entries : Eleanor Carson's journal was almost done. I do not find this surprising. Tired and old and powerless, she turned her face to the wall. She had seen the ruin of the edifice to the raising of which she had subscribed her life. On every side the articles of her faith were being condemned and derided as heathenish stuff. Manners no longer made man, and Tradition was out of date. Though they were as iron in her soul, she could have borne these things—if they had been to the good : for Eleanor Carson was honest as any man. But, of her wisdom, she knew that the truth was being denied. False prophets were spouting the praises of the new order of life. She tried to believe they were fools : she knew in her heart they were knaves. But their doctrines were hailed with delight by millions of dupes. Certain of the Answers of The Catechism

had for long been a thorn in the flesh. Its painless extraction
was almost too good to be true.

The capital sum which Miss Carson had had of the Brabants
was left in Trust for Blue Girl and for the issue, if any, of the
late Viscount Haven of The Horseguards Blue. The sixty-
two volumes of her diary were left to Philip and Vivien, ' to
do with them as they think best '. (In fact, after dinner, they
read them aloud to each other, deriving very great pleasure
from the burden of other days.)

*　　*　　*　　*　　*

Lady Haven died in childbed. The doctors said that she
made no effort to live. The baby—a girl—was saved.
She was named Ildico Vivien. With Miss Vivien Enderby-
Lowe, she shared her family seat. The two were the light
of Vivien's and Philip's eyes.

*　　*　　*　　*　　*

In 1946 Sully and Marion de Guesclin were solemnly
playing back-gammon at Cleveland Row.

At the end of the seventh game, Sully laid down her cup,
and stared at the fire.

" Surplus women," she said. " What the hell do we
do ? "

" Another war," said Marion, " would be the easiest
thing."

" I entirely agree : but they're not going to make one
for us. And yet we must do something, or we shall go
mad."

" That's right," said Marion, slowly. " The plain truth is
that life has lost its charm : take charm from life, and what
do you get ? Existence. You and I and millions of others
are simply existing to-day. And, when you have lived,
existence is very drab. And so we must do something to

309

—to lace the nauseous draught. I mean, in the old days I could stay at Poesy week after week. Now, after two or three days I'm ready to scream. And these imitation parties make me want to burst into tears."

"That's right," said Sully. "The best was good enough for us : so nothing short of the best will ever serve. But that is beside the point—which is that we must do something, if we are not to go mad."

"A job," said Marion. "I'm not afraid of work; but it's got to be something worth doing—and—and not too squalid, Sully. We've had so much to bear, and if I've got to lace my existence with squalor—well, it's rather like drinking water out of a dirty glass."

Sully nodded abruptly.

"You're telling me." She opened her case and took out a cigarette. "I take it you don't *have* to work."

"I gather I don't," said Marion. "It's rather involved. As far as I can make out, I've eight hundred a year to spend. That's three hundred less than the Lavenhams' char and her husband. But then they're paid in notes."

"I seem to have rather more—twelve hundred, I think. But then, of course, there's Blue Girl. The point is, we don't *have* to work—and so we can pick and choose."

"Go on," said Marion. "I see you've something in mind."

Sully regarded her really beautiful hands.

Then—

"Remember the 'Cries of London' we gave to Aunt Ildico ? Well, I sort of managed that. I had a word with Christie's, and then I went to the sale and said my piece."

"To some effect, Sully darling."

"If he's got the money behind him, any fool can rush in. The point is that I was bitten. That autumn I attended most of the sales. I didn't bid, of course, but I got a great deal of pleasure out of the stuff put up. You see, it was all the real thing. The finest silver and china ; exquisite furniture ;

310

Morlands and, once, a Claude; and really precious stones. And I got to know the big dealers—by sight, of course: Gersohn and Miles and Ferrari, and men like that. One day Mr. Stukeley came up. You know. The Stukeley Collection. A hell of a connoisseur. He was a friend of father's and recognized me. They were selling a set of Spode dishes, complete with tray. 'What'll that go for?' he whispered. 'My guess is two hundred,' I said. 'Well done,' he said. 'I've told them that they can go to two hundred and ten.' When he got it for that, we both laughed. Then he crooked his finger at Gersohn, who'd run him up. 'Mr. Gersohn,' he said, 'Mrs. Enderby-Lowe is a friend of mine. Her father was Hubert de Guesclin, of whom I expect you've heard. And her mother is Lady Vivien. She's not a purchaser, but she knows the sheep from the goats and I think it would give her great pleasure to see your stock.' Gersohn bowed from the waist. 'I shall be honoured,' he said.

"Well, I went to his shop the next day, and he gave me two hours of his time. You've no idea of the treasures lying within those walls. And I went again and again, and got to know him quite well.

"Now how such people are doing, I've no idea. But I haven't very much doubt that, if he can possibly do it, Gersohn will take us both on at a nominal wage. Cleaning, arranging, ticketing—things like that. Myself, I wouldn't mind serving: but we'd have to rise to that. The point is— it wouldn't be sordid. Quiet, handsome rooms, full of old masters' work. Living and moving and dealing with lovely things. Bohemian glass and Chippendale furniture; Georgian silver and pictures and Lowestoft bowls. I think it would be very restful. And I'm sure we should be beautifully treated."

"Darling," said Marion, "you've opened a wonderful door. But why, in the name of God, should they let me in?"

" Because we're two of a kind. Neither of us is an expert, but each has two cards to play. One is that we are prepared to labour for nothing at all, simply because we should like to do such work : and the second card is that we have always been used to living with beautiful things. So we know how they should be handled. If they give us some china to wash, they know that it won't be smashed—because, from our point of view, we haven't been given a job, but accorded a privilege."

Marion sat up.

" Sully darling, you're terribly sweet to me. But you must go in and win. I'm not going to cramp your style."

Sully leaned forward.

" If you want my private opinion, Gersohn will jump at us both."

She was perfectly right. After one week on trial, Gersohn engaged the two at excellent salaries. For one thing, they gave full measure—a gift which was rare indeed in 1946 : for another, they could be trusted, as Gersohn trusted himself : finally, their interpretation of duty warmed his heart. His father had pushed his barrow : but, when they were on parade, they always called him ' Sir '.

One winter evening they were summoned.

The dealer received them standing, and begged them to take their seats, before resuming his own.

" May I know which of you ladies advised the Countess of Lodestone to let me look at her things ? "

" Mrs. Enderby-Lowe," said Marion.

" That's not quite fair," said Sully. " We were both dining there, and when she mentioned that she was selling up Haycock, we looked very hard at each other and then I spoke."

" I quite understand. Please believe that I am extremely grateful." Gersohn examined his nails. " Cars are so difficult now. What with petrol and parking and chauffeurs, it's hardly worth while. So I've gone to Geoffrey Thomas

—they always have cars, you know. Very efficient people.
An account has been opened with them for 16 Cleveland Row.
That is the name of their client—16 Cleveland Row. The
bills will be sent to me. Whenever you're dining out, or
going into the country, as sometimes I think you do, you
have only to ring them up and say what car you require. So
you will spare yourselves, and will do your work the better,
because you won't be so tired."

Sully swallowed.

" We don't deserve it, Mr. Gersohn."

" Permit me, madam," said the dealer, " to be the best
judge of that."

" It'll be like old times," said Marion.

" That, madam, was the idea."

As they walked back to the flat—

" Isn't he a lamb ? " said Sully.

" To you the magic, darling. My singularly futile
existence is showing signs of life."

*　　*　　*　　*　　*

Two years and more had gone by, and, largely thanks to
Vivien, the tenor of life at Poesy was even and undisturbed.
The estate, of course, had shrunk. Only the home farm was
left, and that was let to a very decent young yeoman on whom
the two could count. But the eight hundred acres of park-
land stayed as they always had, woodland and spreading
meadows, girt by a gray stone wall. They provided wood
for fires, and grazing for cows and sheep : but, most of all,
they harboured the gray, old mansion and gave nine elderly
people a chance to go down in peace.

Between them, Philip and Vivien, contrived to find the
money to staff the house—not as it should have been staffed,
but well enough. Firkin, the butler, was rising sixty-two ;
but he had been a footman at Grosvenor Square, and he
would have worked for nothing rather than leave his lord.

James, the footman, had only left Philip's service to go to the war. Now he was short of a leg: but he did most faithful duty and did it extremely well. Mrs. Kennet, the cook, confessed to sixty-four : she had started life as a kitchen-maid at Brocade : that she would end it at Poesy, nobody dared deny. But, if she knew her own mind, she knew her master's ways, and, so far as in her lay, Philip and Vivien's table was properly found. Her passionate contempt for rationing knew no law : and there can, I think, be no doubt that, sooner than provoke so fearful a personality, many rendered to Cæsar the things that were God's. Two elderly, excellent housemaids did splendid work, and a devoted nurse cared for the two grand-children with all her heart. Finally, there was Pricket . . . far too old, of course, to be in service at all, but about as movable as the Albert Hall. Left to her own devices, she did remarkably well, washing, mending and keeping my lady's clothes and teaching a great-niece of hers to take her place. Finally, Pulse and a grandson did what they could, and Johnson, the elderly chauffeur, cared for the cars.

The house must be kept in repair, and there were all kinds of expenses which could not be cut. When everything had been paid, brother and sister had very little left. (Arlington Street had gone, and Sully and Marion were paying for Cleveland Row.) But enough was as good as a feast. By being very careful, the two got home. And more than home. The sweet, familiar surroundings had healed their wounds. The ways to which they were accustomed had done much to ease the pain. The sympathy of the old servants had been their rod and their staff.

They were strolling the terrace one proud October morning . . .

Philip stopped to look round, to mark the bulwarks of Poesy—green and silver meadows, and oak and ash and chestnut lifting their lovely heads, the warmth of the copper beech and the sweep of the aged elms that were gracing the

314

southern drive. In the distance a blue-brown haze argued the smoke of Peregrine, hidden by neighbouring timber, embowered as villages were in the fairy-tales.

"Vivvy, you know," he said, " we've a lot to be thankful for."

"We have, indeed, my darling. Somewhere it says in the Bible, ' From him that hath not, shall be taken away even that which he hath.' That awful thing can be said of many people to-day : but we are not among them. We've lost very heavily. But we have still got this."

"That's right. When all is said and done, we always loved Poesy best. And now we're there all the time. Things have changed, of course : but so have we. Old age doesn't ask very much. And the babies are very happy—no doubt about that. Poesy's very gentle. Brocade made demands. But Poesy asks nothing, although she gives so much."

Vivien took Philip's arm.

"Isn't it strange, my darling, that now, when our lives are ending, we've come together again ? Here we are, living together, just as we lived together—oh, fifty-five years ago. We never drifted apart, as brothers and sisters do. But each of us led his own life. Grosvenor Square and Brocade and darling Ildico. Charles Street and Fairing Over and Hubert and then dear Jack. Separate lives and interests for nearly fifty years. And now all that is over, but this remains."

Philip's hand closed upon Vivien's.

"I find it most strange," he said. "I think it must have been written when you and I were born. You had a husband and children, and I had a wife and child. And, one by one, they were taken, but we were left. And so we're alone together, as once we were. Perhaps because of that, the old days are always with me—I daresay they are with you. Astoundingly vivid, too. I see them much more clearly than many more recent times. You with your hair down your back, and Miss Carson sending me off to wash my hands ; Aunt Ursula driving out in the carriage and pair, and Great-

315

uncle Henry taking the head of the table and making all of us laugh. Miss Carson, of course, stands out. She was closer to us than anyone else. We always took her for granted. She might have been bone of our bone."

"I often think," said Vivien, "that she was the greatest woman that I have ever known. Everything was against her, for she was a governess. As such, she was weighted out : yet she won every race. Love, respect, admiration—she had them all. However tricky the going, she never put a foot wrong. She never put herself forward, yet she was always there. Perhaps her greatest triumph was won in the servants' hall, for servants always used her as if she was the lady of the house."

"She was, really," said Philip.

"And yet a governess." Vivien drew in her breath. "How on earth she did it, I've no idea. It must have been sheer personality. And were we fortunate, Pip ? "

"By God, we were. Such as we've been, she made us. And she was wonderfully human. When we were little, we had the time of our lives. Tennis and cubbing and going round the stables and having tea in the hay. . . . Oh, Vivvy, we seem to be poor, but really we're very rich. Such happy memories. . . . And then we've got each other, and we're at home. What more can one ask to-day ? "

"No more, darling," sighed Vivien, regarding the smiling prospect with loving eyes. "We've had our show, and a glorious show it's been. There have been bitter moments for both of us. But now we're in port, tied up. Lying close in the harbour we love so well. . . . D'you remember the water-wheel ? And how we could see his flourish from where we're standing now ? He's quiet now, of course : but, except for that, it's all very much as it was."

"'The same yesterday, to-day and for ever.' Out of all reason to-day—and yet it's true. Our precious vignette has survived." A footfall made them look round, and Philip glanced at his watch. "Hullo, time for lunch."

316

The butler approached and bowed.

" My lady is served."

Vivien inclined her head.

" Thank you, Firkin. We're coming."

" You go in," said Philip. " I must just wash my hands."

" *The* good *that* women *do lives after them."*

Philip began to laugh.

*   *   *   *   *

Two hours had gone by.

Philip had left for the farm. This, on foot : it was a short two miles, and the day and the going were good. Blue Girl must have a new pony—a proper mount : something that she could be proud of—cost what it would. Old Milly would do for the baby—for little Ildico. (Fancy anything ' doing for ' a Brabant. . . . What would Uncle Henry have said ? Oh, well. . . .) But Blue Girl must have a new pony—a good-looking horse. And young Raven had managed to find one. Philip would see it himself this afternoon.

Vivien was writing a letter. In half an hour Johnson would take her to Blackbird, to purchase some wool. She supposed she would find some there. The babies must have new woollies, when winter came in.

Firkin appeared with the paper—the local gazette.

" Oh, thank you, Firkin. Is it James' afternoon off ? "

" Yes, my lady."

" If he'd like to go to Blackbird, let him come round with the car."

" Thank you, my lady. I'm sure he'd be very pleased."

Vivien finished her letter, picked up the paper and moved to the window-seat.

Idly she glanced at the sheet. . . .

HAMPSHIRE DISTRICT SCHEDULED FOR
SATELLITE TOWN

*The Ministry of Town and County Planning has ordered a
preliminary survey to be made of what will be called ' The
Peregrine Extension', that is to say, some five square miles of
country to the north of and including the picturesque village of
Peregrine. Within the perimeter, as scheduled, lies the estate
of Poesy (2,000 acres) the seat of the Earl of Ringwood, whose
only son, Viscount Haven, fell in the war. Compensation will
be paid to Lord Ringwood and to other landowners who are thus
expropriated.*

Vivien was shaking all over.

She let the paper go and felt for the window-sill.

" Steady," she breathed, " steady. It's only shock. . . .
Be . . . all right in a minute."

Breathing most hard, she gripped the stone of the sill with
all her might. . . .

When she had stopped trembling, she let the sill go and
put her head down as low as ever she could.

At last she sat up.

" I'm all right now," she said quietly.

She picked up and folded the paper, moved to the writing-
table and thrust it into a drawer. Then she passed to the
fireplace and rang the bell. . . .

" I think I'll go now, Firkin. That is, as soon as Johnson
can turn out the car."

" Very good, my lady."

" Tell Amy to bring my blue scarf and my lightweight
coat and gloves."

" Certainly, my lady."

The butler withdrew.

Three minutes later, perhaps, Pricket appeared.

" Hullo, Arabella."

Pricket looked at her shrewdly, before she laid the clothes
down.

318

" You all right, my lady? You don't look too good to me."

" Of course I'm all right, Arabella."

" No ' of course ', about it. Here's your scarf."

Vivien stepped to a mirror and bound it about her hair.

" You're always imagining things."

" Did your ladyship have a fall? "

" I swear I didn't," said Vivien. " I'm quite all right."

" Well, something's happened. You're shaken. You can't fool me."

" My dear Arabella," said Vivien, " I'm perfectly well."

" An' that after fifty years. Will you wear your coat, my lady? Or shall I give it to James? "

" Give it to James. I may want it coming back."

Two minutes later the car slipped down the drive.

As they came to the outskirts of Blackbird —

" Welbeck and Mason, Johnson."

The chauffeur touched his hat. . . .

" Mr. Mason's engaged, my lady. He won't be very long."

" All right. I'll wait," said Vivien.

The old clerk ushered her into the dusty waiting-room.

" Here's *The Gazette*, my Lady."

" Oh, thank you so much," said Vivien, taking the sheet.

The Ministry of Town and Country Planning has ordered a preliminary survey to be made of what will be called ' The Peregrine Extension ', that is to say . . .

The solicitor greeted her warmly.

" Pray come in, Lady Vivien."

" Have you seen this, Mr. Mason? "

The other bit his lip.

" I'm afraid I have, Lady Vivien. I don't know how far it's gone. But——"

" It's got to be stopped, Mr. Mason."

The solicitor pulled his moustache.

319

"I'm afraid, Lady Vivien, that's easier said than done. These people are very autocratic. If I may say so, I think our best line would be——"

"Can it be stopped?"

"Not if they mean to go on. Their power is absolute. So we must be very careful to give no offence. They're bound to hear us, of course. And I think the first thing to do . . ."

After nearly an hour of discussion, Vivien got to her feet.

"Then that's arranged. I'll write to Fulford and Willing and tell them they'll hear from you. They'll do what they can in London, and you'll attend to things here."

"That's understood, Lady Vivien. I'll do my very best."

"*But you have no hope.*"

The solicitor flinched. The words caught him unawares : they were like the crack of a whip.

"One can always hope, Lady Vivien. The trouble is that when Labour has made up its mind, it seems to resent . . ."

*　　*　　*　　*　　*

The pony had been approved, and Philip was walking slowly back from the farm.

As he rounded Waterloo Coppice, he saw the theodolite. This was being used by a red-haired youth : a hundred yards ahead, another young man was planting a black and white pole.

Philip stopped in his tracks and fingered his chin.

Then—

"Learning to survey, I suppose. Well, that's all right. Perhaps they asked at the house."

He moved towards the theodolite, slowly enough.

The red-headed youth surveyed him.

"Good afternoon," said Philip.

"Good afternoon."

" You're making a survey, aren't you ? "

" That's right. Preliminary survey." He pointed to the theodolite. " Joo understan' these things ? "

Philip laughed.

" I'm afraid I don't," he said. " They're for measuring angles, aren't they ? "

" Some-ming like that," said the youth. He peered through the telescope. Then he straightened his back and raised his voice to a shout. " Can' see the one after. She's too much down in the dip. Bring 'er back a bit, will you ? "

A yell came back.

" O.K."

The surveyor turned to Philip and lighted a cigarette.

" My boss ought to be here. But he's taking his wife to the pictures this afternoon. ' You go an' do it,' he says. ' It's easy enough.' Maybe, it is to 'im. But I 'aven't 'ad no practice."

" Your boss ? " said Philip, frowning. " Who's your boss ? "

" A.D.E., Town an' Country Planning."

" But why did he send you here ? "

" 'Cause this is a scheduled district. ' The Peregrine Extension ', they call it. Goin' to be a satellite town."

Philip stared.

" There's some mistake," he said. " This is my land."

For a moment the other stared back.

Then he leaned forward.

" You're not the Earl of Ringwood ? "

" That's my name."

The youth clapped a hand to his brow.

" Christ," he said. " An' I never thought I'd meet you. Know all about you, I do. The Reverend Datchet tole me."

" Datchet," said Philip. A hand went up to his head. " The name's familiar, but——"

" Used to be Vicar of Tumbril."

321

" That's right. I remember now. A delightful man."

" Well then he comes to Worthing—that's my home town. Runs a Boys' Club. An' when we was sick of ping-pong, 'e used to talk. Give up Brocade, 'aven't you? "

" Er, yes. But tell me about this—this township. Did you say ' The Peregrine——' ? "

" Is it true you 'ad the King there? An' everyone cried ? "

" At Brocade? Yes. But—that was a long time ago. I want to hear more of this survey."

" Oh, forget it," said the youth. " Any way, I can' do it. 'E'll 'ave to come to-morrow an' do it 'imself." He swung round and shouted again. " Pack up, Fred, an' bring the —— things in." He returned to his host. " That's Fred Alder, that is : an' my name's Erny Balch." He looked Philip up and down. " Christ, I can't believe it. I always thought the Reverend was 'aving me on. An' you stood in Buckin'am Palace, all dressed up ? "

" Yes, once or twice," said Philip, " when I was young. But please let that go for a moment. I want you to tell me——"

" Oh, you'll hear all about that. Haven't you had your notice ? "

" What notice ? " said Philip.

Erny nodded grimly—as one who finds his worst suspicions confirmed.

" There's the office for you. Laziest set of ——s I ever saw." He turned to Fred Alder, coming up with the poles. " What about that, Fred ? 'E's never 'ad 'is notice. Wants to know what we're doin' on his land."

" Pressure of business," said Fred. " He'll get it next year."

The two laughed heartily.

" Oh, I forgot. Meet the Earl of Ringwood, Fred."

" Pleased to meet you—sir."

Philip wrung out a smile.

322

Then—

" I'm rather in the dark about this. Why are you making a survey upon my land ? "

" 'Cause it's part of the scheduled district. Got to have the survey to lay it out. You ought to 'ave 'ad your notice. Then you'd 'ave known."

" Can't you tell me now ? "

" But I keep on telling you. This is ' The Peregrine Extension ', taking in Peregrine village an' four miles north. Satellite towns, they call them. You'll get compensation for being turned out. . . . 'Ere ! "

As Philip swayed, the youth caught him. . . .

Between them they laid him down, and Erny Balch loosened his collar, while the other ran to the truck. . . .

They let the water trickle over his face and head.

Philip opened his eyes. Then he propped himself on an elbow.

" I think I must have fainted," he said.

" That's right," said Fred. " I 'spect you walked too far. An' it's hot, too, for October."

" See here," said Erny. " If you can make the truck, we'll run you back to the 'ouse."

" You're—very kind," said Philip.

The two of them helped him to rise. With Erny's arm about him he moved, at first uncertainly, over the sward. . . .

The air in his face revived him.

" Er, this'll do," he said quietly. " I'll walk from here."

" Sure ? " said Erny, setting a foot on the brake.

" Sure," said Philip. He let himself out of the cab and put up a hand. " You've been—very good to me."

" That's all right. Cheerioh."

" Er, cheerioh," said Philip.

When the truck was gone, he wiped his face and throat and straightened his collar and tie.

Then he walked very slowly up to the house.

*   *   *   *   *

Brother and sister met at half past eight. This, in the Great Hall. Philip, dressed for dinner, was sitting beside the hearth. As Vivien made her appearance, he got to his feet.

" Hullo, Vivvy. Glass of sherry, my dear ? "

" That's all right, darling. I'll help myself."

" Did you—get your wool ? "

" My wool ? Oh, yes. I was lucky. Exactly what I wanted. Tell me about the pony."

" The pony ? Oh, yes." Vivien and Philip sat down. " I—think she'll do very well. She's a polo pony. Not quite up to our standard : but Blue Girl won't care."

" We'll pick out a saddle to-morrow."

" That's right. . . . 'Member the ralli-car ? " Vivien nodded. " I shouldn't have let it go. Then we could have . . . used it again."

" So—so we could. Never mind. What—what's the pony's name ? "

Philip put a hand to his head.

" I think Raven called her ' Sally '."

" Sally. I see. 'Member Sally of the Mill ? "

" Yes, indeed. And Big Ben. Tragic business, that. We never—came back for three years."

Vivien set down her glass.

" We—got very fond of Brocade."

" That's true. Strange how things work out. If we hadn't *had* to live there . . ."

" That's right. *There's a . . . divinity that shapes—our ends.*"

" That's—right."

The door was opened, set wide.

Firkin approached very slowly, as though unsure of his steps.

Philip and Vivien looked up. Then with one accord, they averted their eyes. Each of them knew that the tidings had reached the servants' hall.

324

The butler's face was ravaged ; his eyes had a hunted look. Twice he endeavoured—and failed to say the familiar words.

" It's all right, Firkin," said Philip. " We—understand." The butler bowed and withdrew. . . .

With his eyes on the ground, Philip had gone very white : his hands were holding fast to the arms of his chair.

A dry sob shook Vivien.

" Oh, Pip, Pip," she wailed. " I spoke too soon this morning. . . . ' From him that hath not . . .' "

Philip got to his feet and stepped to her side.

He put her hand to his lips, holding it there for a moment, before he let it go and straightened his back.

Then, with the tenderest smile, he offered his arm.

" Come, my sweet," he said gently. " We'd better go in."

THE END